On Beauty

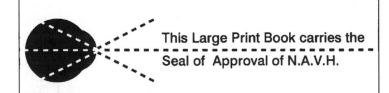

This Large Print Book carries the
Seal of Approval of N.A.V.H.

On Beauty

ZADIE SMITH

Thorndike Press • Waterville, Maine

Published in 2006 by arrangement with The Penguin Press, a member of Penguin Group (USA) Inc.

Thorndike Press® Large Print Basic.

The tree indicium is a trademark of Thorndike Press.

The text of this Large Print edition is unabridged.
Other aspects of the book may vary from the original edition.

Set in 16 pt. Plantin.

Printed in the United States on permanent paper.

Library of Congress Cataloging-in-Publication Data

Smith, Zadie.
    On beauty : a novel / by Zadie Smith.
      p. cm.
    "Thorndike Press large print basic" — T.p. verso.
    ISBN 0-7862-8319-X (lg. print : hc : alk. paper)
    1. College teachers — Fiction.   2. Massachusetts —
Fiction.   3. Domestic Fiction.   4. Large type books.
I. Title.
PR6069.M59O5 2006
  823'.914—dc22   2005029352

2/06

For my dear Laird

As the Founder/CEO of NAVH, the only national health agency solely devoted to those who, although not totally blind, have an eye disease which could lead to serious visual impairment, I am pleased to recognize Thorndike Press⋆ as one of the leading publishers in the large print field.

Founded in 1954 in San Francisco to prepare large print textbooks for partially seeing children, NAVH became the pioneer and standard setting agency in the preparation of large type.

Today, those publishers who meet our standards carry the prestigious "Seal of Approval" indicating high quality large print. We are delighted that Thorndike Press is one of the publishers whose titles meet these standards. We are also pleased to recognize the significant contribution Thorndike Press is making in this important and growing field.

Lorraine H. Marchi, L.H.D.
Founder/CEO
NAVH

⋆ Thorndike Press encompasses the following imprints: Thorndike, Wheeler, Walker and Large Print Press.

contents

acknowledgements

My gratitude to my first readers, Nick Laird, Jessica Frazier, Tamara Barnett-Herrin, Michal Shavit, David O'Rourke, Yvonne Bailey-Smith and Lee Klein. Their encouragement, criticism and good advice got the thing started. Thank you to Harvey and Yvonne for their support and to my younger brothers, Doc Brown and Luc Skyz, who offer advice on all the things I am too old to know. Thank you to my ex-student Jacob Kramer for notes on college life and East Coast mores. Thank you to India Knight and Elisabeth Merriman for all the French. Thank you to Cassandra King and Alex Adamson for dealing with all extra-literary matters.

I thank Beatrice Monti for another stay at Santa Maddelena and the good work that came out of it. Thank you to my English and American editors, Simon Prosser and Anne Godoff, without whom this book would be longer and worse. Thank you to Donna Poppy, the cleverest copy editor a girl could hope for. Thank you to Juliette

Mitchell at Penguin for all her hard work on my behalf. Without my agent, Georgia Garrett, I couldn't do this job at all. Thank you, George. You're a bobby dazzler.

Thank you to Simon Schama for his monumental *Rembrandt's Eyes*, a book that helped me to see paintings properly for the first time. Thank you to Elaine Scarry for her wonderful essay 'On Beauty and Being Just', from which I borrowed a title, a chapter heading and a good deal of inspiration. It should be obvious from the first line that this is a novel inspired by a love of E. M. Forster, to whom all my fiction is indebted, one way or the other. This time I wanted to repay the debt with *hommage*.

Most of all, I thank my husband, whose poetry I steal to make my prose look pretty. It's Nick who knows that 'time is how you spend your love', and that's why this book is dedicated to him, as is my life.

kipps and belsey

We refuse to be each other.

H. J. Blackham

I

One may as well begin with Jerome's e-mails to his father:

To: HowardBelsey@fas.Wellington.edu
From: Jeromeabroad@easymail.com
Date: 5 November
Subject:

Hey, Dad — basically I'm just going to keep on keeping on with these mails — I'm no longer expecting you to reply, but I'm still hoping you will, if that makes sense.

Well, I'm really enjoying everything. I work in Monty Kipps's own office (did you know that he's actually *Sir* Monty??), which is in the Green Park area. It's me and a Cornish girl called Emily. She's cool. There're also three more yank interns downstairs (one from Boston!), so I feel pretty much at home. I'm a kind of an intern with the duties of a PA — organizing lunches, filing, talking to people on the phone, that sort of thing. Monty's work is much more than just the academic stuff:

13

he's involved with the Race Commission, and he has Church charities in Barbados, Jamaica, Haiti, etc. — he keeps me really busy. Because it's such a small set-up, I get to work closely with him — and of course I'm living with the family now, which is like being completely integrated into something new. Ah, the family. You didn't respond, so I'm imagining your reaction (not too hard to imagine . . .). The truth is, it was really just the most convenient option at the time. And they were totally kind to offer — I was being evicted from the 'bedsit' place in Marylebone. The Kippses aren't under any obligation to *me,* but they asked and I accepted — gratefully. I've been in their place a week now, and still no mention of any rent, which should tell you something. I know you want me to tell you it's a nightmare, but I can't — I *love* living here. It's a different universe. The house is just *wow* — early Victorian, a 'terrace' — unassuming-looking outside but massive inside — but there's still a kind of humility that really appeals to me — almost everything white, and a lot of handmade things, and quilts and dark wood shelves and cornices and this four-storey staircase — and in the whole place there's only one television,

14

which is in the basement anyway, just so Monty can keep abreast of news stuff, and some of the things he does on the television — but that's it. I think of it as the negativized image of our house sometimes . . . It's in this bit of North London called 'Kilburn', which sounds bucolic, but boy oh boy is not bucolic in the least, except for this street we live on off the 'high road', and it's suddenly like you can't hear a thing and you can just sit in the yard in the shadow of this *huge* tree — eighty feet tall and ivy-ed all up the trunk . . . reading and feeling like you're in a novel . . . Fall's different here — much less intense and trees balder earlier — everything more melancholy somehow.

The family are another thing again — they deserve more space and time than I have right now (I'm writing this on my lunch hour). But, in brief: one boy, Michael, nice, sporty. A little dull, I guess. *You'd* think he was, anyway. He's a business guy — exactly what business I haven't been able to figure out. And he's huge! He's got two inches on you, at least. They're all big in that athletic, Caribbean way. He must be 6' 5". There's also a very tall and beautiful daughter, Victoria, who I've seen only in photos (she's inter-railing in Europe), but she's coming back for a while on Friday, I think. Monty's wife, Carlene — perfect. She's not from Trinidad, though — it's a small island, St something or other — I'm not sure. I didn't hear it very well the first time she mentioned it, and now it's like it's too late to ask. She's always trying to fatten me up — she feeds me constantly. The rest of the family talk about sports and God and politics, and Carlene floats above it all like a kind of angel — and she's helping me with prayer. She really knows how to *pray* — and it's very cool to be able to pray without someone in your family coming into the room and (a) passing wind (b) shouting (c) analysing the 'phoney metaphysics' of prayer (d) singing loudly (e) laughing.

So that's Carlene Kipps. Tell Mom that she bakes. Just tell her that and then walk away chuckling . . .

Now, listen to this next bit carefully: in the morning THE WHOLE KIPPS FAMILY have breakfast together and a conversation TOGETHER and then get into a car TOGETHER (are you taking notes?) — I know, I know — not easy to get your head around. I never met a family who wanted to spend so much time with each other.

16

I hope you can see from everything I've written that your feud, or whatever it is, is a complete waste of time. It's all on your side, anyway — Monty doesn't do feuds. You've never even really met — just a lot of public debates and stupid letters. It's such a waste of energy. Most of the cruelty in the world is just misplaced energy. Anyway: I've got to go — work calls!

Love to Mom and Levi, partial love to Zora. And remember: I love you, Dad (and I pray for you, too) Phew! Longest mail ever!

Jerome XXOXXXX

To :HowardBelsey@fas.Wellington.edu
From: Jeromeabroad@easymail.com
Date: 14 November
Subject: Hello again

Dad,
Thanks for forwarding me the details about the dissertation — could you phone the department at Brown and maybe get me an extension? Now I begin to see why Zora enrolled at Wellington . . . lot easier to miss your deadline when Daddy's the teacher ☺ I read your one-liner query and then like a fool I searched for a further attachment

(like, say, a letter???), but I guess you're too busy/mad/ etc. to write. Well, I'm not. How's the book going? Mom said you were having trouble getting going. Have you found a way to prove Rembrandt was no good yet? ☺

The Kippses continue to grow on me. On Tuesday we all went to the theatre (the whole clan is home now) and saw a South African dance troupe, and then, going back on the 'tube', we started to hum one of the tunes from the show, and this became full-blown singing, with Carlene leading (she's got a terrific voice) and even Monty joined in, because he's not really the 'self-hating psychotic' you think he is. It was really kind of lovely, the singing and the train coming above ground and then walking through the wet back to this beautiful house and a curried chicken home-cooked meal. But I can see your face as I type this, so I'll stop.

Other news: Monty has honed in on the great Belsey lack: logic. He's trying to teach me chess, and today was the first time in a week when I wasn't beaten in under six moves, though I was still beaten of course. All the Kippses think I'm muddle-headed and poetic — I don't know what they would say if they knew that among   Belseys   I'm   practically Wittgenstein. I think I amuse them, though — and Carlene likes to have me around the kitchen, where my cleanliness is seen as a positive thing, rather than as some kind of anal-retentive syndrome . . . I have to admit, though, I do find it a little eerie in the mornings to wake up to this peaceful silence (people WHISPER in the hallways so as not to wake up other people) and a small part of my backside misses Levi's rolled-up wet towel, just as a small part of my ear doesn't know what to do with itself now Zora's no longer screaming in it. Mom mailed me to tell me that Levi has upped the headwear to FOUR (skullcap, baseball cap, hoodie, duffel hood) *with* earphones on — so that you can only see a tiny, tiny bit of his face around the eyes. Please kiss him there for me. And kiss Mom for me too, and remember that it's her birthday a week from tomorrow. Kiss Zora and ask her to read Matthew 24. I know how she just loves a bit of Scripture every day.

Love and peace in abundance,

Jerome xxxxx

P.S. in answer to your 'polite query', yes, I

19

am still one . . . despite your evident contempt I'm feeling quite fine about it, thanks
. . . twenty is really not that late among
young people these days, especially if
they've decided to make their fellowship
with Christ. It was weird that you asked, because I did walk through Hyde Park yesterday and thought of you losing yours to
someone you had never met before and
never would again. And no, I wasn't
tempted to repeat the incident . . .

To :HowardBelsey@fas.Wellington.edu
From: Jeromeabroad@easymail.com
Date: 19 November
Subject:

Dear Dr Belsey!
I have no idea how you're going to take
this one! But we're in love! The Kipps girl
and me! I'm going to ask her to marry me,
Dad! And I think she'll say yes!!! Are you
digging on these exclamation marks!!!! Her
name's Victoria but everyone calls her
Vee. She's amazing, gorgeous, brilliant.
I'm asking her 'officially' this evening, but I
wanted to tell you first. It's come over us
like the Song of Solomon, and there's no
way to explain it apart from as a kind of
mutual revelation. She just arrived here

20

last week — sounds crazy but it true!!!! Seriously: I'm happy. Please take two Valium and ask Mom to mail me ASAP. I've got no credit left on this phone and don't like to use theirs.

Jxx

2

'What, Howard? What am I looking at, exactly?'

Howard Belsey directed his American wife, Kiki Simmonds, to the relevant section of the e-mail he had printed out. She put her elbows either side of the piece of paper and lowered her head as she always did when concentrating on small type. Howard moved away to the other side of their kitchen-diner to attend to a singing kettle. There was only this one high note — the rest was silence. Their only daughter, Zora, sat on a stool with her back to the room, her earphones on, looking up reverentially at the television. Levi, the youngest boy, stood beside his father in front of the kitchen cabinets. And now the two of them began to choreograph a breakfast in speechless harmony: passing the box of cereal from one to the other, exchanging implements, filling their bowls and sharing milk from a pink china jug with a sun-yellow rim. The house was south facing. Light struck the double glass doors that led to the garden, filtering through the arch that split the kitchen. It rested softly upon the still life of Kiki at the breakfast table, motionless, reading. A dark red Portuguese earthenware bowl faced her, piled high with apples. At this hour the light extended itself even further, beyond the breakfast table, through the hall, to the lesser of their two living rooms. Here a bookshelf filled with their oldest paperbacks kept company with a suede beanbag and an ottoman upon which Murdoch, their dachshund, lay collapsed in a sunbeam.

'Is this for real?' asked Kiki, but got no reply.

Levi was slicing strawberries, rinsing them and plopping them into two cereal bowls. It was Howard's job to catch their frowzy heads for the trash. Just as they were finishing up this operation, Kiki turned the papers face down on the table, removed her hands from her temples and laughed quietly.

'Is something funny?' asked Howard, moving to the breakfast bar and resting his elbows on its top. In response, Kiki's face resolved itself into impassive blackness. It was this sphinx-like expression that sometimes induced their American friends to imagine a more exotic provenance for her than she actually possessed. In fact she was from simple Florida country stock.

'Baby — try being less facetious,' she suggested. She reached for an apple and began to cut it up with one of their small knives with the translucent handles, dividing it into irregular chunks. She ate these slowly, one piece after another.

Howard pulled his hair back from his face with both hands.

'Sorry — I just — you laughed, so I thought maybe something was funny.'

'How am I meant to react?' said Kiki, sighing. She laid down her knife and reached out for Levi, who was just passing with his bowl. Grabbing her robust fifteen-year-old by his denim waistband, she pulled him to her easily, forcing him down half a foot to her sitting level so that she could tuck the label of his basketball top back inside the collar. She put her thumbs on each side of his boxer shorts for another adjustment, but he tugged away from her.

'*Mom,* man . . .'

'Levi, honey, please pull those up just a

little . . . they're so low . . . they're not even covering your ass.'

'So it's *not* funny,' concluded Howard. It gave him no cheer, digging in like this. But he was still going to persist with this line of questioning, even though it was not the tack upon which he had hoped to start out, and he understood it was a straight journey to nowhere helpful.

'Oh, *Lord,* Howard,' said Kiki. She turned to face him. 'We can do this in fifteen minutes, can't we? When the kids are —' Kiki rose a little in her seat as she heard the lock of the front door clicking and then clicking again. 'Zoor, honey, get that please, my knee's bad today. She can't get in, go on, help her —'

Zora, eating a kind of toasted pocket filled with cheese, pointed to the television.

'Zora — get it *now,* please, it's the new woman, Monique — for some reason her keys aren't working properly — I think I *asked* you to get a new key cut for her — I can't be here all the time, waiting in for her — Zoor, will you get off your *ass* —'

'Second arse of the morning,' noted Howard. 'That's nice. Civilized.'

Zora slipped off her stool and down the hallway to the front door. Kiki looked at Howard once more with a questioning

24

penetration, which he met with his most innocent face. She picked up her absent son's e-mail, lifted her glasses from where they rested on a chain upon her impressive chest and replaced them on the end of her nose.

'You've got to hand it to Jerome,' she murmured as she read. 'That boy's no fool . . . when he needs your attention *he sure knows how to get it,*' she said, looking up at Howard suddenly and separating syllables like a bank teller counting bills. 'Monty Kipps's daughter. Wham, bam. Suddenly you're interested.'

Howard frowned. 'That's your contribution.'

'Howard — there's an egg on the stove, I don't know who put it on, but the water's evaporated already — smells nasty. Switch it off, please.'

'*That's* your contribution?'

Howard watched his wife calmly pour herself a third glass of clamato juice. She picked this up and brought it to her lips, but then paused where she was and spoke again.

'Really, Howie. He's *twenty.* He's wanting his daddy's attention — and he's going the right way about it. Even doing this Kipps internship in the first place —

there's a *million* internships he could have gone on. Now he's going to marry Kipps junior? Doesn't take a Freudian. I'm saying, the worst thing we can do is to take this seriously.'

'The Kippses?' asked Zora loudly, coming back through the hallway. 'What's going on — did Jerome move in? How totally insane . . . it's like: Jerome — Monty Kipps,' said Zora, moulding two imaginary men to the right and left of her and then repeating the exercise. *'Jerome . . . Monty Kipps. Living together.'* Zora shivered comically.

Kiki chucked back her juice and brought the empty glass down hard. 'Enough of Monty Kipps — I'm serious. I don't want to hear his name again this morning, I swear to God.' She checked her watch. 'What time's your first class? Why're you even here, Zoor? You know? Why — are — you — *here?* Oh, good morning, Monique,' said Kiki in a quite different formal voice, stripped of its Florida music. Monique shut the front door behind her and came forward.

Kiki gave Monique a frazzled smile. 'We're crazy today — everybody's late, running late. How are you doing, Monique — you OK?'

The new cleaner, Monique, was a squat Haitian woman, about Kiki's age, darker still than Kiki. This was only her second visit to the house. She wore a US Navy bomber jacket with a turned-up furry collar and a look of apologetic apprehension, sorry for what would go wrong even before it had gone wrong. All this was made more poignant and difficult for Kiki by Monique's weave: a cheap, orange synthetic hairpiece that was in need of renewal, and today seemed further back than ever on her skull, attached by thin threads to her own sparse hair.

'I start in here?' asked Monique timidly. Her hand hovered near the high zip of her coat, but she did not undo it.

'Actually, Monique, could you start in the study — *my* study,' said Kiki quickly and over something Howard was starting to say. 'Is that OK? Please don't move any papers — just pile them up, if you can.'

Monique stood where she was, clutching her zip. Kiki stayed in her strange moment, nervous of what this black woman thought of another black woman paying her to clean.

'Zora will show you — Zora, show Monique, please, just go on, show her where.'

Zora began to vault up the stairs three at a time, Monique trudging behind her. Howard came out from behind the proscenium and into his marriage.

'If this happens,' said Howard levelly, between sips of coffee, 'Monty Kipps will be an in-law. Of ours. Not somebody else's in-law. *Ours.*'

'Howard,' said Kiki with equal control, 'please, no "routines". We're not on stage. I've just said I don't want to talk about this now. I *know* you heard me.'

Howard gave a little bow.

'Levi needs money for a cab. If you want to worry about something, worry about that. Don't worry about the Kippses.'

'Kippses?' called Levi, from somewhere out of sight. 'Kippses who? Where they at?'

This faux Brooklyn accent belonged to neither Howard nor Kiki, and had only arrived in Levi's mouth three years earlier, as he turned twelve. Jerome and Zora had been born in England, Levi in America. But all their various American accents seemed, to Howard, in some way artificial — not quite the products of this house of his wife. None, though, was as inexplicable as Levi's. Brooklyn? The Belseys were located two hundred miles north of Brooklyn. Howard felt very close to com-

28

menting on it this morning (he had been warned by his wife not to comment on it), but now Levi appeared from the hallway and disarmed his father with a gappy smile before biting the top off a muffin he held in his hand.

'Levi,' said Kiki, 'honey, I'm interested — do you know who I am? Pay any attention at *all* to anything that goes on around here? Remember Jerome? Your brother? Jerome no here? Jerome cross big sea to place called England?'

Levi held a pair of sneakers in his hands. These he shook in the direction of his mother's sarcasm and, scowling, sat down to begin putting them on.

'So? And what? I know about Kippses? I don't know nothing about no Kippses.'

'Jerome — go to school.'

'Now I'm Jerome too?'

'Levi — *go to school.*'

'Man, why you gotta be all . . . I just ahks a question, that's all, and you gotta be all . . .' Here Levi provided an inconclusive mime that gave no idea of the missing word.

'Monty Kipps. The man your brother's been working for in England,' conceded Kiki wearily. It was interesting to Howard to see how Levi had won this concession, by meeting Kiki's corrosive irony with its opposite.

'See?' said Levi, as if it was only by his efforts that decency and sense could be arrived at. 'Was that hard?'

'So is that a letter from Kipps?' asked Zora, coming back down the stairs and up behind her mother's shoulder. In this pose, the daughter bent over the mother, they reminded Howard of two of Picasso's chubby water-carriers. 'Dad, *please, I*'ve got to help with the reply this time — we're going to *destroy* him. Who's it for? The *Republic*?'

'No. No, it's nothing to do with that — it's from Jerome, actually. Getting married,' said Howard, letting his robe fall open, turning away. He wandered over to the glass doors that looked out on to their garden. 'To Kipps's daughter. Apparently it's funny. Your mother thinks it's hilarious.'

'No, honey,' said Kiki. 'I think we just established that I *don't* think it's hilarious — I don't think we know *what's* happening — this is a seven-line e-mail. We don't know what that even *means,* and I'm not gonna get all hepped up about —'

'Is this *serious?*' interrupted Zora. She yanked the paper from her mother's hands, bringing it very close to her myopic eyes.

'This is a fucking joke, right?'

Howard rested his forehead on the thick glass pane and felt the condensation soak his eyebrows. Outside, the democratic East Coast snow was still falling, making the garden chairs the same as the garden tables and plants and mail-boxes and fence-posts. He breathed a mushroom cloud and then wiped it off with his sleeve.

'Zora, you need to get to class, OK? And you *really* need to not use that language in my house — *Hup! Hap! Nap! No!*' said Kiki, each time masking a word Zora was attempting to begin. 'OK? Take Levi to the cab rank. I can't drive him today — you can ask Howard if he'll drive him, but it doesn't look like that's gonna happen. *I'll* phone Jerome.'

'I don't need drivin',' said Levi, and now Howard properly noticed Levi and the new thing about Levi: a woman's stocking, thin and black, on his head, tied at the back in a knot, with a small inadvertent teat like a nipple, on top.

'You can't phone him,' said Howard quietly. He moved tactically, out of sight of his family to the left side of their awesome refrigerator. 'His phone's out of credit.'

'What did you say?' asked Kiki. 'What are you saying? I can't hear you.'

Suddenly she was behind him. 'Where's

the *Kippses'* phone number?' she demanded, although they both knew the answer to this one.

Howard said nothing.

'Oh, yeah, that's right,' said Kiki, 'it's in the *diary,* the diary that was left in *Michigan,* during the famous *conference* when you had more important things on your mind than your wife and family.'

'Could we not do this right now?' asked Howard. When you are guilty, all you can ask for is a deferral of the judgement.

'Whatever, Howard. Whatever — either way it's me who's going to be dealing with it, with the consequences of your actions, as usual, so —'

Howard thumped their icebox with the side of his fist.

'Howard, please don't do that. The door's swung, it's . . . everything'll defrost, push it properly, *properly,* until it — OK: it's *unfortunate.* That's if it really has *happened,* which we don't know. We're just going to have to take it step by step until we know what the hell is going on. So let's leave it at that, and, I don't know . . . discuss when we . . . well, when Jerome's here for one thing and there's actually something to discuss, agreed? Agreed?'

'Stop arguing,' complained Levi from

the other side of the kitchen, and then re-peated it loudly.

'We're not arguing, honey,' said Kiki and bent her body at the hips. She tipped her head forward and released her hair from its flame-coloured headwrap. She wore it in two thick ropes of plait that reached to her backside, like a ram's unwound horns. Without looking up, she evened out each side of the material, threw her head back once more, spun the material twice round and retied it in exactly the same manner but tighter. Everything lifted an inch, and, with this new, authoritative face, she leaned on the table and turned to her children.

'OK, show's over. Zoor, there might be a few dollars in the pot by the cactus. Give them to Levi. If not, just lend him some and I'll pay you back later. I'm a little short this month. OK. Go forth and learn. Anything. Anything at all.'

A few minutes later, with the door closed behind her children, Kiki turned to her husband with a thesis for a face, of which only Howard could know every line and reference. Just for the hell of it Howard smiled. In return he received nothing at all. Howard stopped smiling. If there was going to be a fight, no fool would bet on him. Kiki — whom Howard had once, twenty-eight years ago, thrown over his shoulder like a light roll of carpet, to be laid down, and laid upon, in their first house for the first time — was nowadays a solid two hundred and fifty pounds, and looked twenty years his junior. Her skin had that famous ethnic advantage of not wrinkling much, but, in Kiki's case the weight gain had stretched it even more impressively. At fifty-two, her face was still a girl's face. A beautiful tough-girl's face.

Now she crossed the room and pushed by him with such force that he was muscled into an adjacent rocking chair. Back at the kitchen table, she began violently to pack a bag with things she did not need to take to work. She spoke without looking at him. 'You know what's weird? Is that you can get someone who is a professor of one thing and then is just so *intensely stupid* about everything else? Consult the ABC of parenting, Howie. You'll find that if you go about it this way, then the exact, but the exact opposite, of what you want to happen will happen. The *exact opposite.*'

'But the exact opposite of what I want,' considered Howard, rocking in his chair, 'is what always fucking happens.'

Kiki stopped what she was doing. 'Right. Because you never get what you want.

Your life is just an orgy of deprivation.'

This nodded at the recent trouble. It was an offer to kick open a door in the mansion of their marriage leading on to an ante-chamber of misery. The offer was declined. Kiki instead began that familiar puzzle of getting her small knapsack to sit in the middle of her giant back.

Howard stood up and rearranged himself decently in his bathrobe. 'Do we have their address at least?' he asked. 'Home address?'

Kiki pressed her fingers to each temple like a carnival mind-reader. She spoke slowly, and, though the pose was sarcastic, her eyes were wet.

'I want to understand what it is you think we've done to you. Your family. What is it we've done? Have we deprived you of something?'

Howard sighed and looked away. 'I'm giving a paper in Cambridge on Tuesday anyway — I might as well fly to London a day earlier, if only to —'

Kiki slapped the table. 'Oh, *God,* this isn't 1910 — Jerome can marry who the hell he wants to marry — or are we going to start making up visiting cards and asking him to meet only the daughters of academics that *you* happen to —'

'Might the address be in the green mole-skin?'

Now she blinked away the possibility of tears. 'I don't *know* where the address *might be,*' she said, impersonating his accent. 'Find it yourself. Maybe it's hidden underneath the crap in that damn *hovel* of yours.'

'Thanks *so* much,' said Howard and began his return journey up the stairs to his study.

3

A tall, garnet-coloured building in the New England style, the Belsey residence roams over four creaky floors. The date of its construction (1856) is patterned in tile above the front door, and the windows retain their mottled green glass, spreading a dreamy pasture on the floorboards whenever strong light passes through them. They are not original, these windows, but replacements, the originals being too precious to be used as windows. Heavily insured, they are kept in a large safe in the basement. A significant portion of the value of the Belsey house resides in windows that nobody may look through or open. The sole original window is the skylight at the very top of the house, a harlequin pane that casts a disc of varicoloured light upon different spots on the upper landing as the sun passes over America, turning a white shirt pink as one passes through it, for example, or a yellow tie blue. Once the spot reaches the floor in mid morning it is a family superstition never to step through it. Ten years earlier you would have found children here, wrestling, trying to force each other into its orbit. Even now, as young adults, they continue to step round it on their way down the stairs.

The staircase itself is a steep spiral. To pass the time while descending it, a photographic Belsey family gallery has been hung on the walls, following each turn that you make. The children come first in black and white: podgy and dimpled, haloed with curls. They seem always to be tumbling towards the viewer and over each other, folding on their sausage legs. Frowning Jerome, holding baby Zora, wondering what she is. Zora cradling tiny wrinkled Levi with the crazed, proprietorial look of a woman who steals children from hospital wards. School portraits, graduations, swimming pools, restaurants, gardens and vacation shots follow, monitoring physical development, confirming character. After the children come four generations of the Simmondses' maternal line. These are placed in triumphant, deliberate sequence: Kiki's great-great-grandmother, a house-slave; great-grandmother, a maid; and then her grandmother, a nurse. It was nurse Lily who inherited this whole house from a benevolent white doctor with whom she had worked closely for twenty years, back in Florida. An inheritance on this scale changes everything for a poor family in America: it makes them middle class. And 83 Langham is a fine middle-class house, larger even than it looks on the outside, with a small pool out back, unheated and missing many of its white tiles, like a British smile. Indeed much of the house is now a little shabby — but this is part of its grandeur. There is nothing *nouveau riche* about it. The house is ennobled by the work it has done for this family. The rental of the house paid for Kiki's mother's education (a legal clerk, she died this spring past) and for Kiki's own. For years it was the Simmondses' nest egg and vacation home; they would come up each September from Florida to see the Color. Once her children had grown and after her minister husband had died, Howard's mother-in-law, Claudia Simmonds, moved into the house permanently and lived happily as landlady to cycles of students who rented the spare rooms. Throughout these years Howard coveted the house. Claudia, acutely aware of this covetousness, determined to pervert its course. She knew well that the place was perfect for Howard: large, lovely and within spitting distance of a half-decent American university that might consider hiring him. It gave Mrs Simmonds joy, or so Howard believed, to make him wait all those years. She tripped happily into her seventies without any serious health problems. Meanwhile, Howard shunted his young family around various second-rate seats of learning: six years in upstate New York, eleven in London, one in the suburbs of Paris. It was only ten years ago that Claudia had finally relented, leaving the property in favour of a retirement community in Florida. It was around this time that the gallery photograph of Kiki herself, a hospital administrator and final inheritor of 83 Langham Drive, was taken. In the photo she is all teeth and hair, receiving a state award for out-reach services to the local community. A rogue white arm clinches what was, back then, an extremely neat waist in tight denim; this arm, cut off at the elbow, is Howard's.

When people get married, there is often

a battle to see which family — the husband's or the wife's — will prevail. Howard has lost that battle, happily. The Belseys — petty, cheap and cruel — are not a family anyone would fight to retain. And because Howard had conceded willingly, it was easy for Kiki to be gracious. And so here, on the first landing, we have a large representation of one of the English Belseys, a charcoal portrait of Howard's own father, Harold, hanging as high up the wall as is decent, wearing his flat-cap. His eyes are cast downward, as if in despair at the exotic manner in which Howard has chosen to continue the Belsey line. Howard himself was surprised to discover the picture — surely the only artwork the Belsey family had ever owned — among the small bundle of worthless bric-a-brac that came his way upon his mother's death. In the years that followed the picture has lifted itself out of its low origins, like Howard himself. Many educated upscale Americans of the Belseys' acquaintance claim to admire it. It is considered 'classy', 'mysterious' and redolent in some mystifying way of the 'English character'. In Kiki's opinion it is an item the children will appreciate when they get older, an argument that ingeniously bypasses the fact that the children are already older and do not appreciate it. Howard himself hates it, as he hates all representational painting — and his father.

After Harold Belsey follows a jolly parade of Howard himself in his seventies, eighties and nineties incarnations. Despite costume changes, the significant features remain largely unchanged by the years. His teeth — uniquely in his family — are straight and of a similar size to each other; his bottom lip's fullness goes some way towards compensating for the absence of the upper; and his ears are not noticeable, which is all one can ask of ears. He has no chin, but his eyes are very large and very green. He has a thin, appealing, aristocratic nose. When placed next to men of his own age and class, he has two great advantages: hair and weight. Both have changed little. The hair in particular is extremely full and healthy. A grey patch streams from his right temple. Just this fall he decided to throw the lot of it violently forward on to his face, as he had not done since 1967 — a great success. A large photo of Howard, towering over other members of the Humanities Faculty as they arrange themselves tidily around Nelson Mandela, shows this off to some effect: he has easily the most hair of any fellow there. The pictures of Howard multiply as we near the ground: Howard in Bermuda shorts with shocking white, waxy knees; Howard in academic tweed under a tree dappled by the Massachusetts light; Howard in a great hall, newly appointed Empson Lecturer in Aesthetics; in a baseball cap pointing at Emily Dickinson's house; in a beret for no good reason; in a Day-Glo jumpsuit in Eatonville, Florida, with Kiki beside him, shielding her eyes from either Howard or the sun or the camera.

Now Howard paused on the middle landing to use the phone. He wanted to speak with Dr Erskine Jegede, Soyinka Professor of African Literature and Assistant Director of the Black Studies Department. He put his suitcase on the floor and tucked his air ticket into his armpit. He dialled and waited out the long ring, wincing at the thought of his good friend hunting through his satchel, apologizing to his fellow readers and making his way out of the library into the cold.

'Hello?'
'Hello, who is this? I am in the library.'
'Ersk — it's Howard. Sorry, sorry —

should have called earlier.'

'Howard? You're not upstairs?'

Usually, yes. Reading in his beloved Carrel 187, on the uppermost floor of the Greenman, Wellington College's library. Every Saturday for years, barring illness or snowstorm. He would read all morning, and then convene with Erskine in the lobby at lunchtime, in front of the elevators. Erskine liked to grip Howard fraternally by the shoulders as they walked together to the library café. They looked funny together. Erskine was almost a foot smaller, completely bald, with his scalp polished to an ebony sheen and a short man's stocky chest, thrust forward like plumage. Erskine was never seen out of a suit (Howard had been wearing different versions of the same black jeans for ten years), and the mandarin impression he gave was perfectly completed by his neat salt-and-pepper beard, pointed like a White Russian's, with a matching moustache and 3-D freckles around his cheeks and nose. During their lunches he was always wonderfully scurrilous and bad tempered about his peers, not that his peers would ever know it — Erskine's freckles did incredible diplomatic work for him. Howard had often wished for a similarly benign face to show the world. After lunch, Erskine and Howard would part, always somewhat reluctantly. Each man returned to his own carrel until dinner. For Howard there was great joy in this Saturday routine.

'Ah, now that is unfortunate,' said Erskine upon hearing Howard's news, and the sentiment covered not only Jerome's situation but also the fact that these two men should be deprived of each other's company. And then: 'Poor Jerome. He's a good boy. It is surely a point he is trying to prove.' Erskine paused. 'What the point is, I'm not sure.'

'But Monty *Kipps,*' repeated Howard despairingly. From Erskine he knew he would get what he needed. This was why they were friends.

Erskine whistled his sympathy. 'My God, Howard, you don't have to tell me. I remember during the Brixton riots — this was '81 — I was on the BBC World Service trying to talk about context, deprivation, etcetera' — Howard enjoyed the tuneful Nigerian musicality of 'etcetera' — 'and that madman Monty — he was sitting there opposite me in his Trinidad cricket-club tie saying, "The coloured man must look to his own home, the coloured man must take responsibility." The coloured man! And he *still* says coloured! Every time it was one step forward, and Monty was taking us all two steps back again. The man is sad. I pity him, actually. He's stayed in England too long. It's done strange things to him.'

Howard was quiet on the other end of the phone. He was checking his computer bag for his passport. He felt exhausted at the prospect of the journey and of the battle that awaited him at the other end.

'And his work gets worse every year. In my opinion, the Rembrandt book was very vulgar indeed,' added Erskine kindly.

Howard felt the baseness of pushing Erskine into unfair positions such as this. Monty was a shit, sure, but he wasn't a fool. Monty's Rembrandt book was, in Howard's opinion, retrogressive, perverse, infuriatingly essentialist, but it was neither vulgar nor stupid. It was good. Detailed and thorough. It also had the great advantage of being bound between hard covers and distributed throughout the English-speaking world, whereas Howard's book on the same topic remained unfinished and strewn across the floor before his printer on pages that seemed to him sometimes to have been spewed from the machine in disgust.

'Howard?'

'Yes — here. Got to go, actually. Got a cab booked.'

'You take care, my friend. Jerome is just . . . well, by the time you get there I'm sure it will have proved to be a storm in a teacup.'

Six steps from the ground floor Howard was surprised by Levi. Once again, this head-stocking business. Looking up at him from beneath it, that striking, leonine face with its manly chin, upon which hair had been growing for two years and yet had not confidently established itself. He was top-less to the waist and barefoot. His slender chest smelt of cocoa butter and had been recently shaved. Howard stretched his arms out, blocking the way.

'What's the deal?' asked his son.

'Nothing. Leaving.'

'Who you on the phone to?'

'Erskine.'

'You *leaving* leaving?'

'Yes.'

'Right *now?*'

'What's the deal with *this?*' asked Howard, flipping the interrogation round and touching Levi's head. 'Is it a political thing?'

Levi rubbed his eyes. He put both arms behind his back, held hands with himself

46

and stretched downwards, expanding his chest hugely. 'Nothin', Dad. It's just what it *is*,' he said gnomically. He bit his thumb.

'So then . . .' said Howard, trying to translate, 'it's an aesthetic thing. For looks only.'

'I guess,' Levi said and shrugged. 'Yeah. Just what it is, just a thing that I wear. You know. Keeps my head warm, man. Practical and shit.'

'It does make your skull look rather . . . neat. Smooth. Like a bean.'

He gave his son a friendly squeeze on the shoulders and pulled him close. 'Are you going to work today? They let you wear it at the wotsit, the record shop?'

'Sure, sure . . . It's not a record shop — I keep telling you — it's a mega-store. There's like seven floors . . . You make me laugh, man,' said Levi quietly, his lips buzzing Howard's skin through his shirt. Levi pulled back now from his father, patting him down like a bouncer. 'So you going now or what? What you gonna say to J? Who you flyin' wid?'

'I don't know — not sure. Air miles — someone from work booked it. Look . . . I'm just going to *talk* to him — have a reasonable conversation like reasonable people.'

'Boy . . .' said Levi and clucked his tongue, 'Kiki wants to *kick* your ass . . . An' I'm with *her.* I think you should just let the whole thing go by, just go *by.* Jerome ain't gonna marry anybody. He can't find his dick with two hands.'

Howard, though duty bound to disapprove of this, did not completely disagree with the diagnosis. Jerome's lengthy virginity (which Howard now presumed had come to an end) represented, in Howard's opinion, an ambivalent relationship to the earth and its inhabitants, which Howard had trouble either celebrating or understanding. Jerome was not quite *of the body* somehow, and this had always unnerved his father. If nothing else, the mess in London surely ended the faint whiff of moral superiority that had so far clung to Jerome through his teens.

'So: someone's about to make a personal mistake,' said Howard, an attempt to widen the conversation. 'A terrible one — and you just let it "go by"?'

Levi considered this proposition for a moment. 'Well . . . even if he *does* get married I don't even get why marrying's so like the bad thing all of a sudden . . . At least he got *some chance* of gettin' some *ass* if he's actually married . . .' Levi released a deep, vigorous laugh that in turn flexed that extraordinary stomach, creasing it like a shirt rather than real flesh. 'You *know* he ain't got no chance in hell right now.'

'Levi, that's . . .' began Howard, but up floated a mental picture of Jerome, the un- even afro and soft, vulnerable face, the women's hips and the jeans always slightly too high in the waist, the tiny gold cross that hung at his throat — the innocence, basically.

'What? I say somethin' that ain't true? You *know* it's true, man — you smiling yourself!'

'Not marriage *per se,*' said Howard crossly. 'It's more complicated. The girl's father is . . . not what we need in this family, put it that way.'

'Yeah, well . . .' said Levi, turning over his father's tie so the front was at the front. 'I don't see what that's got to do with shit.'

'We just don't want Jerome to make a pig's ear of —'

'*We?*' said Levi, with an expertly raised eyebrow — genetically speaking a direct gift from his mother.

'Look — do you need some money or something?' asked Howard. He dug into his pocket and retrieved two crushed twenty-dollar bills, screwed up like balls of tissue. After all these years he was still unable to take the dirty green feel of American money very seriously. He stuffed them in Levi's own low-slung jeans pocket.

' 'Preciate that, Paw,' drawled Levi, in imitation of his mother's Southern roots.

'I don't know what kind of hourly wage they pay you at that place . . .' grumbled Howard.

Levi sighed woefully. 'It's flimsy, man . . . Real flimsy.'

'If you'd only let me go down there, speak to someone and —'

'No!'

Howard assumed his son was embarrassed by him. Shame seemed to be the male inheritance of the Belsey line. How excruciating Howard had found his own father at the same age! He had wished for someone other than a butcher, for someone who used his brain at work rather than knives and scales — someone more like the man Howard was today. But you shift and the children shift also. Would Levi prefer a butcher?

'I mean,' said Levi, artlessly modifying his first reaction, 'I can handle it myself, don't worry about it.'

'I see. Did Mother leave any message or — ?'

'Message? I ain't even *seen* her. I got no idea where she is — she left *early*.'

'Right. What about you? Message for your brother maybe?'

'Yeah . . . Tell him,' said Levi smiling, turning from Howard and holding on to the banister either side of himself, lifting his feet up and then parallel with his chest like a gymnast, 'tell him *"I'm just another black man caught up in the mix, tryna make a dollah outta fifteen cents!"'*

'Right. Will do.'

The doorbell rang. Howard took a step down, kissed the back of his son's head, ducked under one of his arms and went to the door. A familiar, grinning face was there on the other side, turned ashen in the cold. Howard raised a finger in greeting. This was a Haitian fellow called Pierre, one of the many from that difficult island who now found occupation in New England, discreetly compensating for Howard's unwillingness to drive a car.

'Oi — where's Zoor?' Howard called back to Levi from the threshold.

Levi shrugged. 'Eyeano,' he said, that strange squelch of vowels his most frequent response to any question. 'Swimming?'

'In this weather? *Christ.*'

'It's *indoors.* Obviously.'

51

'Just tell her goodbye, all right? Back on Wednesday. No, Thursday.'

'Sure, Dad. Be safe, yo.'

In the car, on the radio, men were screaming at each other in a French that was not, as far as Howard could tell, actually French.

'The airport, please,' said Howard, over this.

'OK, yes. We have to go slow, though. Streets pretty bad.'

'OK, not too slow, though.'

'Terminal?'

The accent was so pronounced Howard thought he heard the name of Zola's novel.

'What's that?'

'You know the terminal?'

'Oh . . . No, I don't . . . I'll find out — it's here somewhere — don't worry . . . you drive — I'll find it.'

'Always flying,' said Pierre rather wistfully, and laughed, looking at Howard via the rear view. Howard was struck by the great width of his nose, straddling the two sides of his amiable face.

'Always off somewhere, yes,' said Howard genially, but it did not seem to him that he travelled so very much, though when he did it was more and further than he wished. He thought of his own father again — compared to him, Howard was Phileas Fogg. Travel had seemed the key to the kingdom, back then. One dreamed of a life that would enable travel. Howard looked through his window at a lamp-post buried to its waist in snow supporting two chained-up, frozen bikes, identifiable only by the tips of their handlebars. He imagined waking up this morning and digging his bike out of the snow and riding to a proper job, the kind Belseys had had for generations, and found he couldn't imagine it. This interested Howard, for a moment: the idea that he could no longer gauge the luxuries of his own life.

Upon returning to the house and before entering her own study, Kiki took her opportunity to look into Howard's. It was half dark, with curtains drawn. He'd left the computer on. Just as she was turning to leave, she heard it waking up, making that heaving, electronic wave-machine sound they produce every ten minutes or so when untouched, as if they're needy, and now sending something unhealthy into the air to admonish us for leaving them. She went over and touched a key — the screen returned. His in-box, with one e-mail waiting. Correctly presuming it was from

Jerome (Howard e-mailed his teaching assistant, Smith J. Miller, Jerome, Erskine Jegede and a selection of newspapers and journals; nobody else), Kiki refreshed the window.

To: HowardBelsey@fas.Wellington.edu
From: Jeromeabroad@easymail.com
Date: 21 November
Subject: PLEASE READ THIS

Dad — mistake. Shouldn't have said anything. Completely over — if it ever began. Please please *please* don't tell anybody, just forget about it. I've made a total fool of myself! I just want to curl up and die.

Jerome

Kiki let out a moan of anxiety, then swore, and turned around twice, clenching her fingers round her scarf, until her body caught up with her mind and ceased its trouble, for there was nothing whatsoever to be done. Howard would already be negotiating with his knees the impossible closeness of the seat in front, torturing himself about which books to retain before placing his bag in the upper storage — it was too late to stop him and there was no way to contact him. Howard had a profound fear of carcinogens: checked food labels for Diethylstilbestrol; abhorred microwaves; had never owned a cellphone.

4

When it comes to weather, New Englanders are delusional. In his ten years on the East Coast Howard had lost count of the times some loon from Massachusetts had heard his accent, looked at him pitiably and said something like: *Cold over there, huh?* Howard's feeling was: look, let's get a few things straight here. England is not warmer than New England in July or August, that's true. Probably not in June either. But it *is* warmer in October, November, December, January, February, March, April and May — that is, in every month when warmth matters. In England letter-boxes do not jam with snow. Rarely does one see a squirrel tremble. It is not necessary to pick up a shovel in order to unearth your rubbish bins. This is because it is never really very cold in England. It is drizzly, and the wind will blow; hail happens, and there is a breed of Tuesday in January in which time creeps and no light comes and the air is full of water and nobody really loves anybody, but still a decent jumper and a waxen jacket lined with wool is sufficient for every weather England's got to give. Howard knew this, and so was suitably dressed for England in November — his one 'good' suit, topped by a lightweight trench coat. Smugly he watched the Boston woman opposite him overheating in her rubber coat, the liberated pearls of sweat emerging from her hairline and slinking down her cheek. He was on the train from Heathrow into town.

At Paddington the doors opened and he stepped into the warm smog of the station. He wound his scarf into a ball and stuffed it in his pocket. He was no tourist and did not look about him, not at the sheer majesty of interior space, nor at that intricate greenhouse ceiling of patterned glass and steel. He walked straight out to the open air, where he might roll a cigarette and smoke it. The absence of snow was sensational. To hold a cigarette without wearing gloves, to reveal one's whole face to the air! Howard rarely felt moved by an English skyline, but today just to see an oak and an office block, outlined by a bluish sky with no interpolation of white on either, seemed to him a landscape of rare splendour and refinement. Relaxing in a narrow corridor of sun, Howard leaned against a pillar. A stretch of black cabs lined up. People explained where they were going and were given generous help lugging bags into back seats. Howard was taken aback to hear twice in five minutes the destination 'Dalston'. Dalston was a filthy East End slum when Howard was born into it, full of filthy people who had tried to destroy him — not least of all his own family. Now, apparently, it was the sort of place where perfectly normal people lived. A blonde in a long powder-blue overcoat holding a portable computer and a pot plant, an Asian boy dressed in a cheap, shiny suit that reflected light like beaten metal — it was impossible to imagine these people populating the East London of his earliest memory. Howard dropped his fag and nudged it into the gutter. He turned back and walked through the station, keeping pace with a flow of commuters, allowing himself to be bustled by them down the steps to the underground. In a standing-room-only tube carriage, pressed up against a determined reader, Howard tried to keep his chin clear of a hardback and considered his mission, such as it was. He had got nowhere with the vital points: what he would say, how he would say it and to whom. The matter was too deeply clouded and perverted for him by the excruciating memory of the following two sentences:

Even given the extreme poverty of the arguments offered, the whole would of course be a great deal more compelling if Belsey knew to which painting I was referring. In his letter he directs his attack at the *Self-Portrait* of 1629 that hangs in Munich. Unfortunately for him, I make it more than clear in my article that the painting under discussion is the *Self-Portrait with Lace Collar* of the same year, which hangs in The Hague.

These were Monty Kipps's sentences. Three months on they clanged, they stung, and sometimes they even seemed to have an actual weight — the thought of them made Howard's shoulders roll forward and down as if someone had snuck up behind and laden him with a backpack filled with stones. Howard got off the train at Baker Street and crossed the platform to the northbound Jubilee line, where the compensation of a waiting train greeted him. And of course, the thing was that in *both* of these self-portraits Rembrandt wears a white collar, for Christ's sake; *both* faces emerge from murky, paranoid shadows with a timorous adolescent look about them — but no matter. Howard had failed to note the differing head position described in Monty's article. He had been going through an extremely difficult time personally and had let his guard down. Monty saw his chance and took it. Howard would have done the same. To enact with one sudden tug (like a boy removing his friend's shorts in front of the opposing team) a complete exposure, a cataclysmic embarrassment — this is one of the purest academic pleasures. One doesn't have to deserve it; one has only to leave oneself open to it. But what a way to go! For fifteen years these two men had been moving in similar circles; passing through the same universities, contributing to the same journals, sometimes sharing a stage — but never an opinion — during panel discussions. Howard had always disliked Monty, as any sensible liberal would dislike a man who had dedicated his life to the perverse politics of right-wing iconoclasm, but he had never *really* hated him until he had heard the news, three years ago, that Kipps too was writing a book about Rembrandt. A book that, even before it was published,

Howard sensed would be a hugely popular (and populist) brick designed to sit heavily atop the *New York Times* bestseller list for half a year, crushing every book beneath it. It was the thought of that book, and of its likely fate (compared to Howard's own unfinished work, which, in the best of all possible worlds, could only ever end up in the bookshelves of a thousand art history students), that had pushed to him to write that terrible letter. In front of the entire academic community Howard had picked up some rope and hanged himself.

Outside Kilburn Station Howard found a phone-box and called directory inquiries. He gave the Kippses' full address and received in return a phone number. For a few minutes he hung about, examining the prostitutes' cards. Strange that there should be so very many of these ladies-of-the-afternoon, tucked away behind the Victorian bay windows, reclining in post-war semis. He noticed how many were black — many more than in a Soho phone-box, surely — and how many, if the photos were to be believed (are they to be believed?), were exceptionally pretty. He picked up the handset again. He paused. In the past year he had grown shyer of Jerome. He feared the new adolescent religiosity, the moral seriousness and silences, always somehow implicitly critical. Howard took courage and dialled.

'Hello?'

'Yes, hello.'

The voice — young-sounding and very London — threw Howard for a moment.

'Hi.'

'Sorry, who's this?'

'I'm . . . who's that?'

'This is the Kipps residence. Who's *that?*'

'Ah — the son, right.'

'Pardon? Who *is* this?'

'Er . . . look, I need to — this is awkward — I'm *Jerome's father* and —'

'Oh, right, let me just call him —'

'No — no — no, wait — one minute —'

' 'Sno trouble — he's having dinner, but I can call him —'

'No, don't — I — look, I don't want to . . . Thing is, I've just come from Boston . . . we only just heard, you see —'

'OK,' said the voice in an exploratory way that Howard couldn't get a handle on.

'Well,' said Howard, swallowing hard, 'I'd quite like to sound out someone in the family a little . . . before I speak properly to Jerome — he didn't explain much — and obviously . . . I'm sure your father —'

'My father's eating too. Do you want to —'

'No . . . no, no, no, no, *no.* I mean, he won't want to . . . *no* . . . no, no — I just . . . whole thing's a bloody mess, of course, it's just a matter of —' began Howard, but then could not think what indeed it was a matter of.

A cough came down the line. 'Look, I don't understand — do you want me to get Jerome?'

'I'm right near you, actually —' Howard blurted.

'Excuse me?'

'Yes . . . I'm calling from a phone-box . . . I don't really know this bit of town and . . . no map, you see. You couldn't . . . pick me up maybe? I'm rather — I'll only get lost if I try to get to you — no sense of direction at all . . . I'm just at the station.'

'Right. It's really an easy walk, I could give you directions.'

'If you *could* just pop up here, it would be very helpful — it's getting dark already and I know I'll take a wrong turn, and . . .'

Howard cringed into the silence.

'I'd just like to ask you a few things, you see — before I see Jerome.'

'All right,' said the voice at last, tetchy now. 'Well — let me get my coat, yeah? Outside the station, right? Queen's Park.'

'Queens . . . ? No, I, er . . . Oh, *Christ,*

62

I'm at Kilburn — is that wrong? I thought *you* were in Kilburn.'

'Not really. We're between the two, closer to Queen's Park. Look, just . . . I'll come and get you, don't worry. Kilburn Jubilee line, right?'

'Yes, that's right — that's very kind of you, thank you. Is it Michael?'

'Yes. Mike. You're . . . ?'

'Belsey, Howard Belsey. Jerome's —'

'Yeah. Well, stay there, then, Professor. I'll be seven minutes, maybe.'

A rough white boy lurked outside the phone-box, with a doughy face and three well-spaced spots, one on his nose, one on his cheek and one on his chin. As Howard opened the door, doing the apologetic smile thing, the boy did the uninterested in outmoded social convention thing, saying 'About fucking *time*', and then made it as difficult as possible for Howard to get out and for the boy to get in. Howard's face glowed. Why this flush of shame, when it is someone else who has been rude, pushing you roughly with their shoulder — why the shame? It was more than shame, though, it was also the physical capitulation — at twenty Howard might have sworn back at him or offered him out; at thirty, even at forty; but not at fifty-six, not now. Fearing an escalation *(What you looking at?)* Howard dug into his pocket and found the requisite three pounds for the nearby photo-booth. He bent his knees and parted the miniature orange curtain as if entering a tiny harem. He sat on the stool, a fist on each knee and his head low. When he looked up, he found himself reflected in the sheet of dirty perspex, his face enclosed by a big red circle. The first flash went off without any planning on Howard's part: he had dropped his gloves and, upon looking down to find them, was then forced to spring back up as he heard the machine begin, his head just that moment raised, his hair obscuring his right eye. He looked cowed, beaten down. For the second flash he lifted his chin and tried to challenge the camera as that boy might — the result was something yet more insecure. There followed a completely unreal smile that Howard would never smile in the course of a normal day. Then the consequences of the unreal smile — sad, frank, abashed, almost confessional, as men often appear in their final years. Howard gave up. He stayed where he was, waiting to hear the boy leave the phone-box and walk away. Then he retrieved his gloves from the floor and left his own small box.

Outside the bare trees lined up along the high road, lopped branches thrust into the air. Howard stepped forward to lean against one of these, careful to avoid the dirty patch around the trunk. From here he could keep an eye on both ends of the street and the mouth of the station. A few minutes later he looked up and saw the man he assumed he was waiting for, rounding the corner of the next street. To Howard's eye, which fancied itself attuned to these things, he looked African. He had that ochre highlight in his skin, most visible where the skin was in tension with bone — at the cheekbones and across the forehead. He wore leather gloves, a long grey topcoat and a dark blue cashmere scarf tied smartly. His glasses were thin-rimmed and gold. His shoes were an item of interest: very grubby trainers of the flat, cheap kind Howard felt sure Levi would never wear. As he came closer to the station, he slowed down and began to cast his eyes around the small gathering of people waiting for other people. Howard thought himself as instantly recognizable as this Michael Kipps, but it was he who had to come forward and hold his hand out.

'Michael — Howard. Hi. *Thanks* for coming to get me, I wasn't —'

'Find it OK?' Michael cut in with extreme shortness, nodding at the station. Howard, who didn't understand the point of this question, grinned stupidly back at him. Michael was quite a bit taller than Howard, which Howard was unused to and disliked. He was broad too; not that freshman muscle that Howard saw in his classes, the kind that begins at the top of the neck and makes young men trapezoid, no, this was more elegant than that. A birthright. He's one of those people, thought Howard, who looks like one quality very much, and the quality in this case is 'noble'. Howard didn't much trust people like that, so full of one quality, like books with insistent covers.

'This way, then,' said Michael, and took a step forward, but Howard caught him by the shoulder.

'Just going to get these — new passport,' he said, as the photos were delivered to the chute, where an artificial breeze began to blow on them.

Howard reached for his pictures, but now Michael's hand stopped him.

'Wait — let them dry — they smudge otherwise.'

Howard straightened up, and they both stood still where they were, watching the photos twitch. Although perfectly content with silence, Howard suddenly heard himself saying 'Soooo . . .' for a long time, with no clear idea of what was to follow 'so'. Michael turned to him, his face sourly expectant.

'So,' said Howard again, 'what is it you do, Mike, Michael?'

'I'm a risk analyst for an equities firm.'

Like many academics, Howard was innocent of the world. He could identify thirty different ideological trends in the social sciences, but did not really know what a software engineer was.

'Oh, I see . . . that's very . . . Is that in the City, or — ?'

'In the City, yeah. Round St Paul's way.'

'But you're still living at home.'

'Just come back weekends. Go to church, Sunday lunch. Family stuff.'

'Live near by or — ?'

'Camden — just by the —'

'Oh, I know *Camden* — once upon a century I used to knock about there a bit — well, do you know where the —'

'Your photos are finished, I think,' said Michael, picking them out of their cubbyhole. He shook them and blew on them.

'You couldn't use the first three; they're not square on your face,' said Michael brusquely. 'They're strict about that now.

Use the last one, maybe.'

He handed them to Howard, who pushed them into his pocket without looking. So he hates the idea of this marriage even more than I do, thought Howard. He can barely even be polite to me.

Together they walked down the street from which Michael had just come. There was something fatally humourless even in the way the young man walked, a status-preserving precision to each step, as if proving to a policeman that he could walk along a straight white line. A minute and then two passed without either man speaking. They walked by houses and more houses, uninterrupted by any conveniences, neither shop nor cinema nor launderette. Everywhere cramped rows of Victorian terraces, the maiden aunts of English architecture, the culture museums of bourgeois Victoriana . . . This was an old rant of Howard's. He grew up in one of these houses. Once free of his own family he had experimented with radical living spaces — communes and squats. And then the children came, the second family, and all of those spaces became impossible. He did not like to remember now exactly how much and for long he had coveted his mother-in-law's house — we forget what we choose to forget. He saw himself instead as a man hustled by circumstance into spaces that he rejected politically, personally, aesthetically, as a concession to his family. One among many concessions.

They turned into a new street, clearly bombed in the last war. Here were mid-century monstrosities with mock-Tudor fronts and crazy-paved driveways. Pampas grass, like the tails of huge suburban cats, drooped over the front walls.

'It's nice round here,' said Howard, and wondered about this instinct of his to offer unsolicited exactly the opposite opinion to the one he held.

'Yeah. You live in Boston.'

'Just outside of Boston. Near a liberal arts place I teach at — Wellington. You probably haven't heard of it over here,' said Howard with false humility, for Wellington was by far the most respected institution he had ever worked in, as close to an Ivy League as he was ever going to get.

'Jerome's there, isn't he?'

'No, no — actually, his *sister's* there — Zora. Jerome's at Brown. Much healthier idea, probably,' said Howard, although the truth was he had been hurt by the choice. 'Breaking free, apron strings, etcetera.'

'Not necessarily.'

'You don't think?'

'I was at the same uni as my dad at one point — I think that's a good thing, when families are close-knit.'

The pomposity of the young man seemed to Howard to be concentrated in his jaw, which he worked round and round as they walked, as if ruminating on the failures of others.

'Oh, absolutely,' said Howard, generously, he felt. 'Jerome and I, we're just not . . . well, we have different ideas about things and . . . you and your father must be closer than us — more able to . . . well, I don't know.'

'We're very close.'

'Well,' said Howard, restraining himself, 'you're very lucky.'

'It's about *trying,*' said Michael keenly — the topic seemed to animate him. 'It's like, if you put the effort in. And I spose my mum's always been at home, which makes a lot of difference, I think. Having the mother figure and all that. Nurturing. It's like a Caribbean ideal — a lot of people lose sight of it.'

'Right,' said Howard, and walked another two streets — past an ice-cream scoop of a Hindu temple and down an avenue of awful bungalows — imagining knocking

70

this young man's head against a tree.

The lamps were lit on every street now. Howard began to be able to make out the Queen's Park to which Michael had referred. It was nothing like the groomed royal parks in the centre of town. Just a small village green with a colourful spot-lit Victorian bandstand at its centre.

'Michael — can I say something?'

Michael said nothing.

'Look, I don't mean in any way to offend anyone in your family, and I can see we agree basically anyway — I can't see the point in arguing over it. Really we need to put our heads together and just think of . . . well, I suppose, some *way,* some *means* of convincing both of them, you know — that this is a bloody *insane* idea — I mean, that's the *key* thing, no?'

'Look, man,' said Michael tersely, quickening his step, 'I'm not an intellectual, right? I'm not involved in whatever the argument is regarding my father. I'm a forgiving Christian, and as far as I'm concerned whatever is between you and him doesn't change the way we feel about Jerome — he's a good kid, man, and that's the main thing — so there's no argument.'

'Yes — of course, of course, of *course,* no one's *saying* there's an argument — I'm just saying, and I'm hoping your father will *appreciate* this, that Jerome's really too young — and he's younger than he *actually* is — emotionally he's much younger, completely inexperienced — much more so than you probably realize —'

'Sorry — am I being stupid — what are you trying to say?'

Howard took a deep, artificial breath. 'I think they're both much, *much* too young to get married, Michael, I really do. That's it, in a nutshell. I'm not old-fashioned, but I do think, by any measure —'

'Marriage?' said Michael, stopping where he was, pushing his glasses up the bridge of his nose an inch. 'Who's getting married? What're you chatting about?'

'Jerome. And Victoria — sorry . . . I thought that surely —'

Michael arranged his jaw in a new way. 'Are we talking about my sister?'

'Yes — sorry — Jerome and Victoria — who are you talking about? Wait — what?'

Michael let out a loud single-burst laugh, and then came closer to Howard's face with his own, seeking some sign of jest. When none came, he took off his glasses and slowly rubbed them against his scarf.

'I don't know where you got that idea, yeah, but just seriously, like, remove it, because it just isn't even . . . Phew!' he said, breathing out heavily, shaking his head and replacing his glasses. 'I mean, I like Jerome, he's fine, yeah? But I think my family wouldn't really . . . *feel safe* thinking of Victoria getting involved with somebody who was so far outside of . . .' Howard watched Michael openly search for a euphemism. 'Well, things we think are important, right? That's just not the plan right now, sorry. You've got the wrong end of something there, mate, but whatever it is, I suggest you get the right end of it before you walk into my father's house, you understand? Jerome is just not the thing at all, *at all.*'

Michael began to walk off at speed, still shaking his head, with Howard angled to his right, trying to keep up. This was interspersed with frequent side glances at Howard and more of this head-shaking, until Howard was considerably wound up.

'Look, *excuse* me — I'm not exactly overjoyed here, right? Jerome's whack bam in the middle of his studies — and anyway, if and when the time comes I imagine he's expecting a woman of similar — how do you want me to say this — *intellectual* — and not the first woman he happens to have got his end away with. Look, I don't want to fall out with you as well — we *agree,* that's fine — you and I both know that Jerome's a *baby* —'

Howard, who had matched Michael's pace at last, halted him once more by laying a firm hand on his shoulder. Michael turned his head quite slowly to look at the hand, until Howard felt compelled to retract it.

'What was that?' said Michael, and Howard noticed a slip in his accent, to something a little rougher, a little more familiar with the street than with the office. 'Excuse me? Get your hands off me, all right? My sister is a *virgin,* yeah? You get me? That's how she was brought up, yeah? Mate, I don't even *know* what your son has been telling you —'

This medieval turn to the conversation was too much for Howard. 'Michael — I don't want to . . . we're on the same *side* here — no one's saying a marriage isn't completely ridiculous — look at my lips, I'm saying completely ridiculous, *completely* — no one's *disputing your sister's honour,* really . . . no need for swords at dawn . . . duel to the . . . or any of that — look, of course I know you and your family have "beliefs",' began Howard uneasily, as if 'beliefs' were a kind of condition, like oral herpes. 'You know . . . and I completely and utterly respect and tolerate that — I didn't realize this was a surprise to you —'

'Well, it is, yeah? It's a *fucking* surprise!' cried Michael, turning about him and whispering the swear word, as if in fear of being overheard.

'So, OK . . . it's a surprise, I appreciate that . . . Michael, please . . . I didn't come here to have a row — let's take it down a notch —'

'If he's *touched* —' began Michael, and Howard, over and above the madness of the conversation itself, began to feel genuinely afraid of him. The flight from the rational, which was everywhere in evidence in the new century, none of it had surprised Howard as it had surprised others, but each new example he came across — on the television, in the street and now in this young man — weakened him somehow. His desire to be involved in the argument, in the culture, fell off. The energy to fight the philistines, this is what fades. Now Howard's eyes turned to the ground, in some expectation of being thumped or otherwise verbally abused. He listened to a sudden curve of wind swoop around the corner they were standing on and rustle the trees.

'Michael —'

'I don't *believe* this.'

The nobility Howard had first thought he detected in Michael's face was rapidly being replaced by a hardening, the nonchalant manner supplanted by its exact opposite, as if some fluid poisonous to his system had been swapped for the blood in his veins. His head whipped back round; now Howard seemed no longer to exist for him. He began to walk with speed, almost to jog, down the street. Howard called out to him. Michael increased his pace, took a sudden, jerky right and kicked open an iron gate. He shouted 'Jerome!' and disappeared under and through a leafless bower that thrust twigs in all directions, like a nest. Howard followed him through the gate and under the bower. He stopped before an imposing double-fronted black door with a silver knocker. It was ajar. He paused again in the Victorian hallway, underfoot those black-and-white diamonds that no one had welcomed him on to. A minute later, upon hearing raised voices, he followed them to the furthest room, a high-ceilinged dining room with dramatic French doors, before which was a long table laid with five dinner settings. He had the sense of being in one of those horrid claustrophobic Edwardian plays, in which the whole world is reduced to one room.

To the right of this scene was his son, presently pressed up against a wall by Michael Kipps. Of other matters, Howard had time to note someone who must be Mrs Kipps with her right hand raised in the direction of Jerome, and someone beside her with their face in their hands and only their intricately plaited scalp on view. Then the tableau came to life.

'Michael,' Mrs Kipps was saying firmly. She pronounced the name so that it rhymed with 'Y-Cal', a brand of sugar substitute that Howard used in his coffee. 'Let Jerome go, please — the engagement is already off. No need for this.'

Howard noticed the surprise on his own son's face as Mrs Kipps said the word 'engagement'. Jerome tried to stretch his head away from Michael's body to catch the eye of the silent, curled-up figure at the table, but this figure did not move.

'Engagement! Since when was there an engagement!' Michael yelled and drew back his fist, but Howard was already there and surprised himself by instinctively reaching out to grab the boy's wrist. Mrs Kipps was trying to stand but seemed to be having difficulty, and, when she called her son's name again, Howard was thankful to feel all the will in Michael's arm dissolve. Jerome, shaking, stepped aside.

'Anyone could see it happening,' said Mrs Kipps quietly. 'But it's over now. All done.'

Michael looked confused for a minute, and then a second thought seemed to come to him and he started to rattle the handle of the French doors. 'Dad!' he shouted, but the doors wouldn't give. Howard stepped forward to help him with the top lock. Michael violently shrugged him off, spotted the fastened lock at last and released it. The French doors flew open. Michael stepped out into the garden, still calling for his father, as the wind chased the curtains up and down. Howard could make out a long stretch of grass and somewhere at the end of it the orange glow of a small bonfire. Beyond that, the ivy-covered base of a monumental tree, the invisible top of which belonged to the night.

'Hello, Dr Belsey,' said Mrs Kipps now, as if all of this were a perfectly normal preamble to a nice social call. She took her napkin off her knees and stood up. 'We've not met, have we?'

She was not all what he'd expected. Howard had for some reason envisioned a younger woman, a trophy. But she was older than Kiki, more like sixty something, and rather rangy. Her hair was set and curled but stray wisps framed her face, and her clothes were not at all formal: a dark purple skirt that reached the floor, and an Indian blouse of loose white cotton with elaborate needlework down its front. Her neck was long (he saw now where Michael had inherited his look of nobility) and deeply creased, and round it was a substantial piece of art deco jewellery with a multifaceted moonstone at its centre, rather than the expected cross. She took both of Howard's hands in her own. At once Howard felt that things were not as absolutely dire as they had appeared to be twenty seconds earlier.

'Please, not "Doctor",' he said. 'I'm — off-duty — it's Howard — please. Hello — I'm *so* sorry about all of —'

Howard looked about him. The person he now assumed to be Victoria (though the sex was not at all clear from the scalp) was still frozen at the table. Jerome had slid all the way down the wall like a stain and now sat on the floor, looking at his feet.

'Young people, Howard,' said Mrs Kipps, as if beginning a Caribbean children's story Howard had no interest in hearing, 'they got their own way of doing things — it's not always our way, but it's a way.' She smiled a purple gummy smile, and shook her head several times with what appeared to be a slight palsy. 'These two are sensible enough, thank the Lord. Did you know Victoria just turned eighteen? Can you *remember* eighteen? I know I can't, it's like another universe. Now . . . Howard, you staying in a hotel, yes? I would offer you to stay here but —'

Howard confirmed the existence of his hotel and his enthusiasm for leaving for it immediately.

'That's a good idea. And I think you should take Jerome —'

At this point Jerome put his head in his hands; at the same moment, in a perfect inversion, the young lady at the table sprang out of that exact position, and Howard registered in his peripheral vision a gamine type with spidery-lashed wet eyes, and arms of sinew and bone like a ballet dancer's.

'Don't worry, Jerome — you can get your things in the morning when Montague is at work. You can write to Victoria when you get home. Let's not have any more scenes today, please.'

'Can I *just* —' offered the daughter, but stopped when Mrs Kipps closed her eyes and with unsteady fingers touched her own lips.

'Victoria, go and see on the stew, please. Go.'

Victoria stood up and slammed her chair into the table. As she left the room, Howard watched her nimble shoulder blades from the back, shifting up and down like pistons driving the engine of her sulk.

Mrs Kipps smiled again. 'We've loved having him, Howard. He's such a good, honest, upright young man. You should be very proud of him, truly.'

All this time she had been holding Howard's hands; now she gave them a final squeeze and released him.

'I should probably stay and talk to your husband?' mumbled Howard, hearing approaching voices from the garden and praying that this would not be necessary.

'I don't think that's a good idea, do you?' said Mrs Kipps, turning, and, with a fugitive breeze lifting her skirt a little, she drifted down the patio steps and vanished into the gloom.

5

We must now jump nine months forward, and back across the Atlantic Ocean. It is

81

the third sultry weekend of August, during which the town of Wellington, Mass, holds an annual outdoor festival for families. Kiki had intended to bring her family, but, by the time she returned from her Saturday-morning yoga class, they had already dispersed, off in search of shade. Outside, the pool stagnated under a shifting layer of maple leaves. Inside, the AC whirred for no one. Only Murdoch was left, she found him flat out in the bedroom, his head or his paws, tongue as dry as chamois leather. Kiki rolled down her leggings and wriggled out of her vest. She threw them across the room into an overflowing wicker basket. She stood naked for a while before her closet, making some astute decisions regarding her weight as it might be placed on an axis against the heat and the distance she would be covering, making her way through Wellington's celebrations alone. On a shelf here she kept a chaotic pile of multipurpose scarves, like something a magician might pull from his pocket. Now she picked out a brown cotton one with a fringe, and wrapped her hair in this. Then an orange square of silk that could be fashioned into a top, tied beneath the shoulder blades. A deep red scarf, of a coarser silk, she wore around her waist as a sarong. She sat on the bed to fiddle with the buckles of her sandals, a hand idly turning over one of Murdoch's ears, from the glossy brown to the crenulated pink and back again. 'You're with me, baby,' she said, heaving him up and on to her chest, the hot sack of his belly in her hand. Just as she was about to leave the house, she heard a noise from the living room. She retraced her steps down the hallway and put her head around the door.

'Hey, Jerome, baby.'

'Hey.'

Her son sat morosely in the beanbag, in his lap a notebook bound in fraying blue silk. Kiki put Murdoch on the floor and watched his maladroit waddle towards Jerome, where he sat upon the boy's toes.

'Writing?' she asked.

'No, dancing,' came the reply.

Kiki let her mouth close and then opened it once more with a mordant puck. Since London he was like this. Sarcastic, secretive, sixteen all over again. And always working away at this diary. He was threatening not to go back to college. Kiki felt that the two of them, mother and son, were now moving steadily in obverse directions: Kiki to forgiveness, Jerome to bitterness. For, though it had taken almost a year, Kiki had begun to release the memory of

Howard's mistake. She had had all the usual conversations with friends and with herself; she had measured a nameless, faceless woman in a hotel room next to what she knew of herself; she had weighed one stupid night against a lifetime of love and felt the difference in her heart. If you'd told Kiki a year ago, *Your husband will screw somebody else, you will forgive him, you will stay,* she wouldn't have believed it. You can't say how these things will feel, or how you will respond, until they happen to you. Kiki had drawn upon reserves of forgiveness that she didn't even know she had. But for Jerome, friendless and brooding, it was clear that one week with Victoria Kipps, nine months ago, had expanded in his mind until it now took up all the space in his life. Where Kiki had felt her way instinctively through her problem, Jerome had written his out, words and words and words. Not for the first time, Kiki felt grateful she was not an intellectual. From here she could see the strangely melancholic format of Jerome's text, italics and ellipses everywhere. Slanted sails blowing about on perforated seas.

'Remember that thing . . .' Kiki said absently, rubbing his exposed ankle with her own shin. *'Writing about music is like dancing about architecture.* Who said that again?'

Jerome crossed his eyes like Howard and looked away.

Kiki hunkered down to Jerome's eye level. She put two fingers to his chin and drew his face to hers. 'You OK, baby?'

'Mom, please.'

Kiki cupped Jerome's face in her hands. She stared at him, seeking a refracted image of the girl who had caused all this misery, but Jerome had not given his mother any details when it happened and he wasn't going to give her any now. It was a matter of an impossible translation — his mother wanted to know about a girl, but it wasn't *about* a girl or, rather, it wasn't about *just* the girl. Jerome had fallen in love with a family. He felt he couldn't tell his own family this fact; it was easier for them to believe that last year was Jerome's 'romantic fuck-up' or — more pleasing to the Belsey mentality — his 'flirtation with Christianity'. How could he explain how pleasurable it had truly been to give himself up to the Kippses? It was a kind of blissful un-selfing; a summer of un-Belsey; he had allowed the Kippses' world and their ways to take him over entirely. He had *liked* to listen to the exotic (to a

85

Belsey) chatter of business and money and practical politics; to hear that Equality was a myth, and Multiculturalism a fatuous dream; he thrilled at the suggestion that Art was a gift from God, blessing only a handful of masters, and most Literature merely a veil for poorly reasoned left-wing ideologies. He had put up a weak show of fighting these ideas, but only so that he might enjoy all the more the sensation of the family's ridicule — to hear once again how typically liberal, academic and wishy-washy were his own thoughts. When Monty suggested that minority groups too often demand equal rights they haven't earned, Jerome had allowed this strange new idea to penetrate him without complaint and sunk further back into the receiving sofa. When Michael argued that being black was not an identity but an accidental matter of pigment, Jerome had not given a traditionally hysterical Belsey answer — 'Try telling that to the Klansman coming at you with a burning cross' — but rather vowed to think less of his identity in the future. One by one the gods of the Belseys toppled. *I'm so full of liberal crap,* Jerome had thought happily, bowed his head low and pressed his knees into one of the little red cushions provided for kneeling in the Kippses' pew of the local church. Long before Victoria arrived in the house, he was already in love. It was only that his general ardour for the family found its correct, specific vessel in Victoria — right age, right gender, and as beautiful as the idea of God. Victoria herself, flush with the social and sexual successes of her first summer abroad without her family, returned home to find a tolerable young man, weighed down by his virginity and satisfyingly unmanned by his desire for her. It seemed petty not to make a gift of her new-found loveliness (she had been what Caribbeans call a *margar* child) to a boy so obviously starved of the same quality. And he'd be gone by August anyway. They spent a week stealing kisses in shaded corners of the house and made love once, extremely badly, under the tree in the Kippses' back garden. Victoria never for a moment considered . . . But of course Jerome did. Considering things too much, all the time, was the definition of who he was.

'It's not healthy, baby,' said his mother now, smoothing his hair to his scalp, watching it spring back. 'You're brooding the hell out of this summer. Summer's almost up.'

'What's your point?' said Jerome, with uncharacteristic rudeness.

'It's a shame, that's all . . .' said Kiki quietly. 'Look, shug, I'm going to the festival — why don't you come?'

'Why don't I,' replied Jerome, without inflection.

'It's a hundred and ten degrees in here, baby. Everybody done gone already.'

Jerome mimed a minstrel's expression to match his mother's intonations. He returned to his task. As he wrote, his womanly mouth drew into a tight, cushioned pout, and this in turn accentuated the family's cheekbones. His prominent forehead — the detail that made him so unpretty — pulled forward, as if in sympathy with the long, horse's lashes that curled up to meet it.

'You just going to sit in all day, write your diary?'

'Not a diary. Journal.'

Kiki made a noise of defeat, stood up. She walked casually around the back of him and then bellyflopped suddenly towards him, hugging him from behind, reading over his shoulder: *'It is easy to mistake a woman for a philosophy . . .'*

'Mom, fuck *off* — I'm serious —'

'Watch your mouth — *The mistake is to be attached to the world at all. It will not thank you for your attachments. Love is the extremely difficult realization —*'

Jerome wrestled the book away from her.

'What is that — proverbs? Sounds *heavy.* You're not gonna put on a trench coat and shoot up your school, now, are you, baby?'

'Ha, ha.'

Kiki kissed the back of his head and stood up. 'Too much recording — try living,' she suggested softly.

'False opposition.'

'Oh, Jerome, *please* — get up out of that nasty thing, come with me. You *live* in that goddamn beanbag. Don't make me go alone. Zora went with her girls already.'

'I'm *busy.* Where's Levi?'

'Saturday job. Come *on.* I'm by myself . . . and Howard left me high and dry — he went off with Erskine an hour ago . . .'

This sneaky mention of his father's negligence had exactly the effect his mother had intended. He groaned and closed the book between his big, soft hands. Kiki reached out her own hands in a cross towards her son. He grabbed both and heaved himself up.

From the house to the town square was a pretty walk: swollen gourds on doorsteps, white clapboard houses, luscious gardens carefully planted in preparation for the famous fall. Fewer American flags than in

Florida but more than in San Francisco. Everywhere the hint of yellow curl on the leaves of the trees, like the catch paper thrown at something about to go up in flame. Here also were some of the oldest things in America: three churches built in the 1600s, a graveyard overrun with mouldy pilgrims, blue plaques alerting you to all of this. Kiki made a cautious move to link arms with Jerome; he let her. People began to join them on the road, a few more at each corner. At the square, the power of independent movement was taken away from them; they were as one mass with hundreds of others. It had been a mistake to bring Murdoch. The festival was at its most populated point, lunchtime, and inside the crush everybody was too hot and grouchy to be interested in stepping aside for a small dog. With difficulty the three of them made their way to the less populated sidewalk. Kiki stopped at a stall selling sterling silver — earrings, bracelets, necklaces. The stallholder was a black man, exceptionally skinny, in a green string vest and grubby blue jeans. No shoes at all. His bloodshot eyes widened as Kiki picked up some hoop earrings. She had only this brief glimpse of him, but Kiki suspected already that this would be one of those familiar exchanges in which her enormous spellbinding bosom would play a subtle (or not so subtle, depending on the person) silent third role in the conversation. Women bent away from it out of politeness; men — more comfortably for Kiki — sometimes remarked on it in order to get on and over it, as it were. The size was sexual and at the same time more than sexual: sex was only one small element of its symbolic range. If she were white, maybe it would refer only to sex, but she was not. And so her chest gave off a mass of signals beyond her direct control: sassy, sisterly, predatory, motherly, threatening, comforting — it was a mirror-world she had stepped into in her mid forties, a strange fabulation of the person she believed she was. She could no longer be meek or shy. Her body had directed her to a new personality; people expected new things of her, some of them good, some not. And she had been a tiny thing for years and years! How does it happen? Kiki held the hoops up to each ear. The stall guy proffered a small oval mirror, raising it up to her face, but not quickly enough for her sensitivities.

'Excuse me, brother — a few inches higher with that — *Thank* you — *they* don't wear jewellery — sorry 'bout that. Just the ears.'

Jerome recoiled from this joke. He dreaded his mother's habit of starting conversations with strangers.

'Honey?' she asked Jerome, turning to him. Again with the shrugging. In comic response, Kiki turned back to the stall guy and shrugged, but he only said 'Fifteen' loudly and stared at her. He was unsmiling and intent upon a sale. He had a brutal, foreign accent. Kiki felt foolish. Her right hand passed quickly over a number of items on the table.

'OK . . . And these?'

'All earring fifteen, necklace thirty, bracelet some ten, some fifteen, different — silver, all silver — all this here silver. You should try necklace, very nice — with black skin, it is good. Do you like earrings?'

'I'm going to get a burrito.'

'Oh, Jerome, please — one minute. We can't spend five minutes together? What do you think of those?'

'Fine.'

'Small hoop or big?'

Jerome made a desperate face.

'OK, OK. Where will you be?'

Jerome pointed directly into the rippling day. 'It's called something hokey . . . like Chicken America or something.'

'God, Jay, I don't know what that is.

What is that? Just meet me in front of the bank in fifteen, OK? And get me one — a shrimp one if they have it, extra hot sauce and sour cream. You *know* I like 'em hot.'

She watched him amble away, pulling his long-sleeved Nirvana T-shirt down over that sloppy English backside, wide and charmless like the rear view of one of Howard's aunts. She turned back to the stall and once again tried to engage the man, but he was busy fiddling with the coins in his fanny pack. Listlessly she picked up this and that and put it down, nodding at prices as they were earnestly re-counted each time her finger made contact with an item. Aside from her money, the guy seemed barely concerned with her, neither as a person nor as an idea. He did not call Kiki 'sister', make any assumptions or take any liberties. Obscurely disappointed, as we sometimes are when the things we profess to dislike don't happen, she looked up abruptly and smiled at him. 'You're from Africa?' she asked sweetly, and picked up a charm bracelet with tiny replicas of international totems hanging from it: the Eiffel Tower, the Leaning Tower of Pisa, the Statue of Liberty.

The man folded his arms across his narrow filleted chest, every rib as visible as it is upon a cat's belly. 'Where do you *think* I am from? You are African — no?'

'No, noooo, I'm from *here* — but of course . . .' said Kiki. She wiped some sweat from her forehead with the back of her hand, waiting for him to finish the sentence as she knew it would be finished.

'We are all from Africa,' said the man obligingly. He made a double outward fan of his hands over the jewellery. 'All of this, from Africa. You know where I am from?'

Kiki was trying to fix something to her wrist, unsuccessfully. Now she looked up as the man took a half step back to give her a fuller view of him. She found she wanted very much *to be right,* and struggled for a minute between a few places she recalled having French history, unsure if she was right about any of them. She wondered about her own boredom. She must be very bored indeed to want to be right before this man.

'Ivory . . .' began Kiki cautiously, but his face repelled this, so she switched to Martinique.

'*Haiti,*' he said.

'*Right.* My —' began Kiki, but realized she did not want to say the word 'cleaner' in this context. She began again, 'There're so many Haitians here . . .' She dared a

94

little further: 'And of course it's so difficult, in Haiti, right now.'

The man put the hub of each hand firmly on the table between them and engaged her eyes. *'Yes.* Terrible. *So terrible.* Now, every day — *terror.'*

The solemnity of this reply forced Kiki to turn her attention back to the bracelet sliding off her wrist. She had only the most vague sense of the difficulty she had made reference to (it had slid off the radar under the stress of other, more pressing difficulties, national and personal) and felt ashamed now to be caught under the pretence of having more knowledge than she possessed.

'This is not for here — for *here,'* he said, suddenly coming around the table and pointing at Kiki's ankle.

'Oh . . . it's like a . . . what do you call that, an *anklet?'*

'Put here — put up here — please.'

Kiki released Murdoch to the floor and allowed this man to lift her foot on to the small bamboo stool. She had to rest her hand on his shoulder for balance. Kiki's sarong opened a little and some of her thigh was revealed. Moisture sprang from the chubby crease behind her knee. The man did not seem to notice but remained purposeful, catching one sweaty loose end of the chain and bringing it round to meet the other. It was in this unorthodox position that Kiki found herself ambushed from behind. Two masculine hands grabbed her round her middle, squeezed — and then a hot red face materialized next to her own like the Cheshire Cat's, kissing her damp cheek.

'Jay — don't be crazy —'

'Keeks, *wow* — you're all leg. What're you trying to do, kill me?'

'Oh, my *God* — Warren — *Hi* . . . You almost killed *me* — *Jesus* — creeping like a *fox* — I thought it was Jerome, he's around here someplace . . . God, I didn't even know you guys were back. How was Italy? Where's —'

Kiki spotted the subject of her question, Claire Malcolm, turning away from a stall selling massage oils. Claire looked confused for a moment, panicked almost, but then raised a hand, smiling. In response Kiki gave Claire the long-distance look of surprise and swept her hand up and down to signify the change in Claire, a little green sundress instead of her winter staples of black leather jacket, black polo neck and black jeans. Thinking about it, she hadn't seen Claire Malcolm since the winter. Now she was speckled a toasty

Mediterranean brown, the pale blue of her eyes intensified by the contrast. Kiki signaled to her to come over. The Haitian man, having fastened Kiki's anklet, dropped his hands and looked anxiously at her.

'Warren, just wait one minute — let me just do this — how much again?'

'Fifteen. For this fifteen.'

'I thought you said *ten* for a bracelet — Warren, sorry about this, just one minute — didn't you say ten?'

'This one fifteen, please, fifteen.'

Kiki hunted in her purse for her wallet. Warren Crane stood beside her, with his hefty head, too large for that neatly muscular blue-collar New Jersey body, his beefy sailor arms crossed and a whimsical look on his face, like that of an audience member waiting for the comedian to get on stage. When you are no longer in the sexual universe — when you are supposedly too old, or too big, or simply no longer thought of in that way — apparently a whole new range of male reactions to you come into play. One of them is humour. They find you funny. But then, thought Kiki, they were brought up that way, these white American boys: I'm the Aunt Jemima on the cookie boxes of their childhoods, the pair of thick ankles Tom and Jerry played around. Of course they find me funny. And yet I could cross the river to Boston and barely be left alone for five minutes at a time. Only last week a young brother half her age had trailed Kiki up and down Newbury for an hour and would not relent until she said he could take her out some time; she gave him a fake number.

'You need a loan, Keeks?' asked Warren. 'Sister, I could spare you a dime.'

Kiki laughed. She found her wallet at last. Money dealt with, she said goodbye to the trader.

'That's pretty,' said Warren, looking down her and then up her again. 'As if you needed to get any prettier.'

And this is another thing they do. They flirt with you violently because there is no possibility of it being taken seriously.

'What did she get — something lovely? Oh, that *is* lovely,' said Claire as she approached, peering down at Kiki's ankle. She tucked her tiny body into a cleft of Warren's. Photographs elongated her, making her appear long and wiry, but in life this American poet was only five foot one and physically prepubescent, even now, at fifty-four. She was neatly made

98

with the minimum of material. When she moved a finger, you could trace the motion through pulleys of veins that went all the way up her slender arms and shoulders to her neck, itself elegantly creased like the lungs of an accordion. Her elfin head with its inch of closely cropped brown hair fitted neatly into her lover's hand. To Kiki they looked very happy — but what did that mean? Wellington couples had a talent for looking happy.

'Incredible day, isn't it? We got back a week ago and it's hotter here than it was there. The sun is a *lemon* today, it *is*. It's like a huge lemon-drop. *God,* it's incredible,' said Claire, as Warren softly palpated the back of her skull. She was babbling a little; it always took her a minute or two to settle. Claire had been at graduate school with Howard, and Kiki had known her thirty years, but never had she felt that they knew each other well. They did not quite gel as friends. There was a part of Kiki that felt every meeting with Claire was like the first time all over again. 'And you look marvellous!' cried Claire now. 'It's so good to *see* you. What an outfit! It's like a sunset — the red, the yellow, the orangey-brown — Keeks, you're *setting*.'

'Honey,' said Kiki, moving her head from

side to side in a manner she understood white people enjoyed, 'I done *set already.*'

Claire made the jangle sound of laughter. Not for the first time, Kiki noted the implacable intelligence of her eyes, the way they did not indulge in the natural release of the act.

'Come on, walk with us,' said Claire plaintively, putting Warren between herself and Kiki, as if he were their child. It was a strange way to walk — it meant they had to talk to each other over Warren's body.

'OK — we got to keep an eye out for Jerome, though — he's about. So how was Italy?' asked Kiki.

'*Amazing.* Wasn't it incredible?' said Claire, looking to Warren with an intensity that fulfilled Kiki's hazy idea of how an artist should be: passionate, attentive, bringing her native enthusiasm to the smallest matters.

'Was it just a vacation?' asked Kiki. 'Weren't you collecting a prize or — ?'

'Oh, a silly . . . nothing, the Dante thing — but that's not interesting — *Warren* spent the whole time in this rape field going crazy over this new theory about airborne pollutants from fields, GM fields — Kiki, my *God* . . . unbelievable ideas he was having out there — he's basically going to be able to prove *definitively* that there's cross — cross — oh, God, cross-dissemination — insemination — you know what I mean — which is what this damn government has been *lying* through its *teeth* about — but it's really the science that's just —' Here Claire made a noise and a gesture to signify the top of one's head coming off, revealing the inner cranium to the universe. 'Warren, tell Kiki about it — I get it all mixed up, but it's absolutely *phenomenal* science — Warren?'

'It's not really so fascinating,' said Warren flatly. 'We're trying to find a way to pin down the government regarding these crops — a lot of the lab work has already been done, but it hasn't been put together — just needs someone to harness the solid evidence — Oh, Claire, it's too damn hot — boring subject . . .'

'Oh, no . . .' protested Kiki faintly.

'It is *not* boring —' cried Claire. 'I had no *idea* about the extent of this technology and what it's actually *doing to the biosphere.* I don't mean in ten years or fifty years, I mean *right now* . . . It's so vile, so vile. "Infernal" is the word I keep getting *caught* on, do you know what I mean? We've reached a new ring somehow. A very low infernal ring. The planet is finished with us, at this point —'

'Right, right,' Kiki kept saying through all of this, as Claire kept talking. Kiki was impressed by her but also slightly wearied — there was no subject she could not enthusiastically dissect or embroider. Kiki was reminded of that famous poem of Claire's about an orgasm that seemed to take apart all the different elements of an orgasm and lay them out along the page, the way a mechanic dismantles an engine. It was one of the few poems by Claire that Kiki had felt she understood without having to be talked through it by her husband or her daughter.

'Honey,' said Warren. He touched Claire's hand lightly but with intent. 'So where's Howard?'

'Missing in action,' said Kiki, and smiled at Warren warmly. 'Probably in a bar with Erskine.'

'God — I haven't seen Howard in *for ever,*' said Claire.

'Working on the Rembrandt still, though?' persisted Warren. He was the son of a fireman, and Kiki liked this best about him, although she knew all the other ideas she connected with this one were romantic notions on her part, not relevant to the real lived existence of a busy biochemist. He asked questions, he was interested and interesting, he rarely spoke of himself. He had a calm voice for the worst accidents and emergencies.

'Uh-huh,' said Kiki, and nodded and smiled but found she could go no further than this without betraying more than she wanted to.

'We saw *The Shipbuilder and His Wife* in London — the Queen lent it out to the National Gallery — nice of her, huh, right? It was fabulous . . . the working up of the paint,' said Claire urgently, and yet practically to herself, 'the *physicality* of it, like he's digging *in* to the canvas to get what's really *in* those faces, in that marriage — that's the thing, I think. It's almost *anti*-portraiture: he doesn't want you to look at the faces; he wants you to look at the *souls.* The faces are just a way *in*. It's the purest kind of genius.'

A tricky silence followed this, not necessarily noticeable to Claire herself. She had a way of saying things that couldn't be answered. Kiki was still smiling, looking down at the rough, hardy skin of her own black toes. And if it were not for the bedside charm of my mother, thought Kiki dreamily, there would have been no inherited house; and if it were not for the house, there would have been no money to send me to New York — would I have met Howard, would I *know* people like this?

'Except I think Howard's actually coming from a contrary position, darling — when he's discussed it, if you remember — he's weighing in against — would we say the culture myth of Rembrandt, his genius, etcetera?' said Warren doubtfully, with the scientist's reticence when using the language of artists.

'Oh, of course that's right,' said Claire tightly — she seemed not to want to discuss the subject. 'He doesn't like.'

'No,' said Kiki, equally glad to pass on to other topics. 'He doesn't like.'

'What *does* Howard like?' asked Warren wryly.

'Therein lies the mystery.'

Just then Murdoch began to yap furiously, and yank on the lead that Warren held in his hand. The three of them tried both cooing and chastising, but Murdoch was moving purposefully towards a toddler who was waddling along with a stuffed frog, held high above his head like a standard. Murdoch cornered the boy between his mother's legs. The child wept. The woman knelt down by the child and hugged him to her, glaring at Murdoch and his handlers.

'That's my husband's fault — sorry

about that,' said Claire, without enough contrition to satisfy. 'My husband's not used to dogs. It's not actually *his* dog.'

'It's a *dachshund,* it's not going to kill anybody,' said Kiki crossly, as the woman marched off, Kiki crouched to pet Murdoch on his flat head. She looked up again to find Claire and Warren squabbling, using only their eyes, each trying to impel the other to speak. Claire lost.

'Kiki . . .' she began, her face as demure as can be managed at fifty-four, 'the term isn't figurative, you know. Not any more. When I said husband just then.'

'What are you talking about?' said Kiki at the same moment that she realized the answer.

'Husband. Warren is my husband. I said it earlier but you didn't pick up. We got married. Isn't it *fabulous?*' Claire's tensile features pulled themselves tight with glee.

'I *thought* something was going on with you — you seemed nervy. Married!'

'Completely and absolutely,' confirmed Warren.

'But you didn't invite anybody or anything? When *was* this?'

'Two months ago! We just did it. You know what? I didn't want anybody rolling their eyes about a couple of old birds like us getting hitched, so we didn't invite any-body and there was no goddamn eye-rolling. Except Warren. He rolled his eyes because I dressed up as Salomé. Now is that something to roll your eyes about?'

Just before an oncoming lamp-post their little chain of three dissolved itself, and Claire and Warren merged into each other again.

'*Claire,* I wouldn't have rolled my eyes, honey — you should have said something.'

'It was utterly last minute, Keeks, really it was,' said Warren. 'You think I would have married this woman if I'd had time to think about it? She called me up and said it's the birthday of St John the Baptist, let's do it, and we did it.'

'Again, please,' said Kiki, although this aspect of the couple, their locally cele-brated 'eccentricity', was not really attrac-tive to her.

'So I have this Salomé dress — red, sequinned, I knew when I saw it that it was my Salomé dress, I bought it in Montreal. I wanted to get married in my Salomé dress and take a man's head with me. And, god-damn it, I did. And it's such a *sweet* head,' said Claire, pulling it gently towards her.

'So full of facts,' said Kiki. She won-dered how many times this exact routine would be repeated to well-wishers in the coming weeks. She and Howard were just the same, especially when they had news. Each couple is its own vaudeville act.

'*Yes,*' said Claire, 'so full of genuine *facts.* And I never had that before, someone who knew *anything real at all.* Apart from "art is truth" — you can't *move* for people in this town who know that. Or *think* they know it.'

'Mom.'

Jerome, in all his gloomy Jeromeity, had joined them. The ill-pitched greetings that compassionate age sings to mysterious youth rang out; hair was almost tousled and then wisely not, the eternal unanswerable question was met with a new and horrible answer ('I'm dropping out.' 'He *means* he's taking a little time out.'). For a moment it seemed that the world had drained itself of all possible subjects that might be gently discussed on a hot day in a pretty town. Then the glorious news of matrimony was recalled and joyfully repeated only to be met with the dispiriting request for specifics ('Oh, well, it's actually my *fourth,* Warren's second'). Through all this Jerome continued to unwrap, very slowly, a silver foil package in his hand. At last the top of a volcanic burrito was revealed; it then promptly erupted in his hand and down his wrist. Their little circle took a collective step back. Jerome caught a shrimp from the side of it with his tongue.

'Anyway . . . enough about the wedding already. In fa-aa-act,' said Warren, taking his phone from the pocket of his khaki shorts, 'yep — it's one fifteen — we've actually got to head off.'

'Keeks — it's been *so nice* — but let's do it indoors at a table soon, OK?'

She was clearly eager to get away; Kiki wished herself more compelling, more artistic or funny or smart, more able to retain the attention of a woman like Claire.

'Claire,' she said, but then could think of nothing interesting. 'Is there anything Howard needs to know? He hasn't been checking his mail — he's trying to work on the Rembrandt; don't think he's even spoken to Jack French yet.'

Claire looked baffled by this tediously practical turn to the conversation.

'Oh — right, right . . . well, we have a cross-faculty meeting on Tuesday — we've got six new lecturers across the Humanities Faculty, including that celebrity asshole, you know the guy, I think, Monty Kipps —'

'Monty Kipps?' repeated Kiki, each word

encased in the double ripple of a dead laugh. She felt shock shudder through Jerome, radiating out.

Claire continued: 'I know, really — he's apparently going to have an office in the Black Studies Department — poor Erskine! It's the only space they could find for him. I *know* . . . I don't understand how many more crypto-fascist appointments this place is going to make, it's actually pretty extraordinary at this point . . . it's just . . . well, what can you say? The whole country's going to hell.'

'Oh, *goddamn,*' said Jerome beseechingly, turning around in a small circle, inviting sympathy from the people of Wellington.

'Jerome, can we talk about this later —'

'What the *fuck* . . .' said Jerome more quietly, shaking his head in wonderment.

'Monty Kipps and Howard . . .' said Kiki evasively, and made an iffy motion with her hand.

Claire, at last aware of a subtext of which she was not the sub, began to effect her exit. 'Oh, Keeks, I really wouldn't worry about it. I heard Howard did have a beef with him a while back, but Howard's *always* having some fight or another.' She smiled awkwardly at this understatement. 'So . . . OK — well, come on — kisses — we gotta go. *So* lovely to see you guys.'

Kiki kissed Warren and was hugged too tightly by Claire; she waved and called goodbye and did all the necessaries on behalf of Jerome, who stood oblivious next to her on the blue doorstep of a Moroccan restaurant. To stave off the inevitable discussion, Kiki watched the couple walk away for as long as she could.

'Fuck,' said Jerome once again, loudly. He sat down where he was.

The sky had misted over slightly, allowing the sun to cast itself in a misleading godly role. It shone beneficence in thin rods of Renaissance light, thrusting through a landscaped cloud that seemed designed for this purpose. Kiki tried to figure the blessing in it all, a way to spin bad news as good. Sighing, she removed her headwrap. Her heavy plait collapsed down her back, but it was good to have the sweat ooze from the scalp down her face. She sat down next to her son. She said his name, but he stood up and began to walk away. A family searching each other's backpacks for some lost item blocked his progress; Kiki caught up.

'Don't do that, don't make me run after you.'

'Er . . . free citizen, moving through the

world?' said Jerome, pointing to himself.

'You know, I was just about to sympathize, but actually I think I want to tell you to grow the hell *up.*'

'Fine.'

'No, it is *not* fine. Baby, I know you were hurt badly —'

'I'm not hurt. I'm embarrassed. Let's skip it.' He pinched his brow with his fingers, a gesture so like one of his father's that it was ridiculous. 'I forgot your burrito, sorry.'

'Forget the burrito — can we talk?'

Jerome nodded, but they walked the left side of Wellington Square in silence. Kiki paused, and made Jerome pause, by a stall selling pin-cushions. These were shaped like fat Oriental gentlemen, complete with two diagonal dashes for their eyes and tiny yellow coolie hats with black fringes. Their pulvinate bellies were red satin, and it was here that the needles pierced. Kiki picked one up, rolling it in her hand.

'These are cute aren't they? Or are they awful?'

'Do you think he'll bring his whole family?'

'Honey, I really don't know. Probably not. But if they do come, we're all going to have to be real grown up about it.'

'You're tripping if you think I'm hanging around.'

'Good,' said Kiki with facetious cheeriness. 'You can go back to Brown, problem solved.'

'No, I mean . . . like maybe I'll go to Europe or whatever.'

The absurdity of this plan — economically, personally, educationally — was debated loudly here in the middle of the road, while the Thai woman who ran the stall grew nervous about the weight of Kiki's elbow as it pressed down beside a pyramid display of her useful little men.

'So I'm just meant to sit around like an *asshole* — pretend nothing happened, is that it?'

'No, it means we'll deal with it politely *as a family who* —'

'Because of course that's the Kiki way of dealing with trouble,' said Jerome over his mother. 'Just ignore the problem, forgive and forget, and poof, it's gone away.'

They stared at each other for a moment, Jerome brazen and Kiki surprised at his brazenness. He was, temperamentally, traditionally, the mildest of her children, the one she had always felt closest to.

'I don't know how you stand it,' said Jerome bitterly. 'He only ever thinks of

112

himself. He doesn't care who he hurts.'

'We're not talking about . . . about that, we're talking about you.'

'I'm just saying,' said Jerome uneasily, apparently scared of his own topic. 'Don't tell me I'm not dealing with my stuff when you're not dealing with yours.'

It surprised Kiki, how angry Jerome was about Howard, apparently on her behalf. It made her envious too — she wished she could muster up such clarity of hate. But she could not feel fury for Howard any more. If she was going to leave him, she should have done so in the winter. But she had stayed and now summer was here. The only account she could give of this decision was that she was not quite done loving him, which was the same as saying she was not yet done with Love — Love itself being coeval with knowing Howard. What was one night in Michigan set against Love!

'Jerome,' she said regretfully, and looked to the ground. But now he was determined to have his parting shot — children in a righteous mood always are. Kiki recalled being invincible and truth-loving and twenty years old; remembered feeling exactly this: that if her family could only speak the truth, together they would emerge, weeping but clear-eyed, into the light.

Jerome said, 'It's like, a family doesn't work any more when everyone in it is more miserable than they would be if they were alone. You know?'

Kiki's kids always seemed to say 'you know' at the end of their sentences these days, but they never waited to find out if she *did* know. By the time Kiki looked up, Jerome was already a hundred feet away, tunnelling into the accepting crowd.

6

Jerome sat in the front seat next to the taxi-driver because the trip was Jerome's treat and Jerome's idea; Levi, Zora and Kiki were in the second row of this people-carrier, and Howard lay flat on his back with a row to himself. The Belsey family car was at the mechanics', having its twelve-year-old engine replaced. The Belseys themselves were on their way to hear Mozart's Requiem performed on Boston Common. It was a classic family outing, proposed at the moment when all the members of the family had never felt less familial. The black mood in the house had been building these past two weeks, ever since Howard learned the news of Monty's appointment.

He saw it as an unforgivable betrayal on the part of the Humanities Faculty. A close personal rival invited on to campus! Who had supported it? He made angry calls to colleagues, trying to uncover the Brutus — with no success. Zora, with her creepily expert knowledge of college politics, poured poison in his ear. Neither paused to recall that Monty's appointment might affect Jerome too. Kiki held her temper, waiting for the two to think of someone other than themselves. When this didn't happen, she exploded. They were only just recovering from the family row that ensued. The sulking and door slamming would have continued indefinitely had not Jerome — ever the peacemaker — thought up this trip as an opportunity for everybody to be nice to each other.

Nobody much wanted to go to a concert, but it was impossible to deter Jerome when he was resolved upon a good deed. So here they were, a protesting silence filling the car: against Mozart, against outings generally, against having to take a taxi, against the hour's drive from Wellington into Boston, against the very concept of quality time. Only Kiki supported it. She believed she understood Jerome's motivation. The word on the college grapevine was that

Monty was bringing his family, which meant the girl was coming. Jerome must behave as if nothing had happened. They must *all* do that. They must be united and strong. She struggled forward now and reached over Jerome's shoulder to turn the radio up. It was not loud enough, somehow, to drown out the collective sulk. She stayed in this position for a minute and squeezed her son's hand. They had escaped outer Boston's network of cement and traffic at last. It was a Friday night. Single-sex clusters of Bostonians made their boisterous way through the streets, hoping to collide with their opposite numbers. As the Belsey taxi passed by a nightclub, Jerome squinted after the many girls in few clothes lining up before it, like the tail of something marvellous that did not exist. Jerome turned away. It hurts to look at what you can't have.

'Dad — get up, we're almost there,' said Zora.

'Howie, you got any money? I can't find my wallet, I don't know where it is.'

They stopped at the top corner of the park.

'Thank God, man. I thought I was gonna be *sick*,' said Levi, yanking open the sliding door.

'Plenty of time for that yet,' said Howard cheerily.

'You might *enjoy* it?' suggested Jerome.

'Of *course* we're gonna enjoy it, baby. That's why we came,' murmured Kiki. Finding her wallet, she paid the driver through the window. 'We'll enjoy it fine. I don't know what's wrong with your father. I don't know why he suddenly acts like he *hates* Mozart. I never heard *that* one before.'

'Nothing's wrong,' said Howard, linking arms with his daughter as they began to walk the pretty avenue. 'If I had my way, we'd do this every night. I don't think enough people listen to Mozart. As we speak his legacy is dying. And if *we* don't listen to him, what will happen to him?'

'Save it, Howie.'

But Howard continued. 'Poor bastard needs all the support he can get, as far as I'm concerned. One of the great unappreciated composers of the last millennium . . .'

'Jerome, *ignore* him, honey. Levi'll like it — we'll *all* like it. We're not animals. We can sit for half an hour like respectable folk.'

'More like an hour, Mom,' said Jerome.

'*Who* likes it? Me?' asked Levi urgently. The mention of his own name was never an occasion for irony or humour for Levi, and, like his own avid lawyer, he took a personal interest in every mention or misuse of it. 'I don't even know who he is! Mozart. He's got a wig, right? Classical,' he said with finality, having satisfied himself that he had diagnosed the correct disease.

'That's right,' agreed Howard. 'Wore a wig. Classical. They made a film about him.'

'I've *seen* that. That film eats my *ass* . . .'

'Quite.'

Kiki began to giggle. Now Howard let go of Zora and held his wife instead, gripping her from behind. His arms could not go entirely around her, but still they walked in this manner down the small hill towards the gates of the park. This was one of the little ways in which he said sorry. They were meant to add up each day.

'Man, look at this line,' said Jerome glumly, for he had wanted the evening to be perfect. 'We should have left earlier.'

Kiki rearranged her purple silk wrap around her shoulders. 'Oh, it's not that long, baby. And at least it's not cold.'

'I could jump that fence like *that,*' said Levi, pulling at the vertical iron rods as they walked beside them. 'You wait in line, you're a fool, seriously. A brother don't need a gate — he jumps the fence. That's street.'

'Again, please?' said Howard.

'Street, street,' bellowed Zora. 'It's like, "being street", knowing the street — in Levi's sad little world if you're a Negro you have some kind of mysterious holy communion with sidewalks and corners.'

'Aw, man, shut *up*. You don't know what the street *looks* like. You ain't never been there.'

'What's this?' said Zora, pointing to the ground. 'Marshmallow?'

'*Please*. This ain't America. You think this is America? This is *toy-town*. I was *born* in this country — trust me. You go into Roxbury, you go into the Bronx, you *see* America. That's *street*.'

'Levi, you don't live in Roxbury,' explained Zora slowly. 'You live in Wellington. You go to *Arundel*. You've got your name ironed into your underwear.'

'I wonder if I'm street . . .' mused Howard. 'I'm still healthy, got hair, testicles, eyes, etcetera. Got *great* testicles. It's true I'm above subnormal intelligence — but then again I *am* full of verve and spunk.'

'*No.*'

'Dad,' said Zora, 'please don't say spunk. Ever.'

'Can't I be street?'

'*No.* Why you always got to make everything be a joke?'

'I just want to be street.'

'*Mom.* Tell him to stop, man.'

'I can be a brother. Check it out,' said Howard, and proceeded to make a series of excruciating hand gestures and poses. Kiki squealed and covered her eyes.

'Mom — I'm going home, I swear to God if he does that for one more second, I swear to God . . .'

Levi was trying desperately to get his hoodie to cover the side of his vision in which Howard was persisting. It was surely only seconds before Howard recited the only piece of rap he could ever remember, a single line he'd mysteriously retained from the mass of lyrics he heard Levi mutter day after day. *'I got the slickest, quickest dick —'* began Howard. Screams of consternation rose up from the rest of his family. *'A penis with the IQ of a genius!'*

'Dat's it — I'm *gone.*'

Levi coolly jogged ahead of them all and tucked himself into the swarm going through the gates into the park. They all laughed, even Jerome, and it did Kiki good to see him laugh. Howard had always been funny. Even when they first met, she had thought of him, covetously, as the kind of father who would

120

be able to make his children laugh. Now she tweaked his elbow affectionately.

'Something I said?' asked Howard, satisfied, and released his arms from their folded pose.

'Well done, baby. Has he got his cell on him?' asked Kiki.

'He's got mine,' said Jerome. 'He stole it from my room this morning.'

As they filed in behind the slow-moving crowd, the park gave off its scent for the Belseys, sap-filled and sweet, heavy with the last of the dying summer. On a humid September night like this the Common was no longer that neat, historic space renowned for its speeches and hangings. It shrugged off its human gardeners and tended once more towards the wild, the natural. The Boston primness Howard associated with these kinds of events could not quite survive the mass of hot bodies and the crepitations of the crickets, the soft, damp bark of the trees and the atonal tuning of instruments — and all this was to the good. Yellow lanterns, the colour of rape seed, hung in the branches of the trees.

'Gee, that's nice,' said Jerome. 'It's like the orchestra's hovering above the water, isn't it? I mean, the reflection from the

121

lights makes it look like that.'

'Gee,' said Howard, looking towards the flood-lit mound beyond the water. 'Gee gosh. Golly gee. Bo diddley.'

The orchestra sat on a small stage on the other side of the pond. It was clear to Howard — the only non-myopic member of his family — that every male musician was wearing a tie with a 'musical notes' design upon it. The women had this same motif printed on a cummerbund-like sash they wore around their waists. From an enormous banner behind the orchestra, a profile of Mozart's miserable, pouchy hamster face loomed out at him.

'Where's the choir?' asked Kiki, looking about her.

'They're underwater. They come up in like a . . .' said Howard, miming a man emerging with a flourish from the sea. 'It's Mozart in pond. Like Mozart on ice. Fewer fatalities.'

Kiki laughed lightly, but then her face changed and she held him tightly by his wrist. 'Hey . . . ah, Howard, baby?' she said warily, looking across the park. 'You want good news or bad news?'

'Hmm?' said Howard, turning round and finding both kinds of news were approaching from across the green and waving at him: Erskine Jegede and Jack French, the Dean of the Humanities Faculty. Jack French on his long playboy legs in their New England slacks. How old was this man? The question had always troubled Howard. Jack French could be fifty-two. He could just as easily be seventy-nine. You couldn't ask him and if you didn't ask him you'd never know. It was a movie-idol face Jack had, cut-glass architecture, angled like a Wyndham Lewis portrait. His sentimental eyebrows made the shape of two separated sides of a steeple, always gently perplexed. He had skin like the kind of dark, aged leather you find on those fellows they dig out, after 900 years, from a peat bog. A thin yet complete covering of grey silk hair hid his skull from Howard's imputations of extreme old age and was cut no differently than it would have been when the man was twenty-two, balanced on the lip of a white boat looking out at Nantucket through one sun-shading hand, wondering if that was Dolly stood square on the pier with two highballs in her hand. Compare and contrast with Erskine: his shining, hairless pate, and those storybook freckles that induced in Howard an unreasonable feeling of joy. Erskine was dressed this evening in a three-piece suit of the yellowest of yellows, the curves of his bumptious body naturally resisting all three pieces. On his small feet he wore a pair of pointed Cuban-heeled shoes. The effect was of a bull doing his initial two-step dance towards you. Still ten yards away, Howard had a chance to switch his position with his wife — quickly and unob-served — so that Erskine would naturally veer towards Howard and French would go the other way. He took this opportunity. Unfortunately French was not given to duologic conversation — he addressed the group, always. No — he addressed the gaps *between* the group.

'Belseys *en masse,*' said Jack French very slowly, and each Belsey tried to ascer-tain which Belsey he might be looking at directly. 'Missing . . . *one*, I believe. Belseys minus one.'

'That's Levi, our youngest — we lost him. He lost us. To be honest, he's *trying* to lose us,' said Kiki coarsely and laughed, and Jerome laughed and Zora laughed and so did Howard and Erskine and after all of them, very slowly, with infinite slowness, Jack French began to laugh.

'My children,' began Jack.

'Yes?' said Howard.

'Spend most of their time,' said Jack.

'Yes, yes,' said Howard, encouragingly.

'*Contriving,*' said Jack.

'Ha, ha,' said Howard. '*Yes.*'

'To lose me at public events,' said Jack finally.

'Right,' said Howard, exhausted already. 'Right. Always the way.'

'We are anathema to our own children,' said Erskine merrily, with his scale-jumping accent, from high to low and back again. 'We are liked only by *other* people's children. *Your* children for example like me so much more than they like *you.*'

'It's true, man. I'd move in with you if I could,' said Jerome in return, for which he got the standard Erskine response to good tidings, even minor ones like the arrival of a new gin and tonic on the table — both of Erskine's hands placed on his cheeks and a kiss on the forehead.

'You will come home with me, then. It is settled.'

'Please, take the rest too. Don't dangle carrots,' said Howard, stepping forward and giving Erskine a jovial slap on the back. He then turned to Jack French and put out his hand, which French, who had turned to gaze upon the musicians, did not notice.

'Wonderful, isn't it?' said Kiki. 'We're so glad to bump into you two. Is Maisie here, Jack? Or the kids?'

'It *is* wonderful,' confirmed Jack, putting his hands on his slim hips.

Zora was elbowing her father in his mid-section. Howard observed the moon-eyes his daughter was making at Dean French. It was typical of Zora that when actually faced with the authority figure she had been cursing out all week she would simply swoon at said authority figure's feet.

'Jack,' tried Howard, 'you've met Zora, haven't you? She's a sophomore now.'

'It is an unusual visitation of wonder,' said Jack, turning back to them all.

'Yes,' said Howard.

'For such a prosaic and,' expanded Jack.

'Hmm,' said Howard.

'*Municipal* setting,' said Jack, and beamed at Zora.

'Dean French,' said Zora, picking up Jack's hand and shaking it for him, 'I'm so excited about this year. It's an incredible line-up you've got this year — I was in the Greenman — I work on Tuesdays in the Greenman, in the Slavic section? And I was looking at the past faculty reports like for the past five years, and every year since you've been Dean we just keep on getting more and more amazing guest *lecturers* and *speakers* and *research fellows* — myself and my friends, we're just really psyched about this semester. And of course *Dad's* giving his incredible art theory class — which I am so taking this year — I'm just so over whatever anybody has to say about that — I mean, in the end you've just got to take the class that will most develop you as a human being at whatever cost, I truly believe that. So I just wanted to say that it's just really exciting for me to feel that Wellington's moving through a new progressive stage. I think the college is really moving in a positive direction, which it needed, I think, after that dismal power struggle in the mid-to-late eighties, which I think really dented morale around here.'

Howard did not know which piece of this horrible little speech the Dean was capable of extracting from the rest, of processing and/or replying to, nor had he any idea how long this might take. Kiki once again came to his rescue.

'Honey — let's not talk shop tonight, OK? It's not polite. We've got all semester for that, haven't we . . . Oh, and before I forget, God, it's our *wedding anniversary* in a week and a half — we're gonna have like a shin-dig, nothing much, some Marvin Gaye, some soul-food — you know, very mellow . . .'

Jack asked the date. Kiki told him. Jack's face gave in to that tiny, involuntary shudder with which Kiki had, in recent years, become familiar.

'But of course it's your actual anniversary, so . . .' said Jack, meaning to have said that to himself.

'Yep — and since by the fifteenth everybody's crazy busy anyway, we thought we might as well just have it on the actual day . . . and it might be an opportunity to . . . you know, everybody say hello, meet the new faces before semester begins, etcetera.'

'Although your own faces,' said Jack, his face alight with private delight at the thought of the rest of his sentence, 'of course, will not be so new to each other, will they? Is it twenty-five years?'

'Honey,' said Kiki, laying her big bejewelled hand on Jack's shoulder, 'confidentially, it's *thirty.*'

Some emotion came into Kiki's voice as she said this.

'Now, in the proverbial way of things,' considered Jack, 'would that be silver? Or is it gold?'

'Adamantine chains,' joked Howard, pulled his wife to him and kissed her wetly on her cheek. Kiki laughed deeply, shaking everything on her.

'But you'll come?' asked Kiki.

'It will be a great —' began Jack, beaming, but just then came the divine intervention of a voice over a tannoy system, asking people to take their seats.

7

Mozart's Requiem begins with you walking towards a huge pit. The pit is on the other side of a precipice, which you cannot see over until you are right at its edge. Your death is awaiting you in that pit. You don't know what it looks like or sounds like or smells like. You don't know whether it will be good or bad. You just walk towards it. Your will is a clarinet and your footsteps are attended by all the violins. The closer you get to the pit, the more you begin to have the sense that what awaits you there will be terrifying. Yet you experience this terror as a kind of blessing, a gift. Your long walk would have had no meaning were it not for this pit at the end of it. You peer over the precipice: a burst of ethereal noise crashes over you. In the pit is a great choir, like the one you joined for two months in Wellington in which you were the only black woman. This choir is the heavenly host and simultaneously the devil's army. It is also every person who has changed you during your time on this earth: your many lovers; your family; your enemies, the nameless, faceless woman who slept with your husband; the man you thought you were going to marry; the man you did. The job of this choir is judgement. The men sing first, and their judgement is very severe. And when the women join in there is no respite, the debate only grows louder and sterner. For it *is* a debate — you realize that now. The judgement is not yet decided. It is surprising how dramatic the fight for your measly soul turns out to be. Also surprising are the mermaids and the apes that persist on dancing around each other and sliding down an ornate staircase during the *Kyrie*, which, according to the programme notes, features no such action, even in the metaphorical sense.

Kyrie eleison.
Christe eleison.
Kyrie eleison.

That is all that happens in the *Kyrie*. No apes, just Latin. But for Kiki, it was apes and mermaids all the same. The experience of listening to an hour's music you barely

know in a dead language you do not understand is a strange falling and rising experience. For minutes at a time you are walking
deep into it, you seem to understand. Then,
without knowing how or when exactly, you
discover you have wandered away, bored or
tired from the effort, and now you are nowhere near the music. You refer to the
programme notes. The notes reveal that the
past fifteen minutes of wrangling over your
soul have been merely the repetition of a
single inconsequential line. Somewhere
around the *Confutatis,* Kiki's careful
tracing of the live music with the literal
programme broke down. She didn't know
where she was now. In the *Lacrimosa* or
miles ahead? Stuck in the middle or nearing
the end? She turned to ask Howard, but he
was asleep. A glimpse to her right revealed
Zora concentrating on her Discman,
through which a recording of the voice of a
Professor N. R. A. Gould carefully guided
her through each movement. Poor Zora —
she lived through footnotes. It was the same
in Paris: so intent was she upon reading the
guide book to Sacré-Cœur that she walked
directly into an altar, cutting her forehead
open.

Kiki tipped her head back on her deckchair and tried to let go of her curious anx-

iety. The moon was massive overhead, and mottled like the skin of old white people. Or maybe it was that Kiki noted many older white people with their faces turned up towards the moon, their heads resting on the back of their deckchairs, their hands dancing gently in their lap in a way that suggested enviable musical knowledge. Yet surely no one among these white people could be more musical than Jerome, who, Kiki now noticed, was crying. She opened her mouth with genuine surprise and then, fearful of breaking some spell, closed it again. The tears were silent and plentiful. Kiki felt moved, and then another feeling interceded: pride. *I* don't understand, she thought, but *he* does. A young black man of intelligence and sensibility, and *I* have raised him. After all, how many other young black men would even come to an event like this — I bet there isn't one in this entire crowd, thought Kiki, and then checked and was mildly annoyed to find that indeed there was one, a tall young man with an elegant neck, sitting next to her daughter. Undeterred, Kiki continued her imaginary speech to the imaginary guild of black American mothers: *And there's no big secret, not at all, you just need to have faith, I guess, and you need*

132

to counter the dismal self-image that black men receive as their birthright from America — that's essential — and, I don't know . . . get involved in after-school activities, have books around the house, and sure, have a little money, and a house with outdoor . . . Kiki abandoned her parental reverie for a moment to tug at Zora's sleeve and point out the marvel of Jerome, as if these tears were rolling down the cheek of a stone madonna. Zora glanced over, shrugged and returned to Professor Gould. Kiki returned her own gaze to the moon. So much more lovely than the sun and you can look at it without fear of harm. A few minutes later, she was preparing to make a final, concentrated effort to match the sung words with the text on the page when suddenly it was over. She was so surprised she came late to the clapping, although not as late as Howard, whom it had only just awoken.

'That it, then?' he said, springing from his chair. 'Everyone been touched by the Christian sublime? Can we go now?'

'We have to find Levi. We can't go without him . . . maybe we should try Jerome's cell . . . I don't know if it's on.' Kiki looked up at her husband with sudden curiosity. 'What, so you hated it?

How can you hate it?'

'Levi's over there,' said Jerome, waving towards a tree a hundred yards away. 'Hey — Levi!'

'Well, *I* thought it was amazing,' pressed Kiki. 'It's obviously the work of a genius —'

Howard groaned at the term.

'Oh, Howard, come *on* — you *have* to be a genius to write music like that.'

'Music like what? Define genius.'

Kiki ignored the request. 'I think the kids were quite moved,' she said, squeezing Jerome's arm lightly but saying no more. She would not expose him to his father's ridicule. 'And *I* was very moved. I don't see how it's possible not to be moved by music like that. You're serious — you didn't like it?'

'I liked it fine . . . it was fine. I just prefer music which isn't trying to fake me into some metaphysical idea by the back door.'

'I don't know what you're talking about. It's like God's music or something.'

'I rest my case,' said Howard, and now turned from her and waved at Levi, who was stuck in the crowd, waving back at them. Levi nodded as Howard pointed to the gate where they should all meet up.

'Howard,' continued Kiki, because she was happiest when she could get him to

134

talk to her about his ideas, 'explain to me how what we just heard wasn't the work of a genius . . . I mean, no matter what you say, there's *obviously* a difference between something like that and something like . . .'

The family set off, continuing their debate, with the voices of the children now added to the dispute. The black boy with the elegant neck who had been sitting next to Zora strained to hear the disappearing remnants of a conversation he had been interested in, although he had not followed all of it. More and more these days he found himself listening to people talk, wanting to add something. He had wanted to add something just then, a point of information — it was from that movie. According to the film, Mozart died before he finished the thing, right? So someone else must have finished it — so that seemed relevant to that genius thing they were discussing. But he wasn't in the habit of talking to strangers. Besides, the moment passed. It always did. He pulled his baseball cap down his forehead and checked in his pocket for his cell. He reached under his deckchair to retrieve his Discman — it was gone. He swore violently, padded his hand around the area in the darkness and found something, a Discman. But not his. His had a faint sticky residue on the bottom that he could always feel, the remains of a long-gone sticker of a silhouetted naked lady with a big afro. Apart from that the two Discmans were identical. It took him a second to figure it out. He rushed to get his hoodie off the back of his chair, but it got caught, and he ripped it slightly. That was his best hoodie. At last it was detached — he hurried as best he could after that heavy-set girl with the glasses. With every step more people seemed to place themselves between him and her.

'Hey! *Hey!*'

But there was no name to put on the end of *Hey* and a six foot two athletic black man shouting *Hey* in a dense crowd does not create easiness wherever he goes.

'She's got my Discman, this girl, this lady — just up there — sorry, 'scuse me, man — yeah, can I just get by here — *Hey! Hey, sister!*'

'ZORA — wait up!' came a voice loud by the side of him, and the girl he'd been trying to stop turned around and gave somebody the finger. The white people near by looked about themselves anxiously. Was there going to be trouble?

'Aw, fuck you too,' said the voice resignedly. The young man turned and saw a boy a little shorter than him, but not much, and several shades lighter.

'Hey, man — is that your girl?'

'What?'

'The girl with the glasses you was just calling? Is she your girl?'

'*Hell,* no — that's my sister, bro.'

'Man, she's got my Discman, my music — she must have picked it up by mistake. See, I got hers. I been trying to call her, but I didn't know her name.'

'For real?'

'This is hers, right here, man. It ain't mine.'

'Wait here —'

Few among Levi's pastoral circle of family and teachers would have believed Levi could launch so promptly into action after an instruction as he did for this young man he had never met before. He pushed swiftly through the crowd, caught his sister by the arm and began to talk to her animatedly. The young man approached more slowly, but got there in time to here Zora say: 'Don't be ridiculous — I'm not giving some friend of yours my player — get off me —'

'You're not listening to me — it's *not* yours, it's his — *his,'* repeated Levi, spotting the young man and pointing at him. The young man smiled weakly under the brim of his baseball cap. Even so small a glimpse of his smile told you that his were perfect white teeth, superbly arranged.

'Levi, if you and your friend want to be *gangstas,* piece of advice: you've got to take, not ask.'

'Zoor — it's not yours — it's this guy's.'

'I *know* my Discman — this is my Discman.'

'Bro —' said Levi, 'you got a disc in here?' The young man nodded.

'Check the CD, Zora.'

'Oh, for God's sake — see? It's a record-able disc. Mine. OK? Bye now.'

'Mine's recordable too — it's my own mix,' said the young man firmly.

'Levi . . . We've got to get to the car.'

'Listen to it —' said Levi to Zora.

'No.'

'Listen to the damn CD, Zoor.'

'What's going on over there?' called Howard, twenty yards away. 'Can we get going, please?'

'Zora, you freak — just listen to the CD, settle this.'

Zora made a face and pressed play. A little spring of sweat burst over her forehead.

'Well, this isn't my CD. It's some kind of hip-hop,' she said sharply, as if the CD it-self were somehow to blame.

The young man stepped forward cautiously, with one hand up as if to show he meant no harm. He turned the Discman over in her hand and showed her the sticky patch. He lifted his hoodie and the T-shirt beneath it to reveal a well-defined pelvic bone and drew a second Discman from his waistband. 'This one's yours.'

'They're *exactly* the same.'

'Yeah, I guess that's where the confusion came from.' He was grinning now and the fact that he was stupidly good-looking could no longer be ignored. Pride and prejudice, however, connived in Zora to make a point of ignoring it anyway.

'Yeah, well, I put mine under *my* chair,' she said tartly, and turned and walked off in the direction of her mother, who stood hands on hips another hundred yards away.

'Phew. Tough sister,' said the young man, laughing lightly.

Levi sighed.

'Yo, thanks, man.'

They clapped hands.

'Who you listening to anyway?' asked Levi.

'Just some hip-hop.'

'Bro, can I check it out — I'm all into that.'

'I guess . . .'

'I'm Levi.'

'Carl.'

How old is this boy, Carl wondered. And where'd he learn that you just ask some strange brother you never seen before in your life if you can listen to his Discman? Carl had figured a year ago that if he started going to events like this he would meet the kind of people he didn't usually meet — couldn't have been more right about that one.

'It's tight, man. There's a nice flow there. Who is it?'

'Actually, that track is me,' Carl said, neither humbly nor proudly. 'I got a very basic sixteen-track at home. I do it myself.'

'You a rapper?'

'Well . . . it's more like Spoken Word, as it happens.'

'Scene.'

They talked all the way over the green towards the gates of the park. About hip-hop generally, and then about recent shows in the Boston area. How few and far they were. Levi asked question after question, sometimes answering himself as Carl opened his mouth to reply. Carl kept on trying to figure out what the deal was, but it seemed like there was no deal — some people just like to talk.

Levi suggested they swap cell numbers, and they did so by an oak tree.

'Just, you know . . . next time you hear about a show in Roxbury . . . You can call me or whatever,' said Levi, rather too keenly.

'You live in Roxbury?' asked Carl doubtfully.

'Not really . . . but I'm there a lot — Saturdays, especially.'

'What are you, fourteen?' asked Carl.

'No, man. I'm sixteen! How old are you?'

'Twenty.'

This answer immediately inhibited Levi.

'You at college or . . . ?'

'Nah . . . I'm not an *educated* brother, although . . .' He had a theatrical, old-fashioned way of speaking, which involved his long, pretty fingers turning circles in the air. His whole manner reminded Levi of his grandfather on his mother's side and his tendency to *speechify,* as Kiki called it. 'I guess you could say I hit my own books in my own way.'

'Scene.'

'I get my culture where I can, you know — going to free shit like tonight, for example. Anything happening that's free in this city and might teach me something, I'm *there.*'

Levi's family were waving at him. He was hoping that Carl would go in another direction before they reached the gate, but

141

of course there was only one way out of the park.

'*Finally,*' said Howard, as they approached.

Now it was Carl's turn to grow inhibited. He pulled his baseball cap down low. He put his hands in his pockets.

'Oh, hey,' said Zora, acutely embarrassed.

Carl acknowledged her with a nod.

'So I'll call you,' said Levi, trying to bypass the introduction he feared was moments away. He was not quick enough.

'Hi!' said Kiki. 'Are you a friend of Levi?'

Carl looked distraught.

'Er . . . this is Carl. Zora stole his Discman.'

'I didn't *steal* any —'

'Are you at Wellington? Familiar face,' said Howard distractedly. He was looking out for a taxi. Carl laughed, a strange artificial laugh that had more anger in it than good humour.

'Do I *look* like I'm at Wellington?'

'Not everybody goes to your stupid college,' countered Levi, blushing. 'People do other shit than go to college. He's a street poet.'

'Really?' asked Jerome with interest.

'That ain't really accurate, man . . . I do some stuff, Spoken Word — that's all. I don't know if I be calling myself a street poet, exactly.'

'Spoken Word?' repeated Howard.

Zora, who considered herself the essential bridge between Wellington's popular culture and her parents' academic culture, stepped in here. 'It's like oral poetry . . . it's in the African-American tradition — Claire Malcolm's all into it. She thinks it's *vital* and *earthy,* etcetera, etcetera. She goes to the Bus Stop to check it out with her little Cult of Claire groupies.'

This last was sour grapes on Zora's part; she had applied for, but not been accepted into, Claire's poetry workshop the previous semester.

'I've done the Bus Stop, several times,' said Carl quietly. 'It's a good place. It's about the only cool place for that stuff in Wellington. I did some stuff there just Tuesday night past.' Now he put a thumb to the brim of his cap and lifted it a little so that he might get a good look at these people. Was the white guy the father?

'Claire Malcolm goes to a bus stop to hear poetry . . .' began Howard, bewildered, busy looking up and down the street.

'Shut up, Dad,' said Zora. 'Do you know Claire Malcolm?'

'Nope . . . can't say I do,' replied Carl, releasing another one of his winning

143

smiles, just nerves probably, but each time he did, you warmed to him further.

'She's like a *poet* poet,' explained Zora.

'Oh . . . A *poet* poet.' Carl's smile disappeared.

'Shut up, Zoor,' said Jerome.

'Rubens,' said Howard suddenly. 'Your face. From the four African heads. Nice to meet you, anyway.'

Howard's family stared at him. Howard stepped off the sidewalk to wave down a cab that passed him by.

Carl pulled his hoodie over his cap and began to look around himself.

'You should meet Claire,' said Kiki enthusiastically, trying to patch the thing up. It's remarkable what a face like Carl's makes you want to do in order to see it smile again. 'She's very respected — everybody says she's very good.'

'Cab!' yelled Howard. 'It's going to pull up on the other side. Come on.'

'Why do you say it like Claire's a country you've never been to?' demanded Zora. 'You've *read* her — so you can have an opinion, Mom, it won't kill you.'

Kiki ignored this. 'I'm sure she'd love to meet a young poet, she's very encouraging — you know actually we're having a party —'

'Come on, come on,' droned Howard.

He was in the middle of the traffic island.

'Why would he even want to go to your party?' asked Levi, mortified. 'It's an *anniversary* party.'

'Well, baby, I can *ask,* can't I? Besides, it's not *just* an anniversary party. And between me and you,' she added faux confidentially to Carl, 'we could do with a few more brothers at this party.'

It had not escaped anybody's attention that Kiki was flirting. *Brothers?* thought Zora crossly, since when does Kiki say *brothers?*

'I got to be going,' said Carl. He passed a flat hand over his forehead, smearing the droplets of sweat. 'I got your man Levi's number — we might hang out some time, so —'

'Oh, OK . . .'

They all waved vaguely at his back and said *bye* quietly, but there was no denying he was walking away from them as fast as he could.

Zora turned to her mother and opened her eyes wide. 'What the hell? *Rubens?*'

'Nice boy,' said Kiki sadly.

'Let's get in the car,' said Levi.

'Not bad-looking either, huh?' said Kiki and watched Carl's retreating figure turn a corner. Howard stood on the other side of the road, one hand on the open mini-van door, the other sweeping from the ground to the sky, ushering his family inside.

8

The Saturday of the Belseys' party arrived. The twelve hours before a Belsey party were a time of domestic anxiety and activity; a watertight excuse was required to escape the house for the duration. Luckily for Levi, his parents had provided him with one. Hadn't they gone on and on about his getting a Saturday job? And so he had got one, and so he was going to it. End of discussion. With joy in his heart he left Zora and Jerome polishing doorknobs and set off for his sales associate position in a Boston music mega-store. The job itself was no occasion for joy: he hated the corny baseball cap he had to wear and the bad pop music he was compelled to sell; the tragic loser of a floor manager who imagined he was the king of Levi; the moms who couldn't remember the name of the artist or the single, and so leaned over the counter to tunelessly hum a little bit of the verse. All it was good for was giving him a reason to get out of the toy-town that was

Wellington and a bit of money to spend in Boston once he got there. Every Saturday morning he caught a bus to the nearest T-stop and then the subway into the only city he had ever really known. It was not New York, sure, but it was the only city he had, and Levi treasured the urban the same way previous generations worshipped the pastoral; if he could have written an ode he would have. But he had no ability in that area (he used to try — notebook after notebook filled with false, cringing rhymes). He had learned to leave it to the fast-talking guys in his earphones, the present-day American poets, the rappers.

Levi's shift finished at four. He left the city reluctantly, as always. He got back on the subway and then the bus. He looked out with dread at Wellington as it began to manifest itself outside the grimy windows. The pristine white spires of the college seemed to him like the watchtowers of a prison to which he was returning. He sloped towards home, walking up the final hill, listening to his music. The fate of the young man in his earphones, who faced a jail cell that very night, did not seem such a world away from his own predicament: an anniversary party full of academics.

Walking up Redwood Avenue with its

147

tunnel of cernuous willows, Levi found he had lost the will even to nod his head, usually an involuntary habit with him when music was playing. Halfway down the avenue he noticed with irritation that he was being watched. A very old black lady sitting on her porch was eyeing him like there was no other news in town. He tried to shame her by staring her out in turn. She just kept right on staring. Framed by two yellow-leaved trees on each side of her house, she sat on her porch in this bright red dress and stared like she was being paid to do it. Man oh man, but didn't she look old and papery. Her hair was really not tied back properly. Like she wasn't being taken care of. Hair every which way. Levi hated to see that right there, old people not taken care of. Her clothes were crazy too. This red dress she had on didn't have a waist; it just went straight down like a queen's gown in a children's book and was held together at the throat by one big brooch in the shape of a golden palm leaf. Boxes all around her on that porch filled with clothes and cups and plates . . . like a bag lady, only with a house. She sure could eyeball, though . . . Jesus. Isn't there anything on TV, lady? Maybe he should buy a T-shirt that just had on it YO — I'M NOT

GOING TO RAPE YOU. He could use a T-shirt like that. Maybe like three times each day while on his travels that T-shirt would come in handy. There was always some old lady who needed to be reassured on that point. And check it out . . . now she's struggling to get out of the chair — her legs like toothpicks in sandals. She's gonna say something. Aw, *shit.*

'Excuse me — young man, excuse me for a minute — *wait a bit* there.'

Levi pushed his headphones to one side on his head. 'Say *what?*'

You'd have thought that after all that effort of standing and calling out, the lady might have something important to say. My house is burning down. My cat is up a tree. But no.

'Now, how *are* you?' she said. 'You don't look so well.'

Levi replaced his headphones and began to walk away. But the lady was still waving her arms at him. He stopped again, took the headphones off and sighed. 'Sister, I've had kind of a long day, a'right, so . . . unless there's something I can do for you . . . You need help or something? Carrying something?'

The lady had managed to move forward now. She took two steps and then supported herself with both hands, gripping the porch fence. Her knuckles were grey and dusty. You could pluck bass notes on those veins.

'I *knew* it. You live near here, don't you?'

'Excuse me?'

'I feel *sure* I know your brother. I can't be mistaken, at least I don't think so,' she said.

Her head wobbled slightly as she spoke. 'No, I'm not mistaken. Your faces are the same underneath. You have exactly the same cheekbones.'

Her accent, to Levi's ears, was a shameful, comic thing. To Levi, black folk were city folk. People from the islands, people from the country, these were all peculiar to him, obstinately historical — he couldn't quite believe in them. Like when Howard took the family to Venice and Levi could not shift the idea that the whole place and everybody in it were having him on. No roads? *Water* taxis? He felt the same way about farmers, anybody who wove anything and his Latin teacher.

'Right . . . OK, well, I gotta go, man . . . got stuff to do . . . So . . . Don't you stand up any more, sister, you'll fall — I'm out now.'

'Wait!'

'Aw, man . . .'

Levi approached her and she did the weirdest thing: she clasped his hands.

'I am interested to know what your mother is like.'

'My moms? *What?* Look, sister —' said Levi, releasing his hands from hers, 'I think you got the wrong guy.'

'I will call on her, I think,' she said. 'I feel that she must be nice, from what I have seen of her family. Is she very glamorous? I don't know why it is that I always imagine her to be very busy and glamorous.'

The thought of a busy and glamorous Kiki made Levi smile. 'You must be thinking of someone else. My mom's big like this' — he stretched his hands wide across the length of the fence — 'and *bored* out of her *mind.*'

'Bored . . .' she repeated, as if this were the most interesting thing anyone had ever told her.

'Yeah, kinda like you — going a little insane in the membrane,' he muttered, low enough so as not to be heard.

'Well, I must confess I am a little bored myself. They are all unpacking inside — but I'm not allowed to help! Of course, I'm not terribly well,' she confided, 'and the pills I take . . . they make me feel strange. It's boring for me — I'm used to being *involved.*'

'Uh-huh, . . well, my mom's having a party later — maybe you should check it out, man, shake your money-maker . . . Look, OK, sister, nice talking to you, but I gotta go now — you stay cool for me now. Stay out the sun.'

9

As sometimes happens, the song playing in Levi's headphones ended the moment he put his hand to the gate of 83 Langham. This afternoon his home appeared more surreal a place to him than ever, as far from his idea of where he lived as seemed possible. It looked glorious. The sun had the Belsey house in her hands. She warmed the wood and made the windows opaque and splendid with reflected light. She offered herself to the brazen purple flowers that grew along the front wall, and they opened their mouths wide to receive her. It was twenty past five. The night was going to be sexy: close and warm but with enough of a breeze so that you didn't have to sweat through it. Levi sensed women getting ready all over New England: undressing, washing, dressing again, in cleaner, sexier things; black girls in Boston oiling their legs and ironing their hair, club floors being swept, barmen turning up for work, DJs kneeling in their bedrooms, picking out records to be placed in their heavy silver boxes — all of which imaginings, usually so exciting to him, were made sour and sad by the knowledge that the only party he was going to tonight would be full of white people three times his own age. He sighed and worked his head round in a slow circle. Reluctant to go indoors, he stayed where he was, halfway up the garden path, with his head tipped forward and the departing sun on his back. Somebody had laced petunias around the triangular base of his grand-mother's statuary, a three-foot piece of py-ramidal stone that sat midway between a pair of sugar maples in the front yard. Strands of lights — not yet lit — had been wound around the trunks of both these trees and laid among their branches.

Levi was thinking how grateful he was that he'd missed having to help with these tasks when he felt his pocket vibrate. He took out his pager. From Carl. It took him a minute to remember who the hell Carl was. The message said: 'That party still on? Might swing by. Peace. C.' Levi was both flattered and concerned. Had Carl forgotten what type of party it was? He was about to phone back when he was surprised out of his solitude by the noise of Zora climbing down from a ladder at the front of the house. Evidently she had just hung four upside-down bunches of dried tea-roses, pinks and whites, above the doorframe. Levi could not explain why he hadn't noticed her a moment before, but he had not. On the third rung down she seemed to notice him too; her head slowly turned towards her brother, but her eyes went beyond him, intent on something across the street.

'Wow,' she whispered, bringing one hand up to her forehead as a visor, 'this one really can't believe her eyes. Check it out — she's having some kind of cognitive failure. She's going to malfunction.'

'Huh?'

'Thank you! Yes, move along now — he *lives* here — yes, that's right — no crime is taking place — thank you for your interest!'

Levi turned round and saw the blushing woman Zora was yelling at, now scurrying by on the other side of the street.

'What's *wrong* with these people exactly?' Zora put both feet on the ground and pulled off her gardening gloves.

'She watching me? Same one from before?'

'No, different woman. And don't you

talk to *me* — you were meant to be here two hours ago.'

'Party don't even start till eight!'

'Starts at six, asshole — and you have once again failed to be of any help *whatsoever.*'

'Zoor, man,' sighed Levi, and walked past her, 'you know when you're just not in the mood?' He pulled off his Raiders vest as he went, winding it into a ball in his hand. His naked back, so broad at the top and so narrow at the bottom, blocked Zora's path.

'You know, I wasn't really in the mood to stuff three hundred tiny little vol-au-vent cases with crab paste,' she said, following her brother through the open front door. 'But I guess I just had to put aside my little existential crisis and get on with it.'

The hallway smelled amazing. Soul food has a scent that fills you up even before your mouth gets near any of it. The sweet dough of the pastries, the alcoholic waft of a rum punch. In the kitchen, many dishes, covered for the moment with Saran Wrap, were laid out along the main table, and, on two small card tables brought up from the basement, a great pile of plates and concentric circles of glasses. Howard stood amidst all this, holding a brandy glass filled with red wine and smoking a baggy roll-up.

He had several stray pieces of tobacco stuck to his bottom lip. He was dressed in his traditional 'cooking' costume. This outfit — a kind of protest against the very concept of cooking — Howard constructed by donning all the discarded cook-wear clothes Kiki had purchased over the years and never used. Today Howard wore a chef's coat, an apron, an oven mitt, several dishcloths tucked into his waistband and one tied in a jaunty fashion around his neck. An improbable quantity of flour covered all this.

'Welcome! We're *cooking*,' said Howard. He put his mitted fingers to his lips and then tapped his nose twice.

'And *drinking*,' said Zora, removing the glass of red from his hand and taking it to the sink.

Howard appreciated the rhythm and comedy of this move and pushed on in the same vein. 'And how was your day, John Boy?'

'Well, someone thought I was *robbin'* you again.'

'Surely not,' said Howard cautiously. He disliked and feared conversations with his children that concerned race, as he suspected this one would.

'And don't be telling me I'm paranoid,'

snapped Levi, slinging his damp vest on the table. 'I just don't want to *live* here any more, man . . . all everybody does is stare.'

'Has anyone seen the cream?' said Kiki, appearing from behind the door of the fridge. '*Not* the canned, not the single, not the half and half — the double English. It was on the table.' She spotted Levi's vest. '*Not* there, young man. In your room — *which,* by the way, is an absolute *disgrace.* If you want to move out of that basement any day soon, you're going to have to make some changes. I'd be *ashamed* to have your room where anybody could see it!'

Levi frowned and continued speaking to his father. 'And then some crazy old lady on Redwood started asking about my mom.'

'Levi,' said Kiki, walking over to him, 'are you here to help or what?'

'How do you mean? About Kiki?' asked Howard with interest, taking a seat at the table.

'This old lady on Redwood — I was minding my business — and she's looking at me, looking at me, all the way down the street, like everybody in this town — she stops me, speaking to me — she looked like she was trying to work out if I was gonna kill her.'

This of course was not true. But Levi

had a point to make, and he would have to bend the truth to make it.

'And then she started talking about my mom this, my mom that. Black lady.'

Howard made a noise of objection, but was overruled.

'No, no, but that don't make no difference. Any black lady who be white enough to live on Redwood thinks *'zackly* the same way as any old white lady.'

'Who *is* white enough,' corrected Zora. 'It's the worst kind of pretension, you know, to fake the way you speak — to steal somebody else's grammar. People less fortunate than you. It's grotesque. You can decline a Latin noun, but apparently you can't even —'

'The cream — anybody? It was *right here.*'

'I think you might be overreacting just a tad,' said Howard, exploring the fruit bowl with his fingers. 'Where was this?'

'On *Redwood.* How many times, yo? This crazy old black lady.'

'I don't know how come it is that I put down something and five minutes later it . . . *Redwood?*' asked Kiki sharply. 'How far down Redwood?'

'Just on the top corner, before the nursery.'

'A *black* old lady? No one like that lives on Redwood. Who was she?'

'I don't *know* . . . There was boxes everywhere — look like she was just moving in — anyway, that ain't even the point — point is, I'm *sick* of people watching me every damn step I —'

'Oh, Jesus — *Jesus* . . . were you rude to her?' demanded Kiki, putting down the bag of sugar she had in her hand.

'What?'

'You know who that is?' asked Kiki rhetorically. 'I'll *bet* you that's the Kippses moving in — I heard their place was right by here. I'll bet you a hundred dollars that was the wife.'

'Don't be *absurd,*' said Howard.

'Levi — what did the woman look like — what did she *look like?*'

Levi, bemused and depressed that his anecdote had met with such a heavy reception, struggled to remember details. 'Old . . . real tall, wearing, like, very bright colours for an old lady —'

Kiki looked hard at Howard.

'Ah . . .' said Howard. Kiki turned back to Levi.

'What did you say to her? You better not have been rude to her, Levi, or I swear to God, I'll tire your *ass* out this evening —'

'*What?* It was just some crazy . . . I don't know — she was asking me all these

159

weird questions . . . I don't remember what I said — I wasn't rude, though — I *wasn't*. I barely said anything, man, and she was crazy! She was ahksing me all these questions about my *mom* and I was just like, I'm late — my mom's having a party, I gotta go, I can't talk now — and that was it.'

'You said we were having a party.'

'Oh, my *gosh* — Mom, it ain't whoever you think it is. It's just some crazy old woman who thought I'm gonna kill her 'cos I'm wearing a doo-rag.'

Kiki put a hand over her eyes. 'It's the Kippses — oh, God — I have to invite them now. I should have told Jack to invite them anyway. I have to invite them.'

'You don't *have* to invite them,' stated Howard slowly.

'Of *course* I have to invite them. I'll go round there when I'm done with the key lime — Jerome's out buying more alcohol — God knows what he's doing, he ought to be back by now. Or Levi can go, drop a note off or something —'

'What are you mad at *me* now? Man, I am *not* going back there. I was just trying to explain to you how I feel when I walk round this neighbourhood —'

'Levi, please, I'm trying to think. Go

160

downstairs and deal with your room.'

'Aw, *fuck* you, man.'

The swearing policy in the Belsey house was not self-evident. They had nothing as twee or pointless as a swear jar (a popular household item among Wellington families), and swearing was, as we have seen, generally accepted in most situations. And yet there were several strange subclauses to this libertarian procedure, rules of practice neither written in stone nor particularly transparent. It was a question of tone and feeling, and, in this case, Levi had misjudged. Now his mother's hand came down hard upon the side of his head, a blow that sent him stumbling back three steps into the kitchen table. He knocked a gravy boat of chocolate sauce over himself. In normal circumstances, faced with the smallest slight to himself or his character, and, in particular, his clothes, Levi would argue for justice for as long as he had breath in his body, even when — especially when — he was in the wrong. But on this occasion he left the room at once without a word. A minute later they heard his door downstairs slamming.

'Good. Nice party,' said Zora.

'You wait till the guests arrive,' murmured Howard.

'I just want to teach him to . . .' began Kiki. She felt exhausted. She sat down at the kitchen table and rested her head on its Scandinavian pine.

'I'll go out and cut you a switch, shall I? Bit of parenting, Florida style,' said Howard, making a show of taking off his hat and his apron. In the family context, whenever Howard saw an opportunity to take the moral high ground he pretty much catapulted himself towards it. These opportunities had been rare recently. When Kiki lifted her head, he had already left the room. *That's right,* thought Kiki, *quit while you're ahead.* Just then Jerome came through the door and paused in the kitchen for a moment to mumble that the wine was in the hallway, before proceeding straight through the sliding doors to the back garden.

'I don't know why everybody in this house has to behave like a goddamn animal,' said Kiki with sudden ferocity. She stood up and went to the sink to wet a cloth, returning to go to work on the spilled chocolate. She could not do distress. Anger was so much easier. And quicker and harder and better. *If I start crying, I'll never stop* — you hear people say that; Kiki heard people say it all the time in the hospital. A backlog of sadness for which there would never be sufficient time.

'I'm done with this,' said Zora, swirling a spoon listlessly through the fruit punch she had helped to make. 'I'm going to get changed or something.'

'Zoor,' said Kiki, 'do you know where I could find a pen and paper?'

'Eyeano. Drawer?'

Zora too wandered away. Kiki heard a great splash from outside, and then glimpsed the dark, curled dome of Jerome's head before it went under the water again. She opened the drawer at her end of the long kitchen table and, among many batteries and fake fingernails, found a pen. She went in search of paper. She recalled a pad that had been squeezed between two paperbacks on a bookshelf in the hallway.

'Chess?' Kiki heard Zora ask Howard. When she came back into the kitchen, she could see them setting up play in the lounge as if nothing at all had happened, as if they didn't have a party to host, Murdoch happily ensconced in Howard's lap. *Chess?* Is that what it's like, wondered Kiki, to be an intellectual? Can the tuned mind tune everything else out? Kiki sat alone in the kitchen. She wrote a short note welcoming the Kippses to town and expressing the hope they might attend a little gathering, any time after six thirty.

10

Turning the corner of Redwood, Kiki was already busy reading the signs. The size of the moving van, the style of the house, the colours of the garden. The light was fading and the streetlamps were not yet lit. It bugged her that she was unable to see more clearly the hanging baskets suspended like censers from the four storeys of balconies. Kiki was quite close to the front gate before she saw the outline of a tall woman sitting in a high-backed chair. Kiki put the letter she held in her hand back into her pocket. The woman was asleep. Kiki understood at once that she would never wish to be seen like this, with her thinning hair fanned out across her cheek, her mouth wide open and half of one fluttering, unseeing eyeball revealed to the world. It seemed rude to walk past her and continue to the doorbell, as if she were nothing more significant than a cat or an ornament. Equally, it didn't seem right to wake her. On the porch now and hesitating, Kiki had the momentary fancy of placing the note in the woman's lap and running away. She took another step towards the door; the woman woke.

'Hi, *hi* — I'm sorry, I didn't mean to alarm you — I'm a neighbour here . . . are you . . . Mrs Kipps or . . .'

The woman smiled lazily and looked at Kiki, around Kiki, apparently assessing her bulk, where it began and where it ended. Kiki pulled her cardigan around herself.

'I'm Kiki Belsey.'

Now Mrs Kipps made a jubilant sound of realization, beginning on a reed-thin high note and slowly making its way down the scale. She brought her long hands together slowly like a pair of cymbals.

'Yes, I'm *Jerome's* mother — I think you bumped into my youngest today, Levi? I hope he wasn't rude at all . . . he can be a little brash sometimes —'

'I *knew* I was right, I *knew* it, you see.'

Kiki laughed in an unhinged way, still concentrating on taking in all the visual information about this much discussed, never before glimpsed entity, Mrs Kipps.

'Isn't it crazy? The coincidence of Jerome, and then you and Levi bumping —'

'No coincidence at all — I knew him by his face the moment I saw him. They're so alive to look at, your sons, so handsome.'

Kiki was vulnerable to compliments concerning her children, but she was also familiar with them. Three brown children of a certain height will attract attention wherever they go. Kiki was used to the glory of it and also the necessity of humility.

'Do you think so? I guess they are — I always think of them still as babies, really, without any —' began Kiki happily, but Mrs Kipps continued over her, unheeding.

'And now this is you,' she said, whistling and reaching out to grab Kiki's hand by the wrist. 'Come here, come down.'

'Oh . . . OK,' said Kiki. She crouched beside Mrs Kipps's chair.

'But I didn't imagine you like this at all. You are not a *little* woman, are you?'

Going over it later, Kiki could not completely account for her own response to this question. Her gut had its own way of going about things, and she was used to its executive decisions; the feeling of immediate safety some people gave her, and, conversely, the nausea others induced. Maybe something in the shock of the question, as well as the natural warmth of it, and the apparently guileless nature of the intention behind it, impelled her to respond in kind — with the first thought she had.

'Uh-uh. Ain't nothing small on me. Not a thing. Got bosoms, got back.'

'I see. And you don't mind it at all?'

'It's just me — I'm used to it.'

'It looks very well on you. You carry it well.'

'Thank you!'

It was as if a sudden gust of wind had lifted and propelled this odd little conversation and now, just as suddenly, let it go. Mrs Kipps looked straight ahead, into her garden. Her breathing was shallow and audible in her throat.

'I . . .' began Kiki, and waited again for some kind of recognition and received none. 'I guess I wanted to say how sorry I was about all that unnecessary fuss last year — it all got so out of proportion . . . I hope we can all just put it . . .' said Kiki, and trailed off as she felt Mrs Kipps's thumb pressing down in the centre of Kiki's own palm.

'I hope you won't offend me,' said Mrs Kipps, her head shaking, 'by apologizing for things that were no fault of yours.'

'No,' said Kiki. She meant to continue, but, once again, everything fell away. She just knew she could no longer crouch. She took her feet out from under her and sat down on the wood.

'Yes, you sit down and we can talk properly. Whatever problems our husbands may have, it's no quarrel of ours.'

Nothing followed. Kiki felt and saw herself in this unlikely position, sitting on the floor beneath a woman she did not know. She looked out over the garden and sighed stupidly, as if the charm of the scene had only this moment struck her.

'Now, what do you think,' Mrs Kipps said slowly, 'of my house?'

This question, implicit in Kiki's social dealings with the women of Wellington, was another she had never been asked outright before.

'Well, I think it's absolutely lovely.'

This answer seemed to surprise the occupant. She moved forward, lifting her chin from where it rested on her chest.

'*Really.* I cannot say that I like it so much. It's so *new.* There's nothing in this house except money, jangling. My house in London, Mrs Belsey —'

'Kiki, please.'

'*Carlene,*' she replied, pressing a long hand to her own, exposed throat. 'It's so full of humanity — I could hear petticoats in the hallway. I *miss* it so much, already. American houses . . .' she said, peering over her right shoulder and down the street. 'They always seem to believe that

168

nobody ever loses anything, has ever lost anything. I find that very sad. Do you know what I mean?'

Kiki instinctively bristled — after a lifetime of bad-mouthing her own country, these past few years she had grown into a new sensitivity. She had to leave the room when Howard's English friends settled into their armchairs after dinner and began the assault.

'American houses? How do you mean? You mean, you'd rather a house with, like, a history?'

'Oh . . . well, it can be put this way, yes.'

Kiki was further wounded by the sense she had said something to disappoint, or, worse, something so dull it was not worth replying to.

'But you know, actually this house does have a kind of history, Mrs — Carlene — it's not a very pretty one, though.'

'Mmm.'

Now this was simply impolite. Mrs Kipps had closed her eyes. The woman was rude. Wasn't she? Maybe it was a cultural difference. Kiki pressed on.

'Yes — there was an older gentleman here, Mr Weingarten — he was a dialysis patient at the hospital where I work, so he got picked up by an ambulance, you know, three or four times a week, and one day they arrived and they found him in the garden — it's terrible, actually — he was burned to death — apparently he had a lighter in his pocket, in his bathrobe — he was probably trying to light a cigarette — which he should *not* have been doing — anyway, he went and set fire to himself, and I guess he just couldn't put it out. It's pretty awful — I don't know why I told you that. I'm sorry.'

This last was untrue — she was not sorry she had told the story. She had wanted to kick-start this woman somehow.

'Oh, no, my dear,' said Mrs Kipps, rather impatiently, dismissive of so obvious a ploy to unbalance her. Kiki noticed for the first time the shake in her head also extended to her left hand. 'I already knew that — the lady next door told my husband.'

'Oh, OK. It's just so *sad*. Living alone and all.'

To this, Mrs Kipps's face responded at once — it crumpled and distorted like a child's when given caviar or wine. Her front teeth came forward as the skin on her jaw pulled back. She looked ghastly. Kiki thought for a moment it was a kind of seizure, but then her face healed over. 'It is so *awful* to me, that idea,' Mrs

170

Kipps said passionately.

Once again she gripped Kiki's hand, this time with both of her own. The deeply lined black palms reminded Kiki of her own mother's. The fragility of the grasp — the feeling that one need only release one's own five fingers from it and this other person's hand would smash into pieces. Kiki was shamed out of her pique.

'Oh, God, I'd *hate* to live alone,' she said, before considering whether this was still true. 'But you'll like it here in Wellington — generally, we all take care of each other pretty well. It's a community-minded kind of a place. Reminds me a lot of parts of Florida that way.'

'But when we drove through town I saw so many poor souls living on the street!'

Kiki had lived in Wellington long enough not to be able to quite trust people who spoke of injustice in this faux naive manner, as if no one had ever noticed the injustice before.

'Well,' she said evenly, 'we've certainly got a situation down there — there's a lot of very recent immigrants too, lot of Haitians, lot of Mexicans, a lot of folk just out there with no place to go. It's not so bad in the winter when the shelters open up. But, no . . . absolutely, and you know, we really need to thank you for helping Jerome with a place to stay in London — it was so generous of you. His hour of need and everything. I was so sad that everything got polluted by —'

'I love a line from a poem: *There is such a shelter in each other.* I think it is so *fine.* Don't you think it's a wonderful thing?'

Kiki was left with her mouth open at being interrupted thus.

'Is it — which poet is it?'

'Oh, I would not actually know that for myself . . . Monty is the intellectual in our family. I have no talent for ideas or memory for names. I read it in a newspaper, that's all. You're an intellectual too?'

And this was possibly the most important question Wellington had never honestly asked Kiki.

'No, actually . . . No, I'm not. I'm really not.'

'Neither am I. But I do *love* poetry. Everything I cannot say and I never hear said. The bit I cannot touch?'

Kiki could not tell at first what kind of question this was or whether she was meant to answer it, but a moment's pause proved it rhetorical.

'I find that bit in poems,' said Mrs Kipps. 'I did not read a poem for years and years — I preferred biographies. And then I read one last year. Now I can't stop!'

'God, that's great. I just never get a chance to read any more. I used to read a lot of Angelou — do you read her? That's autobiography, isn't it? I always found her very . . .'

Kiki stopped. The same thing that had distracted Mrs Kipps distracted her. Just passing by the gate five white teenage girls, barely dressed, were going by. They had rolled-up towels under their arms and wet hair, stuck together in long sopping ropes, like the Medusa. They were all speaking at once.

'There is such a shelter in each other,' repeated Mrs Kipps, as the noise grew fainter, 'Montague says poetry is the first mark of the truly civilized. He is always saying wonderful things like that.'

Kiki, who did not think this especially wonderful, stayed quiet.

'And when I told him this line, from the poem —'

'Yes, the poem line.'

'Yes. When I spoke it to him, he said that that was all very well but I should place it on a scale — a scale of judgement — and on the other side of the scale I should place *L'enfer, c'est les autres*. And then see which had more weight in the world!' She laughed for some time at this, a sprightly laugh, more youthful than her speaking voice. Kiki smiled helplessly. She did not speak French.

'I'm so *glad* we've met properly,' said Mrs Kipps, with real fondness.

Kiki was touched. 'Oh, that's very sweet.'

'*Really* glad. We've just met — and look how cosy we are.'

'We're so happy to have you in Wellington, really,' said Kiki, abashed. 'Actually, I came to invite you to a party we're having tonight. I think my son mentioned it.'

'A party! How *lovely*. And how kind of you to invite an old lady who you don't even know from Adam.'

'Honey, if you're old, *I'm* old. Jerome's only two years older than your daughter, isn't he? Is it Victoria?'

'But you're not old,' she admonished. 'It hasn't even touched you yet. It will, but it hasn't yet.'

'I'm fifty-three. I sure feel old.'

'I was forty-five when I had my last child. Praise the Lord for his miracles. No, anybody can see it — you're a child in your face.'

Kiki had inclined her head to avoid

174

having to come up with any face with which to meet the praising of the Lord. Now she raised it again.

'Well, come to a children's party, then.'

'I will, thank you. I will come with my family.'

'That would be wonderful, Mrs Kipps.'

'Oh, *please* . . . *Carlene,* please call me Carlene. I feel the pull of an office and paperclips whenever anybody calls me Mrs Kipps. Years ago I used to help Montague in his office — there I was Mrs Kipps. In England, if you will believe me,' she said, smiling mischievously, 'they even call me *Lady* Kipps because of Montague's achievements . . . proud as I am of Montague, I have to tell you — being called *Lady Kipps* feels like being dead already. I don't recommend it.'

'Carlene, I got to be honest with you, honey,' said Kiki, laughing, 'I don't think Howard's in any danger of a knighthood any time soon. Thanks for the warning, though.'

'You shouldn't make fun of your husband, dear,' came the urgent reply; 'you only make fun of yourself that way.'

'Oh, we make fun of each other,' said Kiki, still laughing but with the same sorrow she had felt when a hitherto perfectly nice cabbie began to tell her that all the Jews in the first tower had been warned beforehand or that you can't trust Mexicans not to steal the rug from under your feet or that more roads were built under Stalin . . .

Kiki moved to stand up.

'Hold on to the arm of the chair, dear . . . Men move with their minds, and women must move with our bodies, whether we like it or not. That's how God intended it — I have always felt that so strongly. When you're a larger lady, though, I expect that becomes a little more hard.'

'No, I'm cool, I'm fine — *there*,' said Kiki good-humouredly, upright now, and shimmying her hips a little. 'Actually, I'm pretty flexible. Yoga. And, to be honest, I guess I feel men and women use their minds about equally.' She brushed the wood dust off her palms.

'Oh, I don't. No, I *don't*. Everything I do I do with my body. Even my soul is made up of raw meat, flesh. Truth is in a face, as much as it is anywhere. We women know that faces are full of meaning, I think. Men have the gift of pretending that's not true. And this is where their power comes from. Monty hardly knows he has a body at all!'

She laughed and put a hand to Kiki's face. 'You have a marvellous face, for example. And the moment I saw you I knew I would like you.'

The silliness of this made Kiki laugh too. She shook her head at the compliment.

'Well, it looks like we like each other,' she said. 'What *will* the neighbours say?'

Carlene Kipps raised herself up from her chair. Kiki's protesting noises couldn't stop her neighbour walking her to the gate. If Kiki had been in any doubt earlier, she knew now that this woman was unwell. She asked to take Kiki's arm after only a couple of steps. Kiki felt almost the whole of Carlene's weight shift on to her, and this weight was nothing at all to bear. Something in Kiki's heart shifted too, towards this woman. She didn't seem to say anything that she didn't mean.

'Those are my bougainvillea — I got Victoria to plant them today, but I don't know if they will survive. But right now they have the *appearance* of survival, which is almost the same thing. And they do it with such style. I grow them in Jamaica — we have a little house there. Yes, I think the garden will be my solution to this house. Don't you think that's true?'

'I don't know how to answer that.

They're both wonderful.'

Carlene nodded quickly, dismissing the charming nonsense.

She patted Kiki's hand soothingly. 'You must go and organize your party.'

'And you must come.'

With the same incredulous and yet mollifying look, as if Kiki had asked her to the moon, she nodded again, and turned back towards her house.

II

By the time Kiki returned to 83 Langham, her first guest had arrived. It is an unnatural law of such parties that the person whose position on the guest list was originally the least secure is always the first to arrive. Christian von Klepper's invitation had been added by Howard, removed by Kiki, reinstated by Howard, removed by Kiki and then, at some later point, apparently extended once more in secret by Howard, for here was Christian, leaning into an alcove in the living room, nodding devotedly at his host. From where she stood in the kitchen, Kiki could see only a sliver of both men, but you didn't need to see much to get the picture. She watched them, unnoticed, as she took off her cardigan and hung it over a chair. Howard was full of beans. Hands in his hair, leaning forward. He was listening — but *really* listening. It's amazing, thought Kiki, how attentive he can be when he puts his mind to it. In his efforts to make peace with her, Howard had spent months showering some of this attention on Kiki herself, and she knew all about the warmth it afforded, the flattering bliss of it. Christian, under its influence, looked properly young for once. You could see him permitting himself some partial release from the brittle persona that a visiting lecturer of only twenty-eight must assume if he has ambitions of becoming an assistant professor. Well, good for him. Kiki took a lighter from a kitchen drawer and began to kindle her tealights wherever she found them. This should all have been done already. The quiches had not been heated. And where were the children? An appreciative rumble of Howard's laughter reached her. And now he and the boy swapped roles — now it was Howard doing the talking and Christian following every syllable like a pilgrim. The younger man looked modestly to the floor, in response, Kiki assumed, to some piece of flattery of her husband's. Howard was more than generous that way;

179

if flattered he repaid the favour tenfold. When Christian's face resurfaced Kiki saw it was flushed with pleasure, and a second later this shaded into something more calculated: the recognition, maybe, that the compliment was nothing less than his due. Kiki went to the fridge and took out a very good bottle of champagne. She picked up a plate of bang-bang chicken canapés. She hoped these would serve as replacement for any opening bon mots she might be expected to come up with. Her encounter with Mrs Kipps had left her strangely empty of casual conversation. She couldn't remember when she'd felt less like having a party than at this moment.

Sometimes you get a flash of what you look like to other people. This one was unpleasant: a black woman in a headwrap, approaching with a bottle in one hand and a plate of food in the other, like a maid in an old movie. The real staff — Monique, and an unnamed friend of hers who was meant to be handing out drinks — were nowhere to be seen. The living room revealed only one other person, Meredith, a fat and pretty Japanese-American girl, constant — you assumed platonic — companion of Christian. She had an extraordinary outfit on and her back to the room, engrossed in reading the spines of Howard's art books on the opposite wall. Kiki was reminded that, although Howard's fan club within the university was extremely small, it had an intensity in inverse proportion to its size. Because of the stringency of his theories and his dislike of his colleagues, Howard was nowhere near as successful or as popular or as well paid as his peers in Wellington. He had, instead, a miniature campus cult: Christian was the preacher; Meredith was the congregation. If there were others, Kiki had never met them. There was Smith J. Miller, Howard's teaching assistant, a sweet-tempered white boy from the Deep South — but Smith was paid for his services by Wellington. Kiki opened the living-room door wide with her heel, wondering again where Monique, who might have thought to wedge the thing open, was hiding. Christian did not yet turn to acknowledge her, but he was already pretending to like Murdoch playing around his ankles. He leaned forward with the clumsy loom of the natural pet-hater and child-fearer, all the time clearly hoping for an intervention before he reached the dog. His elongated, lean body struck Kiki as a comic, human version of Murdoch's own.

'He bothering you?'

'Oh, no. Mrs Belsey, hello. No, not at all, not really. If anything, I was concerned that he might choke on my laces.'

'Really?' said Kiki, looking down dubiously.

'No, I mean it's fine . . . it's fine.' Christian's features abruptly morphed into his pinched attempt at a 'party-face'. 'And anyway: happy anniversary! It's so amazing.'

'Well, thank *you* so much for coming —'

'My God,' said Christian, with that clipped, puzzlingly European inflection he had. He had been raised in Iowa. 'I'm simply privileged to be invited. It must be a very special occasion for you. What a milestone.'

Kiki sensed that he hadn't said any of this to Howard, and indeed Howard's eyebrows now raised a little, as if he had not heard Christian speak like this before. The banalities, obviously, were saved for Kiki.

'Yeah, I guess . . . and it's just a nice thing — beginning of the semester and everything . . . shall I get the dog away from you?'

Christian had been stepping from side to side, trying to lose Murdoch but instead offering him the kind of challenge he adored.

'Oh, well . . . I don't want to —'

'No trouble, Christian, don't sweat it.'

Kiki nudged Murdoch off with her toe, and then gave him another nudge to direct him out of the room. God forbid Christian should get any dog hairs on those fine Italian shoes. No, that was unfair. Christian slicked down his hair with his palm along that severe parting on the left side of his head, a line so straight it seemed marked out with a ruler. And that too was unfair.

'I got me champ*agne* in one hand and chicken in the other,' said Kiki, excessively jolly as penance for her thoughts. 'What can I do you for?'

'Oh, God,' said Christian. He seemed to know a joke should go here but he was constitutionally unable to provide one. 'Choices, choices.'

'Give them here, darling,' said Howard, taking only the champagne from his wife. 'Proper hellos first might be nice — you know Meredith, don't you?'

Meredith — if one were to remember two facts about each of one's guests in order to introduce them to other guests — was interested in Foucault and costume-wear. At various parties Kiki had listened carefully and yet not understood what

Meredith was saying while Meredith was dressed as an English punk, a *fin de siècle* dame in a drop-waisted Edwardian gown, a French movie star and, most memorably, a forties war bride, her hair set and curled like Bacall's, complete with stockings and stays and that compelling black line curving up the back of both her mighty calves. This evening Meredith's dress was a concoction of pink chiffon, with a wide circle skirt you had to make space for, and a little black mohair cardigan slung over her shoulders. This last was set off by a gigantic diamanté brooch. Her shoes were peep-toe red heels that put at least a three-inch distance between Meredith and her real height as she strode across the room. Meredith stretched out a white kid glove for her hostess to shake. Meredith was twenty-seven years old.

'Of course! Wow, Meredith!' said Kiki, blinking theatrically. 'Honey, I don't even know what to say. I should have some kind of award for best party outfit — I don't know what I was thinking. You look *fine, girl!*'

Kiki whistled, and Meredith, who was still holding one of Kiki's hands, took the opportunity to do a twirl, holding Kiki's hand high and describing a small circle beneath it.

'You like? I would so very much like to tell you I just threw it together,' said Meredith loudly and quickly in her nervous, Californian scream, 'but it takes me a long, *looong* time to look this good. Bridges have been built quicker. Whole hermeneutic systems have coalesced with more speed. Just from here to here,' said Meredith, signalling the space between her eyebrows and her upper lip, 'that's like three hours.'

The bell rang. Howard groaned, as if the present company was more than enough, but went practically skipping off to answer it. Abandoned by their only real connection, the little triangle fell quiet, resorting to smiles. Kiki wondered precisely how far she was from Meredith and Christian's ideal of a leader's appropriate consort.

'We made you a thing,' said Meredith abruptly. 'Did he tell you? We made you this thing. Maybe it's *crap*, I don't know.'

'No . . . no, I hadn't yet —' said Christian, blushing.

'Like a thing — a *present*. Is that corny? Thirty years and all that? Have we just been corny?'

'I'll just . . .' said Christian, crouching down awkwardly to get to his old-fashioned satchel, which rested against the ottoman.

'So we did some half-assed research and it turns out that thirty years is *pearl,* but, as you know, the average grad income doesn't really stretch that far, so we weren't really in the pearl way of things . . .' Meredith laughed maniacally. 'And then Chris thought of this poem and then I like did my arts and craft thing and anyway here it is: see it's like a framed, fabricy, type poem thing — I don't know.'

Kiki felt the warm teak frame delivered into her hands and admired the crushed rose petals and broken shells under the glass. The text was sewn in, like a tapestry. It was the most unusual present she could have expected from these two. It was lovely.

'Full fathom five thy father lies; Of his bones are coral made. Those are pearls that were his eyes —' read Kiki circumspectly, aware that she should know it.

'So, that's the *pearl* thing,' said Meredith. 'It's probably stupid.'

'Oh — it's so gorgeous,' said Kiki, skim-reading the rest to herself in a quick whisper. 'Is it Plath? That's wrong, isn't it.'

'It's Shakespeare,' said Christian, wincing slightly. *'The Tempest. Nothing of him that doth fade, But doth suffer a sea-change, Into something rich and strange.* Plath stripped it for parts.'

'*Shit,*' Kiki laughed. 'When in doubt, say Shakespeare. And when it's sport, say Michael Jordan.'

'That is *totally* my policy,' agreed Meredith.

'This is really gorgeous. Howard will love it. I don't think it comes under his representational art ban.'

'No, it's textual,' said Christian testily. 'That's the point. It's a textual artifact.'

Kiki looked at him inquiringly. She wondered sometimes whether Christian was in love with her husband.

'Where *is* Howard?' said Kiki, revolving her head absurdly round the empty room. 'He'll just love this. He loves to hear that nothing on him doth fade.'

Meredith laughed again. Howard re-entered the room with a clap of his hands, but then the bell rang once more.

'Bloody *hell.* Could you excuse us? Like Piccadilly Circus in here. Jerome! Zora?'

Howard cupped a hand to his ear like a man waiting for a response to his fake bird call.

'Howard,' tried Kiki, holding up the frame, 'Howard, look at this.'

'Levi? No? Have to be us, then. Just excuse us one minute.'

Kiki followed Howard into the hall,

where together they opened the door to the Wilcoxes, one of the rare, genuinely moneyed Wellingtonian couples of their acquaintance. The Wilcoxes owned a preppy clothes chain store, gave generously to the college, and looked like the shells of two Atlantic shrimp in evening wear. Right behind them came Howard's assistant, Smith J. Miller, bearing a home-made apple-pie and dressed like the neat Kentucky gentleman he was. They were all ushered into the kitchen to do their best with the completely unsuitable social pairing of old-school Marxist English professor Joe Rainier and the young woman he was presently dating. There was a *New Yorker* cartoon on the fridge that Kiki now wished she had taken down. An upscale couple in the back of a limo. Woman saying: *Of course they're clever. They have to be clever. They haven't got any money.*

'Just go through, go through,' brayed Howard, making the signal for directing sheep across a country road. 'People in the living room, or the garden's lovely . . .'

A few minutes later they were alone once more in the hall.

'I mean, where's *Zora* — she's been going on about the bloody party for weeks and now neither hide nor hair —'

'She's probably gone to get some smokes or something.'

'I think at least *one* of them should be present. So people don't think we keep them in some kind of child sex prison camp in the attic.'

'I'll go and deal with it, Howie, OK? You just get everybody what they need. Where the *hell* is Monique? Wasn't she meant to be bringing somebody?'

'In the garden jumping up and down on *bags of ice*,' said Howard impatiently, as if she might have figured this out for herself. 'Bloody ice-maker fucked up half an hour ago.'

'Fuck.'

'Yes, darling, *fuck*.'

Howard pulled his wife towards him and put his nose in between her breasts. 'Can't we just have a party here? You and me and the girls?' he asked, tentatively squeezing the girls. Kiki drew back from him. Although peace had broken out in the Belsey household, sex had not yet returned. In the past month Howard had stepped up his flirtatious campaign. Touching, holding and now squeezing. Howard seemed to think the next step inevitable, but Kiki had not yet decided whether tonight was to be the beginning of the rest of her marriage.

'Uh-uh . . .' she said softly. 'Sorry. Turns out they're not coming.'

'Why not?'

He pulled her close to him again and rested his head on her shoulder. Kiki let him. Anniversaries will do that. She gripped a clump of her husband's thick, silky hair in her free hand. The other hand held Christian and Meredith's present, still waiting to be appreciated. And just like this, with her eyes closed, and with his hair escaping her fingers, they could have been standing in any happy day of any of these thirty years. Kiki was not a fool and recognized the feeling for what it was: a dumb wish to go backwards. Things could not be exactly the same as they had been.

'The girls hate Christian Von Asshole,' she said finally, teasingly, but let him rest his head on her bosom. 'They won't go to anything he goes to. You know how they are. I can't do a thing about it.'

The bell rang. Howard sighed lustily.

'Saved by the bell,' whispered Kiki. 'Look, I'm going upstairs. I'm going to try to get the kids down. You answer that — and slow down on the drinks, OK? You gotta hold this whole shebang together.'

'Mmm.'

Howard hurried to the door, but then

turned just before he opened it. 'Oh —
Keeks —' His face was childish, apologetic, completely inadequate. It made Kiki
suddenly despair. It was a face that placed
them right alongside every other middle-
aged couple on the block — the raging
wife, the rueful husband. She thought:
*How did we get to the same place as ev-
erybody else?*

'Keeks . . . Sorry, darling, just . . . I need
to know if you invited them?'

'Who?'

'Who d'you think? The Kippses.'

'Oh, right . . . Sure. I spoke to her. She
was . . .' But it was impossible either to
make a joke of Mrs Kipps or to give her to
Howard in a nutshell, the way he liked
people to be served to him. 'I don't know if
they'll come, but I invited them.'

And again with the bell, Kiki went off towards the stairs, leaving the present upon
the little table under the mirror. Howard
answered the door.

12

'Hey.'

Tall, pleased with himself, pretty, *too* pretty
like a conman, sleeveless, tattooed, languid,

191

muscled, a basketball under his arm, black. Howard kept hold of the half-open door.

'Can I help you?'

Carl had been smiling, now he stopped. He'd come from playing ball on Wellington's big, free, college court (you just walked right in and acted like you belonged there); midway through the game Levi had called him and said the party was tonight. Strange date to pick for a party, but then each to their own. The brother had sounded kind of funny, like he was pissed about something, but he was definitely real adamant about Carl coming down here. Sent him the address, like, three times. Carl *could* have gone back home to change first, but that would have been an epic round trip. He'd figured that on a hot night like this, no one would care.

'Hope so. I'm here for the party.'

Howard watched him put both hands either side of his ball so that the slender, powerful contours of his arms were outlined in the security light.

'Right . . . this *is* a private party.'

'Your man, Levi? I'm a friend of his.'

'I see . . . um, look, well, he's . . .' said Howard, turning and pretending to seek his son in the hallway. 'He's not about just now . . . But if you give me your name, I'll tell him you stopped by . . .'

Howard jerked back as the boy bounced his ball once, hard on the doorstep.

'Look,' said Howard rudely, 'I don't mean to be rude, but Levi shouldn't really have been inviting his . . . friends — this is really quite a small affair —'

'Right. For *poet* poets.'

'Excuse me?'

'Shit, I don't know why I even came here — forget it,' said Carl. He was off immediately down the drive and out the gate, a proud, quick, bouncy walk.

'Wait —' called Howard after him. He was gone.

Extraordinary, said Howard to himself, and closed the door. He went into the kitchen in search of wine. He heard the bell go again, and Monique answer, and people come in, and then more people right behind them. He poured his glass — the bell again — Erskine and his wife, Caroline. And then another crowd could be heard relieving themselves of their coats just as Howard thumped the cork back in the bottle. The house was filling up with people he was not related to by blood. Howard began to feel in the party mood. Soon enough he relaxed into his role of life and soul: pressing food upon his guests, pouring their drinks, talking up his reluctant, invisible children, correcting a quotation, weighing in on an argument, introducing people to each other twice or thrice over. During his many three-minute conversations he managed to be committed, curious, supportive, celebratory, laughing before you had finished your funny sentence, refilling your glass even as beaded bubbles still winked at the brim. If he caught you in the action of putting on or looking for your coat, you were treated to a lover's complaint; you pressed his hand, he pressed yours. You swayed together like sailors. One felt confident to tease him, slightly, about his Rembrandt, and he in turn said something irreverent about your Marxist past or your creative-writing class or your eleven-year-long study of Montaigne, and the goodwill was at such a pitch that you did not take it personally. You placed your coat back on the bed. Finally, when you again persisted with your talk of deadlines and morning starts and made it out of the front door, you closed it with the new and gratifying impression that not only did Howard Belsey not hate you — as you had always previously assumed — but, in fact, the man had long harboured a boundless admiration of you which only his natural English reserve had prevented him from expressing before this night.

At nine thirty, Howard decided it was time to give a little speech in the garden to the assembled company. This was well received. By ten, the intoxication of all this bon vivant business had reached Howard's petite ears, which were quite red with joy. It seemed to him an especially successful little party. In truth it was a typical Wellington affair: always threatening to fill up but never quite doing so. The Black Studies Department's graduate crowd were out in force, mostly because Erskine was well loved by them and they were, anyway, by far the most socialized people at Wellington, priding themselves on their reputation for being the closest replicas on campus to normal human beings. Along with large talk they had small talk; they had a Black Music Library in their department; they knew, and could speak eloquently of, the latest trash television. They were invited to all the parties and came to all of them too. But the English Department was less well represented tonight: only Claire, that Marxist Joe, Smith and a few female Cult of Claire groupies who, Howard was amused to see, were throwing themselves at Warren, one after another, like lemmings. Warren had clearly joined the list of things of which Claire approved — therefore they wanted him. A circle of strange young anthropologists Howard didn't think he knew remained in the kitchen all night, hovering by the food, fearful of going anywhere where there was not an abundance of props — glasses, bottles, canapés — with which to fiddle. Howard left them to it and adjourned to the garden. He walked the rim of the pool, happily holding on to his empty glass, as the summer moon passed behind blushing clouds and all about rose the agreeable animal sound of outdoor conversation.

'Strange date for it, though,' he heard somebody say. And then the usual response: 'Oh, I think it's a wonderful date for a party. You know it's their *actual* anniversary, so . . . And if we don't reclaim the day, you know . . . then it's like *they've* won. It's a reclaiming, absolutely.' This was the most popular conversation of the night. Howard had had it himself at least four times since the clock struck ten and the wine really kicked in. Before that no one liked to mention it.

Every twenty seconds or so, Howard admired a pair of feet as they thrust up through the skin of the water; the curved back that followed, and then the slim brown form in the water doing another speedy, almost silent lap. Levi had evidently decided that if he must stay at this party, he might as well get a work-out. Howard could not figure out exactly how long Levi'd been in the pool, but, as his own speech had ended and the applause faded, everyone had noticed at the same time that there was a lone swimmer, and then almost everyone had asked their neighbour whether they recalled Cheever's story. Academics lack range.

'I should have brought my swimsuit,' Howard had overheard Claire Malcolm saying loudly to somebody.

'And would you have swum if you had?' came the sensible reply.

Without any great urgency, Howard was now looking for Erskine. He wanted Erskine's opinion on his earlier speech. He sat down on the pretty bench Kiki had installed under their apple tree and looked out on to his party. The wide backs and solid calves of women he didn't know surrounded him. Friends of Kiki from the hospital, talking among themselves. Nurses, thought Howard definitively, *not* sexy. And how had his speech gone down with

197

women like this, non-academic, solid, opinionated, Kiki supporters — for that matter,
how had it gone down with everyone? It
had not been an easy speech to give. It was,
in effect, three speeches. One for those who
knew, one for those who didn't know, and
one for Kiki, to whom it was addressed and
who both did and didn't know. The people
who didn't know had smiled and whooped
and clapped as Howard touched upon the
rewards of love; they sighed sweetly when
he expanded on the joys of marrying your
best friend, also the difficulties. Encouraged by this moonlit attention, Howard
had strayed from his prepared script. He
segued into Aristotle's praise of friendship,
and from there to some aperçus of his own.
He spoke of how friendship expands toler-
ance. He spoke of the fecklessness of Rembrandt and the forgiveness of his wife,
Saskia. This was close to the knuckle, but
none of it seemed to be greeted with any
undue attention by the majority of his audience. Fewer people knew than he had
feared. Kiki had not, after all, told the
whole world of what he had done, and tonight he was more grateful for this fact
than ever. Speech concluded, the applause
had settled snug around him like a comfort
blanket. He had hugged the two American

children available to him hard around their shoulders, and felt no resistance. So that's how it was. His infidelity had not ended everything, after all. It had been self-pity to think that, and self-aggrandizement. Life went on. Jerome showed him that first, by having his own romantic cataclysm so soon after Howard's — the world does not stop for you. At first, he had thought otherwise. At first he had despaired. Nothing like this had ever happened to him before — he had no idea what to do, which move to make. Later on, when he retold the story to Erskine — a veteran of marital infidelity — his friend had gifted him with some belated, obvious advice: *Deny everything.* This was Erskine's long-term policy, and he claimed it had never failed him. But Howard had been discovered and confronted in the oldest way — a condom in the pocket of his suit — and she had stood before him holding it between her fingers, alive with a pure contempt he had found almost impossible to bear. He had many choices before him that day, but the truth had simply not been one of them, not if he wanted to retain any semblance of the life he loved. And now he felt vindicated: he had made the right decision. He had not told the truth. Instead he said what he felt he must in order to enable all of this to continue: these friends, these colleagues, this family, this woman. God knows, even the story he ended up giving — a one-night stand with a stranger — had caused terrible damage. It broke that splendid circle of Kiki's love, within which he had existed for so long, a love (and it was to Howard's credit that he knew this) that had enabled everything else. How much worse would it have been had he told the truth? It would only have packed misery upon misery. As it stood, a few of his closest friendships had been imperilled: those people Kiki had spoken to were disappointed in him and had told him so. A year later, this party was the test of their respect for him, and now, realizing that he had passed the test, Howard had to restrain himself from crying with relief before each new person who was kind to him. He had made a silly mistake — this was the consensus — and should be allowed (for who among middle-aged academics would dare to throw the first stone?) to remain in possession of that unusual thing, a happy and passionate marriage. How they had loved each other! Everybody thinks they're in love at twenty, of course; but Howard Belsey had really still been in love at forty — embarrassing but true. He never really got over her *face*. It gave him so much pleasure. Erskine often joked that only a man who had such pleasure at home could be the kind of theorist Howard was, so against pleasure in his work. Erskine himself was on his second marriage. Almost all the men Howard knew were already divorced, had begun again with new women; they told him things like 'you get to the end of a woman', as if their wives had been pieces of string. Is that what happened? Had he finally got to the end of Kiki?

Howard spotted her by the pool now, crouching next to Erskine, both of them talking to Levi, who held himself up in the water with his strong folded arms upon the concrete. They were all laughing. Sadness sidled up to Howard. It was so strange to him, this decision of Kiki's not to pursue him for every detail of his betrayal. He admired the strength of her continued emotional willpower, but he didn't understand it. Had it been Howard, no force on earth could have stopped him knowing the name, the face, the whole history of touches. Sexually, he had always been an intensely jealous man. When he met Kiki she had been a woman of only male friends, hundreds of them (or so it had seemed to Howard), mostly ex-lovers. Just hearing their names, even now, *thirty years later,* plunged Howard into a blue funk. They saw none of these men socially with any regularity, and that had been Howard's doing. He had bullied, threatened and frozen them all out. And this was despite the fact that Kiki had always claimed (and he had always believed her) that love started with him.

Now he put his hand over his empty glass to decline some wine Monique was trying to give him. 'Monique. Good party? Have you seen Zora?'

'Zora?'

'Yes, Zora.'

'I don't see 'er. Before I see, not now.'

'Everything going OK? Enough wine and so on?'

'Enough of everything. Too much.'

A few minutes later, by the doors into the kitchen, Howard spotted his unsubtle daughter hovering by a trio of philosophy graduates. He hurried over to effect her entry into this circle. He could do this kind of thing, at least. They stood leaning against each other, father and daughter: Howard feeling the alcohol and wanting to say something sentimental to her; Zora oblivious. She was focused on the conversation between the grads.

'And of course he was the great white hope.'

'Right. Great things were expected.'

'He was the darling of that department. At twenty-two or whatever.'

'Maybe that was the problem.'

'Right. *Right.*'

'He was offered a Rhodes — didn't take it up.'

'But he's doing nothing now, right?'

'Nope. I don't even think he's attached to anywhere at the moment. I heard he had a baby — so who knows. I think he's in Detroit.'

'Which is where he came from . . . Just one of these brilliant but totally unprepared kids.'

'No guidance.'

'None.'

It was a very average piece of *Schadenfreude,* but Howard saw how Zora was compelled by it. She had the strangest ideas about academics — she found it extraordinary that they should be capable of gossip or venal thoughts. She was hopelessly naive about them. She had not noticed, for example, the fact that philosophy graduate number two was involved in a study of her chest, out on messy display this evening in an unreliable gypsy top. So it was Zora whom Howard sent to the door when the bell went; Zora who opened the door to the family Kipps. The penny did not drop immediately. Here was a tall, imperious black man, in his late fifties, with a pug dog's distended eyes. To his right, his taller, equally dignified son; on the other side, his gallingly pretty daughter. Before conversation, Zora waded around in the visual information: the strangely Victorian get-up of the older man — the waistcoat, the pocket-handkerchief — and again that searing glimpse of the girl, the instantaneous recognition (on both sides) of her physical superiority. Now they moved in a triangle behind Zora through the hallway as she babbled about coats and drinks and her own parents, neither of whom, for the moment, could be found. Howard had vanished.

'God, he was right here. *God.* He's around here some place . . . God, where *is* he?'

It was an ailment Zora inherited from her father: when confronted with people she knew to be religious she began to blaspheme wildly. The three guests stood patiently around her, watching Zora's fireworks of anxiety. Monique passed by and Zora lunged at her, but her tray was empty and she hadn't seen Howard since he'd been looking for Zora, a fact that took a tediously long time to explain.

'Levi in the pool — Jerome upstairs,' offered Monique in sulky mitigation. 'He says him not coming down.'

This was an unfortunate reference.

'This is Victoria,' said Mr Kipps, with the measured dignity of a man taking control of a silly situation. 'And Michael. Of course, they already know your brother, the *elder* brother.'

His Trinidadian *basso profundo* sailed effortlessly through the sea of shame here, pressing forward into new waters.

'Yeah, they totally already met,' said Zora, neither lightly nor seriously, and so falling somewhere unsettling in between.

'They were all *chums* in London and now you will all be *chums* here,' said Monty Kipps, looking out impatiently over her head, like a man constantly on the lookout for the camera he knew must be filming him. 'I really should say hello to your parents. Otherwise it is rather like being smuggled in the wooden horse, and I come as a guest, you see, bearing no dubious gifts. Not tonight, at least.' His politician's laugh left his eyes unaffected by the action.

'Oh, sure . . .' said Zora, laughing along blandly, joining him in the fruitless stationary staring. 'I just don't know where . . . So are you all . . . I mean, have you all moved here, or?'

'Not me,' said Michael. 'This is purely holiday for me. Back to London Tuesday. Work calls, sadly.'

'Ah. That's a shame,' said Zora politely, but she wasn't disappointed. He was striking, but wholly void of sex appeal. She thought, strangely, of that boy in the park. Why can't respectable boys like this look more like boys like that?

'And you're at Wellington, yeah?' asked Michael, without betraying any genuine curiosity. Zora met his eyes, made small and dull behind corrective glass, as her own were.

'Yeah . . . went to my dad's place . . . not very adventurous, I guess. And it looks like I'm going to be an Art History major, actually.'

'Which is, of course,' announced Monty, 'the field in which I started. I curated the first American exhibition of the Caribbean "primitives" in New York in 1965. I have the largest collection of Haitian art in private hands outside of that unfortunate island.'

'Wow. All to yourself — that must be great.'

But Monty Kipps was clearly a man aware of his own comic potential; he was on guard against any irony, attentive to its approach. He had made his statement in good faith and would not allow it to be satirized retrospectively. He gave a long pause before he replied. 'It's satisfying to be able to protect important black art, yes.'

His daughter rolled her eyes.

'Great if you like Baron Samedi staring at you from every corner of the house.'

It was the first time Victoria had spoken. Zora was surprised by her voice, which, like her father's, was loud and low and forthright, out of sync with her coquettish appearance.

'Victoria is currently reading the French philosophers . . .' said her father drily, and began to list contemptuously several of Zora's own lodestars.

'Right, right, I see . . .' murmured Zora through this. She had drunk one glass of wine too many. One extra glass made her like this, nodding in agreement before a person's point was finished, and always aiming for exactly this tone, that of the world-weary almost European bourgeois, for whom, at nineteen, all things were familiar.

'. . . And I'm afraid it's making her hate art in a dull way. But hopefully Cambridge will straighten her out.'

'*Dad.*'

'And in the meantime she will audit some classes here — I'm sure you'll run across each other, from time to time.'

The girls looked at one another without much enthusiasm at the prospect.

'I don't hate "art", anyway — I hate *your* art,' countered Victoria. Her father patted her shoulder soothingly, a move she shrugged off as a much younger child might.

'I guess we don't really hang much stuff around the house,' said Zora, looking around at the empty walls, wondering how she got on to the one topic she had wanted to avoid. 'Dad's more into conceptual art, of course. We have totally extreme taste in art — like most of the pieces we own, we can't really show in the house. He's into the whole evisceration theory, you know — like art should rip your fucking guts out.'

There was not time for the fallout from this. Zora felt a pair of hands on her shoulders. She couldn't remember ever being more pleased to see her own mother.

'Mom!'

'You been taking care of our guests?' Kiki stretched out her invitingly podgy hand, glittering with bangles at the wrist.

'It's Monty, isn't it? In fact, I think your wife was telling me it's now *Sir* Monty . . .'

The smoothness with which she proceeded from here impressed her daughter. It turned out that some of those much maligned (by Zora) traditional Wellington interpersonal skills — avoidance, denial, politic speech and false courtesy — had their uses. Within five minutes everybody had a drink, everyone's coat had been hung, and small talk was proceeding apace.

'Mrs Kipps . . . Carlene, she's not with you?' said Kiki.

'Mom, I'm just going to . . . excuse me, nice to meet you,' said Zora, vaguely pointing across the room and then following her own finger.

'She didn't make it?' repeated Kiki. Why did she feel so disappointed?

'Oh, my wife very rarely attends these things,' said Monty. 'She doesn't enjoy social conflagration. It's fair to say she is more warmed by the home hearth.'

Kiki was familiar with this way of torturing metaphor that the self-consciously conservative occasionally have — but the accent was incredible to her. It flew around the scale — somewhat like Erskine's but the vowels were given a body and depth she had never heard before. *Fair* came as Fee-yer.

'Oh . . . that's a pity . . . she seemed so sure she was going to come.'

'And then later, she was just as sure she would not.' He smiled, and in the smile was a powerful man's assurance that Kiki would not be silly enough to push the topic any further. 'Carlene is a woman of changeable moods.'

Poor Carlene! Kiki dreaded the idea of spending even one night with this man with whom Carlene must spend a lifetime. Fortunately there were many people Monty Kipps wanted to be introduced to. He quickly demanded a list of significant Wellingtonians, and Kiki obligingly pointed out Jack French, Erskine, the various faculty heads; she explained that the college president was invited while failing to explain that there wasn't a chance in hell that he would come. The Kipps children had already disappeared into the garden. Jerome — much to Kiki's annoyance — remained skulking upstairs. Kiki accompanied Monty through the rooms. His meeting with Howard was brief and arch, a stylized circling of each other's more extreme positions — Howard the radical art theorist, Monty the cultural conservative — with Howard coming off the worse because he was drunk and took it too seriously. Kiki separated them, manoeuvring Howard towards the curator of a small Boston gallery who had been trying to catch him all night. Howard only half attended to this small worried man as he pressed him on a proposed Rembrandt lecture season that Howard had promised to organize and done nothing about. Its highlight was to be a lecture from Howard himself, with a wine and cheese event afterwards, part sponsored by Wellington. Howard had neither written this lecture nor looked deeply into the matter of the wine and the cheese. Over the man's shoulder, he watched Monty dominate what was left of his party. A loud, playful debate with Christian and Meredith was being conducted near the fireplace, with Jack French at its borders, never quite quick enough to insert the witticisms he kept on attempting. Howard worried whether he was being defended by his supposed defenders. Maybe he was being ridiculed.

'I suppose I'm asking what the *tenor* of your talk will be . . .'

Howard tuned back into his own conversation, which he was apparently having not with one man but two. The curator, with

211

his moist nose, had been joined by a young bald man. This second fellow had such lucent white skin and so prominent a plate of bone in his forehead that Howard felt oppressed by the sheer mortality of the man. Never had another living being shown him this much skull.

'The tenor?'

' "*Ag'inst* Rembrandt",' the second man said. He had a high-pitched Southern voice that struck Howard as a comic assault for which he had been completely unprepared. 'That was the title your assistant mailed us — I'm just tryna figger what you meant by "ag'inst" — obviously my organization are part-sponsors of this whole event, so —'

'Your organization —'

'The RAS — Rembrandt Appreciation — and I'm sure I'm not an innellekchewl, at least, as a fella like you might think of one . . .'

'Yes, I'm sure you're not,' murmured Howard. He found that his accent caused a delayed reaction in certain Americans. It was sometimes the next day before they realized how rude he had been to them.

'I mean, maybe the "fallacy of the human" is a phrase for innnelekchew-alls, but I can tell you our members . . .'

Across the room, Howard saw that Monty's circle had widened to allow in a clutch of avid Black Studies scholars, led by Erskine and his brittle Atlanta wife, Caroline. She was an extremely wiry black woman, really one muscle from head to toe, and always immaculate — that East Coast moneyed finesse translated into blackness, her hair straight and stiff, her Chanel suit slightly brighter and more shapely than those of her white counterparts. She was one of the few women in his circle whom Howard had not imagined in a sexual context — this fact was unrelated to her attractiveness (Howard often considered the most awful-looking women in this dimension). It was rather a question of impenetrability: there was no way for the imagination to get through the powerful casing of Caroline herself. You had to imagine yourself into a different universe to imagine fucking her; and that would not be how it went anyway — *she* would fuck *you.* She was infamously proud (most women disliked her) and, like any wife of a superficially attentive man, she was admirably self-contained, apparently without external social needs. But Erskine was also helplessly unfaithful, which gave the pride a characterful, impressive edge of which

213

Howard had always been slightly in awe. She expressed herself eccentrically — she referred to Erskine's girls imperiously as *those mulattos* — and gave no clue as to her real feelings. A celebrated lawyer, she was, it was said, extremely close to becoming a Supreme Court judge; she knew Powell personally, and Rice; she liked to explain patiently to Howard that such people 'lifted the race'. Monty was exactly to her taste. Her delicate manicured hand was presently making precise cutting movements in the air in front of him, maybe describing where the buck stopped, or how far there was left to go.

And *still* Howard's conversation continued. He began to see no way out of it.

'Well,' he said loudly, hoping to finish it off with a daunting display of academic pyrotechnics, 'what I *meant* was that Rembrandt is part of the seventeenth-century European movement to . . . well, let's shorthand it — essentially *invent the idea of the human,*' Howard heard himself saying, all of it paraphrased from the chapter he had left upstairs, asleep on the computer screen, boring even to itself. 'And of course the corollary to that is the fallacy that *we* as human beings are central, and that our aesthetic sense in some way *makes* us central — think of the position he paints himself in, right between those two inscribed empty globes on the wall . . .'

Howard kept talking along these almost automatic lines. He felt a breeze from the garden get into his system, deep, through channels a younger body would never permit. He felt very sad, retracing these arguments that had made him slightly notable in the tiny circle in which he moved. The retraction of love in one part of his life had made this other half of his life feel cold indeed.

'Introduce me,' instructed a woman suddenly, gripping the slack muscle in his upper arm. It was Claire Malcolm.

'Oh, God, excuse me — can I steal him, just a moment?' she said to the curator and his friend, ignoring their concerned faces. She pulled Howard some steps away towards the corner of the room. Diagonally across from them Monty Kipps's enormous laugh announced itself first and mightiest over a refrain of hoots.

'Introduce me to Kipps.'

They stood next to each other, Claire and Howard, looking out across the room like parents on the edge of a school football field, watching their boy. It was an oblique angle but also a close one. The

215

peachy flush of alcohol had pushed through Claire's deep tan, and the various moles and freckles of her face and décolletage were ringed by this aroused pinkness; it brought youth back to her like no product or procedure could ever hope to. Howard hadn't seen her in almost a year. They had managed this subtly, without drawing attention to the fact or conferring to achieve it. They had simply avoided each other on campus, giving up the cafeteria entirely and making certain they did not attend the same meetings. As an extra measure, Howard had stopped going to the Moroccan café in which, of an afternoon, one could see almost everybody in the English Department sitting alone, marking piles of essays. Then Claire had gone to Italy for the summer, which he had been thankful for. It was miserable seeing her now. She was in a simple shift dress of very thin cotton. Her tiny yogic body came up against it and then retreated once more — it depended on how she stood. You would have no idea, looking at her like this — make-up free, so simply dressed — no idea at all of the strange, minute cosmetic attentions she gave to other, more private parts of her body. Howard himself had been amazed to discover them. In what position had they been lying when she had offered the peculiar explanation of her mother being Parisian?

'For Godssake, why would you want to meet *him?*'

'Warren's interested in him. And actually so am I. I think public intellectuals are incredibly weird and interesting . . . It's got to be a kind of pathological tension, and then he has the race thing to contend with . . . But I just *adore* his *dapperness.* He's terribly *dapper.*'

'Terribly dapper fascist.'

Claire frowned. 'He's so *compelling,* though. Like what they say about Clinton — charisma overdose. It's probably entirely pheromonal, you know, like *nasal,* in some way Warren could explain —'

'Nasal, anal — it's definitely coming out one orifice or another.' Howard now brought his glass to his mouth so that the next thing he said might be slightly muffled. 'Congratulations, by the way. I hear they're in order.'

'We're very happy,' she said placidly. 'God, I am *so* fascinated by him —' Howard thought for a moment that she meant Warren. 'See how he works the room? He's everywhere, somehow.'

'Yeah, like the plague.'

Claire turned to Howard with an impish face. He saw that she had thought it would be all right now to look at him, now the ironic pace of their conversation had been set. The affair, after all, was so long in the past, had remained undiscovered for so long. In the interim Claire had got married! And that imaginary night at a Michigan conference was now the accepted reality; the three-week affair between Howard and Claire Malcolm in Wellington had never happened. Why shouldn't they talk to each other again, look at each other? But in fact to look was lethal, and the moment she turned they both knew it. Claire did her best to continue, everything grotesquely exaggerated now by fear.

'*I* think,' she began in a ludicrous teasing voice, 'I think you'd quite like to be like him.'

'How much have you drunk?'

He had a cruel wish at that moment that Claire Malcolm might be gone from the planet. Without his doing anything at all — just gone.

'All your silly ideological battles . . .' she said, and then grinned at him foolishly, her lips pulling away from her rosy gums to reveal her expensive American teeth. 'You both know they don't really matter. The country's got bigger fish to fry now. Bigger ideas,' she whispered, 'are *afoot*. Aren't they? Sometimes I don't even know why I stay here.'

'What are we talking about exactly — state of the nation or the state of you?'

'Don't be a wise-ass,' she said sourly. 'I mean all of us, not just me. There's just no point.'

'You sound like you're fifteen. You sound like my kids.'

'Bigger ideas than *these*. It's got down to fundamentals, out there, in the world. *Fundamentals*. We've let down your kids, we've let down *everybody's* kids. Looking at this country the way it is now, I'm *thankful* I never had any kids myself.' Howard, who doubted the veracity of this, hid his disbelief by making a study of the yellowing oak floorboards beneath them. 'God, when I think of this next semester I just feel *sick*. Nobody gives a fuck about *Rembrandt*, Howard —' She stopped herself and began to laugh sadly. 'Or Wallace Stevens. Bigger ideas,' she repeated, finished her wine and nodded.

'It's all interconnected,' said Howard dully, tracing the toe of his shoe around a wood-wormed gap in the flooring. 'We produce new ways of thinking, then other people think it.'

'You don't believe that.'

'Define *believe,*' said Howard and, as he said it, felt shattered. There was almost not enough breath even to complete the sentence. Why wouldn't she go away?

'Oh, dear *God* —' huffed Claire, stamping her little foot and laying a hand flat against his chest, priming up for one of their age-old battles. Essence versus theory. Belief versus power. Art versus cultural systems. Claire versus Howard. Howard felt one of her fingers thoughtlessly, drunkenly, slip under a gap in his shirt to his skin. Just then, they were interrupted.

'What are you two gossiping about?'

Too quickly, Claire removed her hand from Howard's body. But Kiki wasn't looking at Claire; she was looking at Howard. You're married to someone for thirty years: you know their face like you know your own name. It was so quick and yet so absolute — the deception was over. Howard realized it at once, but how could Claire pick up on that tiny piece of tight skin on the left side of his wife's mouth, or know what it meant? In her innocence, thinking she was rescuing the situation, Claire enclosed both of Kiki's hands in her own.

'I want to meet *Sir* Montague Kipps.

Howard's being tricky about it.'

'Howard's always tricky,' said Kiki, flashing him a second steely, confirmatory glance that put the matter beyond doubt. 'He thinks it makes him look clever.'

'God, you look great, Keeks. You should be in a fountain in Rome.'

Howard expected that this flattery of his wife's appearance by Claire was compulsive. All he wanted to do was to stop her saying another word. Wild, violent fantasies took hold of him.

'Oh, you too, honey,' said Kiki calmly, dampening down this false enthusiasm. So there wasn't going to be a scene. Howard had always loved this about his wife, her ability to play things cool — but at this moment he would have been happier to hear her scream. She stood like a zombie, her eyes quite dead to any appeal from him, her smile nailed on. And still they were stuck in this ludicrous conversation.

'Look, I need an opening salvo,' continued Claire. 'I don't want him to have the satisfaction of knowing I actually want to talk to him. What can I get him on?'

'He's got a finger in every pie,' said Howard, converting his personal desperation into anger. 'Take your pick. State of Britain, state of the Caribbean, states of blackness, state of art, state of women, state of the States — you hum it, he'll play it. Oh, and he thinks affirmative action is the work of the devil — he's a charmer, he's a . . .'

Howard stopped. All the drink in his body had turned against him; his sentences were beginning to rush away from him like rabbits down their holes; soon neither the white tip of a thought nor the black hole into which it was vanishing would be visible to him.

'Howie — you're making yourself ridiculous,' said Kiki precisely and bit her lip. Howard could see the battle going on inside her. He saw how determined she was. She would not scream, she would not cry.

'He's anti-affirmative action? That's unusual, isn't it?' asked Claire, watching Monty's nodding head.

'Not really,' replied Kiki. 'He's just a black conservative — thinks it's demeaning for African-American kids to be told they need special treatment to succeed, etcetera. It's terrible timing for Wellington, having him here — there's an Anti-Affirmative Action bill working its way through the Senate and it's gonna cause trouble. We need to stand firm on the issue right now. Well, as you know. You and Howard did all that

222

work together.' Kiki's eyes widened at the end of this, taking in her own realization.

'Ah . . .' said Claire, twirling the stem of her empty wine glass. Small-scale politics bored her. She had served six months, a year and a half ago, as Howard's titular deputy in Wellington's Affirmative Action Committee — this was indeed how the whole thing between them had begun — but her interest had been minimal and her attendance patchy. She'd taken the job because Howard (desperate to avoid the appointment of another despised colleague) had begged her. Claire was only truly excited by the apocalyptic on the world stage: WMD, autocratic presidents, mass death. She detested committees and meetings. She liked to go on marches and to sign petitions.

'You should talk to him about art — I mean, he's a collector, apparently. Caribbean art,' continued Kiki bravely.

'I'm *fascinated* by the children too. They're glorious.'

Howard snorted repulsively. He was desperately drunk now.

'Jerome fell in love with the daughter briefly,' explained Kiki tersely. 'Last year. Her family freaked out a little — Howard made it all a hell of a lot worse than it needed to be. The whole thing was so stupid.'

'What drama you all live in,' said Claire happily. 'I don't blame him — I mean, I don't blame Jerome — I saw her, she's so amazing, looks like Nefertiti. Didn't you think so, Howard? Like one of those statuaries in the bottom of the Fitzwilliam, in Cambridge. You've seen those, right? Such an *anciently wonderful* face. Didn't you think?'

Howard closed his eyes and drank deep from his glass.

'Howard, the music —' said Kiki, turning to Howard at last. It was amazing to see her words and her eyes entirely unconnected to each other, like a bad actress. 'I can't take any more of this hip-hop. I don't know how it even got on there. People can't stand it — Albert Konig just left because of it, I think. Put on some Al Green or something — something everybody can enjoy.'

Claire had already taken a few steps towards Monty. Kiki joined her, but then paused and came back towards Howard and spoke in his ear. Her voice was shaky, but her grip on his wrist was not. She said one name and put a disbelieving question mark at the end of it. Howard felt his stomach fall away.

'You can stay in the house,' continued

Kiki, her voice cracking, 'but that's it. Don't you come near me. Don't you come *near* me. I'll kill you if you do.'

Then she calmly drew away and got in step with Claire Malcolm once more. Howard watched his wife walk away with his great mistake.

Initially, he was quite certain he was about to be sick. He walked purposefully into the hallway towards the bathroom. Then he remembered Kiki's errand and perversely determined to complete it. He paused in the doorway of the empty second living room. There was only one person in there, kneeling by the stereo, surrounded by CDs. That narrow, expressive back he had seen once before was exposed to the night: a clever top, tied up at the neck. One expected her to unfurl and dance the dying swan.

'Oh, all right,' she said, turning her head. Howard had the queer sense that this was a reply to his silent thought. 'Having a good one?'

'Not really.'

'Bummer.'

'It's Victoria, isn't it.'

'*Vee.*'

'Yes.'

She was right back on her heels, with only her top half turned to him. They smiled at each other. Howard's heart spontaneously went out in sympathy to his eldest son. Mysteries of the past year resolved themselves.

'So you're the DJ,' said Howard. Was there a new word for that now?

'Looks like it — you don't mind?'

'No, no . . . although a few of our senior guests were finding the selection . . . maybe a little bit hectic.'

'Right. You've been sent to sort me out.'

It was strange to hear this English phrase said in such an English way.

'To confer, I think. Whose music is this, anyway?'

' "Levi's Mix",' she read from a sticker on the CD case. She shook her head at him sadly. 'Looks like the enemy's within,' she said.

Of course she was bright. Jerome wouldn't be able to stand a stupid girl, not even one this gorgeous. This was a problem Howard had never had in his own youth. It was only later that brains began to mean something to him.

'What was wrong with what was on before?'

She stared at him. 'Were you listening?'

'Kraftwerk . . . nothing wrong with Kraftwerk.'

'Two *hours* of Kraftwerk?'

'There's other stuff, surely.'

'Have you *seen* this collection?'

'Well, yes — it's mine.'

She laughed and shook her hair out. It was new hair, pulled back into a pony-tail and then falling down her back in a cascade of synthetic curls. She shifted her position to face him and then sat down on her heels again. The shiny purple material pulled tight across her chest. She seemed to have large nipples, like the old tenpence coins. Howard looked to the floor, feigning shame.

'Like, how did you come by this one, exactly?' She held up a CD of lyric-less electronica.

'I bought it.'

'You bought it under duress. Gunman leading you to the counter.' She mimed this. She had a dirty, cackling laugh, pitched low like her voice. Howard shrugged. He was annoyed by the lack of deference.

'So we're sticking with hectic?'

' 'Fraid so, Professor.'

She winked. The eyelid came down in slow motion. The lashes were extravagant. Howard wondered whether she was drunk.

'I'll report back,' he said, and turned to

go. He almost tripped over a lifted ridge in the rug, but his second step righted him.

'Whoa, there.'

'Whoa . . . there,' repeated Howard.

'Tell them to calm themselves. It's only hip-hop. It won't kill them.'

'Right,' said Howard.

'Yet,' he heard her say as he left the room.

the anatomy lesson

To misstate, or even merely understate, the relation of the universities to beauty is one kind of error that can be made. A university is among the precious things that can be destroyed.

Elaine Scarry

I

Summer left Wellington abruptly and slammed the door on the way out. The shudder sent the leaves to the ground all at once, and Zora Belsey had that strange, late-September feeling that somewhere in a small classroom with small chairs an elementary school teacher was waiting for her. It seemed wrong that she should be walking towards town without a shiny tie and a pleated skirt, without a selection of scented erasers. Time is not what it is but how it is felt, and Zora felt no different. Still living at home, still a virgin. And yet heading for her first day as a sophomore. Last year, when Zora was a freshman, sophomores had seemed altogether a different kind of human: so very definite in their tastes and opinions, in their loves and ideas. Zora woke up this morning hopeful that a transformation of this kind might have visited her in the night, but, finding it hadn't, she did what girls generally do when they don't feel the part: she dressed it instead. How successful this had been she couldn't say.

Now she stopped to examine herself in the window of *Lorelie's*, a campy fifties hairdressers on the corner of Houghton and Maine. She tried to put herself in her peers' shoes. She asked herself the extremely difficult question: *What would I think of me?* She had been gunning for something like 'bohemian intellectual; fearless; graceful; brave and bold'. She was wearing a long boho skirt in a deep green, a white cotton blouse with an eccentric ruff at the neck, a thick brown suede belt of Kiki's from the days when her mother could still wear belts, a pair of clumpy shoes and a kind of hat. What kind of hat? A *man's hat,* of green felt, that looked like a fedora, a little, but was not one. This was not what she had meant when she left the house. This was not it at all.

Fifteen minutes later Zora peeled it all off again in the women's locker room of Wellington's college pool. This was part of the new Zora Self-Improvement Programme for the fall: wake early, swim, class, light lunch, class, library, home. She crushed her hat into the locker and pulled her bathing-cap down low over her ears. A naked Chinese woman who looked eighteen from the back now turned and surprised Zora with her crumpled face, in which two little obsidian eyes struggled under the pressure of folded skin from above and below. Her pubic hair was very long and straight and grey, like dead grass. *Imagine being her,* thought Zora vaguely, and the thought puttered along for a few seconds, collapsed, vanished. She pinned her locker key to the black fabric of her own functional costume. She walked the long edge of the pool, her flat feet meeting the ceramics with a wet slap. Up beyond the stadium seating, at the very top of this giant room, a glass wall let the autumn sun in and shot it across the room, like the searchlights in a prison yard. From this superior vantage point, a long line of athletes on treadmills was looking down on Zora and all the other people not fit enough for the gym. Up there behind glass the ideal people were exercising; down here the misshapen people were floating around, hoping. Twice a week this dynamic changed when the swim team graced the pool with their magnificence, relegating Zora and everyone else to the practice pool to share lanes with infants and senior citizens. Swim-team people launched themselves from the edge, remade their bodies in the image of darts, and then entered the pool like something the water had been waiting for and gratefully accepted. People like Zora sat carefully down on the gritty tiles, gave the water only their feet and then had a debate with their bodies about committing to the next stage. It was not at all unusual for Zora to get undressed, walk the pool, look at the athletes, sit down, put her toes in, get back up, walk the pool, look at the athletes, get dressed and leave the building. But not today. Today was a new beginning. Zora pushed forward an inch and then launched herself, the water rushed up to her neck like a garment she was wearing. She tread water for a minute and then let herself go under. Blowing water out of her nose, she began to swim slowly, indecorously — never quite able to coordinate her arms and legs but still feeling a partial grace that dry land never offered her. Despite all affectations to the contrary, she was actually racing various women in this pool (she always made sure to pick women near enough her own age and size; she had a strong sense of fairness), and her will to carry on swimming rose and fell depending on how well she was keeping up with her unwitting competitors. Her goggles began to seep water in from their sides. She yanked them off, left them at one end and tried four lengths without, but it is much harder swimming above the surface than beneath it. You have to carry yourself more. Zora made her way back to the side. She felt around blindly for her goggles and, when this yielded nothing, thrust herself up out of the water to look — they were gone. She lost her temper at once; an unlucky freshman lifeguard was made to kneel down by the lip of the pool and be rudely spoken to as if he himself were the thief. After a while Zora gave up her interrogation and paddled away across the pool, scanning the surface of the water. To her right a boy sped by, kicking water into her eyes. She struggled for the side, swallowing water as she went. She looked at the back of the boy's head — the red band of her own goggles. She clung on to the nearest ladder and waited for him. At the other end he performed a fluid somersault in the water as Zora had often dreamed of doing. He was a black boy in a pair of striking bumblebee shorts, yellow-and-black striped and moulded around him with the same elasticity and definition as his own skin. The curved line of his backside turned like a brand new beach-ball cresting the water. When he straightened out again, he swam the length of the pool without once lifting his head to breathe. He was faster than everybody. He was some kind of a swim-team asshole. Between the dip of his lower back — like a scoop taken out of an ice-cream tub — and the curve of his high, spherical ass, a tattoo was inked. Probably a fraternity thing. But the sun and water rippled and distorted its outline, and, before Zora could figure it out, he was right beside her, his arm resting on the dividing rope, gulping for air.

'Umm, excuse me?'

'Huh?'

'I said *excuse me* — I think you'll find those are my goggles.'

'I can't hear you, man — hold up a minute.'

He heaved himself up out of the water and rested his elbows on the side. This brought his groin to meet Zora at eye level. For a full ten seconds, as if there were no material there at all, she was presented with the broad line of *it* running along his thigh to the left, making three-dimensional waves of his bumble-bee stripes. Beneath this arresting sight, his balls pulled at the fabric of his shorts, low and heavy and not quite lifted out of the warm water. His tattoo was of the sun — the sun with a face. She felt she had seen it before. Its rays were thick and fanned out like the mane of a lion. The boy took out two ear-plugs, removed the goggles, left them on the side and returned to Zora's bobbing height.

'Got plugs in, man — couldn't hear a thing.'

'I *said* I think you've got my goggles. I put them down for like a second and they went — maybe you picked them up by mistake . . . my goggles?'

The boy was frowning at her. He shook the water from his face. 'I know you?'

'What? No — look, can I see those goggles please?'

The boy, still frowning, threw his long arm up and over the side and came back with the goggles.

'OK, so those are mine. The red strap is mine — the other one broke and I put that red one on myself, so —'

The boy grinned. 'Well . . . If they yours, I guess you better take 'em.'

He held out his long palm towards her — coloured a rich brown like Kiki's, with all the lines drawn in a still darker shade. The goggles hung from his index finger. Zora moved to snatch them but instead nudged them from his finger. She thrust her hands into the water; they twirled on down to the bottom, the red band spiralling, inanimate, yet dancing. Zora took a shallow asthmatic breath and tried to dive. Halfway down the buoyancy of her own flesh reeled her back up, ass first.

'You want me to — ?' offered the boy and didn't wait for the answer. He curved in on himself and shot down with barely a splash. He resurfaced a moment later with the goggles hanging from his wrist. He dropped them into her hands, another fumbling move, for it took all the energy Zora had to tread water while simultaneously opening her palms to receive them. Without a word she kicked away to the side, trying her best to climb the ladder with dignity, and left the pool. Except she didn't quite leave. For the time it takes to swim one length she stood by the side of the lifeguard's chair and watched the smiling sun make its way through the water, watched the initial seal-pup flip-flop of the boy's torso, the ploughing and lifting of two dark arms in turbine motion, the grinding muscles of the shoulders, the streamlined legs doing what all human legs could do if only they tried a little harder. For a whole twenty-three seconds the last thing on Zora's mind was herself.

★ ★ ★

'I *knew* I knew you — Mozart.'

He was dressed now, the necklines of several T-shirts visible underneath his Red Sox hoodie. His black jeans swamped the white scallop-shell toes of his sneakers. If Zora hadn't just seen him almost as God intended, she would have had no idea of the contours beneath all of this. The only clue was that elegant neck of his, angling the head away from the body like a young animal looking about the world for the first time. He was sitting on the outdoor steps of the gym, legs wide open, earphones on, nodding to the music — Zora almost stood on him.

'Sorry — if I can just . . .' she murmured, stepping round.

He slipped his earphones down to his neck, bounced up and kept pace with her down the stairs.

'Hey, hat girl — yo, I'm talking to you — hey, slow down for a second there.'

Zora stopped at the bottom of the stairs, pushed the brim of her stupid hat up, looked into his face and recognized him at last.

'Mozart,' he repeated, cocking a finger at her. 'Right? You took my player — my man Levi's sister.'

'Zora, right.'

'Carl. Carl Thomas. I *knew* it was you. Levi's sister.'

He stood there nodding and smiling as if together they had just cracked the cure for cancer.

'So . . . umm, do you see Levi . . . or . . . ?' tried Zora, awkwardly. His well-madeness as a human being made her feel her own bad design. She folded her arms across her chest and then refolded them the other way. Suddenly she couldn't stand in a position that was even half normal. Carl looked over her shoulder towards the frizzled corridor of yew trees that led to the river.

'You know, I ain't even seen him since that concert — I guess we was meant to hang at one point but . . .' His attention flipped back to her. 'Which way you walking, you walking down there?'

'Actually, I'm going the other way, just into the square.'

'Cool, I can go that way.'

'Er . . . OK.'

They took a few steps, but here the sidewalk ended. They waited at the traffic lights in silence. Carl had replaced one earphone and was nodding to the beat. Zora looked at her watch, and then around herself in a self-conscious way, assuring the passers-by that she also had no idea what

240

this guy could possibly want with her.

'You're on the swim team?' said Zora when the lights refused to change.

'Huh?'

Zora shook her head and pressed her lips together.

'No, say again.' He took off his earphones once more. 'What was that?'

'Nothing — I just — just wondering if you were on the swim team —'

'Do I *look* like I'm on the swim team?'

Zora's memory of Carl refocused, sharpened. 'Umm . . . it's not an insult — I'm just saying you're fast.'

Carl brought his shoulders down from where they were hitched, up around his ears, but his face held the tension. 'I'll be in the A-Team before I'm on the swim team, believe that. Gotta be in college before you on the swim team, as I understand it.'

Two cabs came parallel with each other now, heading in opposite directions. The drivers slowed down to a halt and yelled happily at each other from their open windows while beeping horns started up around them.

'Those Haitians got a lot of mouth, man. Sound like they screaming all the time. Even when they happy they sound pissed as hell,' reflected Carl. Zora jabbed at the traffic button.

'You go to a lot of classical —' asked Carl at the same time that Zora said, 'So you just go to the pool to steal other people's —'

'Oh, shit —' He laughed loudly, falsely, Zora thought. She pushed her wallet deep into her tote bag and discreetly zipped it up.

'I'm sorry about your goggles, man. You still mad about that? I didn't think nobody was using them. My man Anthony works in the locker room — he gets me in without a pass — so, you know.'

Zora did not know. The sing-song bird call of the traffic lights started up so that the blind might know when to walk.

'I was just saying — you go to a lot of those things?' asked Carl as they crossed the street together. 'Like the Mozart?'

'Umm . . . I guess not . . . probably not as much as I should. Studying takes up a lot of my time, I guess.'

'You freshman?'

'Sophomore. First day.'

'Wellington?'

Zora nodded. They were approaching the main campus building. He seemed to want to slow her down, to put off the moment when she passed through the gate and out of his world.

'*Scene.* Educated sister. That's cool,

man — that's really — that's an amazing thing right there, that's . . . good for you, you're going the right way about your shit and all that — that's the prize, education. We all gotta keep our eyes on the *prize* if we're gonna rise, right? Wellington. Hmph. That's nice.'

Zora smiled feebly.

'No, man, you worked for it, you deserved it,' said Carl, and looked around himself distractedly. He reminded her of the young boys she used to mentor in Boston — taking them to the park, to the movies — back when she had time to do that kind of stuff. His attention span was like theirs. And always the toe-tapping and head-nodding as if stillness was the danger.

' 'Cos the thing about Mozart, right,' he said suddenly. 'This is the thing right here — I mean about the Requiem — I don't know too much about his other shit, but that Requiem, that we were listening to — OK, so you know the *Lacrimosa* part?'

His fingers worked the air like a maestro, hoping to conduct the reaction he wanted out of his new companion.

'The *Lacrimosa* — you *know* it, man.'

'Er . . . no,' said Zora, noting with alarm her fellow students pouring in to register.

She was late already.

'It's like the eighth bit,' said Carl impatiently. 'I sampled it for this tune I made, after I heard it at that show, right — and it's *crazy* — with all the angels singing higher and higher and those violins, man — *swish* dah DAH, *swish* da DAH, *swish* da DAH — it's *amazing* listening to that — and it sounds *mad cool* when you put words over the top and a beat below — you know the part, it's like —' said Carl and began to hum the tune again.

'I *really* don't know it. I'm not really a classical music type of —'

'*No,* man, you remember — 'cos I remember I overheard your people, your moms and everybody — they were discussing whether he was a genius, remember, and —'

'That was like a month ago,' said Zora, confused.

'Oh, I'm very memorizing — like I remember *everything.* You tell me something: I remember it, I never forget a face — you *see* how I don't forget a face. And it was just — you know — inneresting to me, about Mozart, 'cos I'm a musician also —'

Zora allowed herself a tiny smile at the unlikely comparison.

'And then I found out about it a little more — 'cos, I've been reading about clas-

sical music, 'cos you can't do what *I* do
without knowing about other shit outside of
your direct, like, your influences and shit —'

Zora nodded politely.

'*Right,* you under*stand* me,' said Carl
vigorously, as if with this nod Zora had
signed her name to a declaration of undis-
closed principles of Carl's choosing. 'And
so anyway, man, it turns out that that section — it wasn't even by him — I mean, it
was partly him, right? Obviously he passed
away halfway through, and then other
people had to be brought in to finish it off.
And it turns out that the main business of
the *Lacrimosa* was by this guy Süssmayr —
which is the *shit,* man, 'cos it's like the
best thing in the Requiem, and it made me
think *damn,* you can be so close to genius
that it like lifts you up — it's like
Süssmayr, this guy, stepped up to the bat,
right, like a rookie, and then he went and
hit it out of the park — and all these
people be trying to prove that it's Mozart
'cos that fits in with their idea of who can
and who can't make music like this, but
the *deal* is that this amazing sound was
just by this guy Süssmayr, this average Joe
Shmo guy. I was tripping when I read that
shit.'

And all the time, while he spoke, and she

tried, bewilderedly, to listen, his face was doing its silent voodoo on her, just as it seemed to work on everybody passing by him in this archway. Zora could clearly see people stealing a look, and lingering, not wanting to release the imprint of Carl from their retinas, especially if it was only to be replaced by something as mundane as a tree or the library or two kids playing cards in the yard. What a thing he was to look at!

'Anyway,' he said, enthusiasm shading off into disappointment at her silence, 'I been wanting to tell you that and now I told ya, so . . .'

Zora snapped out of it. 'You wanted to tell *me* that?'

'No, no, no — it ain't like that.' He laughed raucously. '*Damn,* girl, I'm not a stalker — sister, seriously —' He patted her softly on her left arm. Nothing less than electricity shot right through her body, into her groin and ended up somewhere round her ears. 'I'm just saying that it stuck in my mind, right — 'cos I go to stuff in the city and usually I'm the only *Negro,* right — don't see many black folk at things like that and I thought: Now, if I ever see that bad-tempered black girl again, I'm gonna lay some of my Mozart thoughts on her head, see how she takes them — that's all. That's college, right? That's what you paying all that money for — just so you get to talk to other people about that shit. That's all you're paying for.' He nodded his head authoritatively. 'That's it.'

'I guess.'

'It's nothing more than that,' Carl insisted.

The college bell started up, pompous and monotonous, then the jollier four-note tune of the Episcopalian church across the road. Zora took a risk: 'You know, you should meet my other brother, Jerome. He's a total music-head and poetry-head — he can be a little bit of an uptight asshole, but you should totally come by some time, I mean, if you want to talk and stuff — He's at Brown right now, but he comes back every few weeks . . . it's a pretty amazing household for talking even though they all kind of drive me a little crazy sometimes . . . my dad's like a professor so —' Carl's head jerked back in surprise. 'No, but he's cool . . . and he's pretty incredible to talk to . . . but seriously, you should really feel free, just to come by and talk and just . . .'

Carl looked frostily at Zora. When a boy brushed past him, Zora saw Carl square his own shoulder, bumping the freshman forward a little; the freshman, seeing as how the bumper was a tall black guy, said nothing and continued on his way.

'Well,' said Carl, staring after the boy he'd pushed, 'actually I *did* come by, but seemed like I wasn't welcome, so —'

'You came by . . . ?' began Zora uncomprehendingly.

In her face Carl recognized authentic innocence. He waved the discussion away. 'Bottom line? I'm not a big *talker.* I don't express shit well when I talk. I write better than I speak. When I be rhyming I'm like BAM. I hit it on the *nail,* through the wood and out the other side. *Believe.* Talkin'? I hit my own finger. Every time.'

Zora laughed. 'You should hear my dad's freshmen. *I was like,*' she said, pitching her voice high and across the country to the opposite coast, *'and then she was like, and then he was like, and I was like, oh, my God.* Repeat ad infinitum.'

Carl looked puzzled. 'Your pops, the professor . . .' he said slowly. 'He white, right?'

'Howard. He's English.'

'English!' said Carl, revealing the chalky sclera of his eyes, and then a moment later, seeming to have taken the concept fully on board, 'I ain't never been to England, man. I've never been out of the States. So . . .'

He was doing a strange rhythmic clicking into his palm. 'He be like a math professor or whatever.'

'My dad? No. Art History.'

'You get on with him, with your pops?'

Again Carl's eyes wandered around the place. Again Zora's paranoia got the better of her. She imagined for a moment that all these questions were a kind of verbal grooming that would later lead — by routes she didn't pause to imagine — to her family home and her mother's jewellery and the safe in the basement. She began to speak rather manically, as was her way when trying to disguise the fact that her mind was elsewhere.

'Howard — he's great. I mean he's my *dad,* so sometimes, you know . . . but he's cool — I mean, he just had this *affair* — yeah, I know, it all came out, it was with this other professor — so everything's pretty fucked up at home right now. My mom's freaking *out.* But I'm really like, hello, what kind of a sophisticated guy in his fifties *doesn't* have an affair? It's basically mandatory. Intellectual men are attracted to intellectual women — big fucking surprise. Plus my mom doesn't do herself any favours — she's like three hundred pounds or something . . .'

Carl looked down, apparently embarrassed for Zora. Zora blushed and pressed her stubby nails deep into the meat of her palms.

'Fat ladies need love too,' said Carl philosophically, and took a cigarette from inside his hoodie, where it had been tucked behind his ear. 'You best be going, huh,' he said and lit up. He seemed bored with her now. Zora was filled with the sad sense that something precious had escaped. Somehow with her blethering she had made Mozart vanish and his pal Sussawhatsit too.

'People to see, places to go, sho' nuff,' he said.

'Oh, no . . . I mean, I've just got a meeting. It's not really —'

'Important meeting,' said Carl ruminatively, taking a moment to envision it.

'Not really . . . more like a meeting about the future, I guess.'

Zora was on her way to Dean French's office to empty her hypothetical future into his lap. She was particularly concerned about her failure to get into Claire Malcolm's poetry class last semester. She hadn't yet seen the boards, but if it happened again then that could have a very adverse effect on her future, which needed to be discussed, along with many other troubling aspects of her future in all its futurity. This was the first of seven meetings that she had taken it upon herself to schedule for the initial week of the semester. Zora was extremely fond of scheduling meetings about her future with important people for whom her future was not really a top priority. The more people were informed of her plans the more real they became to her.

'The future's another country, man,' said Carl mournfully, and then the punchline seemed to come to him; his face surrendered to a smile. 'And I *still* ain't got a passport.'

'That's . . . is that from your lyrics?'

'Might be, might be.' He shrugged, rubbed his hands together, although it wasn't cold, not yet. With deep insincerity he said, 'It was nice talking to you, *Zora*. It was educational.'

He seemed angry again. Zora looked away and fiddled with the zip of her tote. She had an unfamiliar urge to help him. 'Hardly — I didn't say a word, practically.'

'Yeah, but you listen well. That's the same thing.'

Zora looked up at him again, startled. She couldn't remember ever being told that she listened well.

'You're very talented, aren't you?' murmured Zora without thinking about what in God's name she meant. She was lucky — the words slipped under a passing delivery truck.

'Well, *Zora* —' He clapped his hands; was she ridiculous to him? 'You keep studyin'.'

'Carl. It was nice to meet you again.'

'Tell that brother of yours to call me. I'm doing another show at the Bus Stop — you know, it's down Kennedy, on Tuesday.'

'Don't you live in Boston?'

'Yeah, and? It ain't far — we're allowed to come into Wellington, you know. Don't need a pass. *Man.* Wellington's OK — that part of it is, Kennedy Square. It ain't all students — there's brothers too. Anyway . . . Just tell your bro if he wants to hear some rhymes he should come. It might not be *poetry* poetry,' said Carl, walking away before Zora had a chance to answer, 'but it's what I do.'

2

Up on the seventh floor of the Stegner Memorial Building, in an insufficiently heated room, Howard had just finished unpacking a projector. He'd slipped his hands on each side of its bulk, kept the armature steady under his chin and eased the whole ugly contraption out of its box. He always requested this projector for his first presentation of the year, when his class was 'shopped'; it was as much of a ritual as unpacking the Christmas lights. As homely, as dispiriting. In what new way, this year, would it fail to light up? Howard carefully opened the lid of the light-box and placed the too familiar title page (he had been delivering this lecture series for six years), CONSTRUCTING THE HUMAN: 1600–1700, face down on the glass. He picked the page up again, wiped away the accumulated dust and placed it back down. The projector was grey and orange — the colours of the future thirty years ago — and, like all obsolete technology, elicited an involuntary sympathy from Howard. He was not modern any more either.

'*Pah*-point,' said Smith J. Miller, who was standing in the doorway, both hands wrapped around his coffee mug for warmth, eagerly keeping a lookout for the students. Howard knew that this morning would bring more students than the room could handle — unlike Smith, he understood that this didn't mean anything.

They'd have students sitting on the long corporate meeting table and the grim floor, students on the window ledge with their student heels tucked under their student backsides, students lined up against the wall like prisoners waiting to be shot. They'd all take notes like crazed stenographers, they'd be so involved in the movements of Howard's mouth he would have to convince himself that this was not a deaf school and these not lip-readers; they would all, every single one — in all sincerity — write down their names and e-mails, no matter how many times Dr Belsey repeated, 'Please only — *only* — put your names down if you're seriously intending to take this class.' And then next Tuesday there would be twenty kids. And the Tuesday after that, nine.

'It's a *heck* of a lot easier, *pah*-point. Ah could show you.'

Howard raised his eyes from his poor machine. He felt obscurely cheered by Smith's neat tartan bow-tie, his baby face spattered with light freckles, the thin ripple of ash-blond hair. You couldn't ask for a better helpmeet than Smith J. Miller. But he was an eternal optimist. He didn't get how this system worked. He didn't know, as Howard did, that by next Tuesday these kids would have already sifted through the academic wares on display in the form of courses across the Humanities Faculty, and performed a comparative assessment in their own minds, drawing on multiple variables including the relative academic fame of the professor; his previous publications up to that point; his intellectual kudos; the uses of his class; whether his class really meant anything to their permanent records or their personal futures or their grad school potential; the likelihood of the professor in question having any real-world power that might translate into an actual capacity to write that letter which would effectively place them — three years from now — on an internship at the *New Yorker* or in the Pentagon or in Clinton's Harlem offices or at French *Vogue* — and that all this private research, all this *Googling,* would lead them rightly to conclude that taking a class on 'Constructions of the Human', which did not come under their core requirements for the semester, which was taught by a human being himself over the hill, in a bad jacket, with eighties hair, who was under-published, politically marginal and badly situated at the top of a building without proper heating and no elevator, was not in their best interests. There's a reason it's called shopping.

'See, now, with *pah*-point,' persisted Smith, 'the whole class can see what's going on. It's pretty damn sharp, the image you git.'

Howard smiled gratefully but shook his head. He was beyond the point of learning new tricks. He got on his knees and plugged the projector's cord into the wall; a snag of blue light leaped from the socket. He pressed the button on the back of the projector. He twiddled the connected cable. He pressed hard on the light box, hoping to engage some loose connection.

'Ah'll do that,' said Smith. He drew the projector away from Howard, sliding it along the table. Howard stood where he was for a minute, in exactly the same pose as if the projector were still before him.

'Maybe you should close those blinds,' suggested Smith gently. Like most people in the Wellington loop, Smith was fully apprised of Howard's situation. And, personally, he was sorry for Howard's trouble, and had told him so two days earlier when they met to go over which worksheets needed photocopying. *I'm sorry for your trouble.* As if someone Howard loved had died.

'You want some coffee, Howard, some tea? Doughnut?'

With one hand absently holding on to the blinds' strings, Howard looked out of the window on to Wellington's yard. Here was the white church and the grey library, antagonizing each other on opposite sides of the square. A pot-pourri of orange, red, yellow and purple leaves carpeted the ground. It was still warm enough, but only just, for kids to sit on the steps of the Greenman, reclining on their own knapsacks, wasting time. Howard scanned the scene for Warren or Claire. The news was that they were still together. This from Erskine, who got it from his wife Caroline, who was on the board of trustees at the Wellington Institute of Molecular Research where Warren spent his days. It was Kiki who had told Warren; the explosion had happened — but no one had died. It was just walking wounded as far as the eye could see. No packed bags, no final door slams, no relocation to different colleges, different towns. They were all going to stay put and suffer. It would be played out very slowly over years. The thought was debilitating. *Everybody* knew about it. Howard expected that the shorthand, water-cooler version, currently circulating the college would be 'Warren's forgiven her' said with pity mixed with a little contempt — as if that covered it, the feeling. People said 'She's forgiven him' about Kiki, and only

257

now was Howard learning of the levels of purgatory forgiveness involves. People don't know what they're talking about. At the water cooler Howard was just another middle-aged professor suffering the expected mid-life crisis. And then there was the other reality, the one he had to live. Last night, very late, he had peeled himself off the crushing, too short divan in his study and gone into the bedroom. He lay down in his clothes, above the quilt, next to Kiki, a woman he had loved and lived with his entire adult life. On her bedside table he could not avoid seeing the packet of anti-depressants, sitting alongside a few coins, some earplugs, a teaspoon, all crushed in a small wooden Indian box with elephants carved upon its sides. He waited almost twenty minutes, never sure if she was awake or not. Then he put his hand, above the quilt, very softly, somewhere on her thigh. She began to cry.

'Ah got a good feelin' about this semester,' said Smith, and whistled and released his sprightly Southern chuckle. 'Expectin' standing room only.'

On to the blackboard Smith was poster-gumming a reproduction of Rembrandt's *Dr Nicolaes Tulp Demonstrating the Anatomy of the Arm*, 1632, that clarion call of an Enlightenment not yet arrived, with its rational apostles gathered around a dead man, their faces uncannily lit by the holy light of science. The left hand of the doctor, raised in explicit imitation (or so Howard would argue to his students) of the benefactions of Christ; the gentleman at the back staring out at us, requesting admiration for the fearless humanity of the project, the rigorous scientific pursuance of the dictum *Nosce te ipsium,* 'Know thyself' — Howard had a long shtick about this painting that never failed to captivate his army of shopping-day students, their new eyes boring holes into the old photocopy. Howard had seen it so many times he could no longer see it at all. He spoke with his back to it, pointing to what he needed to with the pencil in his left hand. But today Howard felt himself caught in the painting's orbit. He could see himself laid out on that very table, his skin white and finished with the world, his arm cut open for students to examine. He turned back to the window. Suddenly he spotted the small but unmistakable figure of his daughter, clomping a speedy diagonal towards the English Department.

'My daughter,' said Howard, without meaning to.

'Zora? She coming today?'

'Oh, yes — yes, I believe so.'

'She's such a satisfying student, rilly she is.'

'She works terribly hard,' agreed Howard. He saw Zora stop by the corner of the Greenman to speak with another girl. Even from here Howard could see she was standing much too close to this other person, closing in on her personal space in a way Americans do not enjoy. Why was she wearing his old hat?

'Oh, ah know it. Ah was supervising her Joyce class and her Eliot class last semester. Compared to the other freshmen, she was lahk a text-eating *machine* — ah mean, she strips the area of sentiment and goes to *work.* Ah'm dealing with these kids who are still saying *Ah really like the part when* and *Ah love the way* — you know, that's their high-school-analysis level. But *Zora . . .*' Smith whistled again. 'She's *awl* business. Whatever she gits in front of her she rips apart to see how it works. She's gonna go a long way.'

Howard thumped the window lightly and then a little harder. He was having an odd parental rush, a blood surge that was also *about* blood and was presently hunting through Howard's expansive intelligence to find words that would more effectively express something like *don't walk in front of cars take care and be good and don't hurt or be hurt and don't live in a way that makes you feel dead and don't betray anybody or yourself and take care of what matters and please don't and please remember and make sure*

'Hey, Howard? Those windows open only at the very top. Student precaution, ah guess. Suicide proof.'

'Basically, I'm concerned that I'm being unfairly prevented from taking this class due to circumstances beyond my control,' said Zora firmly, to which Dean French could offer no more than the merest preamble to a murmur, 'namely, the fact of my father's relationship with Professor Malcolm.'

Jack French clutched the sides of his chair and leaned back into it. This was not the way things went in his office. In a semi-circle on the wall behind him portraits of great men hung, men who were careful with their words, who weighed them cautiously and considered their consequences, men whom Jack French admired and had learned from: Joseph Addison, Bertrand Russell, Oliver Wendell Holmes, Thomas Carlyle and Henry Watson Fowler, the author of the *Dictionary of Modern English*

Usage, on whom French had written a co-
lossal, almost painfully detailed biography.
But nothing in French's armoury of ba-
roque sentences seemed sufficient for
dealing with a girl who used language like
an automatic weapon.

'Zora. If I understand you correctly . . .'
began Jack, moving donnishly forward across
the desk to speak — not quickly enough.

'Dean French, I just don't see why my
opportunity for advancement in the creative
fields should be stymied' — French raised
his eyebrows at 'stymied' — 'by a vendetta
that a professor appears to have against me
for reasons that are outside the proper
context of academic assessment.' She
paused. She sat very straight in her chair. 'I
think it's inappropriate,' she said.

They had been skirting around this for
ten minutes. Now the word had been used.

'Inappropriate,' repeated French. All he
could do at this point was to aim for damage
limitation. The word had been used. 'You
are referring,' he said, hopelessly, 'to the
relationship to which you referred, which
was, indeed, inappropriate. But what I do
not as yet see is how the relationship to
which you referred —'

'No, you misunderstand me. What happened between Professor Malcolm and my

father doesn't interest me,' Zora cut in. 'What *interests* me is my academic career in this institution.'

'Well, naturally, that would be uppermost in all of —'

'And as for the situation between Professor Malcolm and my father . . .'

Jack wished very much she would stop using that violent phrase. It was drilling into his brain: *Professor Malcolm and my father, Professor Malcolm and my father.* The very thing that was not to be spoken of this fall semester, in order to protect both the participants and the families of the participants, was now being batted around his office like a pigskin filled with blood . . . 'as the situation is no *longer* a situation and has not been for some time, I don't see why Professor Malcolm should be allowed to continue to discriminate against me in this blatantly personal fashion.'

Jack gazed tragically over her head to the clock on the far wall. There was a pecan muffin with his name on it in the cafeteria, but it would be too late for all that by the time he was through here.

'And you feel certain, do you, that this is, as you say, a *personal* discrimination?'

'I really don't know what else it can be, Dean French, I don't know what else to call it. I am in the top three percentile of this college, my academic record is pretty spotless — I think we can both agree on that.'

'Ah!' said French, grabbing at a thin rod of light in this murky discussion. 'But we must also consider, Zora, that this class is a *creative*-writing class. It is not purely, therefore, an academic question, and when we approach questions of the *creative,* we must, to a certain extent, *adapt* our —'

'I have a record of publication,' said Zora, scrabbling around in her tote bag, *'canigetmyballback.com, Salon, eyeshot, unpleasanteventschedule.com,* and, as far as print journals go, I'm waiting on a reply from *Open City.*' She thrust a crumpled bundle of sheets across the desk that seemed to be prints of things from websites — beyond that Jack did not wish to conjecture without his glasses.

'I see. And you have submitted this . . . *work,* naturally, as material to be considered by Professor Malcolm. Yes, of course you have.'

'And at this point,' said Zora, 'I'm having to consider how the stress and adverse emotions attached to taking a matter like this to the advisory board would be likely to impact on me. I'm really worried about that impaction. I just think it's inappropriate for a student to feel victimized in this way, and I wouldn't want it to happen to anybody else.'

So now all the cards were laid out. Jack took a moment to examine them. Twenty years of playing this game left him in no doubt that Zora Belsey had a full hand. Just for the hell of it, he played his own.

'And have you expressed these feelings to your father?'

'Not yet. But I know he will support me in whatever I choose to do.'

So it was time, after all, to stand up and walk slowly around the table, and then to perch on the front of it, folding one long leg over the other. Jack did this.

'I want to thank you for coming here this morning, Zora, and for speaking so honestly and eloquently about your feelings in this matter.'

'Thank you!' said Zora, colour rising proud in her face.

'And I want you to understand that I take what you say very seriously indeed — you're a great asset to this institution, as I think you know.'

'I want to be . . . I try to be.'

'Zora, I want you to leave this with me. I don't think, at the present time, that we need to think about the advisory board. I think we can straighten this thing out on a human scale that we can all comprehend and appreciate.'

'Are you going to —'

'Let me speak to Professor Malcolm about your concerns,' said Jack, succeeding at last at winning that little contest. 'And the moment I feel we're making a progression, I'll have you in here and we'll settle things to everybody's satisfaction. Is that answering your concerns?'

Zora stood up and held her bag to her chest. 'Thank you so much.'

'I saw that you got into Professor Pilman's class — now that *is* wonderful. And what else will you be — ?'

'I'm doing a Plato course and Jamie Penfruck's Adorno half-course and I'm definitely going to Monty Kipps's lectures. I read his piece Sunday in the *Herald* about taking the "liberal" out of the Liberal Arts . . . you know, so it's like now they're trying to tell us that conservatives are an endangered species — like they need protecting on campuses or something.' Here Zora took the time to roll her eyes and shake her head and sigh all at the same time. 'Apparently *everybody* gets special treatment — blacks, gays, liberals, women — everybody except poor white males. It's too crazy. But I *definitely* want to hear what he's got to say.

Know thy enemy. That's my motto.'

Jack French smiled weakly at this, opened the door for her and closed it again when she was gone. He hurried back to his chair and drew the N–Z *Shorter Oxford English* out of his bookshelf. He had an idea that 'stymie' might possibly have a more involved Middle English etymology than the usual M19th-century golfing term popularly ascribed to it. Maybe issuing from *styme,* meaning a glimpse, a glimmer; or possibly from the dangerous bird that Hercules killed, the Stymphalian, or . . . It did not. Jack closed the great book and returned it respectfully to its partner on the shelf. Sometimes these two might not give you what you hoped for, but in a deeper sense they never let you down. He picked up the phone and called Lydia, his Department Administrator.

'Liddy?'

'Here, Jack.'

'And how are you, my dear?'

'I'm dandy, Jack. Busy, you know. First day of the semester's always nuts.'

'Well, you do a remarkable job of making it look otherwise. Does it appear that every soul knows what he's doing?'

'Not *every* soul. We got kids wandering around who couldn't find their own ass in their pants, if you'll pardon my French, Jack.'

Jack did pardon it, and also the unconscious pun. There's a time for careful speech and then there's a time for straight talking, and, although Jack French was incapable of the latter, he appreciated Lydia's salty Boston tongue and the 'enforcing' job it did around the department. Unruly students, difficult UPS men, inexpressive computer technicians, Haitian cleaning staff caught smoking dope in the bathrooms — Lydia dealt with them all. The only reason Jack was able to rise above the fray was because Lydia was right there in the fray, toughing it out.

'Now, Liddy, have you any idea where I could get hold of Claire Malcolm this morning?'

'How do you hold a moonbeam in your hand,' mused Lydia, fond as she was of quoting musicals that Jack had never seen. 'I *know* she has a class in five minutes . . . but that doesn't mean she's on her *way* to it. You know Claire.'

Lydia laughed sardonically. Jack didn't encourage administrative staff discussing faculty in a sardonic manner, but there was no question of calling her up on it. Lydia was her own authority. Without her, Jack's whole department would simply fall into chaos and misery.

'I don't think,' considered Lydia, 'that I've *ever* seen Claire Malcolm set *foot* in this department before noon . . . but maybe that's just me. I'm so busy in the mornings I don't see the latte sitting in front of me till it's as cold as ice, you know?'

To women like Lydia, women like Claire made no sense at all. Everything Lydia had achieved in her life had come as a result of her prodigious organizational abilities and professionalism. There wasn't any institution in the country that Lydia couldn't reorganize and make more efficient, and in a few years, when she was done with Wellington, she knew in her heart of hearts that she would go on to Harvard and from there to anywhere she liked, maybe even the Pentagon. She had the skills, and skills took you places in Lydia's America. You started out with something as lowly as creating a filing system for a Back Bay drycleaning firm, and you ended with organizing and managing one of the most complex databases in the country for the President himself. Lydia knew how she'd got where she was today, and also where she was going. What she didn't get was how Claire Malcolm had got where *she* was today. How was it possible that a woman who lost her own office keys sometimes three times in a week and did not know where the supplies cupboard was after *five years* at the college could yet hold a title as grandiose as Downing Professor of Comparative Literature *and* be paid what Lydia knew she was paid because it was Lydia who sent out the pay stubs? And then, on top of it all, have an inappropriate workplace affair. Lydia knew it had something to do with art, but, personally, she didn't buy it. Academic degrees she understood — Jack's two Ph.D.s, in Lydia's mind, made up for the all times he tipped coffee into his own filing cabinet. But poetry?

'Now, would you have any idea which classroom she's assigned to, Liddy?'

'Jack — give me a minute on that. I got it on the computer somewhere . . . Remember that time she took a class on a bench by the river? She gets some crazy ideas sometimes. Is it an emergency?'

'No . . .' murmured Jack, 'Not an emergency . . . as such.'

'It's the Chapman block, Jack, Room 34C. You want that I get a message to her? I can send one of the kids.'

'No, no . . . I'll go and . . .' said Jack, lost for a minute in pressing the tip of a ballpoint into the soft, giving blackness at the centre of his desk.

'Jack, I got a kid just come in my office looking like someone killed his dog — you OK, honey? Jack, call me later if you need anything.'

'Will do, Liddy.'

Jack eased his blazer off the back of his chair and put it on. His hand was on the doorknob when the phone rang.

'Jack? Liddy. Claire Malcolm just ran by my office faster than Carl Lewis. She'll be in front of yours in about three seconds. I'll send someone over to her class and tell them she's going to be late.'

Jack opened his door and not for the first time marvelled at Lydia's precision.

'Ah, *Claire*.'

'Hey, Jack. I'm just rushing to class.'

'How are *you?*'

'Well!' said Claire, pushing the sunglasses she had taken to wearing up on to her head. She was never too late to talk a little of how she was. 'The war continues, the President's an ass, our poets are failing to legislate, the world's going to hell and I want to move to New Zealand — you know? And I've got a class in five. The usual!'

'These are dark times,' said Jack solemnly, threading his fingers through each other like a parson. 'And yet what can the university

271

do, Claire, but continue its work? Doesn't one have to believe that at times like these the university joins arms with the fourth estate, exercising our capacity for advocacy . . . helping frame political issues . . . that we too sit in that "reporters' gallery yonder" . . .'

Even by Jack's standards this was a circuitous route to get to what he intended to say. He seemed a little surprised himself by the development, and stood opposite Claire, with a face suggestive of a continuation of this thought which never materialized.

'Jack, I wish I had your confidence. We had an anti-war rally last Tuesday in Frost Hall? A hundred kids. Ellie Reinhold told me the Wellington anti-Vietnam rally in '67 brought *three thousand people* to the yard, *and* Allen Ginsberg. I'm kind of in despair at the moment. People round here act more like the first estate than the fourth if you ask me. God, Jack — I'm late, I gotta run. But maybe lunch?'

She turned to go but Jack couldn't let her. 'What's on the menu, creatively speaking, this morning?' he said, nodding at the book she held to her chest.

'Oh! You mean what are we reading? As it happens — me!'

She flipped the thin book over to its

cover, a large photo of Claire, circa 1972. Jack, who had some taste in women, admired once again the Claire Malcolm he had first met, all those years ago. Awful pretty with those provocative schoolgirl's bangs running into light brown waves of sumptuous hair, which curved over her left eye like Veronica Lake's and continued all the way down to her miniature hips. For the life of him Jack could never figure out why women of a certain age cut off all their hair like that.

'God, I look so ridiculous! But I just wanted to copy a poem for class, just an example of something. A pantoum.'

Jack brought his hand to his chin. 'I'm afraid you'll have to freshen my memory as to the precise nature of a *pantoum* . . . I'm rather rusty on my Old French verse forms . . .'

'It's Malay originally.'

'Malay!'

'It travelled. Victor Hugo did use it, but it's Malay originally. It's basically interlinked quatrains, usually rhyming a-b-a-b, and the second and fourth line of each stanza go on to be the first and third . . . is that right? So long since I . . . no, that's right — the first and third lines of the *next* stanza — mine's a broken pantoum, anyway. It's kind of hard to

explain . . . . it's better just to look at one,' she
said and opened the book to the relevant
page, handing it to Jack.

On Beauty
No, we could not itemize the list
of sins they can't forgive us.
The beautiful don't lack the wound.
It is always beginning to snow.

Of sins they can't forgive us
speech is beautifully useless.
It is always beginning to snow.
The beautiful know this.

Speech is beautifully useless.
They *are* the damned.
The beautiful know this.
They stand around unnatural as statuary.

They are the damned
and so their sadness is perfect,
delicate as an egg placed in your palm.
Hard, it is decorated with their face

and so their sadness is perfect.
The beautiful don't lack the wound.
Hard, it is decorated with their face.
No, we could not itemize the list.
                              Cape Cod, May 1974

274

Jack was now faced with a task he dreaded: saying something after reading a poem. Saying something *to the poet.* It was a strange fact of his tenure as Dean of the Humanities Faculty that Jack himself was not overly enamoured of either poetry or fictional prose; his great love was the essay, and, if he were really honest with himself, beyond essays themselves, the tools of the essayist: dictionaries. It was in the shady groves of dictionaries that Jack fell in love, bowed his head in awe and thrilled at an unlikely tale, for example, the bizarre etymology of the intransitive verb 'ramble'.

'Beautiful,' said Jack at last.

'Oh, it's just old crap — but a useful illustration. Anyway — Jack, I *really* have to run —'

'I've sent someone over to your classroom, Claire, they know you're going to be late.'

'You have? Is something wrong, Jack?'

'I do actually need a quick word with you,' said Jack, oxymoronically. 'Just in my office if that's possible.'

3

Here they all were, Howard's imaginary class. Howard indulged in a quick visual catalogue of their interesting bits, knowing that this would very likely be the last time he saw them. The punk boy with black-painted fingernails, the Indian girl with the disproportionate eyes of a Disney character, another girl who looked no older than fourteen with a railroad on her teeth. And then, spread across this room: big nose, small ears, obese, on crutches, hair red as rust, wheelchair, six foot five, short skirt, pointy breasts, iPod still on, anorexic with that light downy hair on her cheeks, bow-tie, *another* bow-tie, football hero, white boy with dreads, long fingernails like a New Jersey housewife, already losing his hair, striped tights — there were so many of them that Smith couldn't close the door without squashing somebody. So they had come, and they had heard. Howard had pitched his tent and made his case. He had offered them a Rembrandt who was neither a rule breaker nor an original but rather a conformist; he had asked them to ask themselves what they meant by 'genius' and, in the perplexed silence, replaced the familiar rebel master of historical fame with Howard's own vision of a merely competent artisan who painted whatever his wealthy patrons requested. Howard asked his students to imagine prettiness as the mask that power wears. To recast Aesthetics as a rarefied language of exclusion. He promised them a class that would challenge their own beliefs about the redemptive humanity of what is commonly called 'Art'. 'Art is the Western myth,' announced Howard, for the sixth year in a row, 'with which we both *console* ourselves and *make* ourselves.' Everybody wrote that down.

'Any questions?' asked Howard.

The answer to this never changed. Silence. But it was an interesting breed of silence particular to upscale liberal arts colleges. It was not silent because nobody had anything to say — quite the opposite. You could feel it, *Howard* could feel it, millions of things to say brewing in this room, so strong sometimes that they seemed to shoot from the students telepathically and bounce off the furniture. Kids looked down at the table top, or out of the window, or at Howard with great longing; some of the weaker ones blushed and pretended to take notes. But not one of them would speak. They had an intense fear of their peers. And, more than that, of Howard himself. When he first began teaching he had tried, stupidly, to coax them out of this fear — now he positively relished it. The fear was respect, the respect, fear. If you didn't have the fear you had nothing.

'Nothing? Have I *really* been so very thorough? Not a single question?'

A carefully preserved English accent also upped the fear factor. Howard let the silence stretch a little. He turned to the board and slowly unpeeled the photocopy, letting tongueless questions pelt his back. His own questions kept him mentally occupied as he rolled Rembrandt into a tight white stick. How much longer on the divan? Why does the sex have to mean everything? OK, it can mean *something,* but why everything? Why do thirty years have to go down the toilet because I wanted to touch somebody else? Am I missing something? Is this what it comes down to? Why does the sex have to mean *everything?*

'I have a question.'

The voice, an English voice like his own, came from his left. He turned — she had been hidden by a taller boy sitting right in front of her. The first thing to note were two spots of radiant highlights on her face — maybe the result of the same cocoa butter Kiki used in the winter. A pool of moonlight on her smooth forehead, and another on the tip of her nose; the kind of highlights, it occurred to Howard, that would be impossible to paint without distorting, without misrepresenting, the solid darkness of her true complexion. And her hair had changed again: now it was wormy dreadlocks going every which way, although none was longer than two inches. The tips of each were coloured a sensational orange, as if she had dipped her head into a bucket of sunshine. Because he was not drunk this time he knew now for certain that her breasts were indeed a phenomenon of nature and not of his imagination, for here were the spirited nipples again, working their way through a thick green ribbed woollen jumper. It had a stiff polo neck, several inches from her own skin, through which her neck and head emerged like a plant from its pot.

'Victoria, yes. I mean — is it Vee? Victoria? Go on.'

'It's Vee.'

Howard could feel the class thrill to this new piece of information — a freshman who was already known to the professor! Of course, the more committed Googlers in this class probably already knew the deal between Howard and the celebrity Kipps, and maybe had gone further and knew that this girl was Kipps's daughter, and that girl over there, Howard's. Maybe they even knew something of the culture war shaping up on the campus. Two days ago Kipps had argued strongly against Howard's Affirmative Action committee in the *Wellington Herald.* He had criticized not only its aims but challenged its very right to existence. He accused Howard and 'his supporters' of privileging liberal perspectives over conservative ones; of suppressing right-wing discussion and debate on campus. The article had been a sensation, as such things are in college towns. Howard's e-mail in-box this morning was full of missives from outraged colleagues and students pledging their support. An army rushing to fight behind a general who could barely get on his horse.

'It's just a small question,' said Victoria, shrinking a little from all the student eyes upon her. 'I was just —'

'No, go on, go on,' said Howard, over her attempts to speak.

'Just . . . what time is the class?'

Howard sensed the relief in the room. At least she hadn't asked anything clever. He could tell that the class as a whole could not abide prettiness *and* cleverness. But she had not tried to be clever. And now they approved of her practicality. Every pen was poised. This was all they really wanted to know, after all. The facts, the time, the place. Vee too had her pen on the page and her head low, and now she flicked her eyes up to meet Howard's, a glance somewhere between flirtation and expectancy. Lucky for Jerome, thought Howard, that he had finally agreed to go back to Brown. This girl was a dangerous commodity. And now Howard realized that he'd been looking at her so absorbedly he'd neglected to answer her question.

'It's three o'clock, Tuesday, in *this* room,' said Smith from behind Howard. 'The reading list is on the website, or you can find a copy of it in the cubbyhole outside Dr Belsey's office. Anybody needs their study cards signed, bring 'em to me and *ah'll* sign 'em. Thank you for coming, people.'

'Please,' said Howard above the noise of scraping chairs and the packing of bags, 'please only — *only* — put your names down if you're seriously intending to take this class.'

'Jack, darling,' said Claire, shaking her head, 'you send these websites your *shopping lists* and they put them up. They'll take *anything*.'

Jack retrieved the printouts from Claire and slipped them back into his drawer. He had tried reason and plea and rhetoric, and now he must introduce reality into the conversation. It was time, once again, to walk round the desk, perch on the end and cross one leg over the other.

'Claire . . .'

'My *God,* what a piece of work that girl is!'

'Claire, I really can't have you making those kind of . . .'

'Well, she *is.*'

'That's as may be, but . . .'

'Jack, are you telling me I have to have her in my class?'

'Claire, Zora Belsey is a very good student. She's an *exceptional* student, in fact. Now, she may not be Emily Dickinson . . .'

Claire laughed. 'Jack, Zora Belsey couldn't write a poem if Emily Dickinson herself rolled out of her grave, put a gun to the girl's head and demanded one. She's simply untalented in this area. She refuses to *read* poetry — and all I get from her are pages from her journal aligned down the left-hand margin. I've got *a hundred and twenty* talented students applying for *eighteen* places.'

'She is in the top three percentile of this college.'

'Oh, I *really* couldn't give a crap. My class rewards *talent.* I'm not teaching molecular biology, Jack. I'm trying to refine and polish a . . . a *sensibility.* I'm telling you: she doesn't have one. She has arguments. That's not the same thing.'

'She believes,' said Jack, using his deepest, most presidential, commencement day timbre, 'that she is being kept from this class for . . . personal reasons that are outside the proper context of academic or creative assessment.'

'*What?* What are you talking about, Jack? You're talking to me like a management manual? This is insane.'

'I'm afraid she went as far to intimate that she believed this was a "vendetta". An *inappropriate* vendetta.'

Claire was quiet for a minute. She too had spent much time in universities. She understood the power of the inappropriate.

'She *said* that? Are you serious? Oh, no, this is such a crock, Jack. Do I have a vendetta against the other hundred kids who didn't get in the class this semester? Is this *serious?*'

'She seems willing to take the matter on to the advisory board. As a case of personal prejudice, if I understand her correctly. She would be referring, of course, to your

283

relations . . .' said Jack, and allowed his ellipsis to do the rest.

'What a piece of work!'

'I think this is serious, Claire. I wouldn't bring it to your attention if I thought otherwise.'

'But Jack . . . the class has already been posted. What's it going to look like when Zora Belsey's name is added at the last minute?'

'I think a minor embarrassment now is worth a far larger, possibly costly embarrassment further down the line before the advisory board — or even in court.'

Every now and then Jack French could be admirably succinct. Claire stood up. She was so tiny that even standing she was only just the equal to Jack's reclining pose. But her small proportions bore no relation to the force of Claire Malcolm's personality, as Jack well knew. He drew his head back a little in preparation for the assault.

'What happened to supporting the faculty, Jack? What happened to privileging the decision of a respected faculty member over the demands of a student with a *pretty glaring* chip on their shoulder? Is that our policy now? Every time they cry wolf we run screaming?'

'Please, Claire . . . I need you to appreciate that I have been placed in an extremely invidious situation in which —'

'*You're* in a situation — what about the situation you're putting *me* in?'

'Claire, Claire — sit down for a moment, will you? I haven't explained myself well, I see that. Sit down for one moment.'

Claire lowered herself slowly into her chair, tucking one leg nimbly underneath her bottom like a teenager. She blinked at him warily.

'I looked at the boards today. Three of the names in your class I did not recognize.'

Claire Malcolm did a double-take at Jack French. Then she lifted her hands and brought them down hard on the arms of the chair. 'And? What are you saying?'

'Who, for example,' said Jack, glancing at a sheet of paper on his desk, 'is Chantelle Williams?'

'She's a receptionist, Jack. For an optician, I believe. I don't know which optician. What's your point?'

'A receptionist . . .'

'She also happens to be one of the most exciting young female talents I've come across in years,' announced Claire.

'Claire, it still remains that she is not a student registered at this institution,' said Jack quietly, neatly meeting hyperbole with sobriety. 'And therefore not strictly speaking eligible for —'

'Jack, I can't believe we're doing this . . . it was agreed *three years ago* that if I wanted to take on extra students, above and beyond my requirements, then that was under my discretion. There are a *lot* of talented kids in this town who don't have the advantages of Zora Belsey — who can't *afford* college, who can't *afford* our summer school, who are looking at the army as their next best possibility, Jack, an army that's presently *fighting a war* — kids who don't —'

'I am well aware,' said Jack, a little tired of being lectured by highly strung women this morning, 'of the educational situation for economically disadvantaged young people in New England — and you know I have always supported your sterling attempts . . .'

'Jack — '

'. . . to offer your impressive abilities . . .'

'Jack, what are you saying?'

'. . . to young people who would not otherwise have these opportunities . . . but the bottom line here is that people are asking questions about the fairness of classes being open to non-Wellington —'

'Who's asking? English Department people?'

Jack sighed. 'Quite a few people, Claire. And I redirect those questions. Have done for a while. But if Zora Belsey is successful in bringing a lot of unwelcome attention to your, shall we say, selective admissions process — then I don't know if I will still be able to continue redirecting those questions.'

'Is it Monty Kipps? I heard he "objected",' said Claire bitterly, and made her fingers quote, unnecessarily, Jack felt, 'to Belsey's Affirmative Action Committee working on campus. God, he hasn't even been here a month! Is he the new authority around here now or something?'

Jack blushed. He could blackmail with the best of them, but he could not involve himself very deeply in personal conflict. He also had a profound respect for public power, that compelling quality that Monty Kipps had in spades. If only, as a young man, Jack's way of expressing himself had been a tad sprightlier, a shade more people-friendly (if one could have imagined, even abstractly, the possibility of having a beer with him), he too might have been a public person in the manner of Monty Kipps, or like Jack's own late father, a senator for Massachusetts, or like his brother, a judge. But Jack was a university man from the cradle. And when he

met people like Kipps, a man who strad-
dled both worlds, Jack always deferred to
them.

'I cannot have you talking about a colleague of ours in that way, Claire, I just
can't. And you know that I can't name
names. I am trying to save you a lot of
pointless pain here.'

'I see.'

Claire looked down at her small brown
hands. They were quivering. The dome of
her speckled grey-and-white head faced
Jack, downy, he thought, like the feathers
in a bird's nest.

'In a university . . .' began Jack, preparing his best impression of a parson, but
Claire stood up.

'I know what happens in universities,
Jack,' she said sourly. 'You can tell Zora
congratulations. She made the class.'

4

'I need a homey, warm, chunky, fruit-
based, *wintery* kind of a pie,' explained
Kiki, leaning over the counter. 'You know
— tasty-looking.'

Kiki's little laminated name tag tapped
on the plastic sneeze-guard protecting the

merchandise. This was her lunch hour.

'It's for my friend,' she said bashfully, incorrectly. She hadn't seen Carlene Kipps since that strange afternoon three weeks ago. 'She's not too well. I need a *down home* pie, do you know what I mean? Nothing French or . . . frilly.'

Kiki laughed her big lovely laugh in the small store. People looked up from their speciality goods and smiled abstractly, supporting the idea of pleasure even if they weren't certain of the cause.

'See that?' said Kiki emphatically, pressing her index finger on the plastic, directly above an open-faced pie. The surrounding pastry was golden and in the centre sat a red and yellow compote of sticky baked fruit. '*That's* what I'm talking about.'

A few minutes later Kiki was striding up the hill with her pie in its recycled cardboard box, tied with a green velvet ribbon. She was taking business into her own hands. For there had been a misunderstanding between Kiki Belsey and Carlene Kipps. Two days after their meeting, somebody had hand-delivered an extremely old-fashioned, unironic and frankly unAmerican visiting card to 83 Langham:

Dear Kiki,

Thank you so much for your kind visit. I should like to repay the call. Please let me know of a time that would be convenient to you.

Yours truly
Mrs C. Kipps

In normal circumstances, of course, this card would have served as an ideal object of ridicule over a Belsey breakfast table. But, as it happened, the card arrived two days after the Belsey world fell apart. Pleasure was no longer on the menu. Ditto communal breakfasts. Kiki had taken to eating on the bus to work — a bagel and a coffee from the Irish store on the corner — and putting up with those disapproving looks that other women give big women when they're eating in public. Two weeks later, upon rediscovering the card tucked in the kitchen magazine rack, Kiki felt somewhat guilty; silly as it was, she had meant to reply. But there was never a good time to broach the subject with Jerome. The important thing at the time had been to keep her son's spirits up, to keep the waters as calm as possible so that he might get in the boat his mother had spent so long carefully constructing and sail off to college. Two days before registration Kiki passed Jerome's bedroom and witnessed him gathering his clothes into a ritualistic-looking mound in the middle of the floor — the traditional prelude to packing his bags. So now everyone was back in school. Everyone was enjoying the sense of new beginnings and fresh pastures that school cycles offer their participants. They were starting again. She envied them that.

Four days ago, Kiki found the visiting card once again, in the bottom of her Alice Walker Barnes and Noble tote bag. Sitting in the bus with the card on her lap, she parsed it into its constitutive parts, examining first the handwriting, then the Anglicized phrasing, then the idea of the maid or cleaner or whoever she was being sent round with it; the thick English notepaper with something about Bond Street stamped in the corner, the royal blue ink of the italics. It was too ridiculous, really. And yet when she looked out of the back window of the bus, seeking any happy memories of the long, distressing summer, moments when the weight of what had happened to her marriage was not crushing her ability to breathe and walk down the street and have breakfast with her family, for some reason, that afternoon on the porch with Carlene Kipps kept rising up.

She tried ringing. Three times. She sent Levi over with a note. The note received no reply. And on the phone it was always him, the husband, with his excuses. Carlene wasn't feeling well, then she was asleep, and then yesterday: 'My wife is not quite up to visitors just now.'

'Could I maybe talk to her?'

'I think it would be preferable if you left a message.'

Kiki's imagination went to work. It was, after all, a good deal easier on her own conscience to envisage a Mrs Kipps kept from the world by dark, marital forces than to acknowledge a Mrs Kipps offended by Kiki's own rudeness. So she had booked a two-hour lunch break today with the purpose of going over to Redwood and seeing about liberating Carlene Kipps from Montague Kipps. She would bring a pie. Everybody loves pie. Now she took out her cell and with a dextrous thumb scrolled down to JAY_DORM and pressed 'Call'.

'Hey . . . Hi, Mom . . . wait a minute . . . getting my glasses.'

Kiki heard a thump and then the sound of water spilling.

'Oh, *man* . . . Mom, wait up.'

Kiki tensed her jaw. She could *hear* the tobacco in his voice. But it was no good attacking on that front, seeing as how she'd started up smoking again herself. Instead she attacked obliquely. 'Every time I call you, Jerome, every time you *always* just getting out of bed. It's amazing, really. Don't matter what time I call, you *still* in bed.'

'Mom . . . please . . . less of the Mamma Simmonds . . . I'm in pain here.'

'Baby, we *all* in pain . . . now, look, Jay,' said Kiki seriously, abandoning her own mother's Southern stylings as too unwieldy for the delicate task at hand, 'quickly — when you were in London . . . Mrs Kipps, her relationship with her husband, with Monty — they were, you know, cool with each other?'

'How do you mean?' asked Jerome. Kiki could feel a little of the jittery anxiety of last year coming through the phone. 'Mom, what's going on?'

'Nothing, nothing . . . Nothing about that . . . It's just every time I try to call her, Mrs Kipps — you know, I just want to see how she is — she *is* my neighbour —'

'Give me some gossip, I *am* your neighbour!'

'Excuse me?'

'Nothing. It's a song,' said Jerome and

293

chuckled gently to himself. 'Sorry — go on, Mom. Neighbourly concern, etcetera . . .'

'Right. And *I just* want to say hello, and every time I call it's like he won't let me speak to her . . . like he's got her locked away or . . . I don't know, it's strange. First I thought she was offended — you know how easy folk like that get offended, they're worse than *white folk* that way — but now . . . I don't know. I think it's more than that. And I was just wondering if you knew anything.'

Kiki heard her son sigh into the phone. 'Mom, I don't think it's time for an intervention. Just because she can't come to the phone doesn't mean the evil Republican is beating her. Mom . . . I *really* don't want to come home at Christmas and find Victoria drinking eggnog in my kitchen . . . Could we just . . . like, could we cool it on the "being neighbourly" vibe? They're pretty private people.'

'Who's bothering them!' cried Kiki.

'OK, then!' echoed Jerome, imitating her.

'Nobody's bothering anybody,' muttered Kiki irritably. She stepped aside to allow a woman with a double stroller to get by. 'I just *like* her. The woman lives near by, and she's obviously not well, and I'd like to see how she's doing. Is that allowed?'

It was the first time she had articulated these motives, even to herself. Hearing them now, she recognized how approximate and shoddy they were when placed alongside the strong, irrational desire she had to be in that woman's presence again.

'OK . . . I just — I guess I don't see why we have to be friends with them.'

'You *have* friends, Jerome. And Zora has friends, and Levi practically *lives* with his friends — and' — Kiki followed the thought to the edge of the cliff and beyond — 'well, we sure as hell know now how close your *father* is to his friends — and what? I can't make friends? Y'all have your life and I have *no* life?'

'No, *Mom* . . . come on, that's not fair . . . I just . . . I mean, I wouldn't have thought she was your type of person . . . Makes it a little awkward for me, that's all. Anyway, whatever. You know . . . you do what you want.'

A mutual bad temper stretched its black wings over the conversation.

'Mom . . .' mumbled Jerome contritely, 'look, I'm glad you rang. How are you? Are you OK?'

'Me? I'm fine. I'm *fine*.'

'OK. . .'

'Really,' said Kiki.

'You don't sound great.'

'I'm *fine*.'

'So . . . what's going to happen? With you . . . you know . . . and Dad.' He sounded almost tearful, anxious not to be told the truth. It was wrong, Kiki knew, to be antagonized by this, but she was. These children spend so much time demanding the status of adulthood from you — even when it isn't in your power to bestow it — and then when the *real shit hits the fan,* when you need them to *be* adults, suddenly they're children again.

'God, I don't know, Jay. That's the truth. I'm getting through the days here. That's about it.'

'I love you, Mom,' said Jerome ardently. 'You're gonna get through this. You're a strong black woman.'

People had been telling Kiki this her whole life. She supposed she was lucky that way — there are worse things to be told. But the fact remained: as a sentence it was really beginning to bore the hell out of her.

'Oh, I *know* that. You know me, baby, I cannot be broken. Takes a giant to snap me in half.'

'Right,' said Jerome sadly.

'And I love you too, baby. I'm just fine.'

'You can feel bad,' said Jerome, and coughed the frog from his throat. 'I mean, that's not illegal.'

A fire engine went by, wailing. It was one of the old, shiny, brass-and-red-paint engines of Jerome's childhood. He could see it and its fellows in his mind's eye: six of them parked in the courtyard at the end of the Belseys' road, ready for an emergency. As a child he used to go over the hypothetical moment when his family would be saved from fire by white men climbing through the windows.

'I just wish I was there.'

'Oh, you're busy. Levi's here. *Not,*' said Kiki cheerily, wiping fresh tears from her eyes, 'that I see hide nor hair of Levi. We just do bed, breakfast and the laundry for that boy.'

'Meanwhile I'm drowning in dirty laundry here.'

Kiki was silent trying to picture Jerome right now: where he was sitting, the size of his room, where the window was and what it looked out upon. She missed him. For all his innocence, he was her ally. You don't have favourites among your children, but you do have allies.

'And Zora's here. I'm *fine.*'

'Zora . . . *please.* She wouldn't piss on

297

somebody if they were on fire.'

'Oh, Jerome, that's not true. She's just angry with me — it's normal.'

'*You're* not the one she should be angry with.'

'Jerome, you just get to class and don't be sweating about *me*. Takes a *giant*.'

'Amen,' said Jerome, in the comic way of the Belseys when they were putting on their ancestral Deep South voices, and Kiki echoed him, laughing. *Amen!*

And then to ruin everything that had gone before Jerome said, in all seriousness, 'God bless you, Mom.'

'Oh, baby, please . . .'

'Mom, just *take* the blessing, OK? It's not viral. Look, I'm late for class — I've got to go.'

Kiki snapped her cell closed and wedged it back into the very small gap between her flesh and her jean pocket. She was on Redwood already. During the conversation she had hung the paper bag with the cake box in it from her wrist; now she could feel the pie shifting around dangerously. She threw the bag away and put both hands under the bottom of the box to steady it. At the door she pressed down the bell with the back of her wrist. A young black girl answered with a dishrag in her hand, with poor English, giving her the information that Mrs Kipps was in the 'leebry'. Kiki didn't have a chance to ask if this was a good time, or to offer up the pie and then withdraw — she was led at once down the hallway and to an open door. The girl ushered her through into a white room lined with walnut bookshelves from floor to ceiling. A shiny black piano rested against the only bare wall. On the floor, on top of a sparse cowhide rug, hundreds of books were arranged in rows like dominos, their pages to the floor, their spines facing up. Sitting among them was Mrs Kipps, perched on the edge of a white calico Victorian armchair. She was bent forward, looking at the floor with her head in her hands.

'Hello, Carlene?'

Carlene Kipps looked up at Kiki, and smiled, slightly.

'I'm sorry — is this a bad time?'

'Not at all, my dear. It's a slow time. I think I've bitten off rather more than I can chew. Please sit down, Mrs Belsey.'

There being no other chair, Kiki took a seat on the piano stool. She wondered what had happened to first names.

'Alphabetizing,' murmured Mrs Kipps. 'I thought it would take a few hours. It's a surprise for Monty. He likes his books in order. But I'm been in here since eight this morning and I'm not past C!'

'Oh, wow.' Kiki picked up a book and pointlessly turned it over in her hands. 'I have to say, we've never alphabetized. Sounds like a lot of hard work.'

'Yes, it is.'

'Carlene, I wanted to give this to you as a way —'

'Now, can you see any B's or C's over there?'

Kiki put her pie down beside her on the stool and bent over. 'Oh-oh. Anderson — there's an Anderson here.'

'Oh, dear Lord. Perhaps we should stop for a while. We'll have a cup of tea,' she said, as if Kiki had been by her side all morning.

'Well, that's just perfect, because I brought some pie. It's humble pie — but it tastes great.'

But Carlene Kipps did not smile. It was clear that she had been offended and couldn't now pretend otherwise.

'There's no need for any such thing, I'm sure. I should not have assumed —'

'No, that's the point — you *should* have assumed,' insisted Kiki, lifting a little out of her seat. 'It was just damn rude of me not to answer your lovely note . . . things have been a little complicated and . . .'

'I can understand that possibly your son feels —'

'No, but that's the stupid thing — he's gone back to college anyway. Jerome — he decided to go back. There's no reason at all why we can't be friends now. I'd like to be. If you'd still like to,' said Kiki, and felt ridiculous, like a schoolgirl. She was new to this. The friendship of other women hadn't mattered to her in a long time. She'd never needed to think about it, having married her best friend.

Her hostess smiled impassively at her. 'I'm sure I would.'

'Good! Life's just too short for —' began Kiki. Carlene was already nodding.

'I very much agree. Much too short. Clotilde!'

'Sorry?'

'Not you, dear. *Clotilde!*'

The girl who had answered the door to Kiki came into the room.

'Clotilde, may we have some tea brought in please, and Mrs Belsey has a pie you can cut up. None for me, please —' Kiki protested, but Carlene shook her head. 'No, I can't digest a thing before three in the afternoon these days. I'll try a piece later, but you go on ahead. Now. It's so good to see you again. How are you?'

'Me? *Fine*. I'm fine. And you?'

'As it happens I've been in bed for quite a few days. I watched the television. A long documentary — a series of programmes — about Lincoln. Conspiracy theories regarding his death and so on.'

'Oh, I'm so sorry you're feeling bad,' said Kiki, looking away with shame at the thought of her own conspiracy theories.

'Don't be. It was a very good documentary. I find it's not true what they say about American television — not all of it, anyway.'

'Why, what do they say about it?' asked Kiki, smiling rigidly. She knew what was coming and she was annoyed by it, but also annoyed at herself for being annoyed.

Carlene shrugged in a fragile way, not quite in control of the movement. 'Well, in England we tend to think of it as awful nonsense, I suppose.'

'Right. We hear that a lot. I guess our TV's not so great.'

'Actually I think it's much of a muchness. I don't really follow any of it any more, it's too *fast* . . . *cut, cut cut,* everything so hysterical and loud . . . but Monty says that even Channel Four can't compete with the

302

kind of liberal programming you find on PBS. He can't *bear* PBS. He sees through it terribly — the way they promote all the usual liberal ideas and pretend it's progress for minorities. He hates all that. Did you know most of the donors live in Boston? Monty says that tells you all you need to know. And yet this Lincoln documentary was really very good.'

'And . . . that was on . . . PBS?' said Kiki despondently. She had lost her grip on her clip-on smile.

Carlene pressed her fingers to her brow. 'Yes. Didn't I say that? Yes. It was very good.'

They were not getting very far, and whatever had moved so felicitously between them three weeks ago appeared to have vanished. Kiki wondered how soon she could make her excuses without seeming rude. As if in response to this silent speculation, Carlene leaned back in her chair and lowered her hand from her forehead to place it over her eyes. A pained murmur, lower than her speaking voice, came from her.

'Carlene? Honey, are you OK?'

Kiki moved to stand, but with her other hand Carlene waved her off.

'It's a little thing. It'll pass.'

Kiki stayed on the edge of her piano

stool, in mid action, looking from Carlene to the door and back.

'Are you sure I can't get you any —'

'It's interesting to me,' said Carlene slowly, removing her hand. 'You were worried too, about their meeting again. Jerome and my Vee.'

'Worried? *No,*' said Kiki, laughing casually. 'No, not really.'

'But you were. I was too, I was very glad to hear Jerome avoided her at your party. It's a silly thing, but I knew I didn't want them to meet again. Why *was* that?'

'Well,' said Kiki and looked down, preparing to say something evasive. Glancing up into the woman's serious eyes, she once more found herself speaking the truth. 'For me, I guess I worry about Jerome taking things hard, you know? He's inexperienced — very. And Vee — she's so *incredibly lovely* — I'd never say it to him, but she was a little out of his league. A *lot*. She's what my youngest son would call *bootylicious.*' Kiki laughed, but, seeing that Carlene was following her words as if they were vital, she stopped. 'Jerome always tends to aim a little high . . . You know what the bottom line is? It just looked like broken-heart territory to me. I mean, the kind of broken heart that keeps on getting *broke.* And this is an important college year for Jay. I mean . . . you just have to *look* at her to see she's a fire sign,' said Kiki, resorting to a system of values that never seemed to let her down. 'And Jerome — Jerome's a water sign. He's a Scorpio, like me. And that's pretty much his character.'

Kiki asked Carlene her daughter's sign and was pleased to find her guess was correct. Carlene Kipps looked perplexed at the astrological turn to the conversation.

'She might burn him up,' she considered, trying to decode what Kiki had just told her. 'And he would put out her fire . . . He'd hold her back — yes, yes, I believe that's right.'

But Kiki bridled at this. 'I don't know about that . . . actually, I know all mothers say this, but my baby's *very* brilliant — if anything, it's always a question of keeping up with him, intellectually speaking. He's a live wire — I know Howie would say that Jerome's probably the brightest of the three of them — I mean Zora works hard, God knows, but Jerome —'

'You mistake what I'm saying. I saw when he was with us. He was so focused on my daughter, he almost couldn't let her live. I suppose you call it obsession. When he has an idea, your son, he holds it very tight. My husband is like that — I recognize it. Jerome's a very *absolute* young man.'

Kiki smiled. *This* was what she had liked about the woman. She put things well: insightfully, honestly.

'Yeah, I know what you mean. All or nothing. All of my children are a little like that, to tell you the truth. They set their mind to something, and my *God,* they don't let go. That's their father's influence. Pig-headed as *hell.*'

'And men become very absolute about pretty girls, don't they?' continued Carlene, inching along her own thread now, which was obscure to Kiki. 'And if they can't possess them, they get angry and bitter instead. It occupies them too much. I was never one of those women. I'm *glad* I wasn't. I used to mind, but now I see how it left Monty free for other interests.'

What could one say to this? Kiki felt in her purse for her lip-balm.

'That's a strange way to think about it,' she said.

'Is it? I've always felt that. I'm sure that's wrong. I've never been a feminist. You would put it more cleverly.'

'No, no — I just — surely, it's about what *both* people want to do,' said Kiki, applying a layer of colourless gloop to her mouth. 'And how they each might . . . I guess *enable* their partners, no?'

'Enable? I don't know.'

'I mean, your husband, Monty, for example,' said Kiki, boldly. 'He writes a lot about — I mean, I've read his articles — about what a perfect mother you are, and he . . . you know, often uses you as an example of the ideal — I guess, the ideal "stay-at-home" Christian Mom — which is amazing of course — but there must also be things you . . . maybe things *you* wanted to do that . . . maybe you wish . . .'

Carlene smiled. Her teeth were the only non-regal thing about her, raggedy and uneven with large childish gaps. 'I wanted to love and to be loved.'

'Yes,' said Kiki, because she could not think of anything else. She listened out hopefully for the footsteps of Clotilde, some sign of imminent interruption, but nothing.

'And Kiki — when you were young? I imagine you did a million things.'

'Oh, God . . . I *wanted* to. I don't know about doing them. For the longest time I wanted to be Malcolm X's private assistant. That didn't work out. I wanted to be a writer. Wanted to sing at one point. My mamma wanted me to be a doctor. *Black woman doctor.* Those were her three favourite words.'

'And were you very good-looking?'

'Wow . . . what a question! Where'd that come from?'

Carlene lifted her bony shoulders once again. 'I always wonder what people were like before I knew them.'

'Was I good-looking . . . Actually, I was!' It was a strange thing to say out loud. 'Carlene, between you and me, I was *hot.* Not for very long. About six years maybe. But I was.'

'You can always tell. You still have a good deal of beauty, I think,' said Carlene.

Kiki laughed raucously. 'You are a *shameless* flatterer. You know . . . I see Zora worrying all the time about her looks, and I want to say to her, honey, any woman who counts on her face is a *fool.* She doesn't want to hear that from me. It's how it is, though. We *all* end up in the same place in the end. That's the *truth.*'

Kiki laughed again, more sadly this time. Now it was Carlene's turn to smile politely.

'Did I tell you?' said Carlene, to end the brief silence, 'My son Michael is engaged. We heard only last week.'

'Oh, that's great,' said Kiki, no longer so

easily wrong-footed by the disconnected turns of Carlene's conversation. 'Who is she? American girl?'

'English. Her parents are Jamaican. A very plain, sweet, quiet girl — a girl from our church. Amelia. She couldn't throw anybody off balance — she'll be a companion. And that's a good thing, I think. Michael's just not strong enough for anything else . . .' She broke off here and turned to look through the window at the backyard. 'They're going to have the wedding here, in Wellington. They'll come at Christmas to look for the right place. You'll excuse me for a moment. I must check on your lovely pie.'

Kiki watched Carlene leave the room, unsteadily, leaning on things as she went. Alone, Kiki put her hands between her knees and pressed in on them. The news that some girl was about to start out on the road she herself had walked thirty years earlier gave her a vertiginous feeling. A clearing opened in her mind, and in it she tried to restage one of her earliest memories of Howard — the night they first met and first slept together. But it could not be conjured so easily; for at least the past ten years the memory had presented itself to her like a stiff tin toy left out in the rain —

so rusty, a museum piece, not *her* toy at all any more. Even the kids knew it too well. Upon the Indian rug on the floor of Kiki's Brooklyn walk-up, with all the windows open, with Howard's big grey feet halfway out the door resting on the fire escape. A hundred and two degrees in the New York smog. 'Halleluiah' by Leonard Cohen playing on her dime-store record player, that song Howard liked to call 'a hymn deconstructing a hymn'. Long ago Kiki had submitted to this musical part of the memory. But it was surely not true — 'Hallelujah' had been another time, years later. But it was hard to resist the poetry of the possibility, and so she had allowed 'Halleluiah' to fall into family myth. Thinking back, this had been a mistake. A tiny one, to be sure, but symptomatic of profound flaws. Why did she always concede what was left of the past to Howard's edited versions of it? For example, she should probably say something when, at dinner parties, Howard claimed to despise all prose fiction. She should stop him when he argued that American cinema was just so much idealized trash. *But,* she should say, *but! Christmas 1976 he gave me* Gatsby, *a first edition. We saw* Taxi Driver *in a filthy dive in Times Square — he loved it.* She did not say those things. She let Howard reinvent, retouch. When, on their twenty-fifth wedding anniversary, Jerome had played his parents an ethereal, far more beautiful version of 'Halleluiah' by a kid called Buckley, Kiki had thought yes, that's right, our memories are getting more beautiful and less real every day. And then the kid drowned in the Mississippi, recalled Kiki now, looking up from her knees to the colourful painting that hung behind Carlene's empty chair. Jerome had wept: the tears you cry for someone whom you never met who made something beautiful that you loved. Seventeen years earlier, when Lennon died, Kiki had dragged Howard to Central Park and wept while the crowd sang 'All You Need is Love' and Howard ranted bitterly about Milgram and mass psychosis.

'Do you like her?'

Carlene shakily passed Kiki a cup of tea, while Clotilde placed a piece of pie on a fussy china plate next to her on the piano seat. Before Clotilde could be thanked, she was backing out of the room, closing the door behind her.

'Like . . . ?'

'Maîtresse Erzulie,' said Carlene, pointing to the painting. 'You were ad-

311

miring her, I thought.'

'She's *fabulous*,' replied Kiki, only now taking the time to look at her properly. In the centre of the frame there was a tall, naked black woman wearing only a red bandanna and standing in a fantastical white space, surrounded all about by tropical branches and kaleidoscopic fruit and flowers. Four pink birds, one green parrot. Three humming birds. Many brown butterflies. It was painted in a primitive, childlike style, everything flat on the canvas. No perspective, no depth.

'It's a Hyppolite. It's worth a great deal, I believe, but that's not why I love it. I got it in Haiti itself on my very first visit, before I met my husband.'

'It's lovely. I just love portraits. We don't have any paintings in our house. At least, none of human beings.'

'Oh, that's terrible,' said Carlene and looked stricken. 'But you must come here whenever you want and look at mine. I have many. They're my company — they're the greater part of my *joy*. I realized that quite recently. But she's my favourite. She's a great Voodoo goddess, Erzulie. She's called the Black Virgin — also, the Violent Venus. Poor Clotilde won't look at her, can't even be in the same room as her

— did you notice? A superstition.'

'*Really.* So she's a symbol?'

'Oh, *yes.* She represents love, beauty, purity, the ideal female and the moon . . . and she's the *mystère* of jealousy, vengeance and discord, *and,* on the other hand, of love, perpetual help, goodwill, health, beauty and fortune.'

'Phew. That's a lot of symbolizing.'

'Yes, isn't it? It's rather like all the Catholic saints rolled into one being.'

'That's interesting . . .' began Kiki shyly, giving herself a moment to remember a thesis of Howard's, which she now wished to reproduce as her own for Carlene. 'Because . . . we're so binary, of course, in the way we think. We tend to think in opposites, in the Christian world. We're structured like that — Howard always says that's the trouble.'

'That's a clever way to put it. I like her parrots.'

Kiki smiled, relieved she did not need to go any further down this uncertain path.

'*Good* parrots. So, does she avenge herself on men?'

'Yes, I believe so.'

'I need to get me some of that,' said Kiki, half under her breath, not really meaning for it to be heard.

'I think . . .' murmured Carlene and smiled tenderly at her guest, 'I think that would be a shame.'

Kiki closed her eyes. 'Wow. I hate this town sometimes. Everybody knows everybody's business. Too small by a *long* way.'

'Oh, but I'm so *glad* to see that your spirits haven't been destroyed by it.'

'Oh!' said Kiki, and felt moved by the unsolicited concern. 'We'll get by. I've been married an awful long time, Carlene. Takes a giant to hurt me.'

Carlene leant back in her chair. Her eyes were pink round their rims and wet.

'But why shouldn't you be hurt by it, dear? It's very hurtful.'

'Yes . . . of course it is — but . . . I guess I mean that's not all my life is about. Right now I'm trying to understand what my life's been *for* — I feel I'm at that point — and what it *will* be for. And . . . that's just a lot more essential for me right now. And Howard's got to ask those questions for himself. I don't know . . . we break up, we don't break up — it's the same.'

'I don't ask myself *what* did I live for,' said Carlene strongly. 'That is a man's question. I ask *whom* did I live for.'

'Oh, I don't believe you believe that.' But, looking into her grave eyes, Kiki saw

314

clearly that this is exactly what the woman opposite her *did* believe, and she felt suddenly vexed by the waste and stupidity of it. 'I have to say, Carlene, you know . . . I'm afraid I just don't believe that. I *know* I didn't live for anybody — and it just seems to me it's like taking us all, all women, certainly all *black* women, three hundred years backwards if you really —'

'Oh, dear, we're arguing,' said Carlene, distressed at the prospect. 'You mistake me again. I don't mean to argue a case. It's just a feeling I have, especially now. I see very clearly recently that in fact I didn't live for an idea or even for God — I lived because I loved *this* person. I am very selfish, really. I lived for love. I never really interested myself in the world — my family, yes, but not the world. I can't make a case for my life, but it *is* true.'

Kiki regretted raising her voice. The lady was old, the lady was ill. It didn't matter what the lady believed.

'You must have a wonderful marriage,' she said in conciliation. 'That's amazing. But for us . . . you know . . . you get to a point where you have an understanding —'

Carlene shushed her and came forward further in her chair. 'Yes, yes. But you staked your *life*. You gave somebody your

315

life. You've been disappointed.'

'Oh, I don't know about disappointed . . . it's not really a surprise. Stuff happens. And I *did* marry a man.'

Carlene looked at her curiously. 'Is there another option?'

Kiki looked straight back at her hostess and decided to be brazen. 'For me, there was, I think . . . yes. At one point.'

Carlene looked uncomprehendingly at her guest. Kiki wondered at herself. She was misfiring recently, and now she was misfiring in Carlene Kipps's library. But she did not stop; she felt an old Kikian urge — once upon a time regularly exercised — to shock and, at the same time, to tell the truth. It was the identical feeling she felt (but rarely acted upon) in churches and upscale stores and courtrooms. Places she sensed the truth was rarely told.

'I guess I mean, there was a revolution going on, everybody was looking at different lifestyles, alternative lifestyles . . . so whether women could live with women, for example.'

'With women,' repeated Carlene.

'Instead of men,' confirmed Kiki. 'Sure . . . I thought for a while that might be the road I was going to go down. I mean, I went down it some way.'

316

'Ah,' said Carlene and brought her wobbling right hand under the control of her left. 'Yes, I see,' she said thoughtfully, blushing only very slightly. 'Maybe that would be easier — that's what you think? I've often wondered . . . it must be easier to know the other person — I imagine that's true. They are as *you* are. My aunt was that way. It's not uncommon in the Caribbean. Of course Monty's always been very harsh on the subject — until James.'

'James?' repeated Kiki sharply. She was irked to find her own revelation passed over so swiftly.

'The Reverend James Delafield. He's a very old friend of Monty — Princeton gentleman. A Baptist — he delivered the benediction at President Reagan's inauguration, I believe.'

'Now, didn't he turn out to be . . . ?' said Kiki, vaguely recalling a *New Yorker* profile.

Carlene clapped her hands and — of all things — giggled. 'Yes! It made Monty think again, yes, it did. And Monty hates to think again. But the choice was between his friend and . . . well, I don't know. The Good News, I suppose. But I knew Monty likes James's conversation — not to mention his cigars — a little too much. I said to him: my dear, life must come first over the

Book. Otherwise, what is the Book *for?* Monty was outraged! Scandalized! It is for *us* to conform to the Book, as he said. He told me I'd got it all wrong — no doubt I have. But I see they still like to spend an evening together with a cigar. You know, between you and me,' she whispered, and Kiki wondered what had happened to not making fun of one's own husband, 'they're very good friends.'

Kiki lifted her left eyebrow in neat, devastating fashion: 'Monty Kipps's best friend is a gay man.'

Carlene gave a little shriek of amusement. 'Goodness, he would *never* say that. Never! You see, he doesn't think of it that way.'

'What other way is there to think about it?'

Carlene wiped tears of mirth from her eyes.

Kiki whistled. 'You sure as hell never hear the brother mention *that* on Bill O'Reilly.'

'Oh, my dear, you're terrible. Terrible!'

She was truly gleeful now, and Kiki marvelled at how this whitened her eyes and tightened her skin. She looked younger, healthier. They laughed together for a while, at quite different things, so Kiki imagined. After a while the glee subsided on both sides, and they fell into more normal conversation. These little mutual revelations reminded them of their common ground, and in this they walked around leisurely, steering clear of anything that might prove an obstacle to easy movement. Both mothers, both familiar with England, both lovers of dogs and gardens, both slightly awed by the abilities of their children. Carlene spoke a great deal of Michael, of whose practicality and money sense she seemed very proud. Kiki in return offered up her own somewhat falsified family anecdotes, consciously smoothing over the rougher edges of Levi, sketching in a slender, mendacious picture of Zora's devotion to family life. Kiki mentioned the hospital several times, hoping to segue into an inquiry as to the nature of Carlene's illness, but each time, at the brink, she hesitated. The time passed. They finished their tea. Kiki found she had eaten three pieces of pie. At the door, Carlene kissed Kiki on both cheeks, at which point Kiki smelt her own workplace, clearly, acutely. She let go of where she held Carlene, under each brittle elbow. She walked the pretty garden path back to the street.

5

A mega-store demands a mega-building. When Levi's Saturday employers blew into

Boston seven years ago, several grand nineteenth-century structures were considered. The winner was the old municipal library, built in the 1880s in brash red brick with glittering black windows and a high Ruskinian arch above the door. The building took up most of the block it stood upon. In this building Oscar Wilde once gave a lecture concerning the superiority of the lily over all other flowers. One opened the doors by twisting an iron hoop in both hands and awaiting the soft heavy click as metal released metal. Now those twelve-foot oak doors have been replaced by triple sets of glass panels that silently part when people approach. Levi walked through these and touched fists with Marlon and Big James in security. He took the elevator to the basement storeroom to change into the branded T-shirt, the baseball cap and the cheap, skinny-legged, tapered-ankle, lint-ball-attracting black polyester pants they made him wear. He rode the elevator up to the fourth floor and made his way to his department, his eyes to the floor, following the repeated brand logo in the synthetic carpet underfoot. He was pissed off. He felt he'd been let down. Along the corridor he traced the genealogy of the feeling. He had taken this Saturday job in good faith, having always admired the global brand behind these stores, the scope and ambition of their vision. He had been particularly impressed by this section of the application form:

Our companies are part of a family rather than a hierarchy. They are empowered to run their own affairs, yet other companies help one another, and solutions to problems come from all kinds of sources. In a sense we are a community, with shared ideas, values, interests and goals. The proof of our success is real and tangible. Be a part of it.

He had wanted to be a part of it. Levi liked the way the mythical British guy who owned the brand was like a graffiti artist, tagging the world. Planes, trains, finance, soft drinks, music, cellphones, vacations, cars, wines, publishing, bridal wear — anything with a surface that would take his simple bold logo. That was the kind of thing Levi wanted to do one day. He'd figured that it wasn't such a bad idea to get a little sales assistant job with this enormous firm, if only to see how their operation worked from the inside. Watch, learn, supplant — Machiavelli style. Even when it turned out to be tough work for bad pay, he'd stuck with it. Because he believed that he was part of a family whose success was real and tangible, despite the $6.89 an hour he was being paid.

Then out of nowhere this morning he received a message on his pager from Tom, a nice kid who worked in the Folk Music section of the store. According to Tom, there was a rumour going around that the floor manager, Bailey, required all floor and counter staff to work Christmas Eve and Christmas Day. It then struck Levi that he had never seriously considered precisely what his employer, the impressive global brand, really meant by these *shared ideas, values, interests and goals* of which he and Tom and Candy and Gina and LaShonda and Gloria and Jamal and all the rest supposedly partook. *Music for the people? Choice is paramount? All music all the time?*

'*Get the money,*' suggested Howard at breakfast. '*No matter what.* That's their motto.'

'I am *not* working Christmas Day,' said Levi.

'Nor should you,' agreed Howard.

'That's just not happening. That's bullshit.'

'Well, if you really feel like that, then you need to get your fellow employees together and implement some kind of direct action.'

'I don't even know what that is.'

Over their toast and coffee, Levi's father explained the principles of direct action as it was practised between 1970 and 1980 by Howard and his friends. He spoke at length about someone called Gramsci and some people called the Situationists. Levi nodded quickly and regularly, as he had learned to do when his father made speeches of this kind. He felt his eyelids tugging low and his spoon heavy in his hand.

'I don't think that's how things go down now,' Levi said at last, gently, not wanting to disappoint his father, but needing to catch the bus. It was a nice enough story, but it was making him late for work.

Now Levi arrived at his sector in the west wing of the fourth floor. He'd been recently promoted, although it was more of a conceptual promotion than a fiscal one. Instead of having to be wherever he was needed, he now worked exclusively in Hip-hop, R & B and Urban; he had been encouraged to believe that this would involve him imparting his knowledge of these genres to knowledge-seeking customers, just as the librarians who once walked this floor had helped the readers who came to them. But that wasn't exactly how it had panned out. *Where are the toilets? Where is Jazz? Where is World Music? Where is the café? Where is the signing?* What he did most Saturdays wasn't all that different from standing on a street corner with an arrow sign, directing people to an army surplus store. And, although the dusty light sifted delicately through the high windows, and the spirit of studious contemplation lingered on in the phoney Tudor-style panelling of the walls and the carved roses and tulips that decorated the many balconies, no one in here was genuinely seeking enlightenment. And that was a shame, for Levi loved rap music; its beauty, ingenuity and humanity were neither obscure nor unlikely to him, and he could argue a case for its equal greatness against any of the artistic products of the human species. Half an hour of a customer's time spent with Levi expressing this enthusiasm would be like listening to Harold Bloom wax lyrical about Falstaff — but the opportunity never arose. Instead he spent his days directing people to novelty rap records from hit movies. Consequently, Levi did not get paid enough or enjoy his time here sufficiently even to contemplate working the Christmas weekend. It just wasn't going down like that.

'Candy! Yo, Candy!'

Thirty feet away from Levi, and not sure, initially, who it was shouting at her, Candy turned from the customer she was dealing with and gave Levi a sign to leave her alone. Levi waited for her customer to move on. Then he jogged up to Candy in the Alt. Rock / Heavy Metal section and tapped her on the shoulder. She turned, already sighing. She had a new piercing. A bolt that went through the skin on her chin, just beneath her bottom lip. That was the thing about working here: you met the kind of people you would never *ever* meet in any other circumstances.

'Candy — I need to talk to you.'

'Look . . . I've been here since *seven* stocking and I'm going to lunch now so don't even *ask*.'

'No, man — I just got here, I'm taking my break at twelve. Did you hear about Christmas Day?'

Candy groaned and rubbed her eyes vigorously. Levi noted the grubbiness of her fingers, the torn cuticles, the little translucent wart on her thumb. When she'd finished her face was purple and blotchy and clashed with the pink-black stripes of her hair.

'Yeah, I heard about it.'

'They're tripping if they think they gonna see me on that weekend. I am *not* working Christmas, it ain't happening.'

'So, what — you going to *quit* or something?'

'Now, why would I do that? That's plain dumb.'

'Well, you can complain, but . . .' Candy cracked her knuckles. 'Bailey really doesn't give a fuck.'

'That's why I'm not gonna complain to Bailey, I'm gonna *do* something, man — I'm gonna take some . . . like some direct *action*.'

Candy blinked slowly at him. 'Oh, right. Good luck with that.'

'Look: just meet me out back in two minutes, a'ight? Get the others — Tom and Gina and Gloria — everybody on our floor. I'll find LaShonda — she's on the counter.'

'*Okay,*' said Candy, managing to make this sound like an overused quotation. '*God* . . . calm down with the Stalinism.'

'Two minutes.'

'*Okay.*'

At the counter Levi found LaShonda at

the far end of the long bank of cash registers, much taller and wider than the six male clerks working beside her. An amazon of retail.

'LaShonda, hey, girl.'

LaShonda waved her talons in a swift, economical move, like the spreading of a fan, each nail clicking off the next. She grinned at him. 'Hey, Levi, baby. How you doing?'

'Oh, I'm cool . . . you know, hustling, doing my thang.'

'You do it well, baby, you do it *well*.'

Levi tried hard to hold the gaze of this incredible woman but failed, as ever. LaShonda hadn't yet cottoned on to the fact that Levi was still only sixteen, living with his parents in the middle-class suburb of Wellington, and therefore not really a viable stand-in father for her three small children.

'Hey, LaShonda, can I speak to you for a minute?'

'Sure, baby — I always got time for you, you know that.'

LaShonda came out from behind the counter, and Levi followed her as she made her way to a quiet corner near the Classical Music chart. For a three-time mom, her body was miraculous. The black long-sleeved shirt clung to the muscles in her stocky forearms; the front buttons strained to contain her bust. LaShonda's big old butt, as it stretched and fought against the nylon of the regulation pants, was, as far as Levi was concerned, the great unspoken perk of this job.

'LaShonda, can you meet us all out back in five minutes? We having a meeting,' said Levi, allowing his accent to slip a few rungs down into closer relation with LaShonda's own. 'Get Tom and anyone else who can get away for a minute. It's about this Christmas Day thing.'

'What's that, baby? What Christmas Day thing?'

'You didn't hear? They making us work Christmas Day.'

'For real? Time and a half?'

'Well . . . I don't know . . .'

'Man, I could do with the extra dollars, I *know* you know what I'm saying.' Levi nodded. This was the other thing. LaShonda had made an assumption early on that they were in similar situations, economically. There are so many different ways to need money. Levi didn't need it like LaShonda needed it. 'I'll definitely work. The morning at least. I can't come to the meeting, but put my name down, a'ight?'

'OK . . . sure . . . Sure, I'll do that.'

'I could do with a little extra, that's no joke — and this year I gotta get my Christmas shit to-*geth*-er. I *always* be sayin' I'm gonna do it early this year and then I *never* do — just leave everything last minute just like always. But it's *expensive* — oh, my *word*.'

'Yeah,' said Levi pensively. 'Shit gets tight for everybody this time of year . . .'

'I *hear* that,' said LaShonda, and whistled. 'And I ain't got no one to do for me. I gotta do for myself, know what I mean? Baby, you taking your break? You want to come get some with me? I'm heading for Subway right about now.'

There was an alternative universe that Levi occasionally entered in his imagination, one in which he accepted LaShonda's invitations, and then later they made love standing up in the basement of the store. Soon after, he moved in with her in Roxbury and took on her children as his own. They lived happily ever after — two roses growing out of concrete, as Tupac has it. But the truth was he wouldn't know what to do with a woman like LaShonda. He wished he *did* know, but he didn't. Levi's girls were typically the giggly Hispanic teenagers from the Catholic school next door to his prep, and those girls had simple tastes: happy with a movie and some heavy petting in one of Wellington's public parks. When he was feeling brave and confident, he sometimes hooked up with one of the exquisite fifteen-year-old LaShondas with the fake IDs that he met in Boston nightclubs, who took him semi-seriously for a week or two until they drifted away, confused by his strange determination not to tell them anything at all about his life or to show them where he lived.

'No . . . thanks, LaShonda . . . my break's not till later.'

'All right, baby. I'll miss you, though. You looking *fine* today — buff and *all* that.'

Levi flexed his bicep obligingly under LaShonda's manicured touch.

'*Damn.* And the rest. Don't be shy, now.'

He lifted his T-shirt up a little.

'Baby, that ain't even a six pack no more. That's like a *thirty-six* pack or something! Ladies gotta look out for my boy Levi . . . *damn.* He ain't a boy no more.'

'You know me, LaShonda, I like to take care of myself.'

'Yeah, but who gonna take care of *you?*' said LaShonda and laughed a good long time. She put her hand on his cheek. 'OK, baby, I'm out. See you next week if I don't see you later. You take care.'

'Bye, LaShonda.'

Levi leaned on a rack of *Madame Butterfly* recordings and watched LaShonda go. Somebody tapped him on the shoulder.

'Er . . . Levi — sorry to . . .' said Tom from Folk Music. 'I just heard that you were . . . is there . . . like a meeting? I just heard you were trying to organize some kind of . . .'

Tom was cool. Levi disagreed with him in matters of music in every possible way two young men can disagree, but he could also see that Tom was cool in a lot of other ways. Cool about this crazy war, cool about not letting customers stress him out — plus he was easy to be around.

'Yo, my man Tom — how's it hanging,' said Levi and tried to knock fists with Tom, always a mistake. 'For real — we're having a meeting. I'm heading there now. This Christmas Day thing is bullshit.'

'Good, it's *total* bullshit,' said Tom, pushing his thick blond bangs back off his face. 'It's cool that you're taking . . . you know . . . a stand and everything.'

But sometimes Levi found Tom a little too fretfully deferential, like right now — always anxious to award Levi a prize that

Levi didn't even know he was in the running for.

It was immediately noticeable that only the white kids had showed up for the meeting. Gloria and Gina, the two Hispanic girls, were absent, as was Jamal, the brother who worked in World Music, and Khaled, a Jordanian, who worked in the music DVD section. It was just Tom, Candy and a short, freckly guy Levi didn't know too well called Mike Cloughessy who worked in Pop on the third floor.

'Where is everybody?' asked Levi.

'Gina said she was coming but . . .' explained Candy. 'She has a supervisor up her ass, following her around, so.'

'But she said she was coming?'

Candy shrugged. Then she looked at him hopefully, as did the others. It was the same weird sense he had in his prep school: that unless he spoke no one else would. He was being gifted with an authority, and it was something complex and unspoken to do with being the black guy — deeper than that he could not penetrate.

'I'm just like, there's *gotta* be a line that we don't cross — where we don't go. And working on Christmas Day is that line, man. That's it, right there,' he said, employing his hands a little more than was natural to him because they seemed to expect it. 'My point is we got to protest, with action. 'Cos right now, as it stands, anybody who's working part time who refuses to work Christmas is looking at losing their job. And that's bullshit — in my opinion.'

'But what does that mean . . . protest with action?' asked Mike. He was jittery, moving a lot when he spoke. Levi wondered what it would be like to be such a small, pink, funny-looking, nervy guy. As he wondered this, he must have been frowning at Mike, for the little guy grew more agitated, putting his hands in and out of his pockets.

'Like a . . . you know, like a sit-in,' suggested Tom. He had a packet of German Drum tobacco in one hand and a cigarette paper in the other and was trying to roll. He angled his bear-like torso into a doorway, protecting his nascent project from the wind. Levi — although he passionately disapproved of tobacco — helped him out by standing in front of him, a human shield.

'Sit-in?'

Tom began describing a sit-in, but Levi, once he saw where he was going with it, cut him off.

'Yo, I am *not* sitting on the floor. I don't *do* floor.'

'You don't have to, you know . . . sitting is not obligatory. We could walk out. Outside the building.'

'Er . . . if we walk out they'll just tell us to keep on walking to the welfare office,' said Candy, digging half a Marlboro from her pocket and lighting it off Tom's match. 'Bailey'll make sure of that.'

'You ain't walking your ass out no-where,' said Levi, cruelly impersonating Bailey's clumsy, jerking rooster head and that half-crouched standing position, which made him look like a four-legged animal only just reared upright, *'Your ass ain't going out of this store unless it's whupped out of this store, 'cos it sure as hell ain't walking out of this store, not now, not no how.'*

Levi's audience laughed ruefully — the impersonation was too accurate. Bailey was in his late forties; unavoidably a tragic figure to the teenagers working under him. They considered such employment for a man over the age of twenty-six to be a humiliating symbol of human limitation. They also knew that Bailey had worked in Tower Records for ten years before this — this heaped tragedy upon tragedy. And then Bailey was painfully overburdened with peculiarities, one of which alone would have sufficed to make him a figure of fun. His overactive thyroid made his eyes start from his head. His jowls gathered like turkey wattle. His uneven Afro often had a foreign object in it — pieces of unidentifiable fluff and, once, a matchstick. His heaving, saddlebag backside looked distinctly female from behind. He had a tendency towards malapropism so extreme even a gang of near-illiterate teenagers could notice it, and the skin on his hands peeled and bled, the worst example of the psoriasis that also showed up in milder patches on his neck and forehead. It boggled Levi's mind that anyone could pull such a short straw from God. Despite these physical difficulties (or maybe because of them) Bailey was a hound-dog. He followed LaShonda around the store and touched her when he didn't need to. He went too far once, putting his arm round her waist and suffering the humiliation of a LaShonda dressing-down ('Don't you *dare* tell me to lower my voice, I swear to God — I'll *scream* this place down, I'll send the roof tiles flying!') in front of everybody. But Bailey never learned; two days later he was hound-dogging her again.

Impersonations of Bailey were the stock-in-trade of the floor staff. LaShonda did one, Levi did one, Jamal did one — the white employees were more hesitant, not wishing to cross the line from imperson-ation to possible racial slur. In contrast, Levi and LaShonda were unrestrained, emphasizing every grotesquerie, as if his ugliness were a personal affront to their own beauty.

'*Fuck* Bailey,' insisted Levi. 'Come on, man, let's walk out. Come on, Mikey, you're with me, right?'

Mike chewed the side of his face like the current President. 'I'm just not really sure what it would achieve. I guess I figure Candy's right — we'll just get fired.'

'What . . . they're gonna fire all of us?'

'Probably,' said Mike.

'You know, man,' said Tom, pulling hard on his rollie, 'I don't want to work Christmas Day either, but maybe we need to think it through a bit more. Just walking out doesn't really seem viable . . . like, if we all wrote a letter to management and signed it maybe . . .'

'*Dear Motherfuckers,*' said Levi, holding an imaginary pen and screwing his Bailey face into a look of comic concentration. '*Thank you for your letter of the twelfth. I really could not give a fuck. Get your asses back to work. Yours sincerely, Mister Bailey.'*

They all laughed, but it was harassed, bullied laughter, as if Levi had reached into their throats and pulled it out. Sometimes Levi wondered if his colleagues were scared of him. 'When you think of how much money this place makes,' said Tom, unifyingly, drawing approving noises from the rest, 'and they can't close for one lousy day? Who even buys CDs on Christmas morning? It's really twisted.'

'That's what I'm saying,' said Levi, and they were all silent for a minute looking out over the deserted back lot, a non-place where nothing happened except lines of trash cans overflowing with discarded polythene packaging and a basketball hoop that no one was allowed to use. A pink-streaked winter sky, with the clarity of heatless sunlight, gave a sting to the bleak prospect of returning to work in the next thirty seconds. The sound of the fire door's bar being shunted downwards ended this quiet. Tom went to help pull it open, thinking it was tiny Gina, but it was Bailey pushing against him, sending him back three steps.

'Sorry — I didn't realize —' said Tom, releasing his own hand from the spot

337

where Bailey's psoriatic fingers were pressing. Bailey came blinking into the sun like a cave animal. He had his megastore cap on backwards. There was a strong streak of perversity in Bailey, born of his isolation, which pushed him to pursue these feeble eccentricities. It was his way of at least knowing the cause of, and therefore in some way controlling, the contempt directed at him.

'So here's where all my staff is at,' he said, his manner, as ever, vaguely autistic, speaking to a point just over their heads. 'I was wondering about that. Everybody come out to smoke at the same time?'

'Yeah . . . yep,' said Tom, throwing his smoke to the floor and stepping on it.

'Kill you dead, that will,' said Bailey sombrely, seeming to predict not warn. 'And you too, young lady — kill you dead.'

'It's a calculated risk,' said Candy quietly.

'Excuse me?'

Candy shook her head and put her Marlboro out against the cement wall.

'So,' said Bailey, smiling strainedly, 'I hear you been organizing a coop against me. Grapevine — little bird told me. Organizing a coop. And here you all are.'

Tom looked confusedly at Mike and vice versa.

'Sorry, Mr Bailey,' said Tom. 'Sorry — what did you say?'

'A coop, you're organizing one. Plotting against me out here. I just came to see how that's working out for you.'

'*A coup —*' said Tom, very quietly correcting Bailey for his own comprehension. 'Like a revolution.'

Levi, who heard him, and had not understood the initial mistake or known the word 'coup' until this moment, laughed loudly.

'Coop? Bailey, that's like some thing for chickens, man. We organizing a coop? How's that work?'

Candy and Mike sniggered. Tom turned away to gulp his laugh down like an aspirin. Bailey's hopeful face, hopeful a moment earlier of triumph, broke down into confusion and anger.

'You know what I mean. Anyway — ain't nothing can be changed about store policy, so if anybody here don't like it, they more than welcome to leave this current employment. No point in plotting nothing. Now everybody get back to work.'

But Levi was still laughing. 'That ain't even legal — you can't coop nobody up. Some of us got girls to go home to, man. Fact is, I *wanna* be cooped up with my girl come Christmas Day — I'm sure you do too, Bailey. So we just want to find some way that we can all come to, like, an arrangement about that. Come on, Bailey — you don't want to coop us up in this store on Christmas. Come on, brother.'

Bailey looked closely at Levi. All the other kids had stepped back a little into the alcove by the door, signalling an intention to leave. Levi stood firmly where he was.

'But there ain't nothing to talk about,' said Bailey in a low, resolved tone. 'That's the instruction — do you get that?'

'Umm, can I?' said Tom, taking a step forward. 'Mister Bailey, we're not trying to irritate you, but we were just considering whether . . .'

Bailey waved him off. There was nobody else in this back lot. Just Levi.

'Do you get that? This comes from above my head and it's done. Can't be changed. You get that, Levi?'

Levi shrugged and turned from Bailey slightly, just enough to show how little this stand-off meant to him.

'I *get* it . . . I just think it's bullshit, that's all.'

Candy whistled. Mike pushed the fire-exit door open and held it, waiting for the others.

'Tom — all of you, get yourselves back to work — *now,*' said Bailey, scratching one hand with the other. The welts were pink and raw. 'Levi, stay where you are.'

'It's not just Levi, we all feel —' tried Tom bravely, but again Bailey held a finger up in the air to stop him.

'Right *now,* if it ain't inconveniating you too much. Somebody's got to work round here.'

Tom offered a look of pity to Levi and followed Mike and Candy back to work. The fire door swung shut, very slowly, pushing out a little of the warm store air into this barren cement place. At last the judder of the lock sounded and echoed across the back lot. Bailey took a few steps closer to Levi. Levi kept his arms folded high on his chest, but Bailey's face this close was a shocking thing and Levi could not help blinking over and over.

'*Don't — act — like — a — nigger — with — me — Levi,*' said Bailey in a whisper, each word with a momentum of its own, like darts he was throwing at a target. 'I see you, acting up, trying to make me look stupid — thinking you're all that, 'cos you're the only brother any of these kids met in they whole lives. Let me tell you something. *I know where you're from, brother.*'

341

'*What?*' said Levi, his belly still turning over after the shocking plummet invoked by the strange word — like a speed bump in the sentence — never before said to him in anger. Bailey turned his back on Levi and reached out for the fire door, his upper body sadly hunched over.

'You know what it means.'

'What are you talking about, man? Bailey, why you talking to me like that?'

'It's *Mister* Bailey,' said Bailey, turning back. 'I'm senior to you here. 'Case you ain't noticed. Why am I talking to *you?* Like what? How did you just talk to me in front of them kids?'

'I was just saying that —'

'I *know* where you're from. Those kids don't know shit, but *I* know. They nice suburban kids. They think anyone in a pair of baggy jeans is a gangsta. But you can't fool me. I know where you *pretend to be from,*' he said, his anger newly virulent, still holding the door but leaning in towards Levi. 'Because that's where *I'm from* — but you don't see me acting like a nigger. You better watch yourself, boy.'

'Excuse me?' Levi's fury was backed on either side by forlorn terror. He was a kid and this was a man, speaking to him in a manner, Levi felt sure, he would not use when speaking to the other kids who worked here. This was not the world of the mega-store any more, where everyone was family and 'Respect' was one of the five daily 'personal conduct' reminders written on the board in the coffee room. They had fallen through a loophole of law and propriety and safety.

'I've said what I had to say, I ain't saying no more. Now get your black ass back in there and do some work. And don't *ever* talk to me like that again in front of those kids. Are we clear?'

Levi made a show of walking past Bailey, shaking his head furiously, supposedly bitching to himself, straight on through the fourth floor, past Candy and Tom, ignoring their questions, performing his exaggerated limp as if a gun were weighing down his left side. And the walk gathered speed and direction: suddenly he was throwing off the baseball cap and punting it with his toe so it flew up over the balcony, tracing a pretty arc before drifting down four storeys. When Bailey shouted after him, asking where in the hell Levi thought he was going, Levi suddenly understood where he was going and gave Bailey the finger. Two minutes later he was in the basement, and five minutes after that he was back on the street in his own clothes. An impulsive decision had pro-pelled him out of the mega-store; now the consequences caught up with him, pressing their heavy hands to his shoulders, slowing his stride. Halfway down Newbury Street he stopped altogether. He leaned against the railings of a small churchyard. Two fat tears welled up; he stopped them in the hub of his palms. *Fuck* that. He took clean cold air into his lungs and put his chin on his chest. On the practical side this was very bad — it was a nightmare, at the best of times, getting a dollar out of either of his parents, but now? Zora said he was crazy to think this was divorce time, but what else was it when two people couldn't even eat a meal together? And then you ask one of them for five dollars and they tell you to go ask the other . . . Sometimes it was like: *Are we rich or aren't we? We live in this big ass house — why do I have to beg for ten dollars?*

A long green leaf, not yet crisp, hung near Levi at eye level. He pulled it down and began discreetly making a skeleton of it, pulling strips of flesh away from its spine. And but the thing was, if he didn't get his measly thirty-five dollars a week, then there was no money to escape

Wellington on a Saturday night, no chance to dance with all those kids, all those *girls* who didn't give a fuck who the hell Gramski was or why whoever — *Rem-bran* — was no good. Sometimes he felt that those thirty-five dollars were the only thing that kept him half normal, half sane, half *black*. Levi held his leaf up to the light for a minute to admire his own handiwork. Then he screwed it into a damp green ball in his hand and dropped it to the floor.

'Par*don*, par*don*, par*don*, par*don*.'

It was a gruff French accent coming from a tall skinny guy. He was edging Levi off his day-dreaming spot by the railings, and now there were half a dozen other guys or more, bustling, laying down huge bed sheets stuffed with goods and knotted at the top like plum puddings; now untying them, revealing CDs, DVDs, posters and, incongruously, handbags. Levi stepped off the sidewalk and watched them, at first absently and then with interest. One of them pressed play on a big boom-box, and summery hip-hop, out of place but welcome on this chill autumn day, blew up into the passing shoppers. Many people tutted; Levi smiled. It was a joint he knew and loved. Slipping effortlessly between the high hat and the drum or whatever machine it is that makes those noises these days, Levi began to nod his head and watch the activity of the men, itself a visual expression of the frantic bass line. Like a patchwork quilt knitting together a zillion computer-generated colours, the DVD covers were lined up in rows, each title more scandalously recent than the last, less likely to be legal. One of the guys swiftly hung the bags off the railings, and these new announcements of colour brought a rush of delight to Levi, so strong because so unexpected, so queerly timed. The men sang and bantered among themselves, as if prospective customers didn't even matter. Their display was so magnificent no further hustling was required. They struck Levi as splendid beings, from quite another planet than the one he had been in only five minutes ago — spring-footed, athletic, carelessly loud, coal-black, laughing, immune to the frowns of Bostonian ladies passing with their stupid little dogs. Brothers. An unanchored sentence of Howard's from his morning lecture — now floating free of the tedious original context — meandered into Levi's consciousness. *Situationists transform the urban landscape.*

'Hey, you want hip-hop? Hip-hop? We got your hip-hop here,' said one of the guys, like an actor breaking the suspended disbelief of the fourth wall. He reached out his long fingers to Levi, and Levi walked towards him at once.

6

'Mom — what are you *doing?*'

Is it unusual, then, to be sat thus on a raised step, half in the kitchen and half in the garden, your feet numb on the chill flagstones, waiting for winter? Kiki had been quite content for the best part of an hour, just like this, watching the pitchy wind bully the last leaves to the ground — now here was her daughter, incredulous. The older we get the more our kids seem to want us to walk in a very straight line with our arms pinned to our sides, our faces cast with the neutral expression of mannequins, not looking to the left, not looking to the right, and not — *please not* — waiting for winter. They must find it comforting.

'Mom — *hello?* It's blowing a gale out there.'

'Oh — morning, baby. No, I'm not cold.'

'*I'm* cold. Can you close the door? What are you doing?'

'I don't know, really. Looking.'

'At?'

'Just looking.'

Zora gawped at her mother crudely and then, just as abruptly, lost interest. She set about opening cabinets.

'Okay . . . Have you had breakfast?'

'No, honey, I ate . . .' Kiki put both hands on her knees to signify a decision; she wanted Zora to feel her mother was not an eccentric. That she had been sitting for a reason and now would rise for a reason. She said, 'That garden could do with a little TLC. The grass is full of dead leaves. Nobody picked up any of the apples, they're just rotting there.'

But Zora could find nothing interesting in this.

'Well,' she replied, sighing, 'I'm going to make toast and scrambled. I can have scrambled once on a Sunday — I feel like I earned it, I swam my butt off this week. We got eggs?'

'Cupboard — far right.'

Kiki tucked her feet back under her. She was cold now, after all. Using the thin rubber edges of the sliding doors as support, she hauled her body up off the ground. A squirrel, whose progress she'd been following, finally succeeded in tearing open the netted ball of fat and nuts Kiki had left for the birds, and now stood just where she'd hoped he would half an hour earlier, right on the flagstones before her, with his question-mark of a tail quivering in the northeaster.

'Zoor, look at this little guy.'

'I never *understand* that — how do eggs not go in the fridge? You're the only person I have ever met who believes that. Eggs — fridge. It's so *basic*.'

Kiki closed the sliding doors and went over to the cork notice board, where bills and birthday cards, photos and newspaper clippings were pinned. She began lifting the layers of paper, looking under receipts and behind the calendar. Nothing ever got taken down from here. There was still a picture of the first Bush with a dartboard superimposed over his face. Still, in the top left-hand corner, a huge button bought in New York's Union Square in the mid eighties: *I myself have never been able to figure out precisely what feminism is. I only know that people call me a feminist whenever I express sentiments that differentiate me from a doormat.* Long ago someone had spilled something on it, and the quote had yellowed and curled like parchment, shrinking between its plastic and metal covers.

'Zoor, do we still have the pool guy's number? I should call him. It's getting out of hand out there.'

Zora shook her head quickly, a vibration of perplexed disinterest.

'Eyeano. Ask Dad.'

'Honey, put the extractor fan on. The smoke alarm'll go.'

Kiki, fearing her daughter's infamous clumsiness, raised her hands to her cheeks as Zora unhooked a frying pan from the collection of same hanging from a rack above the oven. Nothing was dropped. Now the fan machine started up, conveniently loud and insensitive to nuance — mechanical background noise to fill up all the gaps in the room, in the conversation.

'Where is everybody? It's late.'

'I don't even think Levi came home last night. Your dad's asleep, I think.'

'You *think*? You don't know?'

They looked at each other, the older woman closely examining the younger face. She struggled to find a route through this cool, featureless irony Zora and her friends seemed to cherish so.

'What?' said Zora, archly innocent, repelling genuine inquiry. 'I don't know these things. I don't know what's happening with the sleeping arrangements.'

She turned away again and opened the double doors of the fridge, taking a step forward into its cavernous interior. 'I just prefer to leave you two to have your little soap opera. If the drama must continue, it must continue.'

'There's no drama.'

Zora used both hands to lift up a massive carton of juice, high and away from her body, like a cup she'd won.

'Whatever you say, Mom.'

'Just do me a favour, Zoor — just cool it this morning. I'd like to get through the day without everybody yelling.'

'Like I said — whatever you say.'

Kiki sat down at the kitchen table. She worked a wood-wormed groove at its edge with her finger. She could hear Zora's eggs sizzle and spit under the pressure of the cook's impatience, the stench of burning pans already part of the process from the moment the gas was lit.

'So where'd Levi get to?' asked Zora brightly.

'I have no idea. I haven't seen him since yesterday morning. He didn't come back from work.'

'I hope he's using protection.'

'Oh, *God*, Zora.'

'What? You should make a list of the

subjects we're not allowed to talk about any more. So I know.'

'I think he went to a club. I'm not sure. I can't keep him home.'

'No, Mom,' said Zora in a two-note trill, meant to pacify the paranoid, the tediously menopausal. 'Of course no one's saying that.'

'As long as he's in on school nights. I don't know what else I can do. I'm his mother — I'm not a jailer.'

'Look, I don't *care*. Salt?'

'On the side — just there.'

'So, you doing anything today? Yoga?'

Kiki flopped forward in her chair and held her calves in both hands. The weight of herself tugged her further forward than most people. If she wanted, she could put her palms flat on the floor.

'I don't think so. I tore something last time.'

'Well, I won't be here for lunch. I can only really eat one meal a day at this point. I'm going shopping — you should come,' offered Zora, without enthusiasm. 'We haven't done that in for ever. I need some new shit to wear. I *hate* everything I own.'

'You look fine.'

'Right. I look fine. Except I don't,' said Zora, tugging sadly at her man's nightshirt.

This was why Kiki had dreaded having girls: she knew she wouldn't be able to protect them from self-disgust. To that end she had tried banning television in the early years, and never had a lipstick or a woman's magazine crossed the threshold of the Belsey home to Kiki's knowledge, but these and other precautionary measures had made no difference. It was in the *air*, or so it seemed to Kiki, this hatred of women and their bodies — it seeped in with every draught in the house; people brought it home on their shoes, they breathed it in off their newspapers. There was no way to control it.

'I can't face the mall today. I might go and see Carlene, actually.'

Zora swivelled round from her eggs. 'Carlene Kipps?'

'I saw her Tuesday — she's not too well, I think. I might take the lasagne in the icebox.'

'*You're* taking a frozen lasagne to Mrs Kipps,' said Zora, pointing at Kiki with the wooden spoon in her hand.

'I might do.'

'So you're friends now?'

'I think so.'

'OK,' said Zora dubiously and returned her attention to the stove.

'Is that a problem?'

'I guess not.'

Kiki closed her eyes for a long beat and awaited the continuation.

'I mean . . . I guess you know Monty is going for Dad real bad at the moment. He wrote another totally vile piece in the *Herald*. He wants to give his toxic lectures, and he's accusing Howard of — get this — *curtailing his right to free speech*. It freaks me *out* to think about how much that man must just be *torn up* by self-hatred. By the time he's done we won't have any affirmative action policy at *all*, basically. And Howard'll probably be out of a job.'

'Oh, I'm sure it's not as serious as all that.'

'Maybe you were reading a different article.' Kiki heard steel enter Zora's voice. The strength of her daughter's burgeoning will, the adolescent intensity of it, was something they were both discovering together, year on year. Kiki felt herself a whetstone that Zora was sharpening herself against.

'I didn't read it,' said Kiki, flexing her own will. 'I'm kind of trying to run with the idea that there's a world outside Wellington.'

'I just don't really see the point in taking

a lasagne to someone who basically believes you're going to burn in the fires of hell, that's all.'

'No, you wouldn't.'

'Explain it to me.'

Kiki conceded the ground with a sigh. 'Let's drop it, OK.'

'Dropped. Duly dropped. Down the big hole where everything gets dropped.'

'How are your eggs?'

'Spiffing,' said Zora, in the tone of the Woosters and pointedly took a seat at the breakfast bar, her back to her mother.

They sat in silence for a few minutes, with the fan doing its useful work. Then, remotely, the television was roused. Kiki watched, but could not hear, a wild gang of raggedy boys, in the hand-me-down sportswear of wealthier countries than their own, career down a tropical back alley. Halfway between a tribal dance and a riot. They punched their fists in the air and seemed to sing. The next shot was of another boy, hurling a simple home-made firebomb. The camera followed its trajectory, showed the explosion rocking an empty army jeep, which had itself already collided with a palm tree. The channel changed once, twice. Zora settled on the weather: a five-day forecast that showed the numbers plummeting, steadily but severely. This told Kiki exactly how long she had left to wait. By next Sunday, winter would be here.

'How's school?' Kiki attempted.

'Fine. I'm going to need the car Tuesday night — we're going on a kind of *field trip* — to the Bus Stop.'

'The club? That'll be fun, right?'

'I guess. It's for Claire's class.'

Kiki, who had assumed this already, said nothing.

'So, is that cool?'

'I don't know what you're asking me. The car's cool, sure.'

'I mean, you haven't said anything,' said Zora, directing her comment to the television screen. 'I wouldn't even take this class, but it really . . . shit like that counts when it comes to grad school — she's a *name,* and it's stupid, but it makes a difference.'

'I don't have a problem, Zoor. You're the one making it a problem. It sounds great. Good for you.'

They were speaking to each other with tinkling officiousness, like two administrators filling out a form together.

'I guess I just don't want to feel bad about it.'

'Nobody's asking you to feel bad. Have you had your first class?'

Zora skewered a bit of toast on her fork, brought it to her mouth but spoke first. 'We had an initial session — just setting out parameters. Some people read stuff out. It was a pretty mixed bag. Lot of Plath wannabees, I'm not too worried.'

'Right.'

Kiki looked over her shoulder to the garden, and, thinking again about water and leaves and the ways they complicate each other, a memory of the summer rose suddenly to the surface of her mind. 'Didn't that . . . remember that boy — the handsome one, at the Mozart — didn't he do stuff at the Bus Stop?'

Zora chewed tightly on her toast and spoke only from the very corner of her mouth. 'Maybe — I don't really remember.'

'He had *such* a great face.'

Zora lifted up the remote and changed over to the local public access channel. Noam Chomsky was sitting at a desk. He spoke directly to camera, his large expressive hands making swelling circular movements in front of him.

'You don't notice that kind of thing.'

'Mom.'

'Well, it's interesting. You don't. You're very high-minded. That's an admirable quality.'

Zora turned up Noam and leaned towards the screen, ear first.

'I guess I'm just looking for something a little more . . . cerebral.'

'When I was your age I used to follow boys down the street 'cos they looked cute from the back. I liked to watch them shimmy and shake.'

Zora looked at her mother with wonder. 'I'm trying to *eat?*'

A sound of a door opening. Kiki stood up. Her heart, having inexplicably relocated to her right thigh, beat harshly and threatened to unbalance her. She took a step towards the back hallway.

'Was that Levi's door?'

'I saw that guy, as it happens . . . weirdly . . . last week in the street. His name's Carl or something.'

'You did? How was he? *Levi — is that you?*'

'I don't know how he *was*, he didn't give me his life story — he seemed fine. He's a little creepy actually. Full of himself to an extent. I think "street poet" just probably means . . .' said Zora, fading as her mother hurried across the room to greet her son.

'Levi! Good afternoon, baby. I didn't even know you were down there.'

Levi pressed the knuckles of his thumbs

into his sleep-encrusted eyes and met his mother and her relief halfway. Without struggle, he allowed himself to be taken into the expansive familiarity of her chest.

'Honey, you look *bad*. What time you get in?'

Levi looked up weakly for a moment before burrowing back in.

'Zora — make him some tea. Poor honey can't speak.'

'Let him make his own tea. The poor honey shouldn't drink so much.'

This enlivened Levi. He freed himself from his mother and strode over to the kettle. 'Man, shut up.'

'*You* shut up.'

'I di'unt drink anything anyhow — I'm just tired. I got back late.'

'Nobody heard you come in — I worry, you know. Where were you?' asked Kiki.

'Nowhere — I just met some guys, I was hanging with them — we went on to a club. It was cool. Mom, is there any breakfast?'

'How was work?'

'Fine. Same. Is there breakfast?'

'These eggs are *mine*,' said Zora, and hunched over, drawing her plate into her chest. 'You know where the cereal is.'

'Shut *up*.'

'Baby, I'm glad you had a good time, but

that's it now. I don't want you out any night this week, OK?'

Levi's voice leaped several decibels in his defence: 'I don't even *want* to go out.'

'Good, because you got SATs and you got to knuckle down right about now.'

'Oh, wait, man — I got to go out Tuesday.'

'Levi, what did I just say?'

'But I'll be back by eleven. Yo, it's impor'ant.'

'I don't *care.*'

'Seriously — oh, man — these guys I met — they performing — I'll be back by eleven — it's just the Bus Stop — I can get a cab.'

Zora's head perked up from her breakfast. 'Wait — *I'm* going to the Bus Stop on Tuesday.'

'So?'

'So I don't want to see *you* there. I'm going with my class.'

'*So?*'

'Can't you just go some other day?'

'Aw, shut *up,* man. Mom, a'hma be back by eleven. I've got two free periods on Wednesday. Honestly, man. It's cool. I'll come back with Zora.'

'No, you *won't.*'

'Yes, he will,' said Kiki with finality. 'That's the deal. Both back by eleven.'

'*What?*'

Levi performed a little bop of celebration en route to the fridge, adding a special Jacksonesque spin as he passed Zora's chair.

'Wow, that's unfair,' complained Zora. 'This is why I should have gone to college in a different town.'

'You live in this house, you have to help out with family stuff,' said Kiki, getting down to fundamentals in order to defend a decision whose unfairness she had already privately registered. 'That's the deal. You don't pay any rent here.'

Zora brought her hands together in penitent prayer. 'That's *so* gracious, thank you. *Thank* you for letting me stay in my childhood home.'

'Zoor, don't start messing with me this morning — I mean it, don't even —'

Without anyone noting it, Howard had entered the room. He was fully dressed, even shoed. His hair was wet and combed backwards. It was maybe the first time in a week that Howard and Kiki had stood in the same room like this, albeit ten feet apart, and now with full eye-contact, like two formal, unrelated, full-length portraits turned so as to face each other. While Howard asked the kids to leave the room, Kiki took her time, looking. She saw differently now; that was one of the side-effects. Whether the new way of seeing was the truth, she couldn't say. But it was certainly stark, revelatory. She saw every fold and tremble of his fading prettiness. She found she could muster contempt for even his most neutral physical characteristics. The thin, papery, Caucasian nostril holes. The doughy ears sprouting hairs that he was careful to remove and yet whose ghostly existence she continued to catalogue. The only things that threatened to disturb her resolve were the sheer temporal *layers* of Howard as they presented themselves before her: Howard at twenty-two, at thirty, at forty-five and fifty-one; the difficulty of keeping all these other Howards out of her consciousness; the importance of not being sidetracked, of responding only to this most recent Howard, the 57-year-old Howard. The liar, the heart-breaker, the emotional fraud. She did not flinch.

'What is it, Howard?'

Howard had just finished ushering his resistant children out of the room. They were alone. He turned round quickly, his face a very nothing. He was at a loss as to what to do with his hands and feet, where to stand, what to rest upon.

'There's no "it",' he said softly, and

pulled his cardigan around himself. 'Particularly. I don't know what that question means. *It?* I mean . . . obviously, there's everything.'

Kiki, feeling the power of her position, re-established her folded arms. 'Right. That's very poetic. I guess I'm just not feeling too poetic right now. Is there something you wanted to say to me?'

Howard looked to the floor and shook his head, disappointed, like a scientist getting no data from an elaborately set-up experiment. 'I see,' he said finally and made as if to return to his study, but then turned back at the door. 'Umm . . . Is there a time when we could talk, properly? Like human beings. Who know each other.'

For her part, Kiki had been waiting for a hook. That would do. 'Don't you tell *me* how to behave like a human being. I *know* how to behave like a human being.'

Howard looked up at her, eagerly. 'Of *course* you do.'

'Oh, *fuck you.*'

To accompany this, Kiki did something she hadn't done in years. She gave her husband the finger. Howard looked baffled. In a faraway voice he said, 'No . . . This isn't going to work.'

'No, really? Aren't we having good dia-

363

logue? Are we not interfacing as you'd hoped? Howard, go to the library.'

'How can I talk to you when you're like this? There's no way for me to talk to you.'

His real distress was obvious and for a moment Kiki considered matching it with her own. Instead, she grew still harder inside.

'Well, I'm sorry about that.'

Kiki became aware, suddenly, of her own belly and the way it hung over her leggings; she reorganized it under the elastic of her underwear, a move that made her feel more protected somehow, more solid. Howard placed both hands on the sideboard like a lawyer giving his summation to an invisible jury.

'Clearly we need to talk about what's going to happen next. At least . . . well, the kids need to know.'

Kiki released a flare of laughter. 'Sugar, you're the one who makes the decisions. We just roll with the punches as they come. Who knows what you'll do to this family next. You know? Nobody can know that.'

'Kiki —'

'What? What do you want me to *say?'*

'Nothing!' flashed Howard, and then he reconstituted his self-control, lowering his voice, clasping his hands together. 'Nothing . . . the onus is on me, I know

364

that. It's for me to — to — explain my narrative in a way that's comprehensible . . . and achieves an . . . I don't know, explanation, I suppose, in terms of motivation . . .'

'Don't worry — I comprehend your narrative, Howard. Otherwise known as, I got your number. *We're not in your class now.* Are you able to talk to me in a way that means *anything?*'

To this Howard groaned. He abhorred the reference (an old war-wound in this marriage, continually reopened) to a separation between his 'academic' language and his wife's so-called 'personal' language. She could always say — and often did — 'we're not in your class now' and that would always be true, but he would never, *never* concede the point that Kiki's language was any more emotionally expressive than his own. Even now, *even now,* this oldest argument of their union was rousing its furious armies in his mind, preparing for one more appearance in the field. It took an enormous act of will on his part to divert his forces.

'Look, let's not . . . All I want to say is that I feel . . . you know, that we seem to be taking rather a giant step backwards. In the spring it seemed that we were going to . . . I don't know. Survive this, I suppose.'

What came next burst from Kiki's chest like an aria she was singing. 'In the *spring I didn't know you were fucking one of our friends.* In the spring it was just someone, a nameless someone, it was a one-night stand — now it's *Claire Malcolm.* It went on for weeks!'

'*Three* weeks,' said Howard, almost inaudibly.

'I *asked* you to tell me the truth, and you *looked me in the eye and lied to me.* Like every other middle-aged *asshole* in this town lying to his *idiot* wife. I can't believe how much contempt you have for me. *Claire Malcolm is our friend.* Warren is our *friend.*'

'All right. Well, let's talk about that.'

'Oh, can we? Can we really?'

'Of course. If you want to.'

'Do I get to ask the questions?'

'If you like.'

'Why did you fuck Claire Malcolm?'

'Bloody hell, Keeks, please —'

'Sorry, is that too obvious? Does that offend your sensibility, Howard?'

'*No.* Of course not — don't be so fatuous . . . It's obviously painful for me to try to . . . explain something so banal, in a way —'

'Oh, I'm *so* sorry your dick offends your

intellectual sensibilities. It must be terrible. There's your subtle, wonderful, intricate brain and all the time it turns out your dick is a vulgar, stupid little prick. That must be a real bitch for you!'

Howard picked up his satchel, which, Kiki only now noticed, was lying on the floor by his feet. 'I'm going to go now,' he said, and took the route by the right side of the table so he might physically avoid a confrontation. Kiki was not averse, in very bad times, to kicking and punching, and he was not averse to holding her wrists tightly in his hands until she stopped.

'A little *white* woman,' yelled Kiki across the room, unable now to control herself. 'A tiny little white woman I could fit in my *pocket.*'

'I'm going. You're being ludicrous.'

'And I don't know why I'm surprised. You don't even notice it — you *never* notice. You think it's normal. Everywhere we go, I'm alone in this . . . this *sea* of white. I barely *know* any black folk any more, Howie. My whole life is white. I don't see any black folk unless they be cleaning under my feet in the fucking café in your *fucking* college. Or pushing a fucking hospital bed through a corridor. I *staked my whole life* on you. And I have no idea any more why I did that.'

Howard stopped underneath an abstract painting on the wall. Its main feature was a piece of thick white plaster, made to look like linen, crumpled up like a rag someone had thrown away. This action of throwing had been caught, by the artist, in mid-flight, with the 'linen' frozen in space, framed by a white wooden box that thrust out from the wall.

'I can't understand you,' he said, looking at her at last. 'You're not making any sense to me. You're hysterical now.'

'I gave up *my life* for you. I don't even know who I am any more.' Kiki fell into a chair and began to weep.

'Oh, God, please . . . please . . . Keeks, don't cry, please.'

'Could you have found anybody less like me if you'd *scoured* the *earth?*' she said, thumping the table with her fist. 'My *leg* weighs more than that woman. What have you made me *look like* in front of everybody in this town? You married a big black bitch and you run off with a fucking leprechaun?'

Howard picked up his keys from the clay boot on the sideboard and walked purposively to the front door.

'I didn't.'

Kiki leaped up and followed him. 'What?

I can't hear you — what?'

'*Nothing.* I'm not allowed to say it.'

'Say. It.'

'All I said was . . .' Howard shrugged fretfully. 'Well, I married a slim black woman, actually. Not that it's relevant.'

Kiki's eyes widened, allowing what was left of the tears to film themselves over her eyeballs. 'Holy *shit.* You want to sue me for breach of contract, Howard? Product expanded without warning?'

'Don't be ridiculous. It's nothing as trite as that. I don't want to get into that. There's a million factors, clearly. This is not the reason people have affairs, and I don't want to have this conversation on this level, I really don't. It's puerile. It's beneath you — it's beneath me.'

'There you go again. Howard, you should talk to your cock so the two of you are singing from the same hymn book. Your cock is beneath you. Literally.' Kiki laughed a little and then cried — childish, formless yelps that came up from her belly, relinquishing everything she had left.

'Look,' said Howard resolutely, and the more she could sense his sympathy draining away from her, the more she wailed. 'I'm trying to be as honest as I can. If you're asking me, obviously physicality is

369

a factor. You have . . . Keeks, you've changed a lot. I don't *care,* but —'

'I staked my *life* on you. I staked my *life.*'

'And I love you. I've always loved you. But I'm not having this discussion.'

'Why can't you tell me the *truth?*'

Howard passed his satchel from his right hand to his left and opened the front door. He was that lawyer again, simplifying a complex case for a desperate, simple-minded client who would not take his advice.

'It's true that men — they respond to beauty . . . it doesn't end for them, this . . . this *concern* with beauty as a physical actuality in the world — and that's clearly imprisoning and it infantilizes . . . but it's *true* and . . . I don't know how else to explain what —'

'Get *away* from me.'

'Fine.'

'I'm not interested in your aesthetic theories. Save them for Claire. She loves them.'

Howard sighed. 'I wasn't giving you a theory.'

'You think there's some great philosophical I-don't-fucking-know-what because you can't keep your dick in your pants? You're not Rembrandt, Howard. And don't kid yourself: honey, I look at boys *all the time* — all the time. I see pretty boys every day of the week, and I think about their cocks, and what they would look like butt naked —'

'You're being really vulgar now.'

'But I'm an *adult,* Howard. And I've chosen my life. I thought you had too. But you're still running after pussy, apparently.'

'But she's not . . .' said Howard, lowering his voice to an exasperated whisper, 'you know . . . she's *our* age, older, I think — you talk as if it were a student like one of Erskine's . . . or . . . But in fact I didn't —'

'You want a fucking *prize?*'

Howard was intent on slamming the door behind him, and Kiki was equally determined to kick it shut. The force of it knocked the plaster picture to the floor.

7

On Tuesday night a water main burst at the corner of Kennedy and Rosebrook. A dark river filled the street, breaking only towards the high ground at its centre. It sloshed either side of Kennedy Square, massing in dirty puddles tinted orange by the streetlights. Zora had parked the family car a block away, intending to wait for her poetry class on the central traffic island, but this too was lapped on all sides by a slurry lake, more an island than ever. The cars sent up sheets of black spray as they went past. Instead she set herself back on the sidewalk, choosing to lean against a cement post in front of a drug store. Here, in this spot, Zora felt confident she would be aware of her class, when they came, at least a moment or two before they were aware of her (this had also been the point of the traffic island). She held a cigarette and struggled to enjoy the sear of it on desiccated winter lips. She watched a little behavioural pattern develop just across the street. People paused at the doorway of the McDonald's, waited for the passing car to displace its gallon of grimy water and then continued on their way, proudly, swiftly adaptable to anything the city could throw at them.

'Anybody call the water board? Or is this the second flood?' inquired a throaty Boston voice, just by Zora's elbow. It was the purple-skinned homeless guy with his coiled beard of solid, grey clumps, with white panda rings around his eyes, as if half his year was spent in Aspen. He was always here, holding a polystyrene cup to hustle for dimes outside the bank, and now he shook this at Zora, laughing gruffly. When she didn't respond, he made his joke again. To escape, she moved forward to the road's edge and looked into the gutters to imply her concern and further investigation of the situation. A patina of frost had collected on top of the puddles here in the potholes and natural gulleys created by uneven asphalt. Some puddles had already resolved themselves into slush, but others maintained their pristine, wafer-thin ice rinks. Zora threw her cigarette on to one of these and at once lit another. She found it difficult, this thing of being alone, awaiting the arrival of a group. She prepared a face as her favourite poet had it — to meet the faces that she met, and it was a procedure that required time and forewarning to function correctly. In fact, when she was not in company it didn't seem to her that she had a face at all . . . And yet in college, she knew she was famed for being opinionated, a 'personality' — the truth was she didn't take these public passions home, or even out of the room, in any serious way. She didn't feel that she *had* any real opinions, or at least not in the way other people seemed to have them. Once the class was finished she saw at once how she might have argued the thing just as viciously and successfully the other way round; defended Flaubert over Foucault; rescued Austen from insult instead of Adorno. Was anyone ever genuinely attached to anything? She had no idea. It was either only Zora who experienced this odd impersonality or it was everybody, and they were all play-acting, as she was. She presumed that this was the revelation college would bring her, at some point. In the meantime, waiting like this, waiting to be come upon by real people, she felt herself to be light, existentially light, and nervously rumbled through possible topics of conversation, a ragbag of weighty ideas she carried around in her brain to lend herself the appearance of substance. Even on this short trip to the bohemian end of Wellington — a journey that, having been traversed by car, offered no opportunity whatsoever for reading — she had brought along, in her knapsack, three novels and a short tract by De Beauvoir on ambiguity — so much ballast to stop her floating away, up and over the flood, into the night sky.

'The *Zor*meister — rocking with the salt of the *earth*.'

At her right were her friends, greeting her; at her left, the homeless guy, just at her shoulder, from whom she now moved away, laughing stupidly at the idea of any connection between them. She was hugged and shaken. Here were people, friends. A boy called Ron, of delicate build whose movements were tidy and ironic, who liked to be clean, who liked things Japanese. A girl called Daisy, tall and solid like a swimmer, with an all-American ingénue face, sandy hair and more of a salty manner than she required, given her looks. Daisy liked eighties romantic comedies and Kevin Bacon and thrift-store hand-bags. Hannah was red-headed and freckled, rational, hard-working, mature. She liked Ezra Pound and making her own clothes. Here were people. Here were tastes and buying habits and physical attributes.

'Where's Claire?' asked Zora, looking around them.

' 'Cross the street,' said Ron, holding his hand against his hip. 'With Eddie and Lena and Chantelle and everybody — most of the class came. Claire's *loving* it, naturally.'

'She sent you over?'

'I guess. Ooooh, Dr Belsey. Do you smell trauma?'

Happily, Zora rose to the bait. By virtue of who she was she had information other students could not hope to have. She was their vital link to the inner life of professors. She had no qualms about sharing all she knew.

'Are you *serious?* She totally can't look me in the eye — even in class, when I'm reading she's nodding at the window.'

'I think she's just ADD,' drawled Daisy.

'Attention Dick Deficiency,' said Zora, because she was extremely quick. 'If it doesn't have a dick, it's basically deficient.'

Her little audience guffawed, pretending to a worldliness none of them had earned.

Ron gripped her chummily round the shoulders. 'The wages of sin, etcetera,' he said as they began to walk, and then, 'Whither morality?'

'Whither poetry?' said Hannah.

'Whither my ass?' said Daisy, and nudged Zora for one of her cigarettes. They were smooth and bright, and their timing was wonderful, and they were young and hilarious. It was really something to see, they thought, and this was why they spoke loudly and gestured, inviting onlookers to admire.

'*Tell* me about it,' said Zora, and flicked open the carton.

And so it happened again, the daily miracle whereby interiority opens out and brings to bloom the million-petalled flower of being here, in the world, with other people.

Neither as hard as she had thought it might be nor as easy as it appeared.

The Bus Stop was a Wellington institution. For twenty years it had been a cheap and popular Moroccan restaurant, attracting students, the aged hippies of Kennedy Square, professors, locals and tourists. A first-generation Moroccan family ran it and the food was very good, unpretentious and flavoursome. Although there was no Moroccan diaspora in Wellington to appreciate the authenticity of the lamb tagine or the saffron couscous, this had never tempted the Essakalli family into Americanization. They served what they themselves enjoyed eating and waited for the Wellingtonians to acclimatize, which they did. Only the decor nodded to the town's hunger for kitschy ethnic charm: oak tables inlaid with mother of pearl, low banquette seating buried in multicoloured cushions of harsh goat's wool. Long-necked hookah pipes rested on the high shelves like exotic birds come to roost.

Six years ago, when the Essakallis went into retirement, their son Yousef took over with his German-American wife, Katrin. Unlike his parents, who had merely tolerated the students — their pitchers of beer, fake IDs and requests for ketchup — the younger, more American Yousef enjoyed their presence and understood their needs. It was his idea to convert the restaurant's 150-foot basement into a club space where many different classes and events and parties could take place. Here the visuals of *Star Wars* were shown alongside the soundtrack to *Dr Zhivago.* Here a fleshy, dimpled red-headed lady explained to a gang of willowy freshman girls how to move one's abdomen in tiny increments of clockwise motion, the art of the belly dance. Local rappers performed impromptu sets. It was a favourite stop-off for British guitar bands hoping to rid themselves of nerves before their American tours. Morocco, as it was reimagined in the Bus Stop, was an inclusive place. The black kids from Boston were down with Morocco, down with its essential Arab nature and African soul, the massive hash pipes, the chilli in the food, the infectious rhythms of the music. The white kids from the college were down with Morocco too: they liked its shabby glamour, its cinematic history of non-politicized Orientalism, the cool pointy slippers. The hippies and activists of Kennedy Square — without even really being conscious of it — came more regularly to the Bus Stop now than they had before the war started. It was their way of showing solidarity with foreign suffering. Of all the Bus Stop's regular events, the bi-monthly Spoken Word nights were the greatest sensation. As an art form it practised the same inclusiveness as the venue itself: it made everybody feel at home. Neither rap nor poetry, not formal but also not too wild, it wasn't black, it wasn't white. It was whatever anybody had to say and whoever had the guts to get up on the small boxy stage at the back of the basement and say it. For Claire Malcolm, it was an opportunity each year to show her new students that poetry was a broad church, one that she was not afraid to explore.

Because of these visits, and as a regular of the restaurant, Claire was well known and loved by the Essakallis. Spotting her now, Yousef pushed through the line of people waiting to be seated and helped Claire hold open the double doors so that her kids might come in from the cold. With his arm high on the doorframe, Yousef smiled at each student in turn, and each got the opportunity to admire his emerald eyes, set improbably in a dark, unmistakably Arab face, and large silky curls, untended, like an infant's. Once they had all passed through he carefully bent down to Claire's height and allowed himself to be kissed on both cheeks. During this courtly display, he held on to a little embroidered skullcap that sat on the back of his head. Claire's class loved all this. Many of them were freshmen for whom a visit to the Bus Stop, indeed to Kennedy Square, was as exotic as a trip to Morocco itself.

'*Yousef, ça fait bien trop longtemps!*' cried Claire, stepping back but with both her little hands still gripping his own. She tipped her head girlishly to the side. '*Moi, je deviens toute vieille, et toi, tu rajeunis.*'

Yousef laughed, shook his head and looked appreciatively at the tiny figure before him, swathed in many layers of black shawl. '*Non, c'est pas vrai, c'est pas vrai . . . Vous êtes magnifique, comme toujours.*'

'*Tu me flattes comme un diable. Et comment va la famille?*' asked Claire, and looked over the restaurant to the bar at the far end, where Katrin, waiting to be acknowledged, raised her skinny arm and waved. A naturally angular woman, she was dressed today in a sensual brown wrap dress to accentuate the fact that she was heavily pregnant, with the high-sitting, pointed bump that suggests a boy. She was tearing off raffle tickets and giving them to a line of teenagers who each paid their three dollars and descended into the basement.

'*Bien,*' said Yousef simply, and then, encouraged by Claire's delight at this pure and honest description, extended it in a manner less to her taste, prattling happily about this longed-for pregnancy, his parents' second, deeper retirement to the wilds of Vermont, the growth and success of his restaurant. Claire's poetry class, not understanding French, huddled together behind their teacher, smiling shyly. But Claire always grew tired of other people's prose narratives and now patted Yousef several times on the arm.

'We need a table, darling,' she said, in English, looking over his head into the double line-up of booths on each side of a wide aisle, like pews in a church. Yousef, in turn, was instantly businesslike.

'Yes, of course. For how many are you?'

'I haven't even introduced you,' said Claire, and began to point her finger around her bashful class, finding something wonderful — although based only loosely in fact — to say about everybody. If you played the piano a little, you were described as a maestro. Once acted in a college cabaret? The next Minnelli. Everyone warmed themselves in the generous communal glow. Even Zora — described as 'the brains of the outfit' — began to feel a little of the real, unassailable magic of Claire: she made you feel that just being in *this* moment, doing *this* thing, was the most important and marvellous possibility for you. Claire spoke often in her poetry of the idea of 'fittingness': that is, when your chosen pursuit and your ability to achieve it — no matter how small or insignificant both might be — are matched exactly, are fitting. *This,* Claire argued, is when we become truly human, fully ourselves, beautiful. To swim when your body is made for swimming. To kneel when you feel humble. To drink water when you are thirsty. Or — if one wishes to be grand about it — to write the poem that is exactly the fitting receptacle of the feeling or thought that you hoped to convey. In Claire's presence, you were not faulty or badly designed, no, not at all. You were the fitting receptacle and instrument of your talents and beliefs and desires. This was why students at Wellington applied in their hundreds for her class. Poor Yousef ran out of facial expressions of wonder with which to greet this race of giants who had come to eat at his establishment.

'And how many is this?' he asked again, when Claire had finished.

'Ten, eleven? Actually, darling, we're going to need three booths, I think.'

Settling into the tables was a political matter. The booth to sit in was clearly whichever one contained Claire and, failing that, Zora, but when these two unintentionally chose the same booth, an indecorous struggle began for the vacant seats. The two who found themselves in these prime positions — Ron and Daisy — did little to conceal their joy. By contrast the second booth behind this one was despondently quiet. The stragglers' booth across the room — with only three people in it — openly sulked. Claire too was disappointed. Her own affections rested with other students, not at this table. Ron and Daisy's callow, spiky humour did not amuse her. American humour in general left her cold. She never felt less at home in the States than when confronted with one of those bewildering sitcoms: people walking in, people walking out, gags, laugh tracks, idiocy, irony. Tonight, she would really have preferred to be sitting at the stragglers' table with Chantelle, listening to that saturnine young lady's startling ac-

counts of ghetto life in a bad Boston neighbourhood. Claire was spellbound by this
news of lives so different from her own as
to seem interplanetary. Her own background had been imitational, privileged
and emotionally austere; she had grown up
among American intellectuals and European aristocrats, a cultivated but cold mix.
Five languages, went the line in a very
early poem, the kind of doggerel she wrote
in the early seventies. *And no way to say I
love you.* Or, more importantly, I hate you.
In Chantelle's family both expressions
were slung around the house with operatic
regularity. But Claire would learn nothing
of all that this evening. Instead she was to
be the net over which Ron and Daisy and
Zora lobbed wisecracks. She settled into
her cushions and tried to make the best of
it.

The present conversation concerned a
television show so famous even Claire had
heard of it (although she'd never seen it); it
was being satirized by her three students,
taken apart to reveal unpleasant subtexts;
dark political motives were assigned to it,
and complex theoretical tools used to dis-
mantle its simple, sincere façade. Every
now and then the discussion swerved and
slowed down until it ran alongside actual

politics — the President, the administration — at which point the door was opened and Claire invited in for the ride. She was grateful when the waiter came to take their orders. A little hesitation hovered over the ordering of drinks — all but one of her students, a grad, were under the legal limit. Claire made it clear they were free to do as they wished. Stupid, faux sophisticated drinks — all incompatible with a Moroccan meal — were then ordered: a whiskey and ginger, a Tom Collins, a Cosmopolitan. Claire ordered a bottle of white wine for herself. The drinks were brought swiftly. Even after one gulp, she could see her students freeing themselves of the formality of the classroom. It wasn't the drink itself but merely the licence it gave. 'Oh, I so *needed* that,' came from the adjacent booth, as a mousy little thing called Lena lowered a simple bottle of beer from her lips. Claire smiled to herself and looked at the table top. Every year more students, same but different. She listened with interest to the young men from her class ordering whatever it was they wished to eat. Then came the girls. Daisy ordered a starter, claiming to have eaten earlier (an old trick of Claire's youth); Zora — after much hesitation — ordered a fish tagine without rice, and this order Claire could hear femininely echoed three times in the booth behind. Then it was Claire's turn. She did as she had done for thirty years.

'Just the salad please, thank you.'

Claire passed her menu to the waiter and brought both hands, one on top of the other, down hard on the table.

'So,' she said.

'So,' said Ron and boldly mimicked his teacher's movement.

'How's the class working out for everybody?' asked Claire.

'Good,' said Daisy solidly, but then glanced at Zora and Ron for confirmation. 'I think it's good — and the discussion format will come into its own, I'm sure. Right now it's a little . . .' said Daisy, and Ron finished for her:

'. . . stop and start. You know, because it's a little *intimidating*.' Ron leaned confidentially over the table. 'For freshmen I think, particularly. But those of us who've had some experience are more —'

'But even then, you can be very intimidating,' insisted Zora.

For the first time tonight, Claire looked at Zora Belsey directly. 'Intimidating? How so?'

'Well,' said Zora, faltering a little. Her

contempt for Claire was like the black backing on a mirror; the other side reflected immense personal envy and admiration. 'This is quite intimate and, and, *vulnerable,* what we're bringing to you, these poems. And of course we want proper constructive criticism, but you also can be —'

'It's like: you make it clear,' said Daisy, already slightly drunk, 'who you, like, really prefer. And that's a little demoralizing. Maybe.'

'I don't *prefer* anybody,' protested Claire. 'I'm evaluating poems, not people. You have to guide a poem to its greatness, and we're all doing that, together, communally.'

'Right, right, right,' said Daisy.

'There isn't *anybody,*' said Claire, 'who I don't believe deserved to get into this class.'

'Oh, *completely,*' said Ron fervently, and then in the little silence, concocted a new, more pleasing route for the conversation.

'You know what it is?' he suggested. 'It's just we're all looking at you, and you did this thing so young, and so successfully — and that's *awe*-inspiring.' Here he touched her hand, as his old-fashioned camp somehow freed him to, and she threw her shawl once more over her shoulder, allowing herself to be cast in the diva role. 'And so it's a big deal — it would be weird if it *wasn't* this total bull-in-a-china-shop situation in the room.'

'Elephant in the room,' corrected Claire gently.

'*Right.* God! I'm such an idiot. Bull? Aaaargh.'

'But what was it *like?*' asked Daisy, as Ron flushed maroon. 'I mean — you were *so* young. I'm nineteen and it feels like it's too late for me or something. Right? Doesn't it feel like that? We were just saying about how awe-inspiring Claire is and what it must have been like for her to be so successful so young and stuff,' said Daisy, for the sake of Lena, who now knelt awkwardly by the low table, having made a weak pretence of coming over to pick up the condiment tray. Daisy looked over at Claire, waiting for her to continue the thread. They all looked at her.

'You're asking me what it was like when I started.'

'Yeah — was it *amazing?*'

Claire sighed. She could tell these stories all night long — she often did when people asked. But they had nothing to do with her any more.

'God . . . it was '73, and it was a very

strange time to be a woman poet . . . I was meeting all these amazing people — Ginsberg, and Ferlinghetti, and then finding myself in these insane situations . . . meeting, I don't know, Mick Jagger or whoever, and I felt just very *examined,* very picked over, not just mentally but also personally and *physically* . . . and I suppose I felt somewhat . . . disembodied from myself. You could put it that way. But the next summer I was already gone, I went up to Montana for three years, so . . . things normalize quicker than you'd think. And I was in this beautiful country, in this exceptional *landscape,* and the truth is land like that is what fills you up, it's what nourishes you as an artist . . . I'd get involved with a cornflower, for *days* . . . I mean with its actual, essential *blueness* . . .'

Claire talked on in her loopy way about the earth and its poetry, and her students nodded thoughtfully, but an unmistakable torpor had descended. They would have preferred to hear more about Mick Jagger, or Sam Shepard, the man she'd gone to Montana for, as they already knew from their Googling. Land did not interest them too much. Theirs was the poetry of character, of romantic personalities, of broken hearts and emotional warfare. Claire, who had experienced more than enough of this in her life, populated her poems these days with New England foliage, wildlife, creeks, valleys and mountain ranges. These poems had proved less popular than the sexualized verse of her youth.

The food arrived. Claire was still speaking about the land. Zora, who had been clearly brooding on something, now spoke up. 'But how do you avoid falling into pastoral fallacy — I mean, isn't it a depoliticized reification, all this beauty stuff about landscape? Virgil, Pope, the Romantics. Why idealize?'

'Idealize?' repeated Claire uncertainly. 'I'm not sure I really . . . You know, what I've always felt is, well, for instance, in *The Georgics* —'

'The what?'

'Virgil . . . in *The Georgics,* nature and the pleasures of the pastoral are essential to any . . .' began Claire, but Zora had already stopped listening. Claire's kind of learning was tiresome to her. Claire didn't know anything about theorists, or ideas, or the latest thinking. Sometimes Zora suspected her of being barely intellectual. With her, it was always 'in Plato' or 'in Baudelaire' or 'in Rimbaud', as if we all had time to sit around reading whatever we fancied. Zora blinked impatiently, visibly tracking Claire's sentence, waiting for a period or, failing that, a semicolon in which to insert herself again.

'But after Foucault,' she said, seeing her chance, 'where is there to go with that stuff?'

They were having an intellectual argument. The table was excited. Lena bounced on her heels to keep the blood circulating. Claire felt very tired. She was a poet. How had she ever ended up here, in one of these institutions, these universities, where one must make an argument for everything, even an argument for wanting to write about a chestnut tree?

'Boo.'

Claire and the rest of the table looked up. A tall, handsome brown boy, with five or six guys hanging right behind him, stood by their table. Levi, unfazed by this kind of focused attention, acknowledged it with a nod.

'Eleven thirty, out front, a'right?'

Zora agreed quickly, willing him away.

'Levi? Is that you?'

'Oh, hi, Mizz Malcolm.'

'My *God.* Look at you! So *that's* what all that swimming is for. You're *huge!'*

'Getting that way,' said Levi, rounding

out his shoulders. He didn't smile. He knew about Claire Malcolm, Jerome had told him, and, with his usual judicious ability to see both sides of a thing, he had felt quite reasonable about it. He felt bad for his mom, obviously, but he also understood his father's position. Levi too had loved girls dearly in the past and then played away with other girls for less than honourable reasons and saw nothing heinously wrong with the separation of sex and love into two different categories. But, looking at Claire Malcolm now, he found himself confused. It was yet another example of his father's bizarre tastes. Where was the booty on that? Where was the rack? He felt the unfairness and illogic of this substitution. He made a decision to cut the conversation short as a sign of solidarity with his mother's more generous proportions.

'Well, you look great,' chimed Claire. 'Are you performing tonight?'

'Not definitely. Depends. My boys probably will,' said Levi, flicking his head back in the direction of his companions. 'Anyway, I guess I better be getting down there. Eleven thirty,' he repeated to Zora and walked on.

Claire, who had not missed Levi's silent chastisement, poured herself another large glass of wine and put her knife and fork together over her half-eaten salad. 'We should probably go down too,' she said quietly.

8

The ethnography of the basement was not as it had been on previous visits. From where Claire sat she could see only a few other white people, and no one at all of her own age. This state of affairs need not change things particularly, but it was not quite as she'd expected and it would take a little while to feel comfortable. She was thankful for yoga; yoga allowed her to sit cross-legged on a floor cushion like a much younger woman, camouflaged among her students. On stage, a black girl in a tall headwrap rhymed brashly over the bluesy swing of the small live band behind her. *My womb,* she said, *is the TOMB,* she said, *of your precious misconceptions / I KNOW the identity of your serenity / When YOU claim my hero was blond / Cleopatra? Brother, that's plain wrong / I HEAR the Nubian spirit behind the whitewash / Oh, gosh / My redemption has its OWN intention.* And so on. This was not good. Claire listened to her students' lively discussion about why this was not good. In the spirit of pedagogy she tried to encourage them to be less abusive, more specific. She was only partly successful in this.

'At least she's *conscious,*' said Chantelle, a little guardedly. She was shy of the weight of opinion on the other side. 'I mean, at least it's not "bitch" this and "nigger" that. You know?'

'This stuff makes me want to *die,*' said Zora loudly and put both hands on the top of her head. 'It's so *cheesy.*'

'My vagina / In Carolina / Is much finer / Than yours,' said Ron, walking close (Claire felt) to the racial line, with his exaggerated impression of the girl's feisty head movements and sing-song intonation. But the class fell into hysterics, Zora leading the laughter and so, in a vital way, sanctioning it. Of course, thought Claire, they're less sensitive about all that than we were. If it were 1972 this room would be as silent as a church.

Through the laughter and conversation, the ordering of drinks, the opening and closing of toilet doors, the girl kept going. After ten minutes the fact that the girl was not good stopped being amusing and began, as Claire heard her students put it, 'getting old'. Even the most supportive members in the audience stopped nodding. Conversation grew louder. The MC, who sat on a stool by the side of the stage, switched his mike on to intervene; he begged them for quiet and attention and respect, this last word having some currency in the Bus Stop. But the girl was not good, and soon enough the chatter started up again. Finally, with the ominous promise *'And I WILL rise'*, the girl stopped. A spattering of applause came.

'*Thank* you, Queen Lara,' said the MC, holding his mike very close to his lips like an ice-cream. 'Now, I'm Doc Brown, your MC this eve'nin', and I want to hear you *make some noise for Queen Lara* . . . Sister was *brave* to get up on this stage, takes some guts to do that, man . . . to stand up in front of everybody, talk about yo'womb and shit . . .' Doc Brown allowed himself a chuckle here but then played the straight man once more: 'Nah, on the real, tho, that takes some guts, sho' nuf . . . right? Am I right? Oh, come on, man, put yo hands together, now. Don't be like that. Let's hear it for Queen Lara and her conscious lyrics — now that's *better.*'

Claire's class joined in the reluctant clapping. 'Bring on the poetry!' said Ron, meaning it as a joke, just for his friends, but he had pitched it too loud.

'Bring on the poetry?' repeated Doc Brown, wide-eyed, looking into the darkness for the mystery voice. 'Shit, now how often you get to hear that? See, that's why I *love* the Bus Stop. *Bring on the poetry.* I *know* that be a Wellington kid . . .' Laughter detonated through the basement, loudest among Claire's class itself. '*Bring on the poetry.* We got some educated brothers in here tonight. *Bring on the poetry. Bring on the trigonometry. Bring ON the algebra — bring that shit* ON,' he said, in the 'nerd' voice with which black comedians sometimes imitate white people. 'Well . . . you're in luck, young man, 'cos we about to bring on the poetry, the Spoken Word, the rap, the rhyming — we gon' do *alla* that for you. *Bring on the poetry.* I love that . . . Now: tonight it's up to y'all who wins — we got a *jeroboam* of champagne — yeah, thank you, Mr Wellington, there's your vocabulary word-for-the-day — a *jeroboam* of champagne, which basically means a *whole lot of alcohol.* And you guys got to choose who wins it — all you got to do is make some noise for your favourite. We got a show for you to-night. We got some *Caribbean* brothers in the house, we got some *African* brothers in the house, we got people gonna hit it in *French*, in *Portuguese* — I am reliably informed we got the United Nations of Spoken Word up in here tonight, so, you people be privileged in the *extreme.* Yeah, that's right,' said Doc Brown, responding to the whoops and whistles. 'We getting *international* on yo' *ass.* You know how we do.'

Thus did the show begin. There was support for the first artist, a young man who rhymed stiffly but spoke eloquently of America's latest war. After this came a gawky, lanky girl with ears that thrust through the poker-straight curtains of her long hair. Claire suppressed her own hatred of elaborate metaphor and managed to enjoy the girl's cruel, witty verse about all the useless men she'd known. But then three boys, one after the other, recounted macho tales of street life, the final boy speaking in Portuguese. Here Claire's attention petered out. It happened that Zora sat right in front of her at an evocative angle, her face presenting itself to Claire in profile. Without wanting to, Claire found herself examining it. How much of the girl's father was here! The slight over-bite, the long face, the noble nose! She was getting fat, though; inevitably she would go the way of her mother. Claire rebuked herself for this thought. It was wrong to hate the girl, as it was wrong to hate Howard, or to hate herself. Hate would not help this. It was personal insight that was required. Twice a week at six thirty Claire drove into Boston, to Dr Byford's house in Chapel Hill, and paid him eighty dollars an hour to help her seek out personal insight. Together they tried to comprehend the chaos of pain Claire had unleashed. If one good thing had come out of the past twelve months, it was these sessions: of all her psychiatrists over the years, it was Byford who had brought her closest to breakthrough. So far this much was clear: Claire Malcolm was addicted to self-sabotage. In a pattern so deeply embedded in her life that Byford suspected it of being rooted in her earliest babyhood, Claire compulsively sabotaged all possibilities of personal happiness. It seemed she was convinced that it was not happiness that she deserved. The Howard episode was only the last and most spectacular in a long line of acts of emotional cruelty she had felt impelled to inflict upon herself. You only had to look at the timing. Finally, *finally,* she had found this wonderful blessing, this angel, this *gift,* Warren Crane, a man who (she could not help but list his attributes as Byford encouraged her to do):

(a) Did not consider her a threat.
(b) Did not fear or dread her sexuality or gender.
(c) Did not wish to cripple her mentally.
(d) Did not, at a preconscious level, want her dead.
(e) Did not resent her money, her reputation, her talent or her strength.
(f) Did not wish to interfere with the deep connection she had with the earth — indeed, loved the earth as she did and encouraged her love of it.

She had come to a place of personal joy. Finally, at fifty-three. And so naturally it was the perfect time to sabotage her own life. To this end she had initiated an affair with Howard Belsey, one of her oldest friends. A man for whom she had no sexual desire whatsoever. Looking back on it, it was really too perfect. Howard Belsey — of all people! When Claire leaned into Howard's body that day in the conference room of the Black Studies Department, when she clearly offered herself to him, she had not really known why. By contrast, she had felt all the classic masculine impulses and fantasies surge through her old friend back towards her — the late possibility of other people, of living other lives, of new flesh, of being young again. Howard was releasing a secret, volatile, shameful part of himself. And it was an aspect of himself with which he was unfamiliar, that he had always presumed beneath him; she could sense all of this in the urgent pressure of Howard's hands on her tiny waist, the fumbling speed with which he undressed her. He was surprised by desire. In response Claire had felt nothing comparable. Only sorrow.

Their three-week affair never even met with a bedroom. To go to a bedroom would have been a conscious decision. Instead, in the regular course of their college business, their thrice-weekly after-hours meeting in Howard's office, they would lock the door and gravitate to his huge squishy sofa, upholstered in its ostentatiously English, William Morris ferns. Silently and fiercely they fucked among the foliage, almost always sitting up, with Claire sat perfunctorily atop her colleague, her little freckled legs wrapped about his waist. When they had finished he had a habit of pushing her backwards until she was lying beneath him. Curiously, he laid his big flat hands on her body, on her shoulders, on her flat chest, on her stomach, on the backs of her ankles, on the thin, waxed line of her pubic hair. It seemed a kind of wonder; he was checking that she was all there and this was all real. Then they would get up and dress. *How did that happen again?* They often said this or something like it. A stupid, cowardly, pointless thing to say. Meanwhile sex with Warren was newly ecstatic and always completed with guilty tears, which Warren misinterpreted, in his innocence, as joy. The whole situation was vile, the more so because she couldn't defend it, even to herself; the more so because she was terrified and humbled by the long reach of her miserable, unloved childhood. Still clasping its fingers round her throat all these years later!

Three Tuesdays after the affair began Howard came into her office to tell her it was over. It was the first time either properly acknowledged it had begun. He explained he'd been caught with a condom. It was the same, unopened condom at which Claire had laughed, that afternoon of their second assignation, when Howard had produced it, like an anxious, well-intentioned teenage boy ('Howard, *darling* — that's sweet of you, but my reproductive days are over'). Upon hearing his retelling of it, Claire had wanted to laugh again — it was so typically Howard, such an unnecessary disaster. But what followed was not so funny. He told her that he had confessed, telling Kiki the minimum that needed to be told — that he had been unfaithful. He had not mentioned Claire's name. This was kind, and Claire thanked him for it. He looked at her oddly. He had told this lie to save his wife's feelings, not Claire's face. He finished his short, factual speech. He wobbled a little on his feet. This was a different Howard from the one Claire had known these thirty years. No longer the steely academic who'd always (she suspected) found her slightly ridiculous, who never seemed quite certain what the point of poetry was. That day in her office Howard had looked as if a good, comforting piece of verse was just what he needed. Throughout their friendship, Claire had satirized his scrupulous intellectualism, just as he had teased her about her artistic ideals. It was her old joke that Howard was only human in a theoretical sense. This was the general feeling in Wellington too: his students found it near impossible to imagine that Howard should have a wife, a family, that he went to the bathroom, that he felt love. Claire was not as naive as the students; she knew he did love, and intensely, but she also saw that it was not articulated in him in the normal way. Something about his academic life had changed love for him, changed its nature. Of course, without Kiki, he couldn't function – anyone who knew him knew that much. But it was the kind of marriage you couldn't get a handle on. He was bookish, she was not; he was theoretical, she political. She called a rose a rose. He called it an accumulation of cultural and biological constructions circulating around the mutually attracting binary poles of nature / artifice. Claire had always been curious how a marriage like that worked. Dr Byford went so far as to suggest that this was exactly the reason Claire had chosen to get involved with Howard after all these years. At the moment of her own greatest emotional commitment she intervened in the most successful marriage she knew. And it was true: sitting behind her desk, examining this abandoned, rudderless man, she had felt perversely vindicated. Seeing him like that had meant she was right, after all, about academics. (And shouldn't she know? She'd married three of them.) They had no idea what the hell they were doing. Howard had no way of dealing with his new reality. He was unequal to the task of squaring his sense of himself with what he had done. It was not rational, and therefore, he could not comprehend it. For Claire, their affair was only confirmation of what she knew of the darkest parts of herself. For Howard, it was clearly revelation.

It was horrendous thinking about him, having him refracted through Zora's features. Now that Claire's part in Howard's indiscretion was no longer a secret, the guilt had moved from private indulgence to public punishment. Not that she minded the shame; she had been the mistress on other occasions and had not been especially cowed by it then. But this time it was infuriating and humiliating to be punished for something she'd done with so little desire or will. She was a woman still controlled by the traumas of her girlhood. It made more sense to put her three-year-old self in the dock. As Dr Byford explained, she was really the victim of a vicious, peculiarly female psychological disorder: she felt one thing and did another. She was a stranger to herself.

And were they still like that, she wondered — these new girls, this new generation? Did they still feel one thing and do another? Did they still only want to be wanted? Were they still objects of desire instead of — as Howard might put it — desiring subjects? Thinking of the girls sat cross-legged with her in this basement, of Zora in front of her, of the angry girls who shouted their poetry from the stage — no, she could see no serious change. Still starving themselves, still reading women's magazines that explicitly hate women, still cutting themselves with little knives in places they think can't be seen, still faking their orgasms with men they dislike, still lying to everybody about everything. Strangely, Kiki Belsey had always struck Claire as a wonderful anomaly in exactly this sense. Claire remembered when Howard first met his wife, back when Kiki was a nursing student in New York. At that time her beauty was awesome, almost unspeakable, but more than this she radiated an essential female nature Claire had already imagined in her poetry — natural, honest, powerful, unmediated, full of something like genuine desire. A goddess of the everyday. She was not one of Howard's intellectual set, but she was actively political, and her beliefs were genuine and well expressed. *Womanish,* as they said back then, not *feminine.* For Claire, Kiki was not only evidence of Howard's humanity but proof that a new kind of woman had come into the world as promised, as advertised. Without ever becoming intimates, she felt she could honestly say that she and Kiki had always been fond of each other. Never had she resented Kiki or wished her ill. And here Claire emerged out of herself refocused on Zora's features so that hers was again a sovereign face and not a blur of colour and personal thoughts. It was not possible to make the last leap — to consider what it was Kiki now thought of Claire. To do that was to become subhuman before yourself, the person cast out beyond pity, a Caliban. Nobody can cast themselves out.

A commotion was going on by the stage. The next act was waiting for Doc Brown to finish his introduction. The group was huge. Nine, ten boys? They were the kind of boys who make three times as much noise as their actual number. They jostled each other, shoulder to shoulder, on the way up the steps, and struggled to reach a collection of five or so microphones on stands in front of them — there would not be enough for all. One of them was Levi Belsey.

'Looks like your brother's up,' said Claire, poking Zora lightly in the back.

'Oh, God,' said Zora, peeking through a gap in her fingers. 'Maybe we'll get lucky — maybe he's just the hype man.'

'Hype man?'

'Like a cheerleader. But for rap,' explained Daisy helpfully.

Finally all the boys were on the stage. The band was dismissed. This group had their own tape: a heavy Caribbean beat and jangly keyboards over the top. They all began to speak at once in a loud Creole. That wasn't working. Further jostling decided that one guy should begin. A skinny guy in a hoodie came forward and gave it his all. The language barrier had an interesting effect. The ten boys were clearly eager that their audience understand what was being said; they jumped and whooped and leaned into the crowd, and the crowd could not help but respond, although most understood nothing bar the beat. Levi was indeed the hype man, picking up his microphone every few bars and shouting 'YO!' into it. Some of the younger black kids in the audience rushed the stage in response to the sheer energy of this performance, and here Levi came into his own, encouraging them in English.

'Levi doesn't even *speak* French,' said Zora frowning at the performance. 'I don't think he has any idea what he's hyping.'

But then came the chorus — sung by everyone together, including Levi, in English: 'AH-RIS-TEED, CORRUPTION AND GREED. AND SO WE ALL SEE, WE STILL AIN'T FREE!'

'Nice rhymes,' said Chantelle, laughing. 'Nice and basic.'

'Is this *political?*' asked Daisy with distaste. After two outings, the chorus thankfully dropped back into the manic Creole of the verse. Claire struggled to simultaneously translate for her class. She soon gave it up under the weight of too many unfamiliar terms. Instead, she paraphrased: 'They seem to be angry about America's involvement in Haiti. The rhymes are very . . . crude, is the best way to put it.'

'We have something to do with Haiti?' asked Hannah.

'We have something to do with everywhere,' said Claire.

'And how does your brother know those guys?' asked Daisy.

Zora widened her eyes. 'I have absolutely no idea.'

'I can't hear myself think,' said Ron, and got up to go to the bar.

The fattest boy on the stage now took his turn with a solo. He was also the angriest, and the other boys dropped back in order to give him the space he needed for whatever it was he was angry about.

'It's a very worthy effort,' shouted Claire to her class above the unbearable noise of another chorus. 'They have the power of the troubadour voice . . . But I'd say they have a little to learn about integration of idea and form — you break a form in two if you have all this undigested political fury in it. I think I'm going to go up for a cigarette.' Deftly she rose without the need of putting her hands to the floor.

'I'll come up too,' said Zora, and made heavier work of the same movement.

They made their way through the crowds in the basement and restaurant without conversation. Claire wondered what was coming. Outside, the temperature had dropped another few degrees.

'You want to share? Be quicker.'

'Thank you,' said Claire and accepted the cigarette she was passed. Her fingers trembled a little.

'Those guys are wild,' said Zora. 'It's like, you *so* want them to be good, but —'

'Right.'

'Something to do with trying too hard, I

guess. That's Levi all over.'

They were silent for a minute. 'Zora,' said Claire, letting the wine take her along, 'are we OK?'

'Oh, *absolutely,*' said Zora with a certainty and speed that suggested she'd been waiting for the question all night.

Claire looked at her doubtfully and passed back the cigarette. 'You sure?'

'*Seriously.* We're all adults. And I have no intention of not being an adult.'

Claire smiled stiffly. 'I'm glad.'

'Don't mention it. It's all about compartmentalization.'

'That's very mature of you.'

Zora smiled contentedly. Not for the first time when talking to Howard's daughter Claire felt estranged from her own being, as if she were indeed just another of the six billion extras playing in that fabulous stage show, the worldwide hit called Zora's Life.

'What's important,' said Zora, her voice turning excessively diffident, 'is finding out, you know . . . whether I can actually do this thing, writing.'

'That's a daily discovery,' said Claire evasively. She felt Zora's avid stare; she sensed something important was about to be said. But now the door of the restaurant was thrown open. It was Ron. The diners behind him complained of the draught.

'Oh my *God* — you've got to see this guy. He's amazing. Downstairs. He's blowing everybody *away.*'

'This better be good — we're smoking.'

'Zoor — I'm telling you. He's like Keats with a knapsack.'

The three made their way back downstairs. Once in the basement, they could get only a foot further than the double doors and had to stand. They could hear but not see. The whole audience was on its feet swaying together, the music passing through the crowd like wind through a cornfield. The voice that was so exciting this room expressed itself with precision (it was the first time all night that nobody missed a word) and threw out complicated multisyllabic lines with apparent ease. The chorus was a simple repeated line, sung flat, yet sweetly: *But it ain't like that.* The verses, by contrast, spun a witty, articulate tale about the various obstacles in the spiritual and material progress of a young black man. In the first verse, he was trying to prove he had Native American blood in order to get into the top colleges in the country. This — close to the bone in a college town — drew broad laughter. The following verse, concerning a girlfriend who had gone ahead with an abortion without informing him, included the following rhymes, completed without obvious pause for breath, and at incredible speed:

My life to you seems wrong / Here's me trynta to do these songs / When you paged me / To say 'Carl, baby, I'm two weeks gone' / Dropped the pager / In my teacup / start to feel I could redeem this / Now I know I need to treat ya / Neat and sweet and never cheat ya / in a week I went to see ya / No need to drag my ass on 'Leeza' / Was gonna get my Dr Spock on / Dat's the medic, not the Klingon / But you already spoke with yo' girls at work / And done decided I'm a jerk / Now, since when does workin' Macca D's / Make this bitch the new authority / On my goddamn paternity? / Say what, Boo? Excuse me? / And yeah, I know you figured I'd be pleased / Depopulated by decree — But it ain't like that.

It elicited a spontaneous basement-wide gasp, followed by more laughter. People whistled and clapped.

'Oh, that's quite brilliant,' said Claire to Ron, who in response held his head with both hands and pretended to swoon.

Zora found a Moroccan footstool and climbed on to it. From this vantage point, she gasped and wrung Ron's hand by the wrist. 'Oh my *God* . . . I totally know him.'

For it was Carl, dressed in an old fifties-style football sweater and wearing a neat little multicoloured knapsack. He was pacing the stage in the same relaxed, homely manner with which he'd accompanied Zora to the gates of Wellington College, and he smiled prettily as he spoke, the complex rhymes tripping off his luminous teeth as if he were crooning in a barbershop troupe. The only sign of exertion was the river of sweat that came down his face. Doc Brown, in his enthusiasm, had joined Carl on the stage, and now found himself reduced to hype man, Yo-ing like Levi in the tiny syllabic gaps Carl left in his wake.

'What?' said Ron, unable to hear anything, not even Carl any more, over the roars and whistles of the audience.

'I KNOW THAT GUY.'

'THAT GUY?'

'YES.'

'OH MY *GOD*. IS HE STRAIGHT?'

Zora laughed. The alcohol had done its work on all of them now. She smiled in a knowing way about things she did not know, and swayed with the beat as much as her footstool would allow.

'Let's try to get closer to the stage,' suggested Claire, and in the last minute, following Ron's unabashed elbowed course through the audience, they reached their original seats.

'OH — MY — *WORD!*' yelled Doc Brown, as Carl's tape finished. He held up Carl's right hand like a prizefighter's. 'I think we have a winner — correction: I *know* we have a *champion* —' But Carl released himself from Doc's grip and jumped lightly off the stage on to the floor. Somewhere, underneath the cheering, you could hear the discontented boos of rival factions, but the cheers won out. The Creole boys and Levi were nowhere in sight. From all sides people clapped their hands to Carl's back and rubbed his head fondly.

'Hey — you don't want your jeroboam? Brother's shy — don't want his prize!'

'No, no, no — hold my champagne,' shouted Carl. 'Brother got to wash his face, though. Too much sweat is too much.'

Doc Brown nodded sagely. 'Well said, well said — gotta be fresh and clean. Ain't no doubt. DJ, spin it for us in the interim.'

Music started up and the audience

ceased being an audience and softened into a crowd.

'Bring him *over* here,' insisted Ron, and then to the class: 'Zora knows that boy. We need him over here.'

'You know him? He's very talented,' said Claire.

'I know him this much,' said Zora, signifying an inch between her forefinger and thumb. Just as she said this, she turned and found Carl in front of her. He had in his face the elated buzz of the performer, just landed back in the plebeian world of his public. He registered her; he grabbed her face; he delivered an enormous sweaty kiss full on her mouth. His lips were the softest, most luscious part of a human being she had ever felt against her own skin.

'See that?' he said. '*That* was poetry. I got to go to the john.'

He was about to pass on to the next back slap, the next head rub, when tiny Claire moved into his path. Her class, wary of the potential shame here, cringed behind her.

'Hi!' she said.

Carl looked down and found the obstruction.

'Yeah, thank you, man — thanks,' he said, presuming her message was the same as everybody else's. He tried to get by her, but she caught him by the elbow.

'Are you interested in refining what you have?'

Carl stopped and stared at her. 'Excuse me?'

Claire repeated her question.

Carl frowned. 'How d'you mean *refining?*'

'Look, when you get back from the bathroom,' said Claire, 'come and talk to me and my kids. We're a class, a poetry class, in Wellington. We'd like to talk to you. We have an idea for you.' Her class wondered at her absolute confidence — this must be what comes with age and power.

Carl shrugged and then broke into his smile. He'd won at the Bus Stop. He'd *killed* at the Bus Stop. All was good with the world. He had time for everybody.

'A'ight,' he said.

9

Just before Thanksgiving, a lovely thing happened.

Zora was in Boston, leaving a second-hand bookstore she had never visited before. It was a Thursday, her free day, and, despite a prediction of gale-force winds, she'd gone into town on a whim. She bought a thin volume of Irish verse, and was holding on to her hat and stepping out to the sidewalk, when a cross-country bus pulled up in front of her. Jerome stepped off. Home a day early for the Thanksgiving weekend. He hadn't told anyone how he was coming back or when. The two held each other, as much for stability as for delight while a huge gust tore through them, sending dry leaves into the air and tipping over a garbage can. Before they had a chance to speak, a loud cry of 'Yo!' came from behind them. It was Levi, delivered to their feet by the wind.

'No *way,*' said Jerome, and for a while the three simply repeated this phrase, hugging each other, blocking the sidewalk. It was freezing; the wind was enough to upend a small child. They should all have gone inside somewhere and had coffee, but to leave the spot would have been somehow to abandon the miracle of it, and they weren't quite ready to do that yet. They each felt a powerful need to stop people on the street and explain what had happened. But who would believe it?

'This is *insane.* I don't even ever come this way. I usually get the train!'

'Man, that's freaky. That's just not right,'

said Levi, whose mind naturally lent itself to conspiratorial and mystical phenomena. They shook their heads and laughed, and to relieve the sense of freakiness recounted their journeys to each other, taking care to assert common-sense arguments like 'Well, we're often in Boston towards the end of the week' and 'This is nearest to the T-stop we usually use', but nobody was especially convinced by this and the wonder continued. The urge to tell someone became acute. Jerome called Kiki on his cell. She was sitting in her cubicle (decorated with photographs of these three children), typing doctor's notes into the Beecham Urology Ward's patient records.

'Jay? But when d'you get back, baby? You didn't say anything.'

'Just now — but isn't that amazing?'

Kiki stopped typing and concentrated properly on what she was being told. It was so blustery outside. The window by her cubicle was lashed every few minutes by slick leaves plastering themselves across the glass. Every word of Jerome's came to her like a cry from a ship in a storm.

'You bumped into Zoor?'

'*And* Levi. We're all standing here — right now — we're freaking out!'

In the background Kiki could hear both Zora and Levi asking for the phone.

'Well, I can't believe that — that's crazy. I guess there are more things in heaven and earth, Horatio — right?' This was Kiki's sole literary quotation, and she used it for all uncanny incidents and also those that were, in truth, only slightly uncanny. 'It's like what they say about twins. Vibrations. You must feel each other's presence somehow.'

'But isn't that *insane?*'

Kiki grinned into the mouthpiece, but real enthusiasm failed her. There was a residual melancholy connected to the thought of these three newly coined adults walking freely about the world without her assistance, open to its magic and beauty, available for unusual experiences and not, explicitly not, typing doctor's notes into the Beecham Urology Ward's patient records.

'Isn't Levi meant to be in school? It's two thirty.'

Jerome relayed this query to Levi and offered him the cellphone but now Levi stepped back from it as if it were primed to explode. Placing his legs wide apart and trying to keep his balance in a fierce crosswind, he began energetically mouthing two silent words.

'*What?*' said Jerome.

'Levi,' repeated Kiki, 'School. Why isn't he in school?'

'Free period,' said Jerome, correctly translating Levi's mime. 'He's got a free period.'

'Is that so. Jerome, can I talk to your brother, please?'

'Mom? Mom — you're breaking up, I can't hear you. It's like a tornado out here. I'll call you back when I'm out of the city,' said Jerome, which was childish, but for the moment he and his siblings formed an inviolable gang of three, and he would not be the one to break the delicate bond into which a little coincidence had delivered them. The Belsey children repaired to a nearby café. They sat on stools lined up against the windowpane, looking out over the blasted heath of Boston Common. They caught up with each other's news casually, leaving long, cosy gaps of silence in which to go to work on their muffins and coffees. Jerome — after two months of having to be witty and brilliant in a strange town among strangers — appreciated the gift of it. People talk about the happy quiet that can exist between two lovers, but this too was great; sitting between his sister and his brother, saying nothing, eating. Before the world existed, before it was populated, and before there were wars and jobs and colleges and movies and clothes and opinions and foreign travel — before all of these things there had been only one person, Zora, and only one place: a tent in the living room made from chairs and bed-sheets. After a few years, Levi arrived; space was made for him; it was as if he had always been. Looking at them both now, Jerome found himself in their finger joints and neat conch ears, in their long legs and wild curls. He heard himself in their partial lisps caused by puffy tongues vibrating against slightly noticeable buckteeth. He did not consider if or how or why he loved them. They were just love: they were the first evidence he ever had of love, and they would be the last confirmation of love when everything else fell away.

'Remember that?' Jerome asked Zora, nodding at the Common across the way. 'My big reconciliation idea. Dumb idea. How are they anyway?'

The scene of that family outing was presently stripped of all its leaves and colour in such a radical fashion it was diffi-cult to imagine any of it growing green again.

'They're doing OK. They're married, so. They're as good as can be expected,' said Zora, and slid off her stool to get some more half and half and a slice of cheese-

cake. Somehow if you ordered the cheese-
cake as an afterthought it had fewer
calories in it.

'It's hardest on you,' said Jerome, not
looking at Levi but referring to him. 'You
have to *be* there all the time. It's like
you're in the belly of the beast.'

Levi glossed over this accusation of sto-
icism: 'Eyeano. It's all right, man. I'm out
a lot. You know.'

'The stupid thing is,' continued Jerome,
fiddling with a ring on his pinkie finger,
'Kiki still loves him. It's so obvious. I just
don't *get* that — how you can love
someone who says *no* to the world like that
— I mean, so *consistently?* It's only when
I'm away from home and I'm talking to
non-family people that I can see how psychotic he is. The only music in the house
now is, like, *Japanese electro.* Soon we'll
just have to tap on pieces of wood. This is
a guy who wooed his wife by singing half
of The Magic Flute *outside her apartment.*
Now he won't even let her have a painting
she likes in the house. Because of some de-
ranged theory in his head, everybody else
has to suffer. It's such a denial of *joy* — I
don't even know how you can stand living
there.'

Through a straw, Levi blew bubbles in

his Americano. He swivelled on his stool and, for the third time in fifteen minutes, checked the clock on the back wall.

'Like I say, I'm out a lot. I don't see how it goes down.'

'What I've really realized is Howard has a problem with gratitude,' pressed Jerome, more to himself than to his brother. 'It's like he *knows* he's blessed, but he doesn't know where to put his gratitude because that makes him uncomfortable, because that would be dealing in transcendence — and we all know how he hates to do *that*. So by denying there are any gifts in the world, any essentially valuable things — that's how he shortcircuits the gratitude question. If there are no gifts, then he doesn't have to think about a God who might have given them. But that's where joy *is*. I'm on my knees to God every day. And it's amazing, Lee,' he asserted, turning on his stool to look at Levi's impassive profile, 'it really is.'

'Cool,' said Levi, with total equanimity, God being as welcome within the borders of Levi's conversation as any other subject. 'Everybody got they own way of getting through the day,' he added truthfully and commenced picking the blueberries out of his second blueberry muffin.

'Why do you *do* that?' asked Zora, re-claiming her seat between her brothers.

'I like blueberry *flavour,*' explained Levi, betraying a slight impatience; 'I'm just not that into blue*berries.*'

Now Zora swivelled in her seat so that her back was to her younger brother and she might speak more privately with the elder. 'S'funny you mention that concert . . . So you remember that guy?' said Zora, tapping her fingers on the glass in a vague way meant to suggest that what she was about to say had only just occurred to her. 'The concert guy — who thought I stole his thing — remember?'

'Sure,' said Jerome.

'So he's in my class now. Claire's class.'

'*Claire's* class? The guy from the park?'

'He's an amazing lyricist — as it turns out. We heard him at the Bus Stop — all of the class, we went to see him, and then Claire invited him to sit in. He's been to two sessions.'

Jerome looked into his coffee mug. 'Claire's waifs and strays . . . she should try taking care of her own life.'

'And so, yeah, so it turns out that he's pretty amazing,' said Zora, talking over Jerome, 'and I think you'd be really interested in his stuff, you know . . . narrative poetry

. . . I was saying to him, you should probably . . . because he's so talented, you know, you could, like, invite him round or —'

'He ain't all that,' interjected Levi.

Zora spun round. 'You need to deal with your envy?' She turned back to Jerome and filled him in: 'Levi and — who *were* those guys? — like, some guys he just met in the harbour, right off the boat — anyway, they got *destroyed* by Carl at the Bus Stop. De-*stroyed*. Poor baby. He's smarting.'

'That ain't got nothing to do with it,' said Levi very calmly, without raising his voice. 'I'm just saying he's all right, 'cos that's all he is.'

'*Right.* Whatever.'

'He's just the kind of rapper white folk get excited about.'

'Oh, shut *up.* That's so *pathetic.'*

Levi shrugged. 'It's true. He don't do no wilding out, he got no crunk, no hyphy, no East Coast vibe to test what be happening on the West Coast,' he said, thus happily rendering himself incomprehensible both to his siblings and 99.9 per cent of the world's population. 'That's *my* boys, they got the *suffering people* behind them — that dude just got a dictionary, man.'

'Sorry —' began Jerome, shaking his head to clear it. 'Why would *I* want to invite this guy — Carl — round?'

Zora looked startled. 'No reason. I just
. . . you're back in town. I thought it might
be good for you to make a few friends and
maybe —'

'I can make my own friends, thanks.'

'OK, fine.'

'Good.'

'Fine.'

Zora's silent sulks were always oppressive, and as belligerent as if she were
screaming at you from the top of her lungs.
They ended only with your apology or with
Zora's delivery of something a little poisonous, wrapped up in pretty paper.

'Anyway, a good thing is . . . well, that
Mom's been getting out a lot more,' she
said, taking a spoonful of froth from off the
top of her Mocha. 'It's been liberating for
her, in that way, I think. She sees people
and stuff.'

'That's good — I hoped she would.'

'Yeah . . .' Zora slurped the cream into
her mouth. 'She's seeing a lot of Carlene
Kipps. If you can believe that.' Thus was
the present delivered.

Jerome brought his coffee up to his lips
and took a leisurely sip before replying. 'I
know. She told me.'

'Oh, she did. Yeah . . . Looks like they've

totally come to roost. I mean, the Kippses. Except the son — but he's coming over to get married here, apparently. And Monty's lectures begin after Christmas.'

'Michael?' said Jerome, with what appeared to be genuine fondness. 'No way. Who's he marrying?'

Zora shook her head impatiently. This was not her main business. 'I don't know. Some Christian.'

Jerome brought his cup back down to the table, hard and quick. Zora checked for, and found, that worrying accessory that used to come and go with Jerome, but now seemed to be here to stay: a little gold cross around his neck.

'Dad's going to try to block them, the lectures,' she said rapidly. 'I mean, under the hate crime law. He wants to see the text of the lectures before they happen — he thinks he might get him on homophobic material. I don't think he has a chance. I wish he did — but it's going to be tough. So far all we've been given is the title. It's *wild*. It's too perfect.'

Jerome was silent. He continued to examine the windblown surface of the small lake in the park opposite. It swelled and surged like a bath two fat men were getting into over and over, one at each end.

' "The Ethics of the University — colon — Taking the 'Liberal' out of 'Liberal Arts' ". How *perfect* is that?'

Jerome pulled each of the cuffs of his long black trench coat down over his wrists. First one and then the other. He gripped the tips of the fabric with his fore-fingers and then put each of these bunched fists against his cheeks and rested upon them.

'And Victoria?' he said.

'Hmm? How d'you mean?' inquired Zora innocently, although it was too late for this. A faint growl came into Jerome's mild voice. 'Well, you told me about the rest of them with such *glee* — aren't you going to tell me about her?'

Zora denied the glee adamantly; Jerome insisted on the glee; a typical sibling argument began, concerning subtleties of tone and phrasing that could neither be objectively proved nor rationally questioned.

'Believe me,' said Zora stridently, to finish the thing, 'I don't feel any *glee* in relation to Victoria Kipps. None whatsoever. She's auditing my *class. Dad's* class. There're a million freshman classes she could sit in on — she chooses a sophomore seminar. What's her *problem?*'

Jerome smiled.

428

'It's *not* funny. I don't even know why she turns up. She's purely decorative.'

Jerome gave his sister a look heavy with the implication that he expected more from her. He'd been laying this look on her since they were children, and now Zora defended herself as she always did, by attacking.

'I'm sorry, but I don't like her. I can't pretend I like her when I don't. I do not like her. She's just a typical pretty-girl, power-game playing, deeply shallow human being. She tries to hide it by reading one book by *Barthes* or whatever — *all* she does is quote Barthes; it's so tedious — but then the bottom line is, whenever things get sticky for her she just works her *charms* to her advantage. It's disgusting. Oh, my God, and she has this coterie of boys just following her everywhere, which is *fine* — obviously it's pathetic, but whatever you need to make it through the day . . . but don't fuck up the dynamic of the class with stupid questions that go nowhere. You know? And she's vain. Wow, is she vain. You're lucky to be out of that situation.'

Jerome looked pained. He hated hearing anybody bad-mouthed; anyone except Howard, maybe, and even then he preferred to do his own dirty work. Now he folded his muffin wrapper in half and passed it idly between his fingers like a playing card.

'You don't know her at all. She's not really that vain. She just hasn't settled into her looks. She's still young. She hasn't decided what to do with it yet. It's a powerful thing, you know, to look like that.'

Zora guffawed. 'Oh, she's decided. She's using it as a force of evil.'

Jerome threw his eyes back in his head but laughed along.

'You think I'm joking. She's poisonous. She needs to be stopped. Before she destroys somebody else. I'm serious.'

This went too far. Zora sank into her stool a little, realizing.

'You don't have to say any of that — not for me, anyway,' said Jerome crossly, confusing Zora, who had been expressing nothing but her own feelings. 'Because . . . I don't . . . I don't love her any more.' With this simplest of sentences all the air seemed to rush from him. 'That's what I found out this semester. It was hard — I willed myself. I actually thought I'd never get her face out of my system.' Jerome looked down at the table top and then up and directly into his sister's eyes. 'But I did. I don't love her any more.' This was said with such solemnity and earnestness that Zora wanted to laugh, as they had always laughed in the past at moments like these. But nobody laughed.

'I'm out,' said Levi and bounced off his stool.

Levi's family turned to him in surprise.

'I gotta go,' he reiterated.

'Back to school?' asked Jerome, looking at his own watch.

'Uh-huh,' said Levi because there was no point in worrying people unnecessarily. He made his farewells, pulling on his Michelin Man coat, thumping first sister and then brother hard between their shoulder blades. He pressed play on his iPod (the earphones of these had never left his ears). He got lucky. It was a beautiful song by the fattest man in rap: a 400-pound, Bronx-born, Hispanic genius. Only twenty-five years old when he died of a coronary, but still very much alive to Levi and millions of kids like Levi. Out of the coffee shop and down the street Levi bounced to the fat man's ingenious boasts, similar in their formality (as Erskine had once tried to explain) to those epic boasts one finds in Milton, say, or in the *Iliad*. These comparisons meant nothing at all to Levi. His body simply loved this song; he made no attempt to disguise the fact that he was dancing down the street, the wind at his back making him as fleet of foot as Gene Kelly. Soon he could see the church steeple and then, as he got a block closer, a flash of the wash-white bed-sheets, knotted to black railings. He wasn't so late. A few of the guys were still unpacking. Felix — who was the 'leader', or at least the guy who held the purse strings — waved. Levi jogged up to meet him. They knocked fists, clasped hands. Some people's hands are sweaty, most are moist, and then there are a few rare souls like Felix whose hands are as dry and cool as stone. Levi wondered whether it was something to do with his blackness. Felix was blacker than any black man Levi ever met in his life. His skin was like slate. Levi had this idea that he would never say out loud and that he knew didn't make sense, but anyway he had this idea that Felix was like the *essence* of blackness in some way. You looked at Felix and thought: *This* is what it's all about, being *this* different; this is what white people fear and adore and want and dread. He was as purely black as — on the other side of things — those weird Swedish guys with translucent eyelashes are purely white. It was like, if you looked up black in a dictionary . . . It was awesome. And, as if to emphasize his singularity, Felix didn't goof off like the other guys, he didn't joke. He was all business. The only time Levi had seen him laugh was when Levi asked Felix that first Saturday whether he had a job going. It was an African laugh, with the deep, resonant timbre of a gong. Felix was from Angola. The rest were Haitian and Dominican. And there was a Cuban too. And now there was a mixed-race American citizen, much to Felix's surprise and much to Levi's. It had taken a week of persistence to convince Felix he was serious about working with them. But now, looking at the way Felix held Levi's hand and kneaded his back, Levi could tell Felix liked him. People tended to like Levi, and he was thankful for this fact without really knowing whom to be thankful to. With Felix and the guys, the clincher had definitely been that night at the Bus Stop. They just didn't think he'd turn up. No *way* did they think he was going to show. They thought he was fly-by. But he *did* turn up, and they'd respected him for it. He'd done more than turn up — he had demonstrated how helpful he could be. It was his own articulate English — comparatively speaking — that had got their tape played and convinced the MC to let ten guys on stage at the same time and made sure they were given the crate of beer each act is promised. He was *in.* Being *in* was a weird feeling. These past few days, coming to meet the guys after school, hanging with them, had been an eye-opener for Levi. Try walking down the street with fifteen Haitians if you want to see people get uncomfortable. He felt a little like Jesus taking a stroll with the lepers.

'You come back again,' said Felix, nodding. 'OK'.

'OK,' said Levi.

'Saturdays and Sundays you will come. Regular. And Thursdays?'

'No, man — Saturday and Sunday, yes. But not Thursdays. Just *this* Thursday. I got a free day today — if it's cool.'

Felix nodded again, took a little notepad and a pen out of his pocket and wrote something down.

'It's cool if you work. It's fucking cool if you work,' he considered, putting his syllabic emphasis in various unnatural places.

'I'm all about work, Fe.'

'All about work,' repeated Felix appreciatively. 'Very good. You'll work other side,' he said, pointing to the opposite corner of the street. 'We have a new guy.

You work with him. Fifteen per cent. Keep your eye to the city. Fucking cops all over. Keep your eye. The stuff is here.'

Levi obediently picked up two bed-sheet sacks and stepped off the sidewalk, but Felix called him back.

'Take him. Chouchou.'

Felix pushed a young man forward. He was skinny, with shoulders no broader than a girl's; you could rest an egg between each knob of his spine. He had a big natural afro, a small, feathery moustache, and an Adam's apple bigger than his nose. Levi imagined him to be in his mid twenties, maybe as old as twenty-eight. He wore a cheap orange acrylic sweater rolled up to his elbows, despite the chill, and down his right arm there was this knockout scar, rose-pink against his black skin, beginning in a point and then spreading out down his forearm like the wake of a ship.

'That's your name?' asked Levi, as they crossed the street. 'Like a *train?*'

'What does this mean?'

'You know, like a *train,* like, choo choo! Train coming through! Like a *train.*'

'It's Haitian. C-H-O-U-C —'

'Yeah, yeah — I see . . .' Levi considered the problem. 'Well, I can't call you that, man. How about just Choo — that works, actually. It works. Levi and Choo.'

'It's not my name.'

'No, I get that, man — but it just runs better to my ear — Choo. Levi and Choo. You hear that?'

No answer came.

'Yeah, it's street. Choo . . . *The* Choo. That's cool. Put it there — no, not there — like this. *That's* the way.'

'Let's get on with it, shall we?' said Choo, freeing his hand from Levi's and looking both ways down the street. 'We need to weigh everything down in this wind. I have some stones from the churchyard.'

Such an extended piece of grammatically correct English was not what Levi had been expecting. In silent surprise he helped Choo untie his bundle, releasing a pile of colourful handbags on to the side-walk. He stood on the sheet to fight the wind, while Choo placed stones on the handles of the bags. Then Levi began to clip his own DVDs to a similarly weighted bed-sheet with clothes-pegs. He tried to make conversation.

'Bottom line is, Choo, the only thing you got to worry about really is keeping an eye out for the cops and just giving me the holler when you see them. A holler and a hoot. And you got to *see* them before they even there — you got to get that *street* sense so you can *smell* a cop eight blocks away. That takes time, that's an art. But you got to acquire it. That's *street.*'

'I see.'

'I lived on these streets all my life, so it's like second nature to me.'

'Second nature.'

'But don't worry — you'll pick all this shit up in time.'

'I'm sure I will. How old are you, Levi?'

'Nineteen,' said Levi, sensing the older the better. But it didn't seem better. Choo closed his eyes and shook his head, slightly but perceptibly.

Levi laughed nervously. 'Now, Choo . . . don't look too excited, you know, all at once, now.'

Choo looked Levi straight in his eyes, hoping for fellow feeling. 'I really fucking *hate* to sell things, you know?' he said, pretty sorrowfully, Levi thought.

'Choo — you ain't *selling,* man,' said Levi keenly in reply. Now that he understood the problem he was happy — it was so easily solved! It was just a matter of attitude. He said, 'This ain't like working the counter at CVS! You *hustling,* man. And that's a different thing. That's *street.* To hustle is to be alive — you dead if you don't know how to hustle. And you ain't a brother if you can't hustle. That's what joins us all together — whether we be on Wall Street or on MTV or sitting on a corner with a dime-bag. It's a beautiful thing, man. We hustling!'

This, the most complete version of Levi's personal philosophy that he himself had ever articulated, hung in the air awaiting its appropriate *Amen!*

'I don't know what you are talking about,' said Choo, sighing. 'Let's get going.'

This disappointed Levi. Even if the other guys didn't fully understand Levi's enthusiasm for what they did, they always smiled and played along, and they had learned a few of the artificial words that Levi liked to apply to their real-life situation. *Hustler, Playa, Gangsta, Pimp.* The reflection of themselves in Levi's eyes was, after all, a more than welcome replacement for their own realities. Who wouldn't rather be a gangsta than a street-hawker? Who wouldn't rather hustle than sell? Who would choose their own lonely, dank rooms over this Technicolor video, this outdoor community that Levi insisted they were all a part of? The Street, the global Street, lined with hustling brothers working corners from Roxbury to Casablanca, from South Central to Cape Town.

Levi tried again: 'I'm talking about *hustlin'*, man! It's like —'

'Louis Vuitton, Gucci, Gucci, Fendi, Fendi, Prada, Prada,' called Choo, as he had been instructed. Two middle-aged white women paused by his display, and started to boldly haggle him down. Levi noticed that his colleague's English transformed at once into something simpler, monosyllabic. He noted also how much more comfortable the women were dealing with Choo than they were with Levi. When Levi tried to interject a little speech about the quality of the merchandise, they looked at him strangely, almost affronted. Of course, they never want conversation — Felix had explained that. They're ashamed to be buying from you. It was a hard thing to remember, after the mega-store, where people had taken such pride in their capacity as purchasers. Levi zipped his mouth and watched Choo swiftly collect eighty-five dollars for three bags. That was the other good thing about this business: if people were going to buy, they did it quickly and walked on quickly. Levi congratulated his new friend on his sale.

Choo took out a cigarette and lit it. 'It's

Felix's money,' he said, cutting Levi off. 'Not mine. I worked the cabs — it was the same bullshit.'

'We get our cut, man, we get our cut. It's economics, right?'

Choo laughed bitterly. 'Originals — eight hundred dollars,' he said pointing at a store across the street. 'Fakes — thirty dollars. Cost to produce — five dollars, maybe three. That's economics. *American* economics.'

Levi shook his head at the miracle of it. 'Can you *believe* these stupid bitches be paying thirty dollars for a three-dollar handbag? That shit's unbelievable. *That's* a hustle.'

And here Choo looked down at Levi's sneakers. 'How much did you pay for them?'

'A hundred and twenty dollars,' said Levi proudly and demonstrated the shock reducers built into their soles by bouncing up and down on his heels.

'Fifteen dollars to make,' said Choo, blowing horns of smoke from both of his nostrils. 'No more. Fifteen dollars. You're the one being hustled, my friend.'

'Now, how would you know that? That ain't true, man. That ain't true at all.'

'I come from the factory where they make your shoes. Where they *used* to make your shoes. We don't make anything now,' said Choo, and then cried 'PRADA!', hooking another group of women, an expanding group, which kept growing, as if he'd thrown a trawler's net over the sidewalk. *Come from a factory?* How can you *come from* a factory? But there was no time for further inquiry; now, on Levi's side, a group of Goth girls. They were black-haired and white and skinny, linked to each other by strange metal chains — the kind of girls who haunt the Harvard T-stop on a Friday night with a bottle of vodka tucked in their huge pants. They wanted horror movies, and Levi had them. He did some brisk business, and for the next hour or so the two salesmen did not talk to each other much, unless one needed change from the other's fanny pack. Levi, who never could bear bad vibes, still felt the need to make this guy like him, like most guys liked him. At last there came a lull in trade. Levi took his opportunity.

'What's your deal, man? Don't take this strange, but . . . you don't seem like the type of guy who would be doing this kind of thing. You know?'

'How about this?' said Choo quietly, again alarming Levi with his easy use of American idioms, albeit dipped in that exotic accent. 'You leave me alone and I do my very best to leave *you* alone. You sell your movies. I sell these handbags. How would that be?'

'That's cool,' said Levi quietly.

'Best movies, top movies, three for ten dollars!' called Levi into the street. He dug into his pocket and found two individually wrapped Junior Mints. He offered one to Choo, who declined it sniffily. Levi unwrapped his own mint and popped it into his mouth. He *loved* Junior Mints. Minty *and* chocolatey. Just everything you want from a candy, basically. The last of the peppermint slipped down his throat. He tried really hard not to say anything at all. And then he said: 'So you got a lot of friends here?'

Choo sighed. 'No.'

'No one in the city?'

'No.'

'You don't know *anyone?*'

'I know two, three people. They work across the river. At Wellington. In the college.'

'Oh, yeah?' said Levi. 'Which department?'

Choo stopped organizing the money in his fanny pack and looked at Levi curiously. 'They're cleaners,' he said. 'I don't know which department they clean.'

OK, OK, you win, bro, thought Levi, and crouched down to the DVDs to pointlessly rearrange a row of them. He was done with this guy. But now it was Choo who seemed freshly interested.

'And you —' said Choo, pursuing him. 'You live in Roxbury, Felix tells me.'

Levi looked up at Choo. He was smiling, at last.

'Yeah, man, that's right.'

Choo looked down at him like the tallest man who had ever lived.

'Yes. That's what I heard, that you live in Roxbury. And you rap with them too.'

'Not really. I just went along. It's good, though — it's got that political vibe. Real angry. I'm learning more about the . . . like, the political context, that's what I'm into right now,' said Levi, referring to a book on Haiti he had borrowed (though it was as yet unread) from Arundel School's 127-year-old library. It was the first time Levi had ever entered that cloistered, dark little space without the propulsion of a school project or imminent exam.

'But they say they never see you there, in Roxbury. The others. They say they never see you.'

'Yeah, well. I pretty much keep myself to myself.'

'I see. Well, maybe we shall see each other there, Levi,' said Choo, and his smile grew wider, 'down in the hood.'

IO

Katherine (Katie) Armstrong is sixteen. She is one of the youngest students attending Wellington College. She grew up in South Bend, Indiana, where she was by far the brightest student in her high school. Although the great majority of kids from Katie's school either drop out or go on to attend Indiana's fine in-state institution, no one was too surprised to discover that Katie would be attending a fancy East Coast school on a full academic scholarship. Katie is proficient both in the arts and sciences, but her heart — if this makes sense — has always resided in the left side of her brain. Katie loves the arts. Given her parents' relative poverty and limited education, she knows that it would probably have made more sense for her family if she'd tried for medical school or even Harvard Law. But her parents are generous, loving people, and they support her in all her choices.

The summer before Katie turned up at Wellington, she drove herself half crazy wondering whether she would end up an English major or an Art History major. She's still unsure. Some days she wants to be an editor of something. Other days she can imagine running a gallery or even writing a book on Picasso, who is the most amazing human being Katie has ever come across. At the moment, as a freshman, she is keeping her options open. She is in Professor Cork's Twentieth-Century Painting seminar (for sophomores only, but she begged) and two literature classes, English Romantic Poetry and American Post-Modernism. She's learning Russian, she helps man the phones for the eating disorder help-line, and she's doing the set design for a production of *Cabaret*. A naturally shy girl, Katie has to overcome a great deal of nerves, every week, simply to enter the rooms where these various activities take place. One class above all terrifies her: Dr Belsey's class on Seventeenth-Century Art. They are spending most of this semester on Rembrandt, who is the second most amazing human being Katie has ever come across. She used to dream about one day attending a college class about Rembrandt with other intelligent people who loved Rembrandt and weren't ashamed to express this love. She has been to only three classes so far. She did not understand much. A lot of the time she felt the professor to be speaking a different language from the one she has spent sixteen years refining. After the third class she went back to her dorm and cried. She cursed her stupidity and her youth. She wished her high school had given her different kinds of books to read than the ones she has evidently wasted her time on. Presently, Katie calmed down. She looked up some of the mysterious vocab from her class in *Webster's*. The words were not there. She did find 'liminality', but she still didn't understand the way Dr Belsey was using it. However, Katie is not the type of girl to give up easily. Today is the fourth class. She is prepared. Last week, they were given a worksheet with photocopies of the two pictures that would be under discussion today. Katie has spent a week staring at them, thinking deeply about them, and has made notes in her notebook.

The first painting is *Jacob Wrestling with the Angel*, 1658. Katie has thought about the vigorous impasto that works counter-intuitively to create that somnolent, dreamy atmosphere. She makes notes on the angel's resemblance to Rembrandt's pretty son, Titus; on the perspective lines that create the illusions of frozen movement; on the personal dynamic between the angel and Jacob. When she looks at this painting she sees a violent struggle that is, at the same time, a loving embrace. It reminds her, in its homoeroticism, of Caravaggio (since beginning at Wellington she finds a lot of things homoerotic). She adores the earthy colours — Jacob's simple damask, and the angel's off-white farmboy smock. Caravaggio always gave his angels the darkly resplendent wings of eagles; by contrast, Rembrandt's angel is no eagle but he's no dove either. No bird Katie has ever seen really has these imprecise, shabby, dun-coloured wings. The wings seem almost an afterthought, as if to remind us that this painting is meant to be of matters biblical, other-worldly. But in Rembrandt's Protestant heart, so Katie believes, the battle depicted here is really for a man's earthly soul, for his *human* faith in the world. Katie, who lost her faith slowly and painfully two years earlier, finds the relevant passage in the Bible and adds the following to her notes:

And Jacob was left alone; and there wrestled a man with him until the break of day . . . And he said, Let me go for the day breaketh. And the angel said, I will not let thee go, except thou bless me.

This painting Katie finds impressive, beautiful, awe-inspiring — but not truly moving. She can't find the right words, can't put her finger on why that is. All she can say, again, is that this is not a faith battle she is looking at. At least, not of the kind she herself has experienced. Jacob looks like he wants sympathy, and the angel looks like he wants to *give* sympathy. That's not how a battle goes. The struggle isn't really there. Does that make sense?

The second picture, on the other hand, makes Katie cry. It is *Seated Nude*, an etching from 1631. In it a misshapen woman, naked, with tubby little breasts and a hugely distended belly, sits on a rock, eyeing Katie directly. Katie has read some famous commentaries on this etching. Everybody finds it technically good but visually disgusting. Many famous men are repulsed. A simple naked woman is apparently much more nauseating than Samson having his eye put out or Ganymede pissing everywhere. Is she really so grotesque? She was a shock, to Katie, at first — like a starkly lit, unforgiving photograph of oneself. But then Katie began to notice all the exterior, human information, not explicitly *in* the frame but implied by what we see there. Katie is moved by the crenulated marks of absent stockings on her legs, the muscles in her arms suggestive of manual labour. That loose belly that has known many babies, that still fresh face that has lured men in the past and may yet lure more. Katie — a stringbean, physically — can even see her own body contained in this body, as if Rembrandt were saying to her, and to all women: 'For you are of the earth, as my nude is, and you will come to this point too, and be blessed if you feel as little shame, as much joy, as she!' This is what a woman *is:* unadorned, after children and work and age, and experience — *these are the marks of living.* So Katie feels. And all this from cross-hatching (Katie makes her own comics and knows something of cross-hatching); all these intimations of mortality from an inkpot!

Katie comes to class very excited. She sits down excited. She keeps her notebook open before her, determined this time, *determined* to be one of the three or four people who dare to speak in Dr Belsey's class. The class, all fourteen of them, are arranged in a square, the desks fitted together so that everyone can see everyone. They have their names written on pieces of paper that are folded in half and stood atop their desks. They look like so many bank managers. Dr Belsey is speaking.

'What we're trying to . . . *interrogate* here,' he says, 'is the mytheme of artist as autonomous individual with privileged insight into the human. What is it about these texts — these images as narration — that is implicitly applying for the quasi-mystical notion of genius?'

An awful long silence follows this. Katie bites at the skin around her cuticles.

'To reframe: is what we see here really a *rebellion,* a turning away? We're told that this constitutes a rejection of the classical nude. OK. But. Is this nude not a *confirmation* of the ideality of the vulgar? As it is already inscribed in the idea of a specifically gendered, class debasement?'

Another silence. Dr Belsey stands up and writes the word LIGHT very large on the blackboard behind him.

'Both these pictures speak of illumination. Why? That is to say, can we speak of *light* as a neutral concept? What is the *logos* of this light, this *spiritual* light, this supposed illumination? What are we signing up to when we speak of the "beauty" of this "light"?' says Dr Belsey, employing quoting fingers. 'What are these images *really* concerned with?'

Here Katie sees her opportunity and begins the slow process of thinking about possibly opening her mouth and allowing sound to come from it. Her tongue is at her teeth. But it is the incredible-looking black girl, Victoria, who speaks, and as ever she has a way of monopolizing Dr Belsey's attention, even when Katie is almost certain that what she is saying is not terribly interesting.

'It's a painting of its own interior,' she says very slowly, looking down at her desk and then up again in that stupid, flirty way she has. 'Its subject *is* painting itself. It's a painting about painting. I mean, that's the desiring force here.'

Dr Belsey raps on his desk in an interested way, as if to say, *now we're getting to it.*

'OK,' he says. 'Expand.'

But before Victoria can speak again there is an interruption.

'Umm . . . I don't understand how you're using "painting" there? I don't think you can simply just inscribe the history of painting, or even its logos, in that one word "painting".'

The professor seems interested in this

point too. It is made by the young man with the T-shirt that says BEING on one side and TIME on the other, a young man Katie fears more than anybody else in this whole university, much more than she could ever fear any woman, even the beautiful black girl, because he is clearly the third most amazing person she has ever come across. His name is Mike.

'But you've already privileged the term,' says the professor's daughter, whom Katie, who is not given easily to hatred, hates. 'You're already assuming the etching is merely "debased painting". So there's your problematic, right there.'

And now the class escapes Katie; it streams through her toes as the sea and sand when she stands at the edge of the ocean and dozily, *stupidly,* allows the tide to draw out and the world to pull away from her so rapidly as to make her dizzy . . .

At three fifteen, Trudy Steiner hesitantly put her hand up to point out that the class had gone fifteen minutes over. Howard collected his papers into a neat pile and apologized for the overrun but for nothing else. He felt this had been the most successful session to date. The class dynamic was finally beginning to come together, to gel. Mike, in particular, impressed him very much. You need people like that in a class. In fact, he reminded Howard a little of Howard at the same age. Those few, golden years when he believed Heidegger would save his life.

Everybody began packing away their things. Zora gave her father the thumbs-up and rushed off, because of a scheduling glitch she always missed the first ten minutes of Claire's poetry class anyway. Christian and Veronica, who were sitting in as entirely unnecessary teaching assistants (given the small class number), passed out worksheets for the following week. When Christian reached Howard's end of the table he crouched down in his creepily limber way to Howard's level, and with one hand reslicked his side parting.

'That was amazing.'

'Went well, yes, I thought,' said Howard, and took a worksheet from Christian's hands.

'I think the worksheet prompted a dialogue,' began Christian cautiously, awaiting confirmation. 'But it's sincerely the way you then take that dialogue and refashion it — that's the ignition.'

Howard both smiled and frowned at this. There was something strange about Christian's English, despite the fact he was apparently an American. It was as if he were being translated as he spoke.

'Worksheet definitely set us off,' agreed Howard, and received waves of grateful protest from Christian. It was Christian himself who had made these worksheets. Howard always meant to read them more thoroughly but would, this week as ever, end up skimming the pages the morning before the class. They both knew this well.

'Did you get the memo about the faculty meeting being postponed?' asked Christian.

Howard assented.

'It's January tenth, first meeting after Christmas. Will you need me to be there?' asked Christian.

Howard doubted this would be necessary.

'Because, I did all that research, re, the limits of political speech on campus. I mean, not that it matters especially . . . I'm sure you won't need it . . . but I think it'll be helpful, although we would need to know the content of Professor Kipps's proposed lectures to be quite certain,' said Christian and began to pull papers from his satchel. As Christian continued speaking at him, Howard kept an eye out for Victoria. But Christian went on too long; Howard watched with dismay her long-legged coltish stumble out of the door, pressed in on both sides by male friends. Each leg was perfectly wrapped, separated and fetishized in its tube of denim. Her ankles clicked together in those tan leather boots. The last thing he saw was the perfection of her ass — so high, so round — turning a corner, leaving. In twenty years of teaching he had never set eyes on anything like her. The other possibility, of course, was that in fact he had seen many such girls over the years, but it was only this year that he noticed. Either way, he was resigned to it. Two classes ago he had stopped trying not to look at Victoria Kipps. There's no point in trying to do impossible things.

Now young Mike came up to Howard, confidently, like a colleague, to ask about an article Howard had mentioned in passing. Freed from the strange bondage of looking at Victoria, Howard gladly directed him to the journal and the year. More people left the room. Howard bent down under his desk to avoid conversation with any other students and pushed his papers back into his satchel. He got the nasty sensation that someone or another was lingering. Lingering always signalled a cry for pastoral care. *I was wondering if we could*

*just maybe meet for a coffee some time
. . . there's some issues I'm having that I'd
like to discuss . . .* Howard grew more intensely involved with the clasps of his bag.
Still he sensed lingering. He looked up.
That strange ghost girl who never said a
word was making a performance of
packing away her one notebook and pen.
Finally she made it to the doorway and
began lingering there, leaving Howard no
choice but to squeeze by her.

'Kathy — everything good?' asked
Howard, very loudly.

'Oh! Yes . . . I mean, but I was just . . .
Dr Belsey, is it the — the — same room
. . . next week?'

'The very same,' said Howard, and
strode through the hallway, down the
wheelchair ramp and out of the building.

'Dr Belsey?'

Outside, in the small octagonal courtyard, it had begun to snow. Great drifting
sheets of it divided the day, and with none
of the mystique snow has in England: *Will
it settle? Will it melt? Is it sleet? Is it hail?*
This was just snow, period, and by tomorrow morning would be knee-deep.

'Dr Belsey? Could I have a word — just
for a sec?'

'Victoria, yes,' he said, and blinked the flakes from his eyelashes. She was too perfect set against this white backdrop. Looking at her made him feel open to ideas, possibilities, allowances, arguments that two minutes earlier he would have rejected. Just now would be a very good moment, for example, for Levi to ask for twenty dollars or for Jack French to ask him to chair a panel on the future of the University. But then — thank the sweet Lord — she turned her head away.

'I'll catch up with you,' said Victoria to two young men who were walking backwards in front of her, grinning and packing snowballs in raw, pink hands. Victoria fell into step with Howard. Howard noticed how her hair kept the snow differently than Howard's own hair. It sat neatly on top of her head like icing.

'I've never seen it like this!' she said gaily as they passed out of the gate and prepared to cross the small road that led to Wellington's main yard. She had placed her hands in a funny position, in the back pockets of her jeans, her elbows jutting backwards like the stumps of wings. 'It must have got going while we were in class. Bloody *hell*. It's like movie snow!'

'I wonder whether movie snow costs a

million dollars a week to clear.'

'Blimey — that much.'

'That much.'

'That's a shitload.'

'Quite.'

This, only the second private conversation they'd ever had, was the same as the first: dumb and oddly charged with humour, Vee smiling toothily and Howard unsure if he was being ridiculed or flirted with. She had slept with his son — was that the joke? If so, he couldn't say he found it too amusing. But he had taken her lead from the start: this unspoken pretence that they had never met before this semester and had no connection other than that of teacher and student. He felt wrong-footed by her. She was unafraid of him. Any other student in his class would be trawling their brains right now for a brilliant sentence, no, they would never have *approached* him in the first place without some sparkling opener prepared earlier, some tedious little piece of rhetorical flash. How many hours of his life had he spent smiling thinly at these carefully constructed comments, sometimes bred and developed days or even weeks before in the nervous hothoused brains of these ambitious kids? But Vee wasn't like that. Outside of class she seemed to take pride in being somewhat moronic.

'Umm, look — you know this thing that all the college societies have, this stupid dinner?' she said, tilting her face upwards to the white-out skies. 'Each table has to invite three professors — mine's Emerson Hall, and we're not too formal, it's not as poncy as some of the others . . . it's all right, actually — mixed, women and men — it's quite chilled. It's basically just dinner, and there's usually a speech — a *long dull* speech. So. Obviously say no if that's not the sort of thing you do . . . I mean, I don't know — it's my first one. Thought I'd ask, though. No harm in asking.' She stuck her tongue out and ate some snowflakes.

'Oh . . . well — I mean, if you'd like me to go, I will, of course,' began Howard, turning to her tentatively, but Vee was still eating snow. 'But . . . are you sure you wouldn't feel . . . well, obligated to take your father, maybe? I wouldn't want to step on any toes,' said Howard rapidly. It was a tribute to the power of the girl's charm that it didn't for a moment occur to Howard that he had obligations of his own.

'Oh, *God,* no. He's already been asked by about a million different students. Plus

I'm a bit stressed that he'll say Grace at the table. Actually, I *know* he will, which would be . . . *interesting.*'

She was already developing the woozy transatlantic accent of Howard's own children. It was a shame. He liked that North London voice, touched by the Caribbean and, if he was not mistaken, equally touched by an expensive girls' school. Now they stopped walking. This was Howard's turn-off, up the stairs to the library. They stood facing each other, almost the same height thanks to her towering boots. Vee hugged herself and plaintively pulled her lower lip under her large front teeth, the way beautiful girls sometimes pull goofy faces, without any fear that the effects will be permanent. In response Howard put on an extremely serious face.

'My decision would depend very much . . .'

'On what?' She clapped her snowy mittens together.

'. . . on whether there will be a glee club in attendance.'

'A what? I don't know . . . I don't even know what that is.'

'They sing. Young men,' said Howard, wincing slightly. 'They sing. Very close harmony singing.'

'I don't think so. Nobody mentioned it.'

'I can't go to anything with a glee club. It's very important. I had an unfortunate episode.'

Now it was Vee's turn to wonder if fun was being made of her. As it happened, Howard was serious. She squinted at him and chattered her teeth.

'But you'll come?'

'If you're sure you'd like me to.'

'I'm completely sure. It's just after Christmas, ages away, basically — January tenth.'

'No glee club,' said Howard as she began to walk away.

'No glee club!'

It was always the same, Claire's poetry class, and it was always a pleasure. Each student's poem was only a slight variation on the poem they had brought in the week before, and all poems were consistently met with Claire's useful mix of violent affection and genuine insight. So Ron's poems were always about modern sexual alienation, and Daisy's poems were always about New York, Chantelle's were always about the black struggle, and Zora's were the kind that appear to have been generated by a random word-generating machine. It was Claire's great gift as a teacher to find something of worth in all these efforts and to speak to their authors as if they were already household names in poetry-loving homes across America. And what a thing it is, at nineteen years old, to be told that a new Daisy poem is a perfect example of the Daisy oeuvre, that it is indeed evidence of a Daisy at the height of her powers, exercising all the traditional, much loved, Daisy strengths! Claire was an excellent teacher. She reminded you how noble it was to write poetry; how miraculous it should feel to communicate what is most intimate to you, and to do so in this stylized way, through rhyme and metre, images and ideas. After each student had read their work and it had been discussed seriously and pertinently, Claire would finish by reading a poem by a great, usually dead poet, and encourage her class to discuss this poem no differently than they had discussed the others. And in this way one learned to imagine continuity between one's own poetry and the poetry of the world. What a feeling! You walked out of that class if not shoulder to shoulder with Keats and Dickinson and Eliot and the rest, then at least in the same echo chamber, in the same roll-call of history. The transformation was most noticeable on Carl. Three weeks ago he had attended his first class wearing a comic, sceptical slouch. He read his lyrics in a grumpy mumble and seemed angered by the interested appreciation with which they were met. 'It's not even a *poem,*' he countered. 'It's rap.' 'What's the difference?' Claire asked. 'They two different things,' Carl had argued, 'two different art forms. Except rap ain't no art form. It's just *rap.*' 'So it can't be discussed?' 'You can *discuss* it — I ain't stopping you.' The first thing Claire did with Carl's rap that day was show him of what it was made. Iambs, spondees, trochees, anapaests. Passionately Carl denied any knowledge of these arcane arts. He was used to being fêted at the Bus Stop but not in a classroom. Large sections of Carl's personality had been constructed on the founding principle that classrooms were not for Carl.

'But the grammar of it,' Claire had explained, 'is hard-wired in your brain. You're almost thinking in sonnets already. You don't need to *know* it to *do* it — but that doesn't mean you're not doing it.' This is the kind of announcement which cannot help but make you feel a little taller the next day when you're in the Nike store asking your customer if they want to try the same sneaker in a size 11. 'You'll write me a sonnet, won't you?' Claire had asked Carl sweetly. In the second class she asked him, 'How about that sonnet, Carl?' He said, 'It's cooking. I'll let you know when it's ready.' Of course he flirted with her; he always did that with teachers, he'd done it all through high school. And Mrs Malcolm flirted right back. In high school Carl had slept with his geography teacher — that was a bad scene. When he looked back on it, he considered that incident the beginning of when things began going very wrong between him and classrooms. But with Claire you got just the right amount of flirting. It wasn't . . . *inappropriate* — that was the word. Claire had that special teacher thing he hadn't felt since he was a really small boy, back in the days before his teachers started worrying that he was going to mug them or rape them: *she wanted him to do well.* Even though there was nowhere this could go, academically speaking. He wasn't really a student and she wasn't really his teacher, and anyway Carl and classrooms did not mix. And yet. She wanted him to do *well.* And he wanted to do well *for* her.

So in this, the fourth session, he went and brought her a sonnet. Just as she said.

Fourteen lines with ten syllables (or beats, as Carl could not help but think of them) a line. It wasn't such a fabulous sonnet. But everybody in the class made a big fuss like he'd just split the atom. Zora said, 'I think that's the only truly funny sonnet I've ever read.' Carl was wary. He was still not sure that this whole Wellington thing wasn't a kind of sick joke being played on him.

'You mean it's stupid funny?'

Everybody in the class cried *Noooo!* Then she, Zora, said, 'No, no, no — it's *alive.* I mean, the form hasn't restricted you — it always restricts me. I don't know how you managed that.' The class enthusiastically agreed with this judgement, and a whole crazy conversation began, which took up most of the hour, about *his poem,* as if his poem were something real like a statue or a country. During this Carl looked down at his poem every now and then and felt a sensation he'd never experienced in a classroom before: pride. He had written his sonnet out sloppily, as he wrote his raps, with a pencil, on scrap paper crumpled and stained. Now he felt this medium was not quite good enough for this new way of writing his message. He resolved to type the damn thing out sometime if he could get access to a keyboard.

Just as they were packing up to leave, Mrs Malcolm said, 'Are you serious about this class, Carl?'

Carl looked around himself cautiously. This was a strange question to ask in front of everybody.

'I mean, do you want to stay in this class? Even if it gets difficult?'

So that was the deal: they thought he was stupid. These early stages were fine, but he wouldn't be able to manage the next stage, whatever it was. Why'd they even ask him, then?

'Difficult how?' he asked edgily.

'I mean, if other people wanted you *not* to be in this class. Would you fight to be in it? Or would you let *me* fight for you to be in it? Or your fellow poets here?'

Carl glowered. 'I don't like to be where I'm not welcome.'

Claire shook her head and waved her hands to disperse that thought.

'I'm not making myself clear. Carl, you want to be in this class, right?'

Carl was very close to saying that he truly did not give a fuck, but at the last moment he understood that Claire's eager face wanted something quite different from him.

'Sure. It's interesting, you know. I feel like I'm . . . you know . . . learning.'

'Oh, I'm so *glad,*' she said and practically smiled her face off. Then she stopped smiling and looked businesslike. 'Good,' she said firmly. 'That's decided. Good. Then you're going to stay in this class. *Anybody who needs this class,*' she said fervently, and looked from Chantelle to a young woman called Bronwyn who worked at the Wellington Savings Bank, and then to a mathematician boy called Wong from BU, 'is *staying* in this class. OK, we're done here. Zora, can you stay behind?'

The class filed out, everybody a little curious and jealous of Zora's special dispensation. Carl, as he left, punched her gently on the shoulder with his fist. Sunshine broke out over Zora. Claire remembered, recognized and pitied the feeling (for it seemed, to her, a long shot on Zora's part). She smiled to think of herself at the same age.

'Zora — you know about the faculty meeting?' Claire sat down on the desk and looked up into Zora's eyes. Her mascara had been ineptly applied, lashes welded together.

'Of course,' said Zora. 'It's the big one — it's been postponed. Howard's going to come out all guns blazing about Monty Kipps's lectures. Since no one else seems to have the balls.'

'Hmm,' said Claire, made awkward by

the mention of Howard. 'Oh, that, yes.' Claire looked away from Zora and out of the window.

'Everybody's going, for once,' said Zora. 'It's basically got down to a battle for the soul of this university. Howard says it's the most important meeting Wellington's had in a long time.'

This was the case. It would also be the first interdisciplinary faculty meeting since all the mess of last year had come into the open. It was more than a month away, but this morning's memo had set the scene all too clearly for Claire: that chilly library, the whispers, the eyes — averted and staring — Howard in an armchair avoiding her, Claire's colleagues enjoying him avoiding her. And this was not to mention the usual tabling of motions, blocked votes, rabid speech-making, complaints, demands, counter-demands. And Jack French directing it all, slowly, very slowly. It didn't seem to Claire that, in this vital stage of her psychic recovery, she should have to contend with such intense spiritual and mental degradation.

'Yes . . . Now, Zora, you know there are people in the college who don't approve of our class — I mean they don't approve of people like Chantelle . . . people like *Carl,* being a part of our community here at Wellington. It's going to be on the agenda at that meeting. There's a general conservative trend sweeping this university right now, and it really, really *frightens* me. And they don't want to hear from *me*. They've already decided I'm the communist loony-tune anti-war poetess or whatever they think I am. I think we need a strong advocate for this class from the other side. So we're not just arguing the same stupid dialectic over and over. And I think a student would be much more appropriate — to make the case. Somebody who has benefited from the experience of learning alongside these people. Someone who could . . . well, attend in my place. Make a barnstorming speech. About something they believed in.'

Zora's all-time academic fantasy was to address the faculty members of Wellington College with a barnstorming speech.

'You want *me* to go?'

'Only, *only,* if you felt comfortable doing that.'

'Wait — a speech that I'd devised and written?'

'Well, I didn't mean an actual *speech* speech — but I guess as long as you knew what you wanted to —'

'I mean, what are we *doing,*' asked Zora loudly, 'if we can't extend the *enormous* resources of this institution to people who need it? It's so *disgusting.*'

Claire smiled. 'You're perfect already.'

'Just me. You wouldn't be there?'

'I think it would be much more powerful if it was you speaking your own mind. I mean, what I'd *really* like to do is send Carl himself, but you know . . .' said Claire, sighing. 'Depressing as it is, the truth is these people won't respond to an appeal to their consciences in any language other than Wellington language. And you *know* Wellington language, Zora. You of all people. And I don't mean to get overly dramatic here, but when I think of Carl, I'm thinking of someone who doesn't have a voice and who needs someone like you, who has a very powerful voice, to speak for him. I actually think it's that important. I also think it's a beautiful thing to do for a dispossessed person in this climate. Don't you feel that?'

II

Two weeks later Wellington College closed for the Christmas recess. The snow continued. Every night unseen Wellington street workers shovelled it back from the sidewalk. After a while every road was edged with grey ice banks, some over five feet high. Jerome came home. Many dull parties followed: for the Art History Department, drinks at the President's house, and at the Vice-President's, at Kiki's hospital, at Levi's school. More than once Kiki found herself walking around the perimeters of these hot, crowded rooms, champagne in hand, hoping to see Carlene Kipps somewhere among the tinsel and the quiet black maids, circulating with their trays of shrimp. Often enough she spotted Monty, leaning against the wainscoting in one of his absurd nineteenth-century three-piece suits, with his timepiece on a chain, bombastically opinionated, and almost always eating — but Carlene was never with him. Was Carlene Kipps one of these women who promises friendship but never truly delivers it? A friendship flirt? Or was Kiki herself mistaken in her expectations? This, after all, was the month in which families began tightening and closing and sealing; from Thanksgiving to the New Year, everybody's world contracted, day by day, into the microcosmic single festive household, each with its own rituals and obsessions, rules and dreams. You didn't feel you could call people. They didn't feel they could phone you. How does one cry for help from these seasonal prisons?

And then a note arrived at the Belsey house, hand-delivered. It was from Carlene. Christmas was approaching, and Carlene felt she was behind as far as presents were concerned. She had spent another spell in bed of late, and her family had gone to New York for a short break so the children might shop and Monty attend to some of his charity work. Would Kiki think about accompanying her on a shopping trip into Boston? On a drear Saturday morning, Kiki picked up her friend in a Wellington taxi. She put Carlene in the front passenger seat and sat herself in the back, lifting her feet so she didn't have to contend with the ice water swilling around on the floor.

'Where you want?' asked the cab driver, and when Kiki told him the name of the mall, he had not heard of it, although it was a Boston landmark. He wanted the street names.

'It's the biggest mall in town. Don't you know the city at *all*?'

'It not *my* job. You should know where you want to go.'

'Honey, that's *exactly* your job.'

'I don't think they should be allowed to drive with poor English like that,' complained Carlene primly, without lowering her voice.

'No, it's my fault,' mumbled Kiki, ashamed to have started this. She sank back in her seat. The car crossed Wellington Bridge. Kiki watched a swell of birds swoop under the arch and land on the frozen river.

'Are you of the opinion,' asked Carlene worriedly, 'that it is better to go to a lot of different shops or just to find one big shop and stick with it?'

'I'm of the opinion that it's better not to shop at all!'

'You don't like Christmas?'

Kiki considered. 'No, that's not quite true. But I don't have a feeling for it like I used to. I used to *love* Christmas in Florida — it was *warm* in Florida — but that's not it really. My daddy was a minister and he made Christmas meaningful to me — I don't mean in the religious sense, but he thought of it as a "hope for the best things". That was his way of putting it. It was a kind of reminder of what we might be. Now it feels like you just get presents.'

'And you don't like presents.'

'I don't want any more things, no.'

'Well, I'm still putting you on my list,' said Carlene brightly, and from the front seat waved a little white notebook. Then, more seriously, she said, 'I *would* like to give you a gift, as a thank you. I've been rather lonely. And you've thought to visit me and spend a little time with me . . . even though I'm not much fun at the moment.'

'Don't be crazy. It's a pleasure to see you. I wish it were more often. Now take my damn name off that list.'

But the name stayed on, although no present was written beside it. They tramped through an enormous, chilly mall and found a few pieces of clothing for Victoria and Michael. Carlene was an erratic, panicky shopper; spending twenty minutes considering a single lovely item without buying it, and then buying three not so nice things in a flurry. She spoke a lot about bargains and value for money in a manner Kiki found faintly depressing, given the Kippses' clearly robust finances. For Monty, though, Carlene wanted to get something 'really nice', and so they decided to brave three blocks of snow-walking in order to reach a fancier, smaller, specialist boutique that might have the cane with the carved handle that Carlene had in mind.

'What will *you* do at Christmas?' asked Kiki, as they pressed through the crowds on Newbury Street. 'Will you go somewhere — back to England?'

'Usually we have Christmas in the countryside. We have a beautiful cottage in a place called Iden. It's near Winchelsea Beach. Do you know it?'

Kiki confessed ignorance.

'It's the most beautiful spot I know. But this year, we must stay in America. Michael's already over, and he'll stay till January third. I can't wait to see him! Our friends have a house we're to borrow in Amherst — just nearby where Miss Dickinson lived. You'd like it a lot. I've visited it — it's lovely. It's very big, though I think not as pretty as Iden. But the really wonderful thing is their collection. They have three Edward Hoppers, two Singer Sargents and a Miró!'

Kiki gasped and clapped her hands. 'Oh, my God — I *love* Edward Hopper. I can't believe that! He *floors me. Imagine* having things like that in your own private home. Sister, I envy you that, I really do. I'd love to see that. That's *wonderful.'*

'They dropped around the key today. I

wish we were all already there. But I should really wait for Monty and the children to come home.' This last word, said broodingly, brought other things to the forefront of her mind. 'How are things at home now, Kiki? I've thought of you a lot. Worried for you.'

Kiki passed an arm around her friend. 'Carlene, honestly now, please don't worry. It's all fine. Everything's settling down. Although Christmas is *not* the easiest time in the Belsey household,' trilled Kiki, niftily turning the subject. 'Howard can't *stand* Christmas.'

'Howard . . . my *word*. He seems to hate such a lot of things. Paintings, my husband —'

Kiki opened her mouth to counter this with she knew not what. Carlene patted her hand.

'I'm mischievous — I was only being mischievous. So he hates Christmas too. Because he is not a Christian.'

'Well, none of us is that,' replied Kiki firmly, not wishing to mislead. 'But Howard's just pretty determined about it. He won't have it in the house. It used to upset the kids, but they're used to it now, and we make up for it in other ways. But, no, not an eggnog, not a bauble shall cross our threshold!'

'But you make him sound like Scrooge!'

'No . . . He's not at all *stingy*. Actually he's incredibly generous. We eat ourselves into a stupor on the day, and he spoils the kids with a crazy amount of gifts come the New Year — but he just won't *do* Christmas. I think we're going to stay with friends in London — it depends if the kids agree. A couple we've known a long time. We went there two years ago — it was lovely. They're Jewish, so there's no issue. That's just the way Howard likes it: no rituals, no superstitions, no traditions and no images of Santa Claus. It sounds strange, I guess, but we're used to it.'

'I don't believe you — you're having fun with me.'

'It's true! Actually, when you think about it, it's a pretty Christian policy. Thou shalt worship no graven images; thou shalt have no other God but me —'

'I see,' said Carlene, dismayed by the levity with which Kiki was approaching the subject. 'But who *is* his God?'

Kiki was limbering up to answer this difficult question, when she was distracted by the noise and colour of a group of Africans one block along. Taking up half the sidewalk selling their rip-offs, and among them, surely among them —

But, as she called his name, a cross-stream rabble of shoppers blocked her sight line, and by the time they'd passed the mirage had vanished.

'Isn't that weird? I *always* think I see Levi. Never the other two. It's that uniform — cap, hood, jeans. All those boys are wearing exactly the same thing as Levi. It's like this goddamn *army.* I see boys who look like him just about everywhere I go.'

'I don't care what the doctors say,' said Carlene, leaning on Kiki as they walked the short flight of steps to an eighteenth-century townhouse, hollowed out to accommodate goods and their buyers and sellers; 'the eyes and the heart are directly connected.'

In this place they found a cane that was a reasonable approximation of the one in Carlene's mind. Also some monogrammed handkerchiefs, and then the most dreadful cravat. Carlene was satisfied. Kiki suggested they take these gifts to the in-store wrapping service. Carlene, who had never considered that such indulgence might exist, hovered all the while over the girl who was doing the wrapping, and could not restrain herself from occasionally offering her own fingers to press down a bit of tape or help position a bow.

'Ah — a Hopper,' said Kiki, pleased at the coincidence. It was a print of *Road in Maine*, one of a series of poorly reproduced lithographs of famous American paintings meant to signal the classiness of this store in contrast to the mall they'd just been in. 'Someone's just walked down there,' she murmured, her finger travelling safely along the flat, paintless surface. 'Actually, I think it was me. I was moseying along counting those posts. With no idea where I was going. No family. No responsibilities. Wouldn't that be fine!'

'Let's go to Amherst,' said Carlene Kipps urgently. She gripped Kiki's hand.

'Oh, honey, I'd love to go some time! It would be such a treat to see paintings like that, not in a museum. Wow . . . that's such a kind offer, thank you. Something to look forward to.'

Carlene looked alarmed. 'No, dear, *now* — let's go now. I have the keys — we could get the train and be there by lunch. I want you to see the pictures — they should be loved by somebody like you. We'll go right away when this is wrapped. We'll be back for tomorrow evening.'

Kiki looked out of the exit doors at another sidelong sweep of snow. She looked at the sunken, pale face of her friend, felt the wobbling hand in her own.

'Really, Carlene, another time I'd love to go, but . . . it's not really the weather — and it's a little late to start out — maybe next week we could organize a trip, properly, and . . .'

Carlene Kipps let go of Kiki's hand and turned back to her present wrapping. She was annoyed. They left the store soon after. Carlene waited under an awning, while Kiki stood out in the wet to hail a cab.

'You've been very kind and helpful,' said Carlene formally as Kiki opened the passenger door for her, as if they were not both getting in the same cab. The ride home was tense and quiet.

'When do all your people get back?' asked Kiki, and had to ask it twice because it was not heard, or there was a pretence of not hearing.

'It will depend on how long Monty is needed,' replied Carlene grandly. 'There is a church there that he does a lot of work with. He won't leave until they can spare him. His sense of duty is very strong.'

Now it was Kiki's turn to be annoyed.

They parted at Carlene's house, Kiki choosing to walk the rest of the way back. Pushing through the slush, she was struck by the growing, upsetting conviction that she had made a mistake. It had been stupid and perverse to greet such passionate spontaneity with complaints about the weather and the hour. She felt it to be a kind of test, and now she saw she had failed it. It was exactly the kind of offer Howard and the kids would have thought absurd, sentimental and impractical — it was an offer she should have taken up. She spent the late afternoon in a snappy sulk, testy with her family and uninterested in the peace lunch (one of many of the past few weeks) that Howard had cooked for her. After the meal she put on her hat and gloves and walked back round to Redwood Avenue. Clotilde answered the door and said that Mrs Kipps had just left for the Amherst house and wouldn't be back until tomorrow.

In a bit of a panic Kiki jogged as best she could to the bus stop; gave up on the bus, walked to the crossroads and managed to hail a cab. At the station she found Carlene buying a hot chocolate and preparing to board the train.

'Kiki!'

'I want to come — I'd love to — if you'll still have me.'

Carlene put one gloved hand to Kiki's

481

hot cheek in a manner that unexpectedly made her want to weep.

'You'll stay over. We'll eat in town and spend all tomorrow in the house. You're such a funny woman. What a thing to do!'

They were just walking arm in arm up the platform when they heard Carlene's name cried out several times: 'Mum! Hey, Mum!'

'Vee! Michael! But this is . . . hello, my darlings! Monty!'

'Carlene, what on *earth* are you doing here? Come here, let me kiss you, you silly old thing — what about this! So you're feeling better, then.' Here Carlene nodded like a happy child. 'Hello,' said Monty to Kiki, frowning as he did so, and shaking her hand briefly before turning back to his wife. 'We had a New York nightmare — the *incompetent* running that church — it's either incompetence or criminality — anyway, we're back early, and very pleased about it — not a chance Michael's getting married in that place, I can tell you *that* — not a chance — but what are you —'

'I was heading up to Eleanor's house,' said Carlene, beaming, accepting hugs on either side from her two children, one of whom, Victoria, was looking over at Kiki like a jealous lover. Another young girl, plainly dressed, with a blue polo neck and pearls at her throat, held Michael's spare arm. His fiancée, Kiki assumed.

'Kiki, I think we shall have to postpone our trip.'

'The man claimed to know nothing — *nothing* — of the last four letters we sent him about the school in Trinidad. He'd washed his hands of it! Shame he didn't tell anyone at *our* end.'

'And his accounts were *so* dodgy. I went through them. Something was definitely not right there,' added Michael.

Kiki smiled. 'Sure thing,' she said. 'Rain check — another day.'

'Do you need a lift?' Monty asked Kiki gruffly, as the family turned to go.

'Oh — thank you, no . . . there's four of you, and a cab wouldn't . . .'

The happy clan bustled away back down the platform, laughing and speaking over each other, as the Amherst train pulled away and Kiki stood with Carlene's hot chocolate in her hand.

on beauty and being wrong

When I say I hate time, Paul says how else could we find depth of character, or grow souls?

Mark Doty

I

A sprawling North London parkland, composed of oaks, willows and chestnuts, yews and sycamores, the beech and the birch; that encompasses the city's highest point and spreads far beyond it; that is so well planted it feels unplanned; that is not the country but is no more a garden than Yellowstone; that has a shade of green for every possible felicitation of light; that paints itself in russets and ambers in the autumn, canary-yellow in the splashy spring; with tickling bush grass to hide teenage lovers and joint smokers, broad oaks for brave men to kiss against, mown meadows for summer ball games, hills for kites, ponds for hippies, an icy lido for old men with strong constitutions, mean llamas for mean children and, for the tourists, a country house, its façade painted white enough for any Hollywood close-up, complete with a tea room, although anything you buy from there should be eaten outside with the grass beneath your toes, sitting under the magnolia tree, letting the white upturned bells of blossoms, blush-pink at their tips, fall all around you. Hampstead Heath! Glory of London! Where Keats walked and Jarman fucked, where Orwell exercised his weakened lungs and Constable never failed to find something holy.

It is late December now; the Heath wears its austere winter cloak. The sky is colourless. The trees are black and starkly cut back. The grass is hoary with a crunch underfoot, and the only relief is the occasional scarlet flash of the holly-berries. In a tall, narrow house that backs on to all this wonder, the Belseys are spending their Christmas break with Rachel and Adam Miller, very old college friends of Howard who have been married longer even than the Belseys. They have no children and do not celebrate Christmas. The Belseys have always loved visiting the Millers. Not for the house itself, which is a chaos of cats, dogs, half-finished canvases, jars of unidentifiable food, dusty African masks, twelve thousand books, too many knicks and a dangerous density of knacks. But the Heath! From every window the view commands you to come outside and enjoy it. The guests obey despite the cold. They spend half their stay in the Millers' small brambly garden that makes up for its size by ending where the Hampstead ponds begin. Howard, the Belsey children, Rachel and Adam were all in the garden — the kids skimming pebbles into the water, the adults watching two magpies build a nest in a high tree — when Kiki pushed up a triple sash window and walked towards them, holding her hand over her mouth.

'She's dead!'

Howard looked at his wife and felt only slightly alarmed. Everybody he truly loved was right here with him in this garden. Kiki came very close to him and hoarsely repeated her message.

'Who — Kiki, *who's* dead?'

'Carlene! Carlene Kipps, Michael — that was him, the son, on the phone.'

'How on earth did they get this number?' asked Howard obtusely.

'I don't *know* . . . I suppose my office gave . . . I can't believe this is *happening*. I saw her two weeks ago! She's being buried here, in London. In Kensal Green Cemetery. The funeral's on Friday.'

Howard's brow contracted.

'Funeral? But . . . we're not going, surely.'

'YES, we're going!' shouted Kiki and began to cry, alerting her children, who now came over. Howard held his wife in his arms.

'OK, OK, OK, we're going, we're

489

almost hourly for four days.

'*To whom it may concern,*' began Amelia, wide-eyed as a child and employing a babyish whisper. '*Upon my death I leave my Jean Hyp— Hyp—* I can never say that name! — *painting of Maîtresse Er— Erzu . . .*'

'We know which bloody painting it is!' snapped Michael. 'Sorry, Dad,' he added.

'*. . . to Mrs Kiki Belsey!*' announced Amelia as if these were the most remarkable words she'd ever been called upon to say out loud. 'And it's signed by Mrs Kipps!'

'She didn't write that,' said Michael again. 'No way. She never would do something like that. Sorry. No way. That woman obviously had some power over Mum that we weren't aware of — she must have had her eye on that painting for a while — we know she'd been in the house. No, sorry, this is completely out of order,' concluded Michael, although his argument had neatly double-backed on itself.

'She bedevilled Mrs Kipps's mind!' yelped Amelia, whose innocent imagination was infected by some of the more gaudy episodes in the Bible.

'Shut up, Ammy,' muttered Michael. He turned the note over as if its blank side might offer a clue to its provenance.

'This is a family matter, Amelia,' said Monty severely. 'And you are not yet family. It would be preferable if you kept your comments to yourself.'

Amelia held on to the cross at her throat and lowered her eyes. Victoria rose up from her armchair and snatched the paper from her brother. 'This is Mum's handwriting. Absolutely.'

'Yes,' said Monty, sensibly. 'I don't think there is any question of that.'

'Look, that painting is worth, what? About three hundred grand? Sterling?' said Michael, for the Kippses, unlike the Belseys, had no horror of talking frankly about money. 'Now there is absolutely no way, *no way* she would have let this fall out of the family . . . and what confirms it for me is that she'd already sort of mentioned, pretty recently —'

'Giving it to us!' squeaked Amelia. 'As a wedding present!'

'As it happens, she had,' agreed Michael. 'Now you're telling me she left the most valuable painting in the house to practically a stranger? To Kiki Belsey? I don't think so.'

'Wasn't there any other letter, anything else?' asked Victoria bewilderedly.

'Nothing,' said Monty. He passed a hand over his shiny pate. 'I can't understand it.'

Michael whacked the arm of the chaise he sat upon. 'Thinking of that woman taking advantage of somebody as ill as Mum — it's disgusting.'

'Michael — the question is how should we deal with this?'

And now the practical hats of the Kippses were put on. The women in the room were not offered hats and instinctively sat back in their chairs as Michael and his father leaned forward with their elbows on their knees.

'Do you think Kiki Belsey knows about this . . . *note?*' said Michael, barely allowing the last word the credence of its own existence.

'This is what we don't know. She's certainly made no claims. As yet.'

'Whether she knows or not,' flashed Victoria, 'she can't prove a thing, right? I mean she has no written evidence that would stand up in court or whatever. This is our *birthright,* for fuckssake.' Victoria allowed sobs to take her again. Her tears were petulant. It was the first time death in any form had ever forced its way into the pleasant confines of her life. Running alongside the genuine misery and loss was livid disbelief. In every other walk of life when the Kippses were hurt they were given access to recourse: Monty had fought three different libel cases; Michael and Victoria had been brought up to fiercely defend their faith and their politics. But this — this could not be fought. Secular liberals were one thing; death was another.

'I don't want that language, Victoria,' said Monty strongly. 'You'll respect this house and your family.'

'Apparently I respect my family more than Mum did — she doesn't even *mention* us.' She brandished the note and, in the process, dropped it. It floated listlessly to the carpet.

'Your mother,' said Monty, and stopped, shedding the first tear his children had yet seen since this began. To this tear Michael was unequal: his head fell back against the cushions; he let out a shrill, agonized croak and began to weep angry choking tears himself.

'Your mother,' tried Monty again, 'was a devoted wife to me and a beautiful mother to you. But she was very sick at the end — the Lord alone knows how she bore it. And this,' he said, retrieving the note from the floor, 'is a symptom of sickness.'

'Amen!' said Amelia and clutched her fiancé.

'Ammy, *please*,' growled Michael, pushing

her off. Amelia hid her head in his shoulder.

'I'm sorry to have shown it to you,' said Monty, folding the paper in half. 'It means nothing.'

'No one thinks it means anything,' snapped Michael, wiping his face with a handkerchief Amelia had thought to produce. 'Just burn the thing and forget about it.'

Finally the word was out there. A log popped loudly, as if the fire were listening and hungry for new fuel. Victoria opened her mouth but said nothing.

'Exactly,' said Monty. He scrunched up the note in his fist and tossed it lightly into the flames. 'Although we should invite her to the funeral, I think. Mrs Belsey.'

'Why!' cried Amelia. 'She's nasty — I saw her that time in the station and she looked right through me like I didn't even exist! She's uppity. And she's practically a Rastafarian!'

Monty frowned. It was becoming clear that Amelia was not the quietest of quiet Christian girls.

'Ammy has a point. Why should we?' said Michael.

'Clearly, in some way your mother felt close to Mrs Belsey. She'd been left alone a lot in the last few months, by all of us.'

Upon hearing this obvious truth, everyone found a spot on the floor to focus on. 'She made this friend. Whatever we think of it, we should respect it. We should invite her. It's only decent. Are we agreed? I don't suppose she'll be able to make it anyway.'

A few minutes later the children filed out again, feeling a degree more confused as to the true character of the person whose obituary was to appear in tomorrow morning's *Times*: Lady Kipps, loving wife of Sir Montague Kipps, devoted mother of Victoria and Michael, *Windrush* passenger, tireless church worker, patron of the arts.

2

Through the grubby windows of their minicab, the Belseys watched Hampstead morph into West Hampstead, West Hampstead into Willesden. At every railway bridge, a little more graffiti; on each street, fewer trees, and in their branches, more fluttering plastic bags. An acceleration of establishments selling fried chicken, until, in Willesden Green, it seemed every other shop sign made reference to poultry. Written in a giant, death-defying font above the train-tracks, a message: YOUR MUM

RANG. In different circumstances this would have amused.

'It gets kind of . . . more crappy down here,' ventured Zora, in the new, quiet voice she had assumed for this death. 'Aren't they rich? I thought they were rich.'

'It's their home,' said Jerome simply. 'They love it here. They've always lived here. They're not pretentious. That's what I was always trying to explain.'

Howard rapped the thick glass side window with his wedding ring. 'Don't be fooled. There're some bloody grand houses around here. Besides, men like Monty like being the big fish in a small pond.'

'Howard,' said Kiki in such a tone that nothing further was said until Winchester Lane, where their journey ended. The car pulled up beside a little English country church, torn from its village surroundings and dropped into this urban suburb, or so it seemed to the Belsey children. In fact it was the countryside that had receded. Only a hundred years earlier, a mere five hundred souls had lived in this parish of sheep fields and orchards, land that they rented from an Oxford college, which institution still counts much of Willesden Green among its possessions. This *was* a country church. Standing in the pebbled

forecourt under the bare branches of a cherry tree, Howard could almost imagine the busy main road completely vanished and in its place paddocks, hedgerows and eglantine, cobbled lanes.

A crowd was gathering. It pooled around the First World War memorial, a simple pillar with an illegible inscription, every single word smoothed into the recess of its own stone. Most people were wearing black, but there were many, like the Belseys, who were not. A wiry little man, in a street cleaner's orange tabard, was running two identical white bull terriers up and over the small mound of remaining garden between the vicarage and the church. He did not seem to be of the party. People looked after him disapprovingly; some tuts were heard. He continued to throw his stick. The two terriers persisted in bringing it back, their jaws clamped round it at either end, forming a new, perfectly coordinated eight-legged beast.

'Every kind of person,' whispered Jerome, because everybody was whispering. 'You can tell she knew every type of person. Can you imagine a funeral — *any* event — this mixed, back home?'

The Belseys looked around themselves and saw the truth of this. Every age, every colour and several faiths; people dressed very finely — hats and handbags, pearls and rings — and people who were clearly of a different world again, in jeans and baseball caps, saris and duffle coats. And among them — joyfully — Erskine Jegede! It was not appropriate to whoop and wave; Levi was sent over to fetch him. He came over doing his bull's stomp, dressed in natty racing-green tweed and brandishing an umbrella like a cane. All that was missing was the monocle. Looking at him now, Kiki could not work out why she hadn't noticed it before. Despite Erskine's more dandified stylings, sartorially, Monty and Erskine were a match.

'Ersk, thank *God* you're here,' said Howard, hugging his friend. 'But how come? I thought you were in Paris for Christmas.'

'I *was* — we were staying at the Crillon — what a hotel that is, that hotel is a beautiful place — and I got a phone call from Brockes, Lord Brockes,' added Erskine breezily. 'But Howard, you *know* I've known our friend Monty for a *very* long time. Either he was the first Negro at Oxford or I was — we can never agree on that. But even if we haven't always seen eye to eye, he is civilized and I am civilized. So here I am.'

'Of *course*,' said Kiki in rather an emotional way and took hold of Erskine's hand.

'And of course Caroline *insisted*,' continued Erskine mischievously, nodding to his wife's lean form across the way. She was standing in the archway of the church, engaged in conversation with a famous black British newscaster. Erskine looked mock-fondly after her. 'She is an awesome woman, my wife. She is the only woman I know who can power-broke at a funeral.' Here Erskine turned the volume down on his big Nigerian laugh. *'Anybody who's anybody will be there,'* he said, badly impersonating his wife's Atlanta twang, 'though I fear there aren't as many somebodies here as she had hoped. Half these people I have never seen before in my *life*. But there we are. In Nigeria we weep at funerals — in Atlanta apparently they network. It's marvellous! Actually, I'm rather surprised to see *you* here. I thought you and Sir Monty were drawing swords for January.' Erskine's umbrella turned into a rapier. 'So says the college grapevine. Yes, Howard. Don't tell me you're not here for your own ulterior motives, eh? Eh? But have I said the wrong thing?' asked Erskine as Kiki's hand dropped from his own.

'Umm . . . I guess Mom and Carlene were pretty close,' murmured Jerome.

Erskine held a hand dramatically to his breast. 'But you should have stopped me speaking out of turn! Kiki — I had no idea you even knew the lady. Now I am very embarrassed.'

'Don't be,' said Kiki, but looked at him coldly. Erskine was paralysed by social friction of any kind. He looked now as if he were in physical pain.

It was Zora who came to his rescue. 'Hey, Dad — isn't that Zia Malmud? Weren't you guys at school with him?'

Zia Malmud, cultural commentator, ex-socialist, anti-war campaigner, essayist, occasional poet, thorn in the side of the present government and regular TV presence, or, as Howard succinctly put it, 'typical rent-a-quote wanker', was standing by the monument, smoking his trademark pipe. Howard and Erskine quickly made their way through the crowd to say hello to their fellow Oxonian. Kiki watched them go. She saw vulgar relief paint itself in broad strokes all over Howard's face. It was the first time since they arrived at this funeral that he had been able to cease twitching, fiddling in his pockets, messing with his hair. For here was Zia Malmud, in and of himself nothing directly to do with the idea of death, and therefore able to bring welcome news of another world outside of this funeral, *Howard's* world: the world of conversation, debate, enemies, newspapers, universities. Tell me anything but don't talk of death. But the only duty you have at a funeral is to accept that somebody has died! Kiki turned away.

'You know,' she said in frustration, to no child in particular, 'I'm getting really tired of listening to Erskine bad-mouth Caroline like that. All these men ever do is talk about their wives with contempt. With *contempt.* I am *so* sick of it!'

'Oh, Mom, he doesn't mean it,' said Zora wearily, as once again she was called upon to explain how the world works to her mother. 'Erskine loves Caroline. They've been married *for ever.*'

Kiki restrained herself. Instead she opened her purse and began searching through it for her lip-gloss. Levi, who had resorted to kicking pebbles in his boredom, asked her who the guy with all the big gold chains was, with the guide dog. The Mayor, Kiki ventured, but couldn't be sure. *The Mayor of London?* Kiki muttered assent but now turned again, getting up on tiptoe so she might see over the heads of the crowd. She was looking for Monty. She was curious about him. She wanted to see what a man who had so worshipped his wife looked like once he was deprived of her. Levi continued to badger her: *Of the whole city? Like the New York Mayor?* Maybe not, agreed Kiki tetchily, maybe the mayor of just this area.

'Seriously . . . this is *weird,*' said Levi, and yanked his stiff shirt collar from his neck with a hooked finger. It was Levi's first funeral, but he meant more than that. It did seem a surreal gathering, what with the strange class mix (noticeable even to as American a boy as Levi) and the complete lack of privacy that the two-foot perimeter brick wall afforded. Cars and buses went by incessantly; noisy schoolchildren smoked, pointed and whispered; a group of Muslim women, in full hijab, floated by like apparitions.

'It's pretty low rent,' dared Zora.

'Look, it was *her* church, I came here with her — she would have wanted the service in her church,' insisted Jerome.

'Of *course* she would,' said Kiki. Tears pricked her eyes. She squeezed Jerome's hand and he, surprised by this emotion, returned the pressure. Without any announcement, or at least not one the Belseys heard, the crowd began to file into the church. The interior was as simple as the exterior suggested. Wood beams ran between stone walls, and the rood screen was of a dark oak, plainly carved. The stained glass was pretty, colourful, but rather basic, and there was only one painting, high on the back wall: unlit, dusty and too murky to make anything of at all. Yes, when you looked up and around you — as one instinctively does in a church — everything was much as you might have imagined. But then your eyes came to earth again, and at this point all those who had entered this church for the first time suppressed a shudder. Even Howard — who liked to think himself ruthlessly unsentimental when it came to matters of architectural modernization — could find nothing to praise. The stone floor had been completely covered by a thin, orange-and-grey capsule carpet; many large squares of fuzzy industrial felt slotted together. The pattern therein was of smaller orange boxes, each with its own sad grey outline. This orange had grown brownish under the influence of many feet. And then there were the pews, or rather their absence. Every single one had been ripped out and in their place rows of conference chairs — in this same airport-lounge orange — were placed in a timid half-circle meant to foster (so Howard envisioned) the friendly, informal atmosphere in which tea mornings and community meetings are conducted. The final effect was one of unsurpassable ugliness. It was not hard to reconstruct the chain of logic behind the decision: financial distress, the money to be had from selling nineteenth-century pews, the authoritarian severity of horizontal aisles, the inclusiveness of semicircles. But no — it was still a crime. It was too ugly. Kiki sat down with her family on the uncomfortable little plastic chairs. No doubt Monty wanted to prove he was a man of the people, as powerful men so often like to do — and at his wife's expense. Didn't Carlene deserve better than a small ruined church on a noisy main road? Kiki felt herself quiver with indignation. But then, as people took their seats and soft organ music began, Kiki's logic flipped all the way around. Jerome was right: this was Carlene's place of local worship. Really Monty was to be commended. He could have had the funeral somewhere fancy in Westminster, or up the hill in Hampstead, or — who knows — maybe even in St Paul's itself (Kiki did not pause over practicalities here), but no. Here, in Willesden Green, in the little local church she had loved, Monty had brought the woman he loved, before a congregation who cared for her. Kiki now chastised herself over her first, typically Belseyian opinion. Had she become unable to recognize real emotion when it was right in front of her? Here were simple people who loved their God, here was a church that wished to make its parishioners comfortable, here was an honest man who loved his wife — were these things really beneath consideration?

'Mom,' hissed Zora, pulling her mother's sleeve. '*Mom.* Isn't that Chantelle?'

Kiki, thus separated from uneasy thoughts, looked obediently to where Zora was pointing, although the name meant nothing to her.

'That can't be her. She's in my class,' said Zora, squinting. 'Well, not exactly *in* it but . . .'

The double doors of the church opened. Ribbons of daylight threaded through the shady interior, tying up a stack of gilt hymn books in their radiance, highlighting the blonde hair of a pretty child, the brass edging on the octangular font. All heads turned at once, in an awful echo of a wedding, to see Carlene Kipps, boxed in wood, coming up the aisle. Howard alone looked up into the simple concameration of the roof, hoping for escape or relief or distraction. Anything but this. He was greeted instead with a wash of music. It poured down on his head from above, from a balcony. There eight young men, with neat curtains of hair and boyish, rosy faces, were lending their lungs to an ideal of the human voice larger than any one of them.

Howard, who had long ago given up on this ideal, now found himself — in a manner both sudden and horrible — mortally affected by it. He did not even get the opportunity to check the booklet in his hand; never discovered that this was Mozart's *Ave Verum*, and this choir, Cambridge singers; no time to remind himself that he hated Mozart, nor to laugh at the expensive pretension of bussing down Kingsmen to sing at a Willesden funeral. It was too late for all that. The song had him. *Aaaah Vay-ay, Aah, aah, vay* sang the young men; the faint, hopeful leap of the first three notes, the declining dolour of the following three; the coffin passing so close to Howard's elbow he sensed its weight in his arms; the woman inside it, only ten years older than Howard himself; the prospect of her infinite residence in there; the prospect of his own; the Kipps children weeping behind it; a man in front of Howard checking his watch as if the end of the world (for so it was for Carlene Kipps) was a mere inconvenience in his busy day, even though this fellow too would live to see the end of his world, as would Howard, as do tens of thousands of people every day, few of whom, in their lifetimes, are ever able to truly believe in the oblivion to which they are dispatched. Howard gripped the arms of his chair and tried to regulate his breathing in case this was an asthmatic episode or a dehydration incident, both of which he had experienced before. But this was different: he was tasting salt, watery salt, a lot of it, and feeling it in the chambers of his nose; it ran in rivulets down his neck and pooled in the dainty triangular well at the base of his throat. It was coming from his eyes. He had the feeling that there was a second, gaping mouth in the centre of his stomach and that this was screaming. The muscles in his belly convulsed. All around him people bowed their heads and joined their hands together, as people do at funerals, as Howard knew: he had been to many of them. At this point in the proceedings it was Howard's more usual practice to doodle lightly with a pencil along the edge of the funeral programme while recalling the true, unpleasant relationship between the dead man in the box and the fellow presently offering a glowing eulogy, or to wonder whether the dead man's widow will acknowledge the dead man's mistress sitting in the third row. But at Carlene Kipps's funeral Howard kept faith with her coffin. He did not take his eyes from that box. He was quite certain he was making embarrassing noises. He was powerless to stop them. His thoughts fled from him and rushed down their dark holes. Zora's gravestone. Levi's. Jerome's. Everybody's. His own. Kiki's. Kiki's. Kiki's. Kiki's.

'Dad — you OK, man?' whispered Levi and brought his strong, massaging hand to the cleft between his father's shoulders. But Howard ducked this touch, stood up and left the church through the doors Carlene had entered.

It was bright when the service began; now the sky was overcast. The congregation were more talkative departing from the church than they had been before — sharing anecdotes and memories — but still did not know how to end conversations respectfully; how to turn the talk from the invisibles of the earth — love and death and what comes after — to its practicalities: how to get a cab and whether one was going to the cemetery, or the wake, or both. Kiki did not imagine she was welcome at either, but, as she stood by the cherry tree with Jerome and Levi, Monty Kipps came over to them and expressly invited her. Kiki was taken aback.

'Are you sure? We really wouldn't want to *intrude* in any way whatsoever.'

Monty's response was cordial. 'There's no question of intrusion. Any friend of my wife is welcome.'

'I *was* her friend,' said Kiki, perhaps too keenly, for Monty's smile shrank and tightened. 'I mean, I didn't know her real well, but what I knew . . . well, I really loved what I knew. I'm so sorry for your loss. She was an amazing person. Just so generous with people.'

'She was, yes,' said Monty, a queer look passing over his face. 'Of course, one worried sometimes that people would take advantage of exactly that quality.'

'Yes!' said Kiki, and impulsively touched his hand. 'I felt that too. But then I realized that that would always be a deadly shame on the person who *did* it, I mean, who took advantage — *never* on her.'

Monty nodded quickly. Of course he must have many other people to speak to. Kiki drew her hand back. In his low, musical voice he gave her directions to the cemetery and to the Kippses' house, where the wake was to be, nodding briefly at Jerome to acknowledge his prior acquaintance with the place. Levi's eyes widened during the instructions. He had no idea these funeral things had second and third acts.

'*Thank* you, really. And I'm . . . I am *so* sorry about Howard having to leave during the . . . he had a stomach . . . thing,' said Kiki, motioning unconvincingly in front of her own belly. 'I'm really just very sorry about that.'

'Please,' said Monty, shaking his head. He smiled again briefly and moved away into the crowd. They watched him go. He was stopped every few feet by well-wishers and dealt with each of them with the same courtesy and patience he had shown the Belseys.

'What a big man,' said Kiki admiringly to her sons. 'You know? He's just not *petty,*' she said, and here stopped herself, under the aegis of a new resolution not to criticize her husband in front of her children.

'Do we have to go to all that other stuff?' asked Levi and was ignored.

'I mean — what the hell was he *thinking?*' demanded Kiki suddenly. 'How can you walk out of somebody's funeral? What goes on in his head? How is that a way to . . .' she stopped herself again. She took a deep breath. 'And where in the *hell* is Zora?'

Holding hands with both her boys, Kiki walked the edge of the wall. They found Zora by the church doors talking to a shapely black girl in a cheap navy suit. She had a flapper's helmet of ironed hair, a kiss curl glued to her cheek. Both Levi and Jerome perked up at this attractive prospect.

'Chantelle's Monty's new project,' Zora was explaining. 'I *knew* it was you — we're in poetry class together. Mom, this is Chantelle, who I'm always telling you about?'

Both Chantelle and Kiki looked surprised by this.

'New project?' asked Kiki.

'Professor Kipps,' said Chantelle, barely audible, 'attends my church. He asked me to intern for him here over the holidays. Christmas is the busiest time — he has to get all the contributions to the islands that need them before Christmas Day — it's a real good opportunity . . .' added Chantelle, but looked miserable.

'So you're in Green Park,' said Jerome,

stepping forward as Levi hung back, for even this much acquaintance had confirmed for both that this girl was not for Levi. Despite her name and other appearances to the contrary, she was from Jerome's world.

'Excuse me?' said Chantelle.

'Monty's office — in Green Park. With Emily and all those guys.'

'Oh, yeah, that's right,' said Chantelle, her lip trembling so violently that Jerome at once regretted bothering her with the question. 'I'm just helping out a little, really . . . I mean I was *going* to help with that . . . but now it looks like I'm going home tomorrow.'

Kiki reached out and touched Chantelle's elbow. 'Well, at least you'll be home for Christmas.'

Chantelle smiled painfully at this. One sensed that Christmas in Chantelle's house was a thing best avoided.

'Oh, honey — it must have been a shock . . . coming here, and now this awful thing happens . . .'

It was just Kiki being Kiki, offering the simple empathy her children were so used to, but for Chantelle it was exactly too much of what she needed. She burst into tears. Kiki at once put her arms around her and brought her into her bosom.

'Oh, honey . . . oh . . . it's OK. It's OK, honey. There you are . . . you're fine. There's no problem . . . it's OK.'

Slowly Chantelle pulled back. Levi patted her gently on the shoulder. She was the kind of girl you wanted to look out for, one way or another.

'Are you going to the cemetery? Do you want to come along with us?'

Chantelle sniffed and wiped her eyes. 'No — thank you, ma'am — I'm gonna go home. I mean — to the hotel. I was staying at Sir Monty's house,' and she said this very carefully, emphasizing the oddity of the title to the American ear and tongue. 'But now . . . well, I leave tomorrow anyhow, like I said.'

'Hotel? A London hotel? Sister, that's crazy!' cried Kiki. 'Why don't you stay with us — with our friends? It's only one night — you can't pay all that money.'

'No, I'm not —' began Chantelle, but then stopped. 'I have to go now,' she said. 'Nice meeting all of you — I'm sorry about . . . Zora, guess I'll see you in January. Nice to see you. Ma'am.'

Chantelle nodded goodbye to the Belseys and hurried away towards the church gates. The Belseys followed at a slower pace, looking around themselves all the time for Howard.

'I do *not* believe this. He's gone! Levi — give me your cell.'

'It doesn't work here — I ain't got the right contract or whatever.'

'Me neither,' said Jerome.

Kiki ground her court heels into the gravel. 'He's crossed a line today. This was somebody else's day, this was *not* his day. This was somebody's *funeral.* He has just got no borders at all.'

'Mom, calm down. Look, my cell works — but who're you going to call, exactly?' asked Zora, sensibly. Kiki phoned Adam and Rachel, but Howard was not in Hampstead. The Belseys got into a minicab the practical Kippses had thought to call, one of a long line of foreign men in foreign cars, windows down, waiting.

3

Twenty minutes earlier, Howard had walked out of the churchyard, turned left and kept on walking. He had no plans — or at least, his conscious mind told him he had none. His subconscious had other ideas. He was heading for Cricklewood.

By foot he completed the final quarter-mile of a journey he had started by car this morning: down that changeable North London hill, which ends in ignominy with Cricklewood Broadway. At various points along this hill, areas are known to fall in and out of gentrification, but the two extremes of Hampstead and Cricklewood do not change. Cricklewood is beyond salvation: so say the estate agents who drive by the derelict bingo halls and the trading estates in their decorated Mini Coopers. They are mistaken. To appreciate Cricklewood you have to walk its streets, as Howard did that afternoon. Then you find out that there is more charm in a half-mile of Cricklewood's passing human faces than in all the double-fronted Georgian houses in Primrose Hill. The African women in their colourful kenti cloths, the whippet blonde with three phones tucked into the waistband of her tracksuit, the unmistakable Poles and Russians introducing the bone structure of Soviet Realism to an island of chinless, browless potato-faces, the Irish men resting on the gates of housing estates like farmers at a pig fair in Kerry . . . At this distance, walking past them all, thus itemizing them, *not having to talk to any of them,* flâneur Howard was able to love them and, more than this, to feel himself, in his own romantic fashion, to be one of them. We scum, we happy scum! From people like these he had come. To people like these he would always belong. It was an ancestry he referred to proudly at Marxist conferences and in print; it was a communion he occasionally felt on the streets of New York and in the urban out-skirts of Paris. For the most part, however, Howard liked to keep his 'working-class roots' where they flourished best: in his imagination. Whatever the fear or force that had thrust him from Carlene Kipps's funeral out on to these cold streets was what now compelled him to make this rare trip: down the Broadway, past the McDon-ald's, past the halal butchers, second road on the left, to arrive here, at No. 46 with the thick glass panel in the door. The last time he stood on this doorstep was almost four years ago. Four years! That was the summer when the Belsey family had con-sidered returning to London for Levi's sec-ondary education. After a disappointing reconnaissance of North London schools, Kiki insisted upon visiting No. 46, for old times' sake, with the kids. The visit did not go well. And since then only a few phone calls had passed between this house and 83

Langham, along with the usual cards on birthdays and anniversaries. Although Howard had visited London often in recent times, he had never stopped at this door. Four years is a long time. You don't stay away for four years without good reason. As soon as his finger pressed the bell, Howard knew he'd made a mistake. He waited — nobody came. Radiant with relief, he turned to go. It was the perfect visit: well intended but with no one at home. Then the door opened. An elderly woman he did not know stood before him with a nasty bunch of flowers in her hand — many carnations, a few daisies, a limp fern and one wilted star-gazer lily. She smiled coquettishly like a woman a quarter of her age greeting a suitor half Howard's.

'Hello,' said Howard.

'Hello, dear,' she replied serenely, and pressed on with her smile. Her hair, in the manner of old English ladies, was both voluminous and transparent, each golden curl (blue rinses having recently vanished from these isles) like gauze through which Howard could see the hallway behind.

'Sorry — is Harold in? Harold Belsey?'

'Harry? Yes, 'course. These are his,' she said, shaking the flowers, rather roughly. 'Come in, dear.'

'*Carol,*' Howard heard his father call from the little lounge they were swiftly approaching, '*who is that? Tell them <u>no</u>.*'

He was in his armchair, as usual. With the telly on, as usual. The room was, as ever, very clean and, in its way, very beautiful. It never changed. It was still frowsty and badly lit, with only one double-glazed window facing the street, but everywhere there was colour. Bright and brazen yellow daisies on the cushions, a green sofa, and three dining chairs painted pillar-box red. The wallpaper was an elaborate, almost Italianate paisley swirl of pinks and browns, like Neapolitan ice-cream. The carpet was hexagons of orange and brown and, in each hexagon, circles and diamonds had been drawn in black. A three-bar fire, portable, tall, like a little robot, had its metal back painted blue, bright as the Virgin's cloak. There was probably something richly comic about all this 1970s exuberance (left by the previous tenant) settling itself around the present, grey-suited, elderly tenant, but Howard couldn't laugh. It hurt his heart to note the unchanging details. How circumscribed must a life have become when a candy-coloured postcard of Mevagissey Harbour, Cornwall, is able to hold its place on the mantelpiece for four years! The pictures of Howard's mother, Joan, were likewise unmoved. A series of photos of Joan at London Zoo remained gathered in the one frame, overlapping each other. The one of her holding a pot of sunflowers still rested on top of the television. The one of her being blown about with her bridesmaids, veil flapping in the wind, remained hanging right by the light switch. She had been dead forty-six years, but every time Harold switched the light on, he saw her again.

Now Harold looked up at Howard. The older man was already crying. His hands shook with emotion. He struggled to get up from his chair and, when he did, embraced his son delicately around his middle, for Howard towered above him, now more than ever. Over his father's shoulder, Howard read the little notes resting on the mantelpiece, written on scraps of paper in a faltering hand.

Gone to Ed's for my haircut. Back soon.
To the Co-op to return kettle.
Back in 15 mins.
Gone shopping for nails. Back in 20 mins.

'I'll make the tea, then. Put these in a vase,' said Carol shyly behind them, and went off to the kitchen.

Howard put his hands on Harold's. He felt the little rough patches of psoriasis. He felt the ancient wedding ring embedded in skin.

'Dad, sit down.'

'Sit down? How can I sit *down?*'

'Just . . .' said Howard, pressing him back softly into his chair and taking the sofa for himself. 'Just, sit down.'

'Are the family with you?'

Howard shook his head. Harold assumed his vanquished position, hands in lap, head bowed, eyes closed.

'Who's that woman?' asked Howard. 'That's not the nurse, surely. Who are those notes for?'

Harold sighed profoundly. 'You didn't bring the family. Well . . . there it is. They didn't want to come, I'm sure . . .'

'Harry, that woman in there — who *is* that?'

'Carol?' repeated Harold, his face the usual mix of perplexity and persecution. 'But that's Carol.'

'Right. And who's Carol?'

'She's just a lady who comes by. What does it matter?'

Howard sighed and sat down on the green sofa. The moment his head connected with the velvet he felt like he'd been sitting here with Harry these forty years, the both of them still tied up in the terrible incommunicable grief of Joan's death. For they fell into the same patterns at once, as if Howard had never gone to university (against Harry's advice), never left this piss-poor country, never married outside his colour and nation. He'd never gone anywhere or done anything. He was still a butcher's son and it was still just the two of them, still making do, squabbling in a railway cottage in Dalston. Two Englishmen stranded together with nothing in common except a dead woman they had both loved.

'Anyway, I don't want to talk about *Carol,*' said Harry anxiously. 'You're here! I want to talk about that! You're *here.*'

'I'm just *asking* you who she *is!*'

Now Harold was exasperated. He was a little deaf and when troubled his voice could suddenly get very loud, without his realizing it. 'She's church-GOING. Pops round few times a week for tea. Just looks in, SEE IF I'M ALL RIGHT. Nice woman. Now, but how are *you?*' he said, adopting an anxiously jovial smile. 'That's what we're all wanting to know, aren't we? How's New York?'

Howard clenched his jaw. 'We pay for a nurse, Harry.'

'What, son?'

'I said *we pay for a nurse.* Why do you let these bloody people in? They're just bloody proselytizers.'

Harold rubbed his hand over his forehead. It took almost nothing to work him into a state of physical and mental panic, the kind normal people suffer when they can't find their child and then a policeman comes to the door.

'Prosler-what? What are you SAYING?'

'Christian nutters — pushing their crap on you.'

'But she doesn't mean anything by it! She's just a nice woman! Besides, I didn't like the nurse! She was a harpy — mean and bony. Bit feminist, you know. She wasn't nice to me, son. She was unhinged . . .' A few tears, here. Wiping them sloppily with the sleeve of his cardigan. 'But I stopped the service — last year I stopped it. Your Kiki did it for me. It's in me little book. You ain't paying for it. There's no . . . no . . . bugger, WHAT *IS* THE NAME OF IT? Debit . . . my mind goes . . . debit . . .'

'*Direct debit,*' supplied Howard, raising his own voice and hating himself now. 'It's not the bloody money, is it, Dad? It's about a standard of care.'

'I care for meself!' And then, under his breath, '*I bloody have to . . .*'

So how long was that? Eight minutes? Harry on the edge of his seat, pleading, and always pleading with the wrong words. Howard already incensed, looking at the rose in the ceiling. A stranger could come in now and think them both completely insane. And neither man would be able to give an account of why what had just happened had happened, or at least no account that would be shorter than sitting down with the stranger and taking them through an oral history — with slides — of the past fifty-seven years, day by day. They didn't mean it to be like this. But it *was* like this. Both had other intentions. Howard had knocked on the door eight minutes ago filled with hope, his heart loosened by music, his mind stunned and opened by the appalling proximity of death. He was a big malleable ball of potential change, waiting on the doorstep. Eight minutes ago. But once inside, everything was the same as it had always been. He didn't mean to be so aggressive, or to raise his voice or to pick fights. He meant to be kind and tolerant. Equally, four years ago, Harry surely hadn't meant to tell his only son that you couldn't expect black people to develop mentally like white people do. He had *meant* to say: I love you, I love my grandchildren, please stay another day.

'Here you are,' sang Carol, and put two unappetizing milky teas before the Belseys. 'No, I won't stay. I'll be going.'

Harold wiped yet another tear away. 'Carol, don't go! This is my son. Howard, I've told you about him.'

'Charmed, I'm sure,' said Carol, but she did not look charmed and now Howard regretted having spoken so loudly.

'Dr Howard Belsey.'

'Doctor!' cried Carol, without smiling. She crossed her arms across her chest, waiting to be impressed.

'No, no . . . not medical,' clarified Harold and looked defeated. 'He didn't have the patience for medical.'

'Oh, well,' said Carol, 'we can't all save lives. Nice, though. Nice to meet you, Howard. Next week, Harry. May the good Lord go with you. Otherwise known as, don't do nothing I wouldn't. Now you won't, will you?'

'Chance'd be a fine thing!'

They laughed — Harry still wiping tears — and walked to the front door together, continuing with these banal little English catchphrases that never failed to drive Howard up the bleeding wall. His childhood had been shot through with this meaningless noise, just so many substitutes for real conversation. *Brass monkeys out there. Don't mind if I do. I don't fancy yours much.* And on. And on. This was what he had been running from when he escaped to Oxford and every year since Oxford. Half-lived life. *The unexamined life is not worth living.* That had been Howard's callow teenage dictum. Nobody tells you, at seventeen, that examining it will be half the trouble.

'Now: how much do you want to put on it as a reserve?' asked the man on the television. 'Forty quid?'

Howard wandered into the golden-yellow galley kitchen to pour his tea down the sink and make an instant coffee. He hunted in the cupboards for a biscuit (when did he ever eat biscuits? Only here! Only with this man!) and found a couple of HobNobs. He filled his cup and heard Harold settling back into his chair. Howard turned round in the tiny space allowed him and knocked something off the sideboard with his elbow. A book. He picked it up and brought it through.

'This yours?'

He could hear his own accent climbing down the class ladder a few rungs to where it used to be.

'Oh, bloody hell . . . look at him. He *is* a right ponce,' said Harold, referring to the television. He tuned in to Howard: 'I dunno. What is it?'

'A book. Unbelievably.'

'A book? One of mine?' said Harold blithely, as if this room housed half the Bodleian rather than three *A–Z*s of varying sizes and a free Koran that had come in the post. It was a hardback royal blue library book that had been relieved of its dust jacket. Howard looked at the spine.

'A *Room with a View*. Forster.' Howard smiled sadly. 'Can't stand Forster. Enjoying it?'

Harold screwed up his face in distaste. 'Ooh, no, not mine. Carol's I should think. She's always got a book on the go.'

'Not such a bad idea.'

'What's that, son?'

'I said it's not such a bad idea. Reading something — every now and then.'

'No doubt, no doubt . . . that was always more your mum, though, weren't it? Always had a book in her hand. Walked into a lamp-post once reading a book in the street,' said Harold, a story Howard had heard and heard and heard, as he had heard the bit that came next and came now. 'Spose that's where *you* got it from

528

. . . Oh, blimey, look at this big tart. Look at him! I mean, purple and pink? He's not serious, though, is he?'

'Who?'

'*Him* — whatsisname . . . he's a bloody fool. Wouldn't know an antique if it was being shoved up his arse . . . But it was funny yesterday 'cause he was doing the bit where you guess the price the thing'll go for before it goes — I mean, it's mostly tat, I wouldn't give you ten bob for most of it, if I'm honest, and we had better stuff than that just knocking around me mum's house . . . never gave it a first thought never mind a second, but there you are . . . I've forgotten what I was on about now . . . oh, yeah, so it's usually couples or mother and daughter that he gets on, but yesterday he's got these two women — like bloody buses, both of 'em huge, hair very short, dressed like blokes of course, like they do, ugly as *sin* and looking to buy some military stuff, medals and that, 'cos they were in the bloody army, weren't they, and they're holding hands, oh dear . . . I was *laughing,* oh, dear . . .' And here Harold chuckled mirthfully. 'And you could tell *he* didn't know what to say . . . I mean, he's not exactly kosher himself, now is he?' Harold laughed some more, and then grew serious, noting, possibly, the lack of laughter elsewhere in the room. 'But then there's always been that aspect in the army, hasn't there? I mean, that's the main place you find them, the women . . . I spose it must suit them more, mentally . . . as it were,' said Harold, this last being his only verbal pretension. *Now, Howard, as it were* . . . He'd started using it when Howard came home for the summer after his first year in Oxford.

'Them?' asked Howard, putting his HobNob down.

'You what, son? Look, you've broken your biscuit. Should have brought a saucer for crumbs.'

'Them. I was just wondering who "they" are.'

'Oh, now Howard, don't get angry about nothing. You're always so angry!'

'No,' said Howard, in a tone of pedantic insistence, 'I'm just trying to understand the point of the story you just told me. Are you trying to explain to me that the women were lesbians?'

Harold's face creased into the picture of distressed aesthetic sensitivity, as if Howard had just put his foot through *The Mona Lisa. The Mona Lisa.* A painting Harold loves. When Howard was having his first pieces of criticism printed in the sorts of papers Harold never buys, a customer of Harold's had shown the butcher a cutting of his son writing enthusiastically about Piero Manzoni's *Merda d'Artista*, Harold closed the shop and went down the road with a handful of twopence to use the phone. 'Shit in a jar? Why can't you write about somefing lovely, like *The Mona Lisa*? Your mum would be so proud of that. *Shit in a jar?*'

'There's no need for that, Howard,' said Harold soothingly now. 'It's just my way of talking — I ain't seen you in so long, just happy to see you, aren't I, just trying to find something to say, you know . . .'

Howard, with what he considered to be superhuman effort, said nothing further.

Together they watched *Countdown*. Harold passed his son a little white pad on which to do his calculations. Howard scored well through the word round, doing better than both the contestants of the show. Meanwhile Harold struggled. His highest was a five-letter word. But in the numbers round, the power changed hands. There are always a few things our parents know about us that nobody else does. Harold Belsey was the only person who knew that when it came to the manipulation of numbers, Dr Howard Belsey, M.A., Ph.D., was a mere child. Even the most basic of multiplications required a calculator. He had been able to hide this for more than twenty years in seven different universities. But in Harold's living room the truth would out.

'One hundred and fifty-six,' announced Harold, which was the target amount. 'What you got, son?'

'A hundred and . . . No, I'm nowhere. Nothing.'

'Got you, Professor!'

'You did.'

'Yeah, well . . .' agreed Harold, nodding as the contestant on the television explained her rather convoluted 'workings out'. ' 'Course you *can* do it that way, love, but mine's a damn sight prettier.'

Howard laid down his pen and pressed his hands to his temples.

'You all right, Howard? You've had a face like a smacked arse since you got in here. Everything all right at home?'

Howard looked up at his father and decided to do something he never did. Tell him the truth. He expected nothing from this course of action. He was talking to the wallpaper as much as to this man.

'No, it's not all right.'

'No? What's the matter? Oh, God, no one's dead, are they, son? I couldn't stand it if anyone's dead!'

'*No* one's dead,' said Howard.

'Bloody out with it, then — you'll give me a heart attack.'

'Kiki and me . . .' said Howard using a grammar older than his marriage, 'we're . . . not good. Actually, Harry, I think we're finished.' Howard put his hands over his eyes.

'Now that can't be right,' said Harold cautiously. 'You've been married — what is it now? Twenty-eight years — summink like that?'

'Thirty, actually.'

'There you are, then. It don't just fall apart, just like that, does it?'

'It does when you . . .' Howard released an involuntary moan as he took his hands from his eyes. 'It's got too hard. You can't carry on when it gets this hard. When you can't even *talk* to someone . . . You've just lost what there was. That's how I feel now. I can't believe it's happening.'

Harold now closed his eyes. His face contorted like a quiz-show contestant's. Losing women was his specialist subject. He did not speak for a while.

' 'Cos she wants to finish it or you do?' he said finally.

'Because she wants to,' confirmed Howard, and found that he was comforted by the simplicity of his father's questions. 'And . . . because I can't find enough reasons to stop her wanting to.'

And now Howard succumbed to his heritage — easy, quick-flowing tears.

'There, son. It's better out than in, isn't it,' said Harold quietly. Howard laughed softly at this phrase: so old, so familiar, so utterly useless. Harold reached forward and touched his son's knee. Then he leaned back in his chair and picked up his remote control.

'She found a black fella, I spose. It was always going to happen, though. It's in their nature.'

He turned the channel to the news. Howard stood up.

'Fuck,' he said frankly, wiping his tears with his shirtsleeve and laughing grimly. 'I never *fucking* learn.' He picked up his coat and put it on. 'See you, Harry. Let's leave it a bit longer next time, eh?'

'Oh, no!' whimpered Harold, his face stricken by the calamity of it. 'What are you saying? We're having a nice time, ain't we?'

Howard stared at him, disbelievingly.

'No. Son, *please.* Oh, come on and stay a bit longer. I've said the wrong thing, have

I? I've said the wrong thing. Then let's sort it! You're always in a rush. Rush 'ere, rush there. People these days think they can outrun death. It's just time.'

Harry just wanted Howard to sit down, start again. There were four more hours of quality viewing lined up before bedtime — antique shows and property shows and travel shows and game shows — all of which he and his son might watch together in silent companionship, occasionally commenting on this presenter's overbite, another's small hands or sexual preference. And this would all be another way of saying: *It's good to see you. It's been too long. We're family.* But Howard couldn't do this when he was sixteen and he couldn't do it now. He just did not believe, as his father did, that time is how you spend your love. And so, to avoid a conversation about an Australian soap actress, Howard moved into the kitchen to wash up his cup and a few other things in the sink. Ten minutes later he left.

4

The Victorians were terrific cemetery designers. In London we used to have seven,

'The Magnificent Seven': Kensal Green (1833), Norwood (1838), Highgate (1839), Abney Park (1840), Brompton (1840), Nunhead (1840) and Tower Hamlets (1841). Rangy pleasure gardens in the daytime, necropolises by night, they crawled with ivy and sprung daffodils from their rich mulch. Some have been built over; others are in an appalling state of disrepair. Kensal Green survives. Seventy-seven acres, two hundred and fifty thousand souls. Space for Anglican Dissenters, Muslims, the Russian Orthodox, one famous Zoroastrian and, next door in St Mary's, the Catholics. Here are angels without their heads, Celtic crosses missing their extremities, a few sphinxes toppled over into the mud. It is what La Cimetière du Père Lachaise would look like if nobody knew it was there or went to visit it. In the 1830s Kensal Green was a peaceful spot, northwest of the city, where the great and the good might find their final rest. Now, on all sides, this 'country' cemetery greets the city: flats on one side, offices on the other, the railway trains vibrate the flowers in their cheap plastic pots, and the chapel cowers under the gas holder, a mammoth drum stripped of its skin.

Behind a line of yew trees in the

northern part of this cemetery, Carlene Kipps was buried. Walking away from the grave, the Belseys kept a distance from the rest of the party. They felt themselves to be in a strange social limbo. They knew no one except the family, and yet they were not close to the family. They had no car (the cabbie having refused to wait), and no clear idea of how to get to the wake. They kept their eyes to the ground and tried to walk at the proper funereal pace. The sun was so low that the stone crosses on one line of graves cast their spectral shadows on the plots of graves in front of them. In her hand Zora held a little leaflet she'd taken out of a box at the entrance. It featured an incomprehensible map of the cemetery and a list of the notable dead. Zora was interested in seeking out Iris Murdoch or Wilkie Collins or Thackeray or Trollope or any of the other artists who, as the poet put it, went to paradise by way of Kensal Green. She tried suggesting this literary detour to her mother. Through her tears (that had not stopped since the first scattering of earth was thrown over the coffin), Kiki glared. Zora tried falling behind a little, veering slightly off course to check out any grave that looked likely. But her instincts were all wrong. The twelve-foot mausoleums with winged angels on top and laurels at their base are for sugar merchants, property dealers and military men — not writers. She could have searched all day and not found Collins's grave, for example: a simple cross atop a block of plain stone.

'Zora!' hissed Kiki, in that powerful scream of hers that yet had no volume. 'I'm not going to tell you again. Keep *up*.'

'*Okay.*'

'I want to get out of here tonight.'

'*Okay!*'

Levi tucked his arm around his mother. She was not right in herself, he could tell. Her long plait swung against his hand like a horse's tail. He grabbed it and gave it a playful tug.

'I'm sorry about your friend,' he said.

Kiki brought his hand from behind her back and kissed the knuckles.

'Thank you, baby. It's crazy . . . I don't even know why I'm so upset. I barely knew the woman, you know? I mean, I really didn't know her at all.'

'Yeah,' said Levi thoughtfully, as his mother pulled his head softly into her shoulder. 'But sometimes it's like you just meet someone and you just know that you're totally connected, and that this person is, like, your brother — or your sister,' adjusted Levi, for he had been thinking of somebody else entirely. 'Even if they don't, like, recognize it, *you* feel it. And in a lot of ways it don't matter if they do or they don't see that for what it is — all you can do is put the feeling out there. That's *your* duty. Then you just wait and see what comes back to you. That's the deal.'

There was a little silence here that Zora felt the need to puncture.

'*Amen!*' she said, laughing. 'Preach it, brother, preach it!'

Levi punched Zora in her upper arm, and then Zora punched him back, and then they ran, weaving through the graves, Zora racing from Levi. Jerome called after them both to have some respect. Kiki knew she should stop them, but she could not help feeling it was a relief to hear curses and laughter and whoops fill the darkening day. It took one's mind off all the people underfoot. Now Kiki and Jerome paused on the white stone steps of the chapel and waited for Zora and Levi to join them. Kiki heard her children's clattering footsteps reverberate through the archways behind her. They rushed towards her like the shadows of people escaped from their graves, and came to a halt by her feet, panting and laughing. She could no longer see their features in this dusk, only the outlines and movements of beloved faces she knew by heart.

'OK, that's enough now. Let's get out of here, please. Which way?'

Jerome took his glasses off and wiped them on the corner of his shirt. Hadn't the burial been just to the left of this very chapel? In which case they had walked in a teasing circle.

After taking leave of his father, Howard walked across the Street and into the Windmill pub. Here he ordered and began drinking a perfectly reasonable bottle of red wine. His chosen seat was, he thought, in a neglected corner of the bar. But two minutes after he sat down, a huge flat screen that he had not noticed was lowered down near his head and switched on. A football game commenced between a white team and a blue team. Men gathered round. They seemed to accept and like Howard, mistaking him for one of those dedicated souls who come early to get the best seat. Howard allowed this misinterpretation and found himself taken up in the general fervour. Soon he was cheering and complaining with the rest. When a stranger, in his enthusiasm, tipped some beer down Howard's shoulder, Howard smiled, shrugged and said nothing. A little while later this same fellow bought Howard a beer, saying nothing when he put it down in front of Howard and seeming to expect nothing in return. At the end of the first half another man beside him knocked glasses with Howard in a very jolly way, in approval of Howard's random decision to cheer the blue team, although the game itself was still 0–0. This score never changed. And after the game finished nobody hit each other or got angry — it didn't seem to be that kind of game. 'Well, we got what we needed,' said one man philosophically. Three other men smiled and nodded at the truth of this. Everybody seemed satisfied. Howard also nodded and polished off the end of his bottle. It takes a lot of practice to ensure that a whole bottle of Cabernet and a pint of beer makes only a slight dent in your sobriety, but Howard felt he had reached this stage of accomplishment. All that happened these days was a pleasant imprecision that settled itself around him like a duvet, padding, protecting. He'd got what he needed. He went down the hall to use the phone opposite the loos.

'Adam?'

'Howard.' Said in a tone of a man who can finally call off the search party.

'Hi. Look, I've been separated from everyone . . . Have they called?'

There was a silence at the end of the phone that Howard correctly identified as concern.

'Howard . . . are you drunk?'

'I'm going to pretend you didn't say that. I'm trying to find Kiki. Is she with you?'

Adam sighed. 'She's looking for you. She left an address. She said to tell you they're going to the wake.'

Howard rested his forehead on the wall next to the pinned-up list of minicabs.

'Howard — I'm painting. I'm getting it all over the phone. Do you want the address?'

'No, no . . . I have it. Did she sound — ?'

'Yes, *very*. Howard, I've got to go. We'll see you back at the house later.'

Howard ordered a minicab and went outside to wait for it. When it arrived, the driver's door opened and a young Turk in the literal sense leaned out and asked Howard a rather metaphysical question:

'Is it you?'

Howard stepped forward from the pub wall. 'Yes, it's me.'

'Where you go?'

'Queen's Park, please,' said Howard, and walked unsteadily round the car to get into the front seat. As soon as he sat down he realized that this was not the usual procedure. It was surely uncomfortable for a driver to have a passenger sitting so close to him, wasn't it? Or was it? They drove in silence, a silence that Howard experienced as unbearably fraught with homoerotic, political and violent implications. He felt he must say something.

'I'm not trouble, you know, I'm not one of those English thugs — I'm a bit pissed, that's all.'

The young driver looked at him with a defensive, uncertain air. 'You trying to be funny?' he said in his thick accent, which yet possessed a fluency that made *You trying to be funny?* sound like a Turkish homily.

'Sorry,' said Howard, blushing. 'Ignore me. Ignore me.' He put his hands between his knees. The cab swung by the tube station where Howard had first met Michael Kipps.

'Straight down, I think,' said Howard very quietly. 'Then maybe a left at the main road — yes, and then over the bridge and then it's on your right, I think.'

'You talk quiet. I can't hear.'

Howard repeated himself. His driver

turned and looked at him incredulously. 'You don't know *name of street?*'

Howard had to admit he did not. The young Turk grumbled something furiously in Turkish, and Howard felt one of those English minicab tragedies coming on in which customer and cabbie drive round and round, and the fare rises and rises, finally you reach the ugliness of being sworn at and cast out on to the street, further from your destination than ever.

'There! That's it! We just passed it!' cried Howard and opened the door while the cab was still moving. A minute later, the young Turk and Howard parted on frosty terms, not much warmed by Howard's twenty-pence tip, the only extra change he had in his pocket. It is on journeys like this — where one is so horribly misunderstood — that you find yourself longing for home, that place where you are entirely understood, for better or for worse. Kiki was home. He needed to find her.

Howard pushed open the Kippses' front door, ajar once again, though for quite a different reason than the last time. The chequered hallway was busy with sombre faces and black suits. Nobody turned to look at Howard except one girl with a tray of sandwiches who came forward and offered him one. Howard took an egg and cress and wandered into the living room. It was not one of those wakes in which the tension of the funeral is released and dissipated. No one here was laughing softly at an affectionate memory or retelling a scurrilous story. The atmosphere was as solemn as it had been in the church, and that lively, surprising woman whom Howard had met a year ago in this very room was presently being piously preserved in the aspic of low voices and bland anecdote, pickled in perfection. *She was always,* Howard heard one woman say to another, *thinking of other people, never of herself.* Howard picked up somebody else's large glass of wine from the dining table and went to stand by the French doors. From here he had a good view of the living room, the garden, the kitchen and the hallway. No Kiki. No kids. No Erskine, even. He could see half of Michael Kipps opening the oven door and taking out a large tray of sausage rolls. Suddenly Monty came into the room. Howard turned towards the garden and looked out on that huge tree where, unbeknown to him, his eldest son had lost his innocence. Not knowing what else to do, he stepped out and closed the door quietly behind him. Instead of walking down the long garden where, as the sole person out here, he would only make himself more conspicuous, Howard walked round the side return, a thin alley between the Kippses' place and next door. Here he paused, rolled a thin cigarette and smoked it. The combination of this new, sweet white wine in his hand, the bitter air and the tobacco made him feel light-headed. He walked further down the alley to a side door and sat down on its cold step. From this perspective the suburban opulence of five neighbouring gardens announced itself: the knobby branches of the hundred-year-old trees, the corrugated roofs of the sheds, the moneyed amber glow of halogen bulbs. So quiet. A fox keening somewhere like a crying child, but no cars, no voices. Would his family have been happier here? He had run from a potentially bourgeois English life straight into the arms of an actual American one — he saw that now — and, in the disappointment of the attempted escape, he had made other people's lives miserable. Howard put out his cigarette on the pebbled ground. He gulped thickly but did not cry. He was not his father. He heard the Kippses' doorbell go. He rose up halfway, listening out hopefully for his wife's voice. Not her. Kiki and the kids must have come and gone. He pictured his family like a Greek chorus, repulsed and outraged by him, rushing from the stage the moment he stepped on it. Maybe he would spend the rest of his life trailing them from house to house.

Now he stood up properly and opened the side door behind him. He found himself in a kind of utility room packed with appliances for washing, drying, ironing and vacuuming. This room led back on to the hallway, and from here Howard kept his head down and turned with the banister, climbing the stairs two by two. On the upper landing he was confronted by six identical doors and no clues as to which of them might open on to a bathroom. He opened one at random — a pretty bedroom, as clean as a room in a show house, without sign of habitation. Two side tables. A book on each. This was sad. He closed the door and opened the next. What he glimpsed was a wall painted like an Italian fresco, with birds and butterflies and winding vines. He could not imagine such fancy anywhere but a bathroom, so he opened the door a little wider. A bed with a pair of bare human feet at its far end.

'Sorry!' said Howard and pulled the door too strongly towards him. This had the effect of making it slam and then bounce right back to where it had been and beyond, clattering against the inner wall. Victoria, dressed in her funeral black down to the waist. But the knee-length skirt had been replaced by a very small pair of green velveteen sports shorts with a silver trim. She had been crying. Her long legs were flat out in front of her; now she gathered them up in her arms in surprise.

'Fucking hell!'

'Oh, God, I'm sorry! Sorry,' said Howard. He had to step deep into the room to grab the doorknob. He tried to look in the opposite direction as he did so.

'Howard *Belsey?*' Victoria flipped round on the bed and knelt up.

'Yes, sorry. I'll just close this.'

'Wait!'

'What?'

'Just — wait.'

'I'll just . . .' said Howard and began to close the door, but Victoria jumped up now and held the door from the other side.

'You're *in* now, so come *in*. You're already *in,*' she said angrily and pushed the door shut with her flat hand. They stood close together for a second; then she retreated to

548

the bed and glared at him. Howard held his wine glass with both hands and looked into it.

'I'm . . . sorry for your loss, I . . .' he began absurdly.

'What?'

Howard looked up and watched Victoria take a swig out of a tall glass filled with red wine. He saw now that there was an empty wine bottle next to her.

'I should go. I was looking for the —'

'Look, you're *in* now. Just sit *down.* We're not in your class now.'

She pushed herself up to the bedstead, and sat leaning against it with crossed legs, her toes in each hand. She was excited, or at least excitable; she fidgeted around on her seat. Howard stayed where he was. He could not move.

'Thought it was the bathroom,' he said very quietly.

'*What?* I can't hear you, whatever you're saying.'

'The walls — thought it was the bathroom.'

'Oh. Well, no. It's a boudoir,' explained Victoria and performed a sloppy, sarcastic flourish with her free hand.

'I see that,' said Howard, looking about at the vanity table, the sheepskin rug and the chaise covered in a fabric print that seemed to have been the original inspiration for whoever had painted the walls. It did not appear to be a Christian girl's bedroom.

'And so now,' said Howard steadily, 'I'm going to go.'

Victoria reached behind her for a huge furry cushion. She threw this violently at Howard, getting him on the shoulder and spilling a little of his wine across his hand.

'Hello? I'm in *mourning?*' she said with that nasty transatlantic twang Howard had noted before. 'The very *least* you can do is sit down and give me a bit *of pastoral care,* Dr. Look, if it makes you happier,' she said springing from the bed and tip-toeing across the room to the door, 'I'll put the lock on so no one can disturb us.' She tiptoed back to the bed. 'Is that better?'

No, it was not better. Howard turned to leave.

'Please, I need to talk to someone,' came the breaking voice behind him. 'You're here. Nobody else is here. They're all praising the Lord downstairs. You're *here.*'

Howard put his fingers to the lock. Victoria thumped her bedcovers.

'*God!* I won't *hurt* you! I'm asking you to *help* me. Isn't that part of your *job?* Oh, forget it, OK? Just forget it. Fuck off.'

She started to cry. Howard turned around.

'Shit, shit, shit. I'm so *bored* with crying!' said Victoria through tears, and then began to laugh at herself a little. Howard moved to the chaise opposite the bed and slowly sat down. It was actually a relief to sit down. He was still experiencing an unhelpful head rush from his cigarette. Victoria wiped her tears with the sleeves of her black shirt.

'Blimey. That's far away.'

Howard nodded.

'Bit unfriendly.'

'I'm not a friendly man.'

Victoria took a deep gulp from her tumbler. She touched the silver edges of her green shorts.

'I must look like a total freak. But I just *have* to be comfy once I'm in the house — I've always been like that. Couldn't take that skirt any longer. *Have* to be comfy.'

She bounced her knees up and down against the mattress. 'Is your family here?' she asked.

'I was looking for them. That's what I was doing.'

'I thought you said you were looking for the loo,' said Victoria accusingly, closing one eye, stretching out her arm and pointing one unsteady finger at him.

'That too.'

'Hmm.' She swivelled round again and now bellyflopped towards him, so her feet were against the bedstead and her head not far from Howard's knees. She balanced her glass hazardously on top of the duvet and rested her chin on her hands. She examined his face and, after a time, softly smiled, as if something she found there had amused her. Howard followed her eyes with his own as they roved, trying to focus them on the matter at hand.

'My mother died,' he attempted, quite unable to hit the note he meant to. 'So I know what you're going through. I was younger than you when she died. Much younger.'

'That would probably explain it,' she said. She lost her smile and replaced it with a thoughtful scowl. 'Why you can't say *I like the tomato.*'

Howard frowned. What game was this? He took out his pocket of tobacco. 'I — like — the — tomato,' he said slowly and pulled the Rizlas from the bag. 'May I?'

'I don't care. Don't you want to know what that means?'

'Not terribly. I've got other things on my mind.'

'It's a Wellington thing — it's a student

thing,' said Victoria rapidly, coming up on her elbows. 'It's our shorthand for when we say, like, Professor Simeon's class is "The tomato's nature versus the tomato's nurture", and Jane Colman's class is "To properly understand the tomato you must first uncover the tomato's suppressed Herstory" — she's *such* a silly bitch that woman — and Professor Gilman's class is "The tomato is structured like an aubergine", and Professor Kellas's class is basically "There is no way of proving the existence of the tomato without making reference to the tomato itself", and Erskine Jegede's class is "The post-colonial tomato as eaten by Naipaul". And so on. So you say, "What class have you got coming up?" and the person says "Tomatoes 1670–1900." Or whatever.'

Howard sighed. He licked one side of his Rizla.

'Hilarious.'

'But your class — your class is a cult classic. I *love* your class. Your class is all about never *ever* saying *I like the tomato.* That's why so few people take it — I mean, no offence, it's a compliment. They can't handle the rigour of never saying *I like the tomato.* Because that's the worst thing you could ever do in your class, right? Because the tomato's not there to be *liked.* That's what I *love* about your class. It's properly intellectual. The tomato is just totally revealed as this phoney construction that can't lead you to some higher truth — nobody's pretending the tomato will save your life. Or make you happy. Or teach you how to live or *ennoble* you or be a *great example of the human spirit.* Your tomatoes have got nothing to do with *love* or *truth.* They're not fallacies. They're just these pretty pointless tomatoes that people, for totally selfish reasons of their own, have attached cultural — I should say *nutritional* — weight to.' She chuckled sadly. 'It's like what you're always saying: let's *interrogate* these terms. What's so beautiful about this tomato? Who decided on its worth? I find that really challenging — I wanted to tell you before; I'm *glad* I've told you. Everybody's so scared of you they don't say anything and I always think *Look, he's just a guy, professors are just people — maybe he'd like to hear that we appreciate this class,* you know? Anyway. Definitely your class is the most rigorous, intellectually . . . Everybody knows it, really, and Wellington is such a nerd heaven so that's basically a serious compliment.'

Here Howard closed his eyes and pulled

his fingers through his hair. 'Out of interest, what is your father's class?'

Victoria considered this a moment. She swigged the rest of her wine down. 'Tomatoes Save.'

'Of course.'

Victoria rested her head in her palm and sighed. 'I can't believe I told you about the tomatoes. I'm going to be excommunicated when we get back.'

Howard opened his eyes and lit his cigarette. 'I won't tell.'

They smiled at each other, briefly. Then Victoria seemed to recall where she was and why — her face fell, her lips pulled tight and vibrated with the effort of holding back the water in her eyes. Howard sat back into the sofa. For a few minutes they said nothing. Howard puffed away steadily.

'Kiki,' she said suddenly. And how awful the corruption when you hear the name of your heart in the mouth of the person you are about to betray her with! 'Kiki,' she repeated, 'your wife. She's amazing. Looking. She's like a queen. Imperious-looking.'

'Queen?'

'She's very beautiful,' said Victoria impatiently, as if Howard were being particularly dense about an obvious truth. 'Like an African queen.'

Howard pulled harshly on the tight end of his fag. 'She wouldn't thank you for that description, I'm afraid.'

'Beautiful?'

Howard blew out his smoke. 'No. African queen.'

'Why not?'

'I think she finds it patronizing, not to mention factually inaccurate — look, Victoria.'

'*Vee.* How many times!'

'Vee. I'm going to go now,' he said, but made no move to stand. 'I don't think I can help you tonight. I think you've drunk a little too much and you're under a great emotional —'

'*Give* us some of that.' She pointed to his wine and pushed herself forward. Something she had done with her elbows had squeezed her breasts together, and the peaks of both, shiny with some kind of body cream, now began to communicate with Howard independently of their owner.

'Give us some, go on,' she said.

In order for her to drink his wine, Howard would have to bring the glass to her lips.

'One sip,' she said looking over the rim

into his eyes. So he tipped it towards her and she drank it tidily. When she drew away from the glass, her mobile, unreasonably large mouth was wet. The ridges in the thick dark lips were like his wife's — plum-coloured in the creases and almost black elsewhere. What was left of her lipstick had retreated back to the corners, as if this were simply too much lip for it to scale.

'She must be remarkable.'

'Who?'

'Bloody hell, keep up. Your wife. She must be remarkable.'

'Must she?'

'Yeah. Because my mum doesn't — *didn't* — make friends with just anybody,' said Victoria, her voice catching at this change of tense. 'She was particular about people. She was hard to get to know. I've been thinking that maybe I didn't get to know her very well . . .'

'I'm sure that's not —'

'No, shush,' said Victoria drunkenly and let some tears slip down her face untended, 'that's not the point — what I was saying is, she didn't suffer fools, you know? They had to be special in some way. They had to be *real people.* Not like you and me. Real, special. So Kiki must be special. Would you say,' said Victoria, 'that she was special?'

Howard dropped his fag in Victoria's empty glass. Breasts or no breasts, it was time to leave.

'I'd say . . . that she has enabled my existence in the form that it has taken. And that form is special to us, yes.'

Victoria shook her head ruefully and reached out a hand, which she now placed on his knee.

'There you are, see? You can never just say . . . *I like the tomato.*'

'I thought we were talking about my wife, not a vegetable.'

Victoria tapped a correcting finger against his trousers. 'Fruit, actually.'

Howard nodded. 'Fruit.'

'Come on, Dr, give me some more.'

Howard held his glass up and away. 'You've had enough.'

'Give me some more!'

She did it. She jumped off the bed and into his lap. His erection was blatant, but first she coolly drank the rest of his wine, pressing down on him as Lolita did on Humbert, as if he were just a chair she happened to sit on. No doubt she had read *Lolita.* And then her arm went round the back of his neck and Lolita turned into a temptress (maybe she had learned from Mrs Robinson too), lasciviously sucking his ear, and then from temptress she moved to affectionate high-school girlfriend, sweetly kissing the corner of his mouth. But what kind of sweetheart was this? He had barely started to return her kiss when she commenced groaning in a disconcertingly enthusiastic manner, and this was followed by a strange fluting business with her tongue, catching Howard off guard. He kept trying to regulate the kiss, to return it back to what he knew of kissing, but she was determined to flicker her tongue in the top of his mouth while keeping a zealous and frankly uncomfortable grip on his balls. Now she began to unbutton his shirt slowly, as if accompanying music were playing, and seemed disappointed not to find a pornographic rug of hair here. She rubbed it conceptually, as if the hair were indeed there, tugging at what little Howard possessed while — could it be? — purring. She pulled him on to the bed. Before he had a chance to consider removing her shirt she had already done the job for him. And then came more of this purring and moaning, although his hands had not yet reached her breasts, and he was presently struggling, at the other end of the bed, to kick one shoe off by means of attacking it with the other. He lifted up slightly, the better to bend his arm back to reach the resistant shoe. On the bed she seemed to be continuing on without him, writhing in a skittish manner and pulling her fingers through her short dreads, as one might muss hair much longer and blonder.

'Oh, Howard,' she said.

'Yes, one minute,' said Howard. *That's* better. He turned back to her with visions of pulling her up to face him and kissing that wonderful mouth in a more restful manner, then feeling along her torso, her shoulders, her arms, hugging her meaty backside and pulling the whole wonderful creation close to him. But she had already turned over on to her stomach, her head pressed against the bed as if an invisible hand were restraining her with a plan to suffocation, her legs splayed, her shorts off, her hands either side of her buttocks pulling them apart. The tiny rosy knot in the centre presented Howard with a dilemma. Surely she didn't mean — or did she? Was that the fashion these days? Howard took off his trousers, his erection faded somewhat.

'*Fuck* me,' said Victoria, once, and then again, and then again. Downstairs Howard could hear the tinkle and murmur of the wake for this girl's dead mother. Clutching his own forehead he brought himself up behind her. At the slightest touch of him to her, she wailed and seemed to quiver with preorgasmic passion, and yet she was, as Howard discovered at his second attempt, completely dry. In the next moment she had licked her hand and brought it round. She rubbed herself with this fiercely and rubbed Howard. Obediently his erection returned.

'Put it *in* me,' said Victoria. 'Fuck me. Put it in me up to the hilt.'

Very specific. Tentatively Howard reached forward to touch her breasts. She licked his hand and asked him several times if he liked doing what he was doing, to which he could only answer with the obvious affirmative. She then began to tell him just how much he liked it. Tiring a little of the running commentary, Howard moved his hand lower along her belly. She raised it at once like a cat stretching, she held her stomach in — seemed to hold her breath, in fact — and only when he ceased touching her there did she breathe again. He had the sense that every time he touched an area of her body that area was at once moved out of his reach and then returned to his hand a moment later, restyled.

'Oh, I so need you *inside* me,' said

Victoria and pushed her backside yet higher in the air. Howard tried to stretch over her, to touch the skin of her face; she moaned and took his fingers in her mouth, as if they were somebody else's cock, and proceeded to suck them.

'Tell me you want me. Tell me how much you want to fuck me,' said Victoria.

'I do . . . I . . . you're so very . . . beautiful,' whispered Howard, rising up on his heels a little and kissing the only bit of her that was really accessible to him, the small of her back. With a strong hand she pushed him back on to his knees.

'Put it in me,' she said.

OK, then. Howard took hold of his cock and began the breach. He had imagined it would be hard to top the moaning that had already occurred, but, as he entered Victoria, she managed it, and Howard, who was not used to so much congratulation so early on in the procedure, feared he might have hurt her and now hesitated as to whether to push deeper.

'Fuck me deeper!' said Victoria.

And so Howard pressed deeper three times, offering about half of his ample eight and a half inches, that happy accident of nature which, Kiki once suggested, was the true, primal reason why Howard was not still working as a butcher on the Dalston High Street. But with his fourth push the nerves and the tightness and the wine overpowered him, and he came in a small, shivery way that gave him no great pleasure. He fell forward on to Victoria and waited morosely for those familiar sounds of feminine disappointment.

'Oh, God! Oh, God!' said Victoria and convulsed dramatically. 'Oh, I love it when you fuck me!'

Howard slid himself out and lay next to her on the bed. Victoria, now completely composed again, rolled over and kissed him maternally on the forehead.

'That was delicious.'

'Mmm,' said Howard.

'I'm on the pill, so.'

Howard grimaced. He had not even asked.

'Do you want me to blow you? I'd love to taste your cock.'

Howard sat up and made a grab for his trousers. 'No, that's all right, I . . . Jesus Christ.' He looked at his watch, as if lateness were the problem here. 'We have to get downstairs . . . I don't know what just happened. This is insane. You're my student. You slept with *Jerome*.'

Victoria sat up in bed and touched his face. 'Look, I hate to be cheesy, but it's true: Jerome's lovely, but he's a *boy,* Howard. I need a man right now.'

'Vee — please,' said Howard, grabbing her hand by the wrist and passing her the shirt she had been wearing. 'We need to go downstairs.'

'All right, all right — keep your hair on.'

Together they got dressed, Howard hurriedly and Victoria languidly, with Howard taking a moment to marvel at the fact that the dream of many weeks — to see this girl naked — was now replaying in dramatic reverse. He'd do absolutely anything to see her with all her clothes on. Finally, after they had both fully dressed, Howard found his boxer shorts tucked in a pillowcase. These he stuffed into his pocket. At the door, Victoria stopped him by putting a hand to his chest. She breathed deeply and encouraged him to do the same. She unlocked the door. Slicked his cowlick down with a finger and straightened his tie.

'Just try not to look like you love tomatoes,' she said.

5

In the early years of the last century, Helen Keller embarked on a lecture tour of New

England, enthralling audiences with her life story (and occasionally surprising them with her socialist views). En route she made a stop at Wellington College, and there named a library, planted a tree and found herself the recipient of an honorary degree. Hence the Keller Library: a long, draughty room on the ground floor of the English Department with a green carpet, red walls and too many windows — it is impossible to heat. On one wall hangs a life-sized portrait of Helen dressed in academic cap and gown, sitting in an armchair, her blind eyes demurely directed into her lap. Her companion Annie Sullivan stands behind her, a hand resting tenderly on her friend's shoulder. It is in this chilly room that all faculty meetings for the Humanities are conducted. Today is January tenth. The first faculty meeting of the year is due to begin in five minutes. As when an especially important vote comes up in the House of Lords, even the most reluctant college members are present this morning, including the octogenarian tenured hermits. It's a full house, although nobody hurries; they arrive in staggered fashion, scarves stiff and wet with the snow, with salty tide marks on their leather shoes, with handkerchiefs and ostentatious coughs and wheezes. Umbrellas, like dead birds after a shooting party, pile up in the far corner. Professors and research fellows and visiting lecturers gravitate towards the long tables at the back of the room. These are laid out with pastries wrapped in cellophane and steaming pots of coffee and decaf in their steel industrial tankards. Faculty meetings — especially those chaired by Jack French, as this one will be — have been known to go on for three hours. The other priority is to try to get a chair as near the exit as possible, so as to enable discreet departure halfway through. The dream (so rarely achieved!) is that one might then be able to leave both early and unnoticed.

By the time Howard arrived at the doors of Keller Library all escape-route seating had already been taken. He was forced right up to the front of the room, directly underneath the portrait of Helen and six feet from where Jack French and his assistant Liddy Cantalino were fussing over an ominously large pile of paper, spread out across two empty chairs. Not for the first time at a faculty meeting, Howard wished himself as sensorially deprived as Keller herself. He would give a lot not to have to look at Jane Colman's pointy little witch face, her mane of parched frizzy blonde hair and the way it thrust out from beneath the kind of beret you find in the 'Be a European!' ads in the *New Yorker*. Ditto the student favourite: 36-year-old, already tenured Jamie Anderson, specialist in Native American history, with his expensive tiny laptop, which he now balanced on the arm of his chair. Most of all Howard wished he could not hear the poisonous mutterings of Professors Burchfield and Fontaine, two portly *grandes dames* of the History Department, squeezed up together on the only sofa, wrapped in their swathes of curtain fabric, and presently giving Howard the evil eye. Like Matrushka dolls they were almost identical, with Fontaine, the slightly smaller of the two, seeming to have sprung fully formed from the body of Burchfield. They sported utilitarian bowl cuts and bulky plastic eyewear dating back to the early seventies, and yet they remained radiant with the almost sexual allure that comes with having written — albeit fifteen years ago — a handful of books that became set texts in every college in the country. No faddish punctuation for these gals: no colons, no dashes, no subtitles. People still spoke of Burchfield's Stalin and Fontaine's Robespierre. And so in the eyes of

Burchfield and Fontaine, the Howard Belseys of this world were mere gadflies, flitting from institution to institution with their fashionable nonsense, meaning nothing, amounting to nothing. After ten years of service they had still opposed Howard's tenure when it was put forward last fall. They would oppose it once more this year. That was their right. And it was also their right, in their capacity as 'lifers', to ensure that the spirit and soul of Wellington — of which they considered themselves guardians — was protected from abuse and distortion by men like Howard, whose presence at the institution could only ever, in the greater scheme of things, be temporary. It was to keep Howard in check that they had raised themselves from their desks to attend this meeting. He could not be allowed to make any unsupervised decision regarding this college that they both loved. Now, as the clock struck ten and Jack stood before them all delivering his preliminary coughs, Burchfield and Fontaine seemed to ruffle and settle, like two big hens bedding down upon their eggs. They gave Howard a last, contemptuous glance. Howard, in preparation for the usual verbal roller coaster of Jack's opening speech, closed his eyes.

'There are,' said Jack, bringing his hands together, 'a dyad of reasons why last month's meeting was delayed, rescheduled . . . maybe in fact it would be more accurate to say *repositioned,* for this date, for January tenth, and I feel that before we can proceed with this meeting, to which, by the way, I warmly welcome you all after what I sincerely hope was a pleasurable — and most importantly — a *restful* Christmas break — yes, and as I say, before we *do* proceed with what promises to be a really rather packed meeting as far as the printed agenda is concerned — *before* starting I just wanted to speak briefly about the reasons for this repositioning, for it was, in itself, as many of you know, not entirely without controversy. Yes. Now. First, it was felt by several members of our community that the issues to be discussed in that upcoming — now realized — meeting were of a magnitude and a complexity that required — nay, *demanded* — proper, considered presentations of both sides of the argument presently under our collective spotlight — which is *not* to suggest the argument before us is of a plainly binary nature — I personally have no doubt that we will find quite the contrary is the case and that, in fact, we may find ourselves this morning aligned along several different points along the, the, the, the *funnel,* if it can be put that way, of the discussion we are about to have. And so in order to create that space for formulation we took it on advice — without a faculty vote — to delay that meeting, and naturally anyone who feels that the decision taken regarding that delay was taken without due discussion can make a notation of their objection in our online file system, which our own Liddy Cantalino has set up expressly for these meetings . . . I believe the cache is situated at Code SS76 on the Humanities web page, the address of which I should hope you are all already familiar with — is that . . . ?' queried Jack, looking to Liddy, who sat on a chair beside him. Liddy nodded, stood up, repeated the mysterious code and sat back down. 'Thank you, Liddy. So, yes. So there is a forum for complaint there. Now. The second reason — a far less fraught one, thank goodness — was the matter of simple time management, which had come to the attention of many of you and of myself and of Liddy, and it was her opinion, and the opinion of many of our colleagues who brought the issue to her attention, that at the very *least* the extreme — if you'll excuse the hackneyed analogy — *gridlock* of events in the December calendar — both academic and social — was leaving very little time for the usual and necessary preparation that faculty meetings — if they are to have any real effect at all — really require, if not demand. And I think Liddy has a few words for us with regard to how we will go about future scheduling of this crucial meeting. Liddy?'

Liddy stood once more and executed a brisk reshuffle of her bust. On her sweater reindeer were travelling unevenly, left to right.

'Hey, folks — well, basically just to repeat what Jack just said there, we ladies on the admin side of things are rushed off our behinds in December, and if we're gonna keep on with this hoo-hah of each department having a Christmas party as was pretty much decided last year, not to mention that we got practically every one of these kids chasing some kind of a recommendation in the week before Christmas, even though *God only knows* they get warned all through the fall not to leave recommendations to the last minute, but anyhoo — we just felt that it made more basic *horse sense* to give ourselves a little breathing space in the last week before the vacation so that I for one can know which way my ass is pointing come the New Year.' This occasioned a polite laugh. 'If you'll excuse my French.'

Everybody did. The meeting began. Howard pushed himself a little lower in his chair. He was not up to bat yet. He was third on the agenda, absurdly, although everybody in the room had surely come to hear the Monty and Howard road show. But first, the Welsh-born classicist and temporary Housing Officer Christopher Fay in his harlequin waistcoat and red trousers must speak for an unendurable amount of time about meeting-room facilities for graduates. Howard took out his pen and began to doodle on his notes, all the time straining to simulate a pensive look on his face that would suggest an activity more serious than doodling. *The right to freedom of speech on this campus, though strong, must yet contend with other rights, rights that protect students at this institution from verbal and personal attack, from conceptual denigration, blatant stereotyping and any other manifestation of the politics of hate.* Around this opening gambit, Howard drew a series of interlocking curlicues, like elegant branches, in the style of William

Morris. Once the outlines were completed he got on to the business of shading. Once the shading was completed, more curlicues suggested themselves; the pattern grew until it took up most of the left-hand margin. He lifted the paper up from his lap and admired it. And then once more with the shading, taking a childish joy in not exceeding the lines, in submitting to these arbitrary principles of style and form. He looked up and pretended to stretch; this movement gave him an excuse to turn his head from right to left and to study the room for supporters and detractors. Erskine was sitting right across the room, surrounded by his Black Studies Department, Howard's cavalry. No Claire, or no Claire that he could see. Zora, he knew, was sitting on a bench in the hallway going through her own speech, waiting to be called. Howard's Art History colleagues were widely spaced but all present and correct. Monty — and this was a nasty shock — was a mere knight's move behind him. He smiled and acknowledged Howard with a little bow, but Howard, shamefully undeserving of such courtesy, could only whip back round and press his pencil into his own knee. There is a word for taking another man's wife — to cuckold. But what is the word for taking another man's daughter? If there were such a word, Howard felt certain that Christopher Fay, with his publisher-friendly, highly sexualized perspective on the mores of the ancient world, would know it. Howard looked up at Christopher now, still on his feet, nimble as a jester, speaking spiritedly, the little rat's tail at the back of his head flicking from side to side. He was the only other Brit on the faculty. Howard had often wondered what impression of the British, as a nation, his American colleagues must glean from their acquaintance with the two of them.

'*Thank* you, Christopher,' said Jack and then took a very long time to introduce Christopher's replacement as temporary Housing Officer (Christopher was soon to be off on sabbatical to Canterbury), a young woman who now stood to speak of the recommendations Christopher had already outlined at great length. A wide-reaching, yet subtle movement, like a Mexican wave, passed through the room as almost everyone repositioned their backsides on their seats. One lucky sod now escaped through the squeaky double-doors — a feckless novelist on a visiting fellowship — but she did not retire unobserved. Beady

Liddy watched her go and made a note. Howard now surprised himself by getting nervous. He went through his notes quickly, too agitated to follow his material sentence by sentence. It was almost time. And then it was time.

'And now if you would turn your attention to the third item on our agenda for this morning, which relates to a proposed lecture series for this coming semester . . . and if I can ask Dr Howard Belsey, who is tabling a motion in relation to, to, to, this proposed lecture series — I refer you all to the notes that Howard has attached to your agendas, which I do hope you have given the proper time and consideration, and . . . yes. So. Howard, if you could . . . ?'

Howard rose.

'Maybe it would be more . . . if you . . . ?' suggested Jack. Howard made his way through chairs to stand next to Jack, facing them all.

'You have the floor,' said Jack; he sat down and began to gnaw fretfully on his thumbnail.

'The right to freedom of speech,' began Howard, his right knee quivering uncontrollably, *'on this campus, though strong, must yet contend with other rights . . .'*

Here Howard made the mistake of

looking up and around him as public speakers are advised to do. He caught sight of Monty, who was smiling and nodding, like a king at a fool who has come to entertain him. Howard stumbled once, twice, and then, to remedy the problem, fixed his eyes on his sheet of paper. Now, instead of embroidering lightly around his notes, improvising, throwing out witty asides and employing all the other loose, from-the-hip sophisms he had intended, he read rigidly and with great speed from his script. He came to a close abruptly and looked blankly at the next pencilled note he had left for himself, which said *After outlining broad issues, get to point.* Somebody coughed. Howard looked up and got another eyeful of Monty — the smile was demonic — and then back at his paper. He pushed his hair away from where the sweat was sticking it to his forehead.

'Let me, um . . . Let me . . . I want to state my concern clearly. When Professor Kipps was invited, by the Humanities Faculty, to Wellington, it was to take part in the communal life of this institution and to offer a series of *instructive* lectures in one of his many, many, *many* areas of expertise . . .' Here Howard got the light laugh he'd been hoping for and the fillip his confidence needed. 'What he was expressly *not* hired to do was to make political speeches that potentially alienate and deeply offend a variety of groups on this campus.'

Monty now stood, shaking his head in apparent amusement. He raised his hand. 'Please,' he said, 'may I?'

Jack looked pained. How he hated such conflict in his faculty!

'Well, now, Professor Kipps — I think if we can just, just, just . . . if we can let Howard finish his pitch, as it were . . .'

'Of course. I shall be patient and tolerant as my colleague defames me,' said Monty with this same grin and sat back down.

Howard pressed on: 'I will remind the committee that last year members of this university lobbied successfully to ban a philosopher who had been invited to read here, but who, it was decided by these members, could not have a platform at this institution because he expressed, in his printed work, what were deemed to be "Anti-Israeli" views and arguments that were offensive to members of our community. This objection (although not an opinion with which I concurred) was democratically passed, and the gentleman was kept from Wellington on the grounds that his views were likely to be offensive to elements of this community. It is on *exactly the same grounds* that I stand before you this morning, with one key difference. It is not my habit or to my taste to ban speakers of different political colours from my own from this campus, which is why I am not requesting such a ban outright but rather asking to see the text of these lectures so that they may be considered by this faculty — *with* the view that any material that appears to us, as a community, to contravene the internal "hate laws" of this institution — as laid out by our own Equal Opportunities Commission of which I am the chair — can be excised. I have asked Professor Kipps, in writing, for a copy of his text — he has refused. I ask again, today, at the very least, for an outline of the lectures he intends to give. My grounds for concern are two: first, the reductive and offensive public statements the Professor has made about homosexuality and race and gender throughout his career. Second, his lecture series "Taking the Liberal Out of the Liberal Arts" shares a title with an article he recently published in the *Wellington Herald*, which itself contained sufficient homophobic material to convince the Wellington LesBiGay group to picket and obstruct any lectures that the Professor might give at this college. For those of you who missed that article, I have photo-copied it — I believe Lydia will give these out to anyone who wishes to read it at the end of our session. So, to conclude,' said Howard, folding his papers in half, 'my proposal to Professor Kipps himself is as follows: that we will be given the text of the lectures; that, failing this, we will be given a proposed outline of these lectures; or, failing that, we shall be told this morning what the intention of the lectures is.'

'Is that . . . ?' queried Jack, 'That's the meat of your . . . so, I suppose we must turn to the Professor and . . . Professor Kipps, could you possibly . . .'

Monty stood and held the back of the chair in front of him, leaning into it as if it were a lectern.

'Dean French, it would be a *pleasure*. How *entertaining* all that was. I love liberal fairytales! So restful — they put no undue strain upon one's mind.' A nervous giggle from the faculty. 'But, if you don't mind, I will stick to fact for a moment and answer Dr Belsey's concerns as directly as I possibly can. In answer to his requests I fear I must decline all three, given the free country I stand in and the freedoms of speech I claim as my inalienable right. I will remind Dr Belsey that neither of us is in England any more.' This raised an actual laugh, stronger than the one Howard had received. 'If it will make him feel better — I know how much the liberal mind likes to *feel better* — I hold myself completely responsible for the contents of the lectures I give. But I am afraid I am quite unable to answer his frankly bizarre request for their "intention". In fact, I admit it surprises and delights me that a self-professed "textual anarchist" like Dr Belsey should be so passionate to know the *intention* of a piece of writing . . .'

A sprinkle of mirthless intellectual laughter, of the kind one hears at bookshop readings.

'I had no idea,' continued Monty gaily, 'what a stickler he was for the absolute nature of the written word.'

'Howard, do you want to . . . ?' said Jack French, but Howard was already speaking over him.

'Look, my point here is this,' declaimed Howard, turning to face Liddy as the nearest interlocutor, but Liddy was not interested. She was reserving her energies for Item 7 on the agenda, the History Department's application for two new photocopiers. Howard turned back to the crowd. 'How *can* he at one and the same time claim responsibility for his text and yet not be able to tell us what *intention* he has for the text?'

Monty put his hands on each side of his own belly. 'Really, Dr Belsey, this is too stupid to answer. Surely a man can write a piece of prose without "intending" any particular reaction, or at least he can and will write without presuming every end or consequence of that piece of prose.'

'You tell me, mate — you're the constitutional originalist!'

This got a wider, more sincere laugh. For the first time, Monty began to look a little ruffled.

'I will be writing,' pronounced Monty, 'of my beliefs concerning the state of the university system in this country. I will be writing employing my knowledge *as well as* my moral sense —'

'*With* the clear intention of antagonizing and alienating various minority groups on this campus. Will he be responsible for that?'

'Dr Belsey, if I may refer you to one of your own liberal lodestars, Jean-Paul Sartre: "We do not know what we want and yet we are responsible for what we are — that is the fact." Now is it not *you*, Dr, who speaks of the instability of textual meaning? Is it not *you,* Dr, who speaks of the indeterminacy of all sign systems? How, then, can I possibly predict *before* I give my lectures how the "multivalency",' said Monty, enunciating the word with obvious disgust, 'of my own text will be received in the "heterogeneous consciousnesses" of my audience?' said Monty, sighing heavily. 'Your entire line of attack is a perfect model of my argument. You photocopy my article but you do not take the time to read it properly yourself. In that article I ask: "why is there one rule for the liberal intellectual and another rule entirely for his conservative colleague?" And I ask you now: why should I offer the text of my lectures to a committee of liberal interrogators and thus have my own — much vaunted in this very institution — right to free speech curtailed and threatened?'

'Oh, for *fucks*sake —' flashed Howard. Jack leaped from his chair.

'Umm, Howard, I'm going to have to ask you to mind your p's and q's there.'

'No need, no need — I am not so delicate, Dean French. I was under no illusion that my colleague was a gentleman . . .'

'Look,' said Howard, his face budding rouge, 'what I want to know —'

'Howard, please,' said Monty scoldingly, 'I did do you the courtesy of listening until you had finished. *Thank* you. Now: two years ago, at Wellington, in this great freedom-loving institution, a group of Muslim students requested the right to have a room given over to their daily prayers — a request Dr Belsey was instrumental in rebuffing, with the result that this group of Muslims is presently pursuing Wellington College through the courts — *FOR THE RIGHT,*' intoned Monty over Howard's remonstrations, '*for the right* to practise their faith —'

'And of course your *own* defence of the Muslim faith is legendary,' taunted Howard.

Monty assumed a face of historical gravity. 'I support any religious freedom against the threat of secular fascism.'

'Monty, you know as well as I do that that case has *nothing to do* with what we're discussing today — this college has always maintained a policy of, of, non-religious activity — we do not discriminate —'

'HA!'

'We do *not* discriminate, but *all* students are asked to pursue their religious interests outside of the confines of the university. But that case is an irrelevance today — what we're discussing today is a cynical attempt to force upon our students what is basically an explicitly right-wing agenda disguised as a series of lectures on the —'

'*If* we are to speak of explicit agendas, we might discuss the under-the-counter manner in which class admissions are organized here at Wellington — a policy that is a blatant corruption of the Affirmative Action bill (which, by the way, is itself a corruption) — whereby students who are NOT enrolled at this college are yet taught in classes here, by professors who, at their own "discretion" (as it is so disingenuously put), allow these "students" into their classes, choosing them over *actual* students better qualified than they — NOT because these young people meet the academic standards of Wellington, no, but because they are considered *needy cases* — as if it helps minorities to be pushed through an elite environment to which they are not yet suited. When the truth is that the liberal — as ever! — *assumes* there is benefit, only because doing so makes the liberal *herself,*' said Monty with mischievous emphasis, 'feel good!'

Howard clapped his hands and looked to Jack French in exasperation.

'Sorry — *which* case are we arguing now? Is there anything in this university that Professor Kipps is *not* on a crusade against?'

Jack French looked distraughtly at the agenda notes Liddy had just passed him.

'Umm, Howard is correct there, Montague — I understand you have a concern about class admissions but that issue comes fourth, I think you'll find, on our agenda. If we could just stick with the . . . I suppose the question, as it has been framed by Howard, is: Will you give your text to the community?'

Monty pushed his chest up and out, and held his pocket-watch in his hand. 'I will not.'

'Well, will you submit to putting it to the vote?'

'Dean French, with all due respect to your authority, I will not. No more than I would accept a vote on whether a man might be allowed to cut out my tongue — a vote is completely irrelevant in this context.'

Jack looked hopelessly at Howard.

'Opinions from the floor?' suggested exasperated Howard.

'Yes . . .' said Jack, with great relief. 'Opinions from the floor? Elaine — did you want to say something?'

Professor Elaine Burchfield pushed her glasses up her nose. 'Is Howard Belsey *really* suggesting,' she said with patrician disappointment, 'that Wellington is such a terribly *delicate* institution that it fears the normal cut and thrust of political debate within its halls? Is the liberal consciousness (which it pleases Professor Kipps to ridicule) *really* so very slight that it cannot survive a series of six lectures that come from a perspective other than its own? I find that prospect very alarming.'

Howard, glowing with anger now, addressed his answer to a high spot on the back wall. 'I'm obviously not making myself clear. Professor Kipps is *on record,* alongside his "kindred spirit" Justice Scalia, denouncing homosexuality as an evil —'

Monty sprang from his seat once more. 'I *object* to that characterization of my argument. In print I defended Justice Scalia's view that it is *within the right* of committed Christian people to hold such an opinion of homosexuality — and furthermore that it is an infringement of the rights of Christian people when their personal objection to gay people, *which* they hold to be a moral principle, is translated into the legal category of "discrimination". That was my exact case.'

Howard watched with satisfaction as Burchfield and Fontaine shrank in distaste at this clarification. Which made it all the more astonishing to Howard when Fontaine now raised her infamous lesbian baritone to say: 'We may find these views objectionable, even repulsive — but this is an institution that defends intellectual discussion and debate.'

'Jesus Christ — Gloria, this is the *opposite* of thought!' cried the head of the Social Anthropology Department. Thus began a verbal ping-pong, which collected more players as the argument ranged the room and continued without the need for Howard as umpire.

Howard sat down. He listened to his argument get lost in accounts of other cases, some similar, some tediously irrelevant. Erskine, meaning well, gave a long and exhaustive history of the civil rights movement, the point of which seemed to be that given Kipps's rigid views of the constitution, Kipps himself would have never voted with the majority on Brown v. Board of Education. It was a good point, but it got lost in Erskine's emotional delivery. Half an hour passed this way. At last Jack brought the debate under control. Gently he pressed Monty with Howard's request. Once more, Monty refused to share the text of his lectures.

'Well,' conceded Jack, 'given that clear determination on Professor Kipps's part . . . but we do still have the right to vote on whether these lectures should take place at all. I know that wasn't your original intention, Howard, but given the circumstances . . . We do have that power.'

'I have no objection to a democratic vote where there is right and power, which there is here,' said Monty in stately mode. 'It is clearly the members of this faculty who ultimately decide who shall or shall not be free to speak at their college.'

Howard, in response to this, could offer only a sulky nod.

'All in favour — I mean, in favour of the lectures going ahead, without prior consultation.' Jack put his glasses on to count the vote. There was no need. With the exception of Howard's small pockets of support, all hands went up.

Howard, dazed, made his way back to his chair. On the way, he was passed by his daughter, who had just entered the room. Zora squeezed his arm and grinned at him, presuming he had just acquitted himself as well as she was about to. She took a chair next to Liddy Cantalino. She held a pristine pile of paper in her lap. She looked powerful, lit from within by her own fearsome youth.

'Now,' said Jack, 'one of our students, as you see, is with us — she is going to be talking to us about an issue she feels passionate about, as I understand it, and which Professor Kipps touched on earlier — our "discretionary" students, if we can put it that way . . . but before we get on to that, there's some standard college business to be attended to . . .' Jack reached out for a piece of paper that Liddy had already drawn from the pile and extended to him. 'Thank you, Liddy. Publications! Always happy news. And publications next year will include Dr J. M. Wilson's *"Windmills of My Mind": Pursuing the Dream of Natural Energy*, Branvain Press, which is due for publication in May; Dr Stefan Guilleme's *"Paint It Black": Adventures in Minimalist America*, Yale University Press, in October; *Borders and Intersections, or Dancing with Anansi: A Study in Caribbean Mythemes* by Professor Erskine Jegede, published by our own Wellington Press this August . . .'

Through this list of triumphant forthcoming publications Howard doodled his way through two sides of paper, waiting for the inevitable, now almost traditional reference to himself.

'And we await . . . we await,' said Jack

wistfully, 'Dr Howard Belsey's *Against Rembrandt: Interrogating a Master*, which . . . which . . .'

'No date as yet,' confirmed Howard.

6

At one thirty the doors were opened. The 'funnel' that Jack French had predicted now manifested itself, in the doorway, as many faculty members forced themselves through a small gap. Howard packed in with the rest and listened to the gossip, much of which was of Zora, and her successful address. His daughter had managed to postpone the decision on discretionary students until the next meeting, a month from now. Within the Wellington system, achieving a postponement of this kind was akin to adding a new amendment to the constitution. Howard was proud of her and her speechifying, but he would congratulate her later. He had to get out of this room. He left her chatting to well-wishers and launched a determined assault on the exit. In the hall, he turned left, avoided the crowd heading for the lunch room. He escaped into one of the corridors that came off the main lobby. The wall along here was lined with glass cases, each with its booty of rusty trophies and curling certificates, photos of students in outmoded sportswear. He walked to the end and leaned against the fire door. You weren't allowed to smoke anywhere in this building. He wasn't going to smoke; he was just going to roll one and then take it outside. Patting the pockets of his suit jacket, he found the comforting green and gold pouch in the breast. You can only buy this brand in England, and at Christmas he had stocked up, buying twenty pouches in the airport. *What's the New Year's resolution,* Kiki had asked, *suicide?*

'*There* you are!'

The worm of tobacco nestling in Howard's palm jumped on to his shoe.

'Oops,' said Victoria and knelt down to rescue it. She stood up again with grace, her spine seeming to uncurl notch by notch until she was straight as a post and right next to him. 'Hello, stranger.'

She placed the tobacco back in his hand. There was a visceral shock in this closeness. He had not seen her since that afternoon. And with the miracle that is male compartmentalization he had barely thought of her either. He had watched old films with his daughter and taken peaceful, meditative walks with his wife; he had worked a little on his Rembrandt lectures. He had recalled, with the mawkish tenderness of the disloyal, how very lucky and blessed he was to have his family. In fact, taken as a concept, as a *premise,* 'Victoria Kipps' had done a world of good for Howard's marriage and for Howard's general mental state. The concept of Victoria Kipps had put the blessings of his own life in perspective. But Victoria Kipps was not a concept. She was real. She patted his arm.

'Been looking for you,' she said.

'Vee.'

'What's the occasion?' she asked and touched the lapels of his suit. 'Oh, 'course — faculty meeting . . . *Very* nice. You can't out-dress Dad, though. It'll only end in tears.'

'Vee.'

She looked at him with the same amused face he had just seen on her father. '*Yes.* What?'

'Vee . . . What . . . what are you *doing* here?'

He scrunched up the Rizla and tobacco and threw them in a nearby trash can.

'Well, Dr Belsey, actually I study here.' She lowered her voice. 'I tried to call you.' She thrust both hands deep into his trouser pockets. Howard grabbed her hands and removed them. He got her by the elbow and pulled her through the fire door, which led into the secret interior of the building: emergency stairs and cleaning closets and stockrooms. Below them, the sound of a photocopier huffing and shaking. Howard skipped down a few steps to look through the spiral of the stairwell to the basement, but there was no one. The photocopier was on autopilot, disgorging pages and stapling them together. He walked back slowly to meet Victoria.

'You shouldn't be back in school so soon.'

'Why not? What's the point of staying at home? I've been trying to call you.'

'Don't,' he said. 'Don't try to call me. It's better if you don't.'

Down here, in this grotty stairwell, the natural light came in through two grated windows in a manner both penal and atmospheric, reminding Howard, incongruously, of Venice. The light fell perfectly on the sculptural construction of lines and planes that was her face. It moved Howard to an emotional urgency he had not felt, or had not felt until this moment.

'Just forget about me, all of it. Please — do that.'

'Howard, I —'

'No — Vee, it was insane,' he said, holding on to both her elbows. 'And it's over. It was *insanity.*'

Even in the panic and horror of this situation Howard stopped to wonder at this drama, of the sheer energizing fact of being returned to drama such as this, properly the preserve of youth, with the hiding and the low voices and the surreptitious touches. But now Victoria drew away from him and folded her arms across that drum-tight adolescent stomach.

'Umm, I'm talking about *tonight,*' she said tartly. 'That's why I was calling you. Emerson Hall dinner? We're meant to be going together? It's not a proposal of marriage — why do *all* your family always think someone wants to marry you? Look . . . I just wanted to know if you're still coming. It's just a pain if I have to find someone else to go with now. Oh, God . . . this is embarrassing — forget it.'

'Emerson Hall?' repeated Howard. The fire door opened. Howard flattened himself against the wall as Vee pressed herself against the banister. A kid in a knapsack came between them, passed by the photocopier, and then through a door that led to who knew where.

'God, you are *so* vain,' said Victoria in a

wearisome way that returned to Howard some of the reality of that afternoon in the boudoir. 'It's a simple question. And, you know: don't *flatter* yourself. I didn't think we were going to run off into the sunset. You're really *not that great*.'

These words momentarily kicked up a little psychic dust between them, but it was inert somehow, it was just noise. They didn't know each other at all. It wasn't like it had been with Claire. That was a case of two old friends losing their nerve at the same time, both on the last lap of their lives. And Howard had *known,* even as it was happening, that they were switching lanes out of fear, just to see if it felt different, better, easier, to run in this new lane — scared as they were of carrying on for ever in the lane they were in. But this girl hadn't even stepped into the race. She wasn't to be belittled for that — God knows, Howard himself had only heard the starting gun in his late twenties. But he had underestimated the strangeness of talking about the future of his life with someone for whom the future still seemed unbounded: a pleasure palace of choices, with infinite doors, in which only a fool would spend his time trapped in one room.

'No,' agreed Howard, because the concession did not mean anything. 'I'm not that great.'

'No . . . but . . . well, you're not *awful,*' she said, coming closer to him and then at the last minute, flipping her body so she was by his side and against the wall as he was. 'You're all right. Compared to some of the wankers round here.'

She nudged him in his gut with her elbow. 'Anyway, if you *are* about to leave me for ever, thanks for the memento. It was very "courtly love" of you.'

Victoria held up a strip of photos. Howard took them in his hands without recognition.

'I found them in my room,' she whispered. 'They must've fallen out of your trouser pocket. That suit you're wearing now. Do you only have one suit or what?'

Howard brought the strip closer to his face.

'You're such a *poseur!*'

Howard peered closer. The images were faint, ageing.

'I have no idea when those were taken.'

'Sure,' said Victoria. 'Tell it to the judge.'

'I've never seen them before.'

'You know what I thought when I saw them? Rembrandt's portraits. Right? Not that one — but look at *that* one, with your hair all over your eyes. And it works because you look older in that one than *that* one . . .' She was leaning into him, shoulder to shoulder. Howard touched one of his faces softly with his own thumb. It was Howard Belsey. This was what people saw as he moved through the world.

'Anyway . . . they're mine now,' she said, snatching them back. She folded the strip in half and put it in her pocket.

'So tonight — you picking me up? Like in the movies — I'll wear a *corsage* and then later I'll throw up on your shoes.'

She moved away from him and took one step up, her arms stretched between the banister and the wall, swaying forward and back, fatally like one of Howard's own children back in 83 Langham.

'I don't think . . .' began Howard, and then started again. 'What is it that we're meant to be going to?'

'Emerson Hall. Three professors a table. You're mine. Food, drink, speeches, go home. Not complicated.'

'Does your . . . Monty — does he know you're going with me?'

Victoria rolled her eyes. 'No — but he'll think it's *perfect*. He thinks Mike and I should always put ourselves in the paths of liberals. He says you learn how not to be stupid that way.'

'Victoria,' said Howard and made an effort to look her in her eyes, 'I think you should find someone else to go with. I think it's inappropriate. And, to be honest, I'm really not in the right state at the moment to go to some —'

'Oh, my *God* — hello? Girl whose mother just died. You are *so* bloody self-obsessed.'

Victoria climbed back up the stairs and put her hand to the fire door. Her eyes filmed over with ready tears. Howard felt sorry for her, naturally, but mostly he felt extremely anxious that if she were to cry it should be far away from here and him, before anyone came down these stairs or through that door.

'Of course, I recognize that . . . of *course* . . . but I'm just saying . . . you know, we've made this . . . *awful mess* and the best thing now is to stop it exactly where it — just draw a line before more people are hurt.'

Victoria laughed horribly.

'But isn't that true?' Howard pleaded in a whisper. *'Wouldn't that be best?'*

'Best for who? Look,' she said, marching back down three steps, 'if you cancel now it's actually going to look even more suspicious. It's booked — I'm head of my table,

I have to go. I've had three weeks of sympathy cards and bollocks — I just wanted to do something *normal*.'

'I understand,' said Howard, and looked away. He considered saying something else here about her bizarre choice of the word 'normal', but, for all Victoria's glamour and chutzpah, the quality that she truly exuded right now was breakability. She was wholly breakable, and there was a threat there, in her shaky bottom lip; there was a warning. If he broke her, where would the pieces fly?

'So just meet me at eight in front of Emerson, OK? Are you going to wear that suit? It's meant to be black tie but —'

The fire door opened.

'And I'll need that essay by Monday,' said Howard loudly, his face cringing. Victoria mimed exasperation, turned and left. Howard smiled and waved at Liddy Cantalino, coming to get her photocopies.

That evening, when Howard returned home at dinner-time, there was no dinner — it was one of those nights when everybody was heading out. The search was on for keys, hairpins, coats, bath towels, cocoa butter, bottles of perfume, wallets, those five dollars that were on the sideboard earlier, a birthday card, an envelope. Howard, who intended to head back out in the suit he had on, sat on the kitchen stool like a dying sun his family were orbiting. Even though Jerome had returned to Brown two days earlier, the noisy clamour had not lessened, nor had the populated feel of the hallways and stairs. Here was his family and they were legion.

'*Five dollars,*' said Levi, suddenly addressing his father. 'It was on the *sideboard.*'

'I'm sorry — I haven't seen it.'

'So what am I meant to *do?*' demanded Levi.

Kiki swept into the kitchen. She looked lovely in a green silk suit with a Nehru collar. The bottom half of her long plait had been unwound and oiled so the free curls fell separately. In each ear she wore the only gems Howard had ever been able to give her: two simple emerald drops that had belonged to his mother.

'You look great,' said Howard genuinely.

'*What?*'

'Nothing. You look great.'

Kiki frowned and shook her head, dismissing this unexpected break in her chain of thought.

'Look, I need you to sign this card. It's for Theresa from the hospital. It's her birthday — I don't know which birthday but Carlos is leaving her and she's feeling awful. Me and some of the girls are taking her out for drinks. You *know* Theresa, Howard — she's one of the people who exist on this planet who isn't you. *Thank* you. Levi, you too. Just sign, you don't have to write anything. And it's ten thirty for you — no later. School night. Where's Zora? She better sign this too. Levi, have you put money in that phone yet?'

'How can I put money in it if people keep on stealing my greens from the counter? Tell me that!'

'Just leave a number where I can find you, OK?'

'I'm going out with my *friend*. He ain't got no phone.'

'Levi, what kind of friend doesn't have a phone? Who *are* these people?'

'Mom, be honest,' said Zora, walking backwards into the room in electric blue satin with her hands above her head. 'What's the ass situation in this dress?'

Fifteen minutes later, possible rides and buses and taxis were being discussed. Howard quietly slipped off his stool and put his overcoat on. This surprised his family.

'Where're *you* going?' asked Levi.

'College thing,' said Howard. 'Dinner in

one of the club halls.'

'One of the dinners?' said Zora quizzically. 'You never said. I thought you weren't going this year. Which hall?' She was pulling a long pair of debutante's elbow-length gloves on to her hands.

'Emerson,' said Howard haltingly. 'But I won't see you, will I? You're going to Fleming.'

'Why are *you* going to Emerson? You never go to Emerson.'

It seemed to Howard that all of his family were overly interested in this question. They stood in a semicircle, putting on their coats, awaiting his reply.

'Some ex-students of mine wanted —' began Howard but Zora was talking over him.

'Well, I'm head of table — I asked Jamie Anderson. I'm late, actually — I gotta run.' She came forward to kiss her father on the cheek, but Howard drew back from her.

'Why would you ask Anderson? Why wouldn't you ask me?'

'*Dad,* I went with you last year.'

'*Anderson?* Zora, he's a complete fraud. He's barely post-adolescent. He's moronic, actually, that's what he is.'

Zora smiled — she was flattered by this show of jealousy.

602

'*He's* really not that bad.'

'He's ridiculous — you *told* me how ridiculous that class is. Post-Native American protest pamphlets or whatever it is. I just don't understand why you would want to —'

'Dad, he's OK. He's . . . fresh — he's got new ideas. I'm taking Carl too — Jamie's interested in oral ethnicity.'

'I bet he is.'

'Dad, I have to go.'

She kissed him gently on his cheek. No hug. No rubbing of his head.

'Wait up!' said Levi. 'I need a ride!' and followed his sister to the door.

And now Kiki was to abandon him too, without a goodbye. But then, on the threshold, she turned back and came towards Howard and held his arm at the slack bicep. She pulled his ear close to her mouth.

'Howard, Zoor adores you. Don't be dumb about this. She wanted to go with you, but people in the class have been suggesting she gets some kind of . . . I don't know . . . favourable treatment.'

Howard opened his mouth to protest, but Kiki patted his shoulder. 'I know — but they don't need an excuse. I think some people are being pretty nasty. She's been upset by it. She mentioned it in London.'

'But why didn't she talk about it with me?'

'Honey, to be honest, you seemed a little self-absorbed in London. And you were writing, and she likes it when you're working — she didn't want to hassle you with it. No matter what you think,' said Kiki, giving his arm a little squeeze, 'we all want you to work well. Look, I've got to go.'

She kissed him on the cheek as Zora had, nostalgically. A reference to earlier affection.

7

In January, at the first formal of the year, the tremendous will-power of Wellington's female students is revealed. Unfortunately for the young women, this demonstration of pure will is accredited to 'femininity' — that most passive of virtues — and, as a result, does not contribute to their Grade Point Average. It is unfair. Why are there no awards for the girl who starves herself through the Christmas period — refusing all sweetmeats, roasts and liqueurs offered to her — so that she might appear at the January formal in a backless dress and toe-less shoes, although the temperature is near to freezing and the snow is heavy upon the ground? Howard, who wore a floor-length overcoat, gloves, leather shoes and a thick college scarf, stood by Emerson's front gate and watched with real awe the mist of white flakes falling upon bare shoulders and hands, the clothed men holding their near-naked, decorative partners as together they stepped around puddles and snowdrifts like ballroom dancers on an assault course. They all looked like princesses — but what steel must lurk within!

'Evening, Belsey,' said an old historian of Howard's acquaintance. Howard nodded his greeting and let the man pass. The historian's companion for the evening was a young man. Howard thought they both looked happier than the mixed-sex student–faculty partners passing intermittently through the gateway. It was an old tradition, this dinner, but it was not quite a comfortable one. It was never the same teaching the student in question after seeing them in their glad rags — though of course, in Howard's case, that line had already been crossed and then some. Howard heard the first dinner bell go. This was the call for people to take their seats. He kept his hands in his pockets and waited. It was too cold even to smoke a cigarette. He looked up and across at Wellington Square, at the glinting white spires of the college and the evergreen trees still strung with Christmas lights. In this bitter weather Howard's eyes watered incessantly. For him, all electric light spread and twinkled; street-lamps sent out fountains of sparks; traffic signals transformed into natural phenomena, glowing and pulsing like the aurora borealis. She was ten minutes late now. A wind was blowing the snow up off the ground in horizontal sweeps. The quad behind him looked like an arctic tundra. Another five minutes. Howard wandered across to Emerson Hall itself, and stationed himself just inside the doors, where he would not miss her. With everybody already seated, he was left with the waiting staff, so black in their white shirts, holding high those trays of Wellington shrimp that always looked much better than they tasted. They were informal back here, laughing and whistling, speaking their boisterous Creole, touching each other. Nothing like the silent docile servers they became in hall. Now a queue of them lined up just near Howard with their platters, jiggling impatiently like footballers in a tunnel, ready to run on to the pitch. A loud clatter of a side door made everyone turn to look at the same time, Howard included. Fifteen white young men in matching black suits and gold waistcoats walked into the hallway. They quickly arranged themselves in a staggered formation on the main stairs. The fattest of them now sang a clear, steady note with which the rest harmonized, until there was an almost unbearably pleasant chord in the air. It vibrated so brutally that Howard felt it in his body, like standing beside a loud sound system. The front door opened.

'Shit! Sorry I'm late — sorry. Clothes crisis.'

Victoria, dressed in a very long overcoat, brushed the snow from her shoulders. The young men, apparently satisfied with their sound check, stopped singing and trooped back into the room from which they had come. A spatter of applause — which sounded distinctly ironic — came from the waiters.

'You're very late,' said Howard, frowning after the retreating singers, but Victoria did not answer. She was busy taking off her coat. Howard turned back round.

'What do you think?' she asked, although there could be no question of the answer. She wore a shimmering white trouser suit, cut low. Apparently there was nothing underneath it. The waist was as neat as neat could be; her backside was impertinent. Her hair had changed again. This time it was parted on the side and slicked down with pomade like in those old photos of Josephine Baker. Her lashes appeared longer than usual. Every man and woman in the line of waiters fixed their eyes upon her.

'You look —' attempted Howard.

'Yeah, well . . . I thought one of us should wear a nice suit.'

They walked into the hall at the same time as the servers and were thankfully obscured by them. Howard feared all activity and conversation in this room would cease if these diners were squarely confronted with this impossible beauty walking beside him. They took their seats at a long table that ran along the east wall. There were four professors at this table with their Emerson student dates, the rest of the places being taken by freshmen from other halls who had paid for their tickets. This pattern was repeated throughout the hall. At a table near the front stage, Howard spotted Monty. He was sitting with a black girl who wore her hair in a similar style to Victoria's. She and all the other students at the table were focused on Monty, presently speechifying in familiar style.

'Your *father's* here?'

'Yes,' said Victoria innocently, spreading her white napkin over her white lap. 'He's Emerson — didn't you know?'

For the first time it occurred to Howard that this gorgeous, single nineteen-year-old giving her attention to a 57-year-old married man (albeit with a full head of hair) might have other motives besides pure animal passion. Was he — as Levi would put it — being played? But Howard was disrupted from further thought on this subject by an old man in cap and gown who rose, welcomed them all and then said something long in Latin. The bell rang again. The servers entered. The overhead lights dimmed, allowing the table candles to offer their flickering illumination. The wine waiters went round, bending delicately over the diners' left shoulders, and finishing each pour with an elegant twist of the bottle. The starter followed. This consisted of two of the shrimp Howard had spotted in the hall laid next to a bowl of clam chowder with its accompanying packet of croutons. Howard had spent ten years wrestling with these little packets of Wellington Town Croutons and had learned to leave them alone. Victoria ripped hers open and sent three flying into Howard's chest. This made her laugh. Her laugh was charming — she was *off-duty* somehow when she laughed. But then the performance continued; she broke open her bread roll and spoke to him in that arch, satirical style she seemed to think was flirtatious. On his other side, a shy, plain girl visiting from M.I.T. was attempting to explain to him the kind of experimental physics she did. As he ate, Howard tried to listen. He made a point of asking her many interested questions; he hoped this would lessen the effect of Victoria's frank disinterest. But after ten minutes he ran out of viable questions. Physicist and Art Historian met their match in technical terms that could not be translated, in two worlds that would not coalesce. Howard drank down his second glass of wine and excused himself to go to the toilet.

'Howard! Hahahahaha! A nice place to meet. God, these things, eh? These *fucking* things. Once a year and it's still too bloody often!'

It was Erskine, drunk, swaying. He came and stood beside Howard, unzipped himself. Howard could not piss next to people he knew. He pretended he had just finished and moved to the sink.

'You look like you're coping. Ersk, how

did you manage to get that much drink down your neck already?'

'I've been drinking for an hour just to prepare myself. John Flanders — know him?'

'Don't think so.'

'You are lucky. My most boring, ugliest, *stupidest* pupil. Why? *Why* is it always the students you least want to spend time with who want to spend time with you?'

'It's passive-aggressive,' joked Howard, soaping his hands. 'They *know* you don't like them. And they're trying to catch you out — get you off your guard and tight enough, so you'll admit it.'

Erskine finished his strenuous piss with a sigh, zipped up and joined Howard at the sinks. 'And you?'

Howard looked up at his own image in the mirror. 'Victoria Kipps.'

Erskine whistled lasciviously, and Howard knew what was coming. Talk of attractive women always stripped Erskine's mask of charm from his face. It was a side of him Howard had always known but chosen not to dwell upon. Drink made it worse. 'That girl,' Erskine whispered, shaking his head. 'She makes my eyes *sting*. You have to have your cock strapped to your leg when you pass that girl in a corridor. Don't *you* roll your eyes at *me*. Come

611

on — you're not such an angel, Howard, we all know that now. She is something! You'd have to be blind not to see it. How she can be related to a walrus like Monty!'

'She's a good-looking girl,' agreed Howard. He put his hands under the dryer, hoping the noise would shut Erskine up.

'Boys these days — they're lucky. Do you know that? Their generation of girls know how to use their bodies. They *understand* their own power. When I married Caroline, she was beautiful, yes, of course. *Like a Southern schoolgirl in bed.* Like a *child.* And now we're too old. We dream, but we can't touch. To *have* Miss Kipps! But those days are gone!'

Erskine hung his head in cod misery, and followed Howard out of the restroom. It took some restraint on Howard's part not to tell Erskine that he *had* touched, that *his* day was not yet over. He quickened his step a little, eager to return to his table. Hearing another man speak of Victoria that way had made him want her again.

'Once more into the breach,' said Erskine at the door to the hall, rubbed his hands together and left Howard for his own table. A stream of servers was leaving as they came in. Howard felt his whiteness as they all pressed past him; he was like a tourist making his way through a crowded Caribbean alleyway. At last he made his seat. He had a passing pornographic thought, as he sat down, of slipping his fingers into Vee under this table, of bringing her in this way to climax. Reality asserted itself. She was wearing trousers. And she was busy, speaking very loudly, addressing the shy girl, the boy next to her, and the boy next to him. Their faces suggested to Howard that Victoria had not stopped speaking since he left the table.

'But then, that's just the kind of person I *am,*' she was saying. 'I'm the kind of person who feels that kind of behaviour is beyond the pale, that's just the way I am. I don't make any apologies. I feel I deserve that respect. I'm very *clear* about my boundaries . . .'

Howard picked up the piece of card in front of him to find out what was to follow on the menu.

Singing

Corn-fed chicken wrapped in parma ham on a bed of sweet-pea risotto

The company is addressed by Dr Emily Hartman

Key Lime Pie

Of course, Howard had known it was coming. But he had not known it would come so soon. He felt he had not had the chance to compose himself properly. It was too late now to leave again; the bell was ringing. And here they came, those boys in their gold waistcoats with their F. Scott Fitzgerald heritage haircuts and ruddy faces. They made their way to the stage amid much applause — one might say they *jogged* towards it. Once again they arranged themselves in staggered formation, tallest at the back, blonds in the middle and the fat guy front and centre. The fat guy opened his mouth and let out that bell-like note, alive with Old Boston money. His fellows harmonized perfectly. Howard felt the familiar trouble coming on, behind his eyes, which had instantly filled with water. He bit his lip and pressed his knees together. This was all going to be made much worse by the fact he had not emptied his bladder. Around his table, nine perfectly straight faces directed themselves to the stage, awaiting entertainment. The room was silent apart from the tremulous chord. Howard felt Victoria touch his knee under the table. He removed her hand. He had to concentrate all his energies now into bringing his overdeveloped sense of the ridiculous under the control of his will. How strong was his will?

There are two different kinds of glee club in this world. The first type sing barbershop favourites and Gershwin tunes, they swing gently, moving from side to side and sometimes clicking their fingers and winking. Howard could basically deal with that type. He had got through occasions graced by glee clubs of that type. But these boys were not of that type. Swaying and clicking and winking were just how they got *warmed up.* Tonight this glee club had chosen as their opener 'Pride (In the Name of Love)' by U2, which they had taken the trouble to transform into a samba. They swayed, they clicked, they winked. They did coordinated spins. They switched places with each other. They moved forward, they moved back — always retaining their formation. They smiled the kind of smile you might employ when trying to convince a lunatic to quit holding a gun to your mother's head. One of the boys, with his lungs, began to reproduce the bass line on the record. And now Howard could hold out no longer. He began to shudder, and, making a choice between tears and noise, he chose tears. In a few seconds his face was soaked. His shoulders were rolling. The effort of not making noise was turning his face purple. One of the boys stepped out of his formation to do the moonwalk. Howard held a thick cotton serviette to his face.

'*Stop* it!' whispered Victoria and pinched his knee. 'Everybody's *looking*.'

It surprised Howard that a girl so used to being looked at should hate so much this other kind of stare. Howard apologetically removed the handkerchief, but this had the effect of releasing the noise. A squealing laugh announced itself in the room. It drew the attention of Howard's own table and the four tables beside it. It even reached Monty's table, where all of the diners turned their heads, seeking — but not yet able to locate — the insolent disturbance.

'What are you *doing?* Are you serious? *Stop* it!'

Howard mimed incapacity. His squeal turned to a honk.

'Excuse me,' said a dour female professor on the table behind him whom he did not know, 'but you're being very rude.'

But Howard could not find a place to put his face. He could either turn to look at the glee club or turn to face his own dining companions, all of whom were now trying to disassociate themselves from him, leaning far back in their chairs, doggedly focusing on the stage.

'Please,' said Victoria urgently, 'this isn't funny. You're actually *embarrassing* me.'

Howard turned to look at the glee club. He tried to think of unfunny things: death, divorce, taxes, his father. But something about the fat guy's handclaps pushed Howard over the brink. He lurched from his chair, knocked it over, picked it up and escaped down the middle aisle.

When Howard got home, he was in that middling state of drunkenness. Too drunk for work, not drunk enough to sleep. The house was empty. He went into the living room. Here was Murdoch, curled in on himself. Howard bent down and stroked his little hound face, tugging the brown-pink skin of his jaw away from harmless, blunted teeth. Murdoch stirred crossly. When Jerome was a baby, Howard liked to go into the nursery and touch his son's crêpey head, knowing he would wake, *wanting* him to. He had liked that warm, talc-scented company resting in his lap, little baby fingers stretching for the key-board. Was it a computer, back then? No: a typewriter. Howard lifted Murdoch from his stinking basket, hooked him under one arm and brought him to the bookcase. He passed a restless eye over the rainbow of spines and titles. But every one met with resistance in Howard's soul — he did not want fiction or biography, he didn't want poetry or anything academic written by anyone he knew. Sleepy Murdoch barked softly and got two of Howard's fingers in his mouth. With his free hand Howard took a turn-of-the-century edition of *Alice in Wonderland* off the shelf and brought it with Murdoch to the couch. As soon as he was released, Murdoch retreated to his basket. He seemed to look at Howard resentfully as he did so and, once he was in his former position, hid his head between his paws. Howard placed a cushion at one end of the couch and stretched out along it. He opened the book and was drawn to a handful of capitalized phrases.

VERY

　　TOOK A WATCH OUT OF
　　　　ITS WAISTCOAT-POCKET

　　ORANGE MARMALADE

　　　　　　DRINK ME

He read a few lines. Gave up. Looked at the pictures. Gave up. Closed his eyes. The next thing was a soft, heavy mass, weighing down the couch by his thigh, and then a hand on his face. The porch light was on, bathing the room in amber. Kiki took the book from his hands.

'Complex stuff. You staying down here?'

Howard shunted up a little. He brought his hand to his eye and dug from it a hard piece of yellow sleep. He asked the time.

'Late. Kids are back — didn't you hear them?'

Howard had not.

'Did you get back early? I wish you'd told me — I would have asked you to walk the Doc.'

Howard shunted up further and grasped her wrist. 'Nightcap,' he said, and had to repeat it because the first time it was just a croaking sound.

Kiki shook her head.

'Keeks, please. Just one.'

Kiki pressed her palms into her eye sockets. 'Howard, I'm real tired. I've had an emotional evening. And for me, it's a little late to drink.'

'Please, darling. One.'

Howard stood and went over to the drinks cabinet by the stereo. He opened the little door and turned to see Kiki standing. He looked at her pleadingly. She sighed and sat down. Howard brought over a bottle of amaretto and two brandy glasses. It was a drink Kiki loved, and she inclined her head in grudging admission of a good choice. Howard sat close to his wife.

'How was Tina?'

'Theresa.'

'Theresa.'

Nothing followed. Howard accepted the thrum of silent anger, waves of it, coming off Kiki. She tapped her fingers on the couch's leather. 'Well, she's pissed off — *'course* she's pissed off. Carlos is a fucking asshole. He's got the lawyers in already. Theresa doesn't even know who the woman is. Blah, blah, *blah.* Little Louis and Angela are devastated. Now they're heading to court. I have no *idea* why. They haven't even got any money to fight about.'

'Ah,' said Howard, disqualified from saying another word. He poured out two glasses of amaretto, passed one to Kiki and brought his glass to hers. He held his own glass up in the air. She thinned her eyes at him but clinked the glass.

'So. There goes another one,' she said, looking through the French doors to the silhouette of their willow tree. 'This year

. . . just everybody falling apart around us. It's not just us. It's *everyone.* That's the fourth since the summer. Dominoes. Plop, plop, plop. It's like everybody's marriage was on a timer. It's pathetic.'

Howard leaned forward with her but said nothing.

'It's worse than that — it's *predictable.*' Kiki sighed. She kicked off her slip-on shoe and reached her bare foot out towards Murdoch. She traced the line of his spine with her big toe.

'We do need to talk, Howard,' she said. 'It can't go on like this. We need to talk.'

Howard drew his lips into his mouth and looked at Murdoch. 'Not now, though,' he said.

'Well, we *need* to talk.'

'I'm agreeing with you. I'm just saying not now. Not now.'

Kiki shrugged and continued to stroke Murdoch. She worked her toe under his ear and flipped it over. The porch light now switched itself off and left them in suburban darkness. The only light remaining was the little bulb under the extractor fan in the kitchen.

'How was your dinner?'

'Embarrassing.'

'Why? Claire there?'

'*No.* That's not even . . .'

They were silent again. Kiki breathed out heavily. 'Sorry. Why was it embarrassing?'

'There was a glee club.'

In the shadow, Howard could see Kiki smile. She did not look at him but she smiled. 'Oh, Jesus. There was *not.*'

'Full glee club. Gold waistcoats.'

Kiki, still smiling, nodded rapidly several times. 'Did they sing "Like a Virgin?"'

'They sang a U2 song.'

Kiki passed her plait around to the front of her body and wound its end around her wrist.

'Which one?'

Howard told her. Frowning, Kiki finished her amaretto and poured herself another. 'No . . . I don't know that one — how's it go?'

'Do you mean how does it *actually* go or how did they sing it?'

'Wasn't worse than that time, though. Couldn't be. Oh, God, I almost *died* that time.'

'Yale,' said Howard. He had always been the repository of their dates, their names, their places. He supposed he was feminine that way. 'The dinner for Lloyd.'

'Yale. The revenge of white boy soul. Oh, my Lord. I had to leave the room. I was weeping tears. He *still* barely speaks to me, 'cause of that one night.'

'Lloyd's a pompous arse.'

'That's true. . . .' mulled Kiki, twirling the stem of her glass in her hand. 'But you and I still did *not* behave ourselves well that evening.'

Outside a dog howled. Howard was aware of Kiki's knee in its rough green silk resting against his own. He could not tell yet whether she was similarly aware.

'This was worse,' he said.

Kiki whistled. 'No,' she said, 'no, you are *not* sitting here and telling me it was as bad as Yale. That's just not even possible.'

'Worse.'

'I don't believe you, I'm sorry.'

Here Howard, who had a tuneful voice, began an effective impersonation.

Kiki held her jaw. Her bosom shook. She was giggling into her bosom, but now her head jerked back and out came her big bellow of a laugh. 'You are *making* this shit up.'

Howard shook his head in denial. He kept singing.

Kiki wagged her finger at him. 'No, no, no — I need to see the *hand* signals. It ain't the same without all that business.'

Howard rose from his seat, still singing,

and turned to face the couch. He did nothing physical yet; he had first to envisage the moves and then fit them to his own badly coordinated body. He panicked for a moment, not able to grasp the idea and the muscles in the same thought. Suddenly it came together. His body knew what to do. He began with a spin and a click.

'Oh, shut your *mouth. I* do *not* believe you! No! No they did *not!*'

Kiki fell back into the cushions, everything on her wobbling. Howard upped the tempo and the volume, growing more confident and fancy in his footwork.

'Oh, my *gosh.* What did you *do?*'

'Had to leave,' said Howard quickly, and carried on singing.

The door of Levi's basement room opened. 'Yo! Keep it *down,* man. Some of us trying to sleep!'

'Sorry!' whispered Howard. He sat down, picked up his glass and brought it to his mouth, still laughing, hoping to hold her, but at the same moment Kiki stood up, agitated, like a woman reminded of a task she hadn't completed. She was also still laughing, but not happily, and, as the laughter slowed, it became a kind of groan, and then a wispy sigh, and then nothing. She wiped her eyes.

'Well,' she said. Howard put his glass down on the table, ready to say something, but she was already at the doorway. She told him there was a clean sheet for the divan to be found in the upstairs closet.

8

Levi needed his sleep. He had to get up early in order to pay a call in Boston and be back in school by midday. By eight thirty he was in the kitchen, keys in his pocket. Before leaving, he stopped by the larder, not quite sure what he was looking for. As a child he had accompanied his mother as she paid calls in Boston neighbourhoods, visiting sick or lonely people she knew from the hospital. She would always arrive with food. But Levi had never paid this kind of call before, not as an adult. He looked blankly into the larder. He heard a door open upstairs. He grabbed three packets of Asian noodle soup and a box of rice pilaf, stuffed them in his knapsack and left the house.

The uniform of the streets comes into its own during the January freeze. While others shivered, Levi was cosy in his sweatshirts and hoods, wrapped up in there with his music. He stood by the bus stop, unconsciously reciting, listening to a tune that really called for a girl to be right in front of him, moving when he moved, fitting her curves into his sculpted crevices, bouncing. But the only female in sight was the stone Virgin Mary behind him in the courtyard of St Peter's. She was, as ever, missing both her thumbs. Her hands were full of snow. Levi studied her pretty, sorrowful face, familiar to him from so many waits at this bus stop. He always liked to have a look at what she was holding. In late spring she held flower petals, which had rained down from the trees above her. When the weather grew less volatile, people put all kinds of weird stuff in her mutilated hands — little chocolates, photos, crucifixes, a teddy bear, once — or sometimes they tied a silk ribbon round her wrist. Levi had never put anything in her hands. He didn't feel it was his place to do so, not being a Catholic. Not being an anything.

The bus approached. Levi did not notice it. At the last minute he stretched out his hand. The bus screeched and stopped a few feet ahead of him. He did his funky limp towards it.

'Hey, man, how about a little more

wah-ning next time?' said the bus guy. He had one of those broad-as-hell Boston accents. *Hah-vahd,* for Harvard. Made cost sound like *cast.* He was one of those fat old Boston guys with stains on their shirts that work for the city and liked to call brothers *man.*

Levi slotted his four quarters into the box.

'I *said* how about a little more time there, young man, so I can stop safely?'

Levi slowly removed one ear of his cans. 'You talking to me?'

'Yeah, I'm talking to you.'

'Hey, buddy, can we close that door and get this bus moving?' called somebody from the back.

'Ahlright, *ahl — right!*' shouted the bus guy.

Levi put his cans back on, scowled and walked to the back of the bus.

'Jumped-up little . . .' began the bus guy, but Levi didn't hear the rest. He sat down and leaned the side of his head against the cold glass. He silently rooted for a girl who was tearing down the snowy hill to meet the bus at the next stop, her scarf fluttering behind her.

When the bus reached Wellington Square it connected with its overhead cables and went underground, winding up outside the

T-stop that takes you into Boston. Here, in the subway, Levi bought a doughnut and a hot chocolate. He got on his train and switched off his iPod. He opened a book on his lap and held its pages flat with his elbows, leaving both hands free to hold the drink for warmth. This was Levi's reading time, this half-hour trip into town. He'd read more on the subway than he'd ever read in class. Today's book was the same one he'd been reading since way before Christmas. Levi was not a fast reader. He read maybe three volumes a year, and only in exceptional circumstances. This was the book about Haiti. He had fifty-one pages left to go. If asked to write a book report, he'd have to say that the main impression he'd gleaned from it so far was that there's this little country, a country *real close to America that you never hear about,* where thousands of black people have been enslaved, have struggled and died in the streets for their freedom, have had their eyes gouged out and their testicles burned off, have been macheted and lynched, raped and tortured, oppressed and suppressed and every other kind of pressed . . . and all so some guy can live in the only decent-looking house in the whole country, a big white house on a hill. He couldn't say

if that was the *real* message of the book —
but that's how it seemed to Levi. These
brothers had an *obsession* with that white
house. Papa Doc, Baby Doc. It was like
they'd seen white people in the white
house for so long that now it seemed reasonable to them that everybody should die
so that they got a chance to live in it too. It
was pretty much the most depressing book
Levi had ever read. It was even more depressing than the last book he got all the
way through, which was about who killed
Tupac. The experience of reading both
books had wounded him. Levi had been
raised soft and open, with a liberal suscep-
tibility to the pain of others. While all the
Belseys shared something of this trait, in
Levi — who knew nothing of history or
economics, of philosophy or anthropology,
who had no hard ideological shell to protect him — it was particularly pronounced.
He was overwhelmed by the evil that men
do to each other. That white men do to
black. How does this shit happen! Each
time he returned to the Haiti book he felt
impassioned; he wanted to stop Haitians
on the streets of Wellington and make it
better for them somehow. And, conversely,
he wanted to stop the American traffic,
stand in front of the American cars, and

demand that somebody do *something* about this wretched, blood-stained little island a mere hour's boat trip from Florida. But Levi was also a fair-weather friend when it came to books of this kind. He need only leave the book on Haiti in a forgotten knapsack in his closet for a week, and the whole island and its history grew obscure to him once more. He seemed to know no more about it than he ever had. Haitian Aids patients in Guantánamo, drug barons, institutionalized torture, state-sponsored murder, enslavement, CIA interference, American occupation and corruption. It all became a haze of history to him. He retained only the searing, unwelcome awareness that somewhere, not far from him, a people were suffering greatly.

Twenty minutes and five pages of impenetrable statistics later, Levi got off at his stop and switched his music back on. At the exit to the T he looked around him. The district was busy. How strange it was to see streets where everybody was black! It was like a homecoming, except he'd never known this home. And yet they all hurried past him as if he were a local — nobody looked at him twice. He asked an old guy by the exit for directions. The man wore an old-fashioned hat and a bow-tie. As soon as he started speaking Levi realized he was going to be of no use what-soever. Very slowly, the old guy told him to take a right here, walk three blocks, past the blessed Mr Johnson — *Beware of them snakes!* — and then take a left into the square because the street he was looking for was someplace around there if he was not mistaken. Levi had no idea what the guy was talking about, but he thanked him and took the right. It began to rain. The one thing Levi was not was waterproof. If all this gear got wet, it would be like drag-ging another boy his own weight around on his back. Three blocks down, under the awning of a pawnshop, Levi stopped a young brother and was directed precisely in language he recognized. He ran diago-nally across the square and soon found the street and the house. It was a big square property with twelve windows out front. It looked like it had been sliced in half. The sliced side was raw brick red. Shrubs and garbage grew up against this wall, along-side a burned-out car, turned upside down. Levi walked to the front of the prop-erty. Three defunct commercial properties faced him. A locksmith, a butcher and a lawyer had all failed to make a go of it here. Each doorway had multiple bells for the apartments above. Levi checked his piece of paper. 1295, Apartment 6B.

'Hey, Choo?'

There was silence. Levi knew someone was there because the intercom had come on.

'Choo? You there? It's Levi.'

'Levi?' Choo sounded half awake, his sleepy accent Gallic and smooth, like Pepe le Pew. 'What are you doing here, man?'

Levi coughed. The rain was now coming down hard. It made a harsh metallic sound as it hit the sidewalk. Levi put his mouth close to the intercom. 'Bro, I was passing, 'cos I live not so far and . . . and this shit's coming *down* outside, yo, so . . . well, you gave me your address that time, so, as I was passing . . .'

'You want to come into my place?'

'Yeah, man . . . I was just . . . Look, Choo, it's chilly out here, man. You gonna let me in or what?'

Silence again.

'Stay there, please.'

Levi released the intercom and tried to get both his feet on the thin doorstep, which afforded him about three inches of cover from the overhang of the roof. When Choo opened the door, Levi practically fell on top of him. Together they stepped into a concrete stairwell that smelled bad. Choo met Levi's fist with his own. Levi noticed that his friend's eyes were red. Choo jerked his head upwards to signify that Levi should follow him. They began to climb the stairs.

'Why did you come here?' asked Choo. His voice was dull and quiet, and he did not turn to look at Levi as he spoke.

'You know . . . I just thought I'd pay you a call,' said Levi awkwardly. It was the truth.

'I don't have a phone.'

'No, I mean,' said Levi, as they reached a landing and a damaged door, patched up with a panel of unpainted wood, '*pay a call.* It's like in America when you go visit someone to see how they are, you know.'

Choo opened his front door. 'You wanted to see how I am?'

This too was true, but Levi now acknowledged that it sounded a little weird. How to explain it? He wasn't sure himself. Simply: Choo had been on his conscience. Because . . . because Choo wasn't like the other guys in the team. He didn't travel with the pack, didn't screw around or go dancing, and he seemed, by contrast, lonely, isolated. Basically, Levi figured that

Choo was just plain *smarter* than all the people around him, and Levi, who lived with people similarly cursed, felt that his own experience in this area (as a carer of smart folk) made him especially qualified to help Choo out. And then the book on Haiti had conspired in Levi's mind with the little he had surmised about Choo's personal life. The tatty clothes he wore, the way he never bought a sub or a can of Coke like the others. His raggedy hair. His unfriendliness. That scar along his arm.

'Yeah . . . basically . . . I was thinking, well, we *down,* ain't we? I mean, I know you don't talk too much when we be working, but . . . you know, I consider you my friend. I do. And brothers look out for each other. In America.'

For what felt like an awful long time, Levi thought Choo was about to kick his ass. Then he began to chuckle and put his hand heavily on Levi's shoulder. 'You have nothing to do, I think. You need to be more busy.'

They came into a reasonably sized room, but now Levi noted that the kitchen units, the bed and the table were all compressed into this one space. It was cold and it stank of marijuana.

Levi slipped off his rucksack. 'I brought

you some stuff, man.'

'Stuff?' Choo picked up a fat joint from his ashtray and relit it. He offered Levi the only chair and took for himself the corner of the bed.

'Like, food.'

'*NO,*' said Choo indignantly, cutting the air with his hand. 'I'm not starving. Forget about charity. I worked this week — I don't need help.'

'No, no, it ain't like that — I just . . . it's like, when you go see someone, you bring something. In America — that's how we do. Like a muffin. My mom always takes muffins or pie.'

Choo stood up slowly, reached over and took the offered packets from Levi's hands. He seemed unsure as to what exactly they were, but he thanked Levi and, peering at them curiously, walked across the room to put them on the kitchen counter.

'I didn't have no muffins and I just thought . . . Chinese soup. Good for when it's cold,' said Levi and mimed coldness. 'So. How you been? I didn't see you Tuesday evening.'

Choo shrugged. 'I have a few jobs. I did a different job on Tuesday.'

Outside on the street came the loud voice of someone crazy, cursing a lot. Levi

tened to *Fear of a Black Planet* all the way through. Choo, though very stoned, knew it well and repeated all the words, and tried to describe to Levi the effect first hearing a bootleg of this album had had on him. *'Then we knew,'* he said eagerly, bending his bony fingers back on the floor. 'That's when we knew, we understood! *We were not the only ghetto.* I was only thirteen but suddenly I understood: America has ghettos! And Haiti is the ghetto of America!'

'Yeah . . . that's deep, bro,' said Levi, nodding largely. He felt stoned just breathing in this room.

'Oh, *man,* YES!' cried Choo when the next song began. He did this whenever the songs changed. He didn't nod his head like Levi; he did this strange shaking of his torso — like he was hanging on one of those elastic straps that vibrate and make you thin. Every time he did it Levi cracked up all over the place.

'I wish I could play you some of our music, Haitian music,' said Choo mournfully, as the album ended and Levi used his thumb to flick through other possibilities. 'You would like it. It would move you. It's political music, like reggae — you understand? I could tell you things about my country. They would make you weep. The music makes you weep.'

'Scene,' said Levi. He wanted — but did not feel sufficiently confident — to speak of the book he'd been reading. Now Levi brought his little music machine close to his face, looking for a particular track whose name he had slightly mistaken, making it impossible to find in the alphabetical lists.

'And I know you don't live near here, Levi,' added Choo. 'Are you listening to me? I'm not an idiot.' He was sitting on his heels and now laid his back right along the floor. His T-shirt rode up his rigid chest. There was not an extra piece of flesh on his body. He blew a large smoke ring into the air and then another one that fit into that. Levi kept flicking through his thousand songs.

'You think we're all peasants,' said Choo, but without any sign of rancour, as if objectively interested in the proposition. 'But we don't all live in dumps like this. Felix lives in Wellington — no, you didn't know that. Big house. His brother runs the taxis there. He saw you there.'

Levi knelt up, still with his back to Choo. He never could lie straight to someone's face. 'Well, that's 'cos my *uncle,* see, *he* lives there . . . and, I like, I do small jobs

639

for him, stuff around his yard and —'

'I was there Tuesday,' said Choo, ignoring him. 'In the *college*.' He treated this word like ink upon his tongue. 'Fucking serving like a monkey . . . teacher becomes the servant. It's painful! I can tell you, because I know.' He thumped his breast. 'It hurts in here! It's fucking painful!' He sat up straight suddenly. 'I teach, I am a teacher, you know, in Haiti. That's what I am. I teach in a high school. French literature and language.'

Levi whistled. 'Bro, I *hate* French, man. We have to do that shit. I *hate* that.'

'And now,' continued Choo, 'my cousin says — come and do this, serve them one night, thirty dollars in the hand, swallow your pride! Wear a monkey suit and look a monkey and serve them their shrimps and their wine, the big white professors. We didn't even get thirty dollars — we had to pay to dryclean our own uniforms! Which leaves twenty-two dollars!'

Choo passed Levi the joint. Once more Levi declined it.

'How much do you think their professors get paid? How much?'

Levi said he didn't know and it was true, he didn't. All he knew was how hard it was to get even twenty bucks out of his own father.

'And then they pay us in cents to serve them. The same old slavery. Nothing changes. *Fuck* this, man,' said Choo, but it sounded harmless and comic in his accent. 'Enough American music. Put some Marley on! I want to hear some Marley!'

Levi obliged with the only Marley he had — a 'Best Of' collection copied off his mother's CD.

'And I saw him,' said Choo, kneeling and staring past Levi, his bloodshot eyes acute and fixed upon some demon not in this room. 'Like a lord at the table. *Sir* Montague Kipps . . .' Choo spat on his own floor. Levi, for whom cleanliness had long superseded godliness, was repelled. He had to move position to where the phlegm was not in his sightline.

'I *know* that guy,' said Levi as he shuffled across the carpet. Choo laughed. 'No, I do . . . I mean I don't *know* him know him, but he's this guy that . . . well, my pops *hates* his ass, he's like, you even mention his *name* and he's like —'

Choo pointed his long forefinger right in Levi's face. 'If you know him, know this: that man is a liar and a thief. We know all about him, in our community, we follow his progress — writing his lies, claiming his glories. You rob the peasants of their art and it makes you a rich man! A rich man! Those artists died poor and hungry. They sold what they had for a few dollars out of desperation — they didn't know! Poor and *hungry!* I served him his wine —' Here Choo lifted his hand and pretended to pour out a glass, with a crude servile look on his face. 'Don't ever sell your soul, my brother. It isn't worth twenty-two dollars. I was weeping inside. Don't ever sell it for a few dollars. Everybody tries to buy the black man. *Everybody,*' he said, pounding the carpet with a fist, 'tries to buy the black man. But he can't be bought. His day is coming.'

'I hear you,' confirmed Levi and, not wanting to be an ungrateful guest, took the joint that was, once again, offered to him.

This same morning, in Wellington, Kiki also paid an unannounced call.

'It's Clotilde, isn't it?'

The girl stood shivering, holding the door ajar. She gazed at Kiki vacantly. She was so slender Kiki could see her hip bones through her jeans.

'I'm Kiki — Kiki Belsey? We met before.'

Now Clotilde opened the door a little wider and, upon recognizing Kiki, became distressed. She gripped the door handle, twisting the plank of her upper body. She had no English words to convey her news. *'Oh . . . madame, oh, mon Dieu, Meeses Kipps — Vous ne le savez pas? Mme Kipps n'est plus ici . . . Vous comprenez?'*

'Sorry, I —'

'Meeses Kipps — elle a été très malade, et tout d'un coup elle est morte! Dead!'

'Oh, no, no, I know . . .' said Kiki, fanning her hands up and down, putting out the fire of Clotilde's anxiety. 'Oh, God, I should have called ahead — yes, Clotilde, yes, I comprehend . . . I was at the funeral . . . no, it's OK . . . honey, I just wondered whether *Mister* Kipps was here, Professor Kipps. Is he in?'

'Clotilde!' came Kipps's voice from somewhere deeper in the house. 'Close the door — *fermé* — must we all freeze? *C'est froid, c'est très froid.* Oh, for goodness sake —'

Kiki saw his fingers curl round the edge of the door; the door swung wide; he stood before her. He looked astonished and not quite as dapper as usual, although his three-piece suit was in place. Kiki sought the anomaly and found it in his eyebrows, which were wildly overgrown.

'Mrs *Belsey?*'

'Yes! I — I . . .'

His huge head, with its glossy pate and

brutal, protruding eyes, proved too much for Kiki. She lost her words. Instead she held up the wrist of her left hand, around which one of the thick paperbags of Wellington's favourite bakery hung.

'For me?' asked Monty.

'Well, you were so . . . so *kind* to us in London and I . . . well, really I just wanted to see how you were and bring you —'

'Cake?'

'*Pie.* I just think sometimes when people suffer a —'

Monty, having processed his astonishment, now took control. 'Wait — come in — it's Baltic outside — there is no point talking out here — come in — Clotilde, out of the way, take the lady's coat —'

Kiki stepped into the Kippses' hallway.

'Oh, thank you — *yes,* because I think when people suffer a loss, well, the temptation is for folk to stay away — and I know when my own mother died, *everybody* stayed away and I felt most resentful of that, and bottom line, I felt, you know, *abandoned,* and so I just wanted to come by and see how you and the kids were doing, bring some pie and . . . I mean, I know we've had our differences, as families, but when something like this happens I just really feel . . .'

Kiki saw that she was talking too much. Monty had snatched the briefest of glimpses at his pocket-watch.

'Oh! But if this is a bad time —'

'No, not at all, no — I am on my way into college, but. . .' He looked over his shoulder, and then put a hand to her back, ushering Kiki forward. 'But I am just in the middle of something — if you could possibly — could I leave you here, for two minutes only, while I . . . Clotilde will make you some tea and . . . yes, just make yourself comfortable here,' he said, as they stepped on to the cow-hide rug of the library. *'Clotilde!'*

Kiki sat down on the piano stool as she had before and, with a sad smile to herself, checked the shelf nearest to her. All the N's were in perfect order.

'I'll be back in one minute,' murmured Monty, turning to go, but just then there was a loud noise in the house and the sound of someone charging up the hallway. The someone stopped at the library's open door. A young black girl. She had been crying. Her face was full of rage, but now, with a start, she spotted Kiki. Surprise supplanted anger on her features.

'Chantelle, this is —' said Monty.

'Can I get out? I'm leaving,' she said and walked on.

'If you wish to do that,' said Monty calmly, and followed her a few steps. 'We'll continue our discussion at lunchtime. One o'clock in my office.'

Kiki heard the front door slam. Monty stayed where he was for a moment and then turned back to his guest. 'I'm sorry about that.'

'*I'm* sorry,' said Kiki, looking at the rug beneath her feet. 'I didn't realize you had company.'

'A student . . . well, actually that is the question,' said Monty, walking across the room and taking the white armchair by the window. Kiki realized she had never really seen him like this, sitting down, in a normal, domestic setting.

'Yes, I think I met her before — she knows my daughter.'

Monty sighed. 'Unreal expectations,' he said, looking at the ceiling and then at Kiki. '*Why* do we give these young people unreal expectations? What good can come from it?'

'Sorry, I don't . . . ?' said Kiki.

'Here is a young African-American lady,' explained Monty, bringing his signet-ringed right hand down solidly on the arm of the Victorian chair, 'who has *no* college education and *no* college experience, who did not *graduate from her high school,* who yet believes that somehow the academic world of Wellington *owes* her a place within its hallowed walls — and why? As restitution for her own — or her family's — misfortunes. Actually, the problem is larger than that. These children are being encouraged to claim reparation *for history itself.* They are being used as political pawns — they are being fed lies. It depresses me terribly.'

It was strange being spoken to like this, as if in an audience of one. Kiki wasn't sure how to reply.

'I don't think I . . . what was it she wanted from you, exactly?'

'In the simplest terms: she wants to continue taking a Wellington class for which she does not pay and for which she is entirely unqualified. She wants this because she is black and poor. What a demoralizing philosophy! What message do we give to our children when we tell them that they are not fit for the same meritocracy as their white counterparts?'

In the silence that followed this rhetorical question, Monty sighed again.

'And so this girl comes to me — into my house, this morning, without warning — to ask me to recommend to the board that she be kept in a class that she is illegally attending. She thinks because she is in my church, because she has helped with our charity work, that I will bend the rules for her. Because I am, as they say here, her "brother"? I told her I was unwilling to do that. And we see the result. A tantrum!'

'Ah . . .' said Kiki, and folded her arms. 'Now, I know about this. If I'm not mistaken, my daughter's fighting in the opposite corner.'

Monty smiled. 'So she is. She gave an *extremely* impressive speech. I fear she might give me a run for my money.'

'Oh, honey,' said Kiki, shaking her head the way people do in church, 'I *know* she will.'

Monty nodded graciously.

'But what about your pie?' he asked, affecting a heartbroken face. 'I suppose this means the houses of Kipps and Belsey are once again at war.'

'No . . . I don't see why that should be so. All's fair in love and . . . and academia.'

Monty smiled again. He checked his watch and rubbed a hand over his belly. 'But unfortunately it is *time*, not ideology, that comes in the way of your pie and me. I must get to college. I wish we could spend the morning eating it. It was truly thoughtful of you to bring it.'

'Oh, another time. But are you walking into town?'

'Yes, I always walk. Are you going that way?' Kiki nodded. 'In which case, let us perambulate together,' he said rolling his *r* magnificently. He put both hands on his knees and stood up, and, as he did, Kiki noticed the blank wall behind him.

'Oh!'

Monty looked up at her inquiringly.

'No, it's just — the painting — wasn't there a painting there? Of a woman?'

Monty turned to look at the blank space. 'As a matter of fact there was — how did you know that?'

'Oh, well — I spent some time with Carlene in here and she spoke about that painting. She told me how much she loved it. The woman was a goddess of some kind, wasn't she? Like a symbol. She was so beautiful.'

'Well,' said Monty, turning back to face Kiki, 'I can assure you she is still beautiful — she has simply moved location. I decided to hang her in the Black Studies Department, in my office. It's . . . well, she's good company,' he said sadly. He held his forehead for a moment in his hand. Then he crossed the room and opened the door to let Kiki out.

'You must miss your wife *so* much,' said Kiki zealously. She would have been shocked to be accused of emotional vampirism here, for she meant only to show this bereaved man that she empathized, but, either way, Monty did not oblige her. He said nothing and passed Kiki her overcoat.

They left the house. Together they walked along the thin strip of sidewalk the neighbourhood's snow shovels had collectively unearthed.

'You know . . . I was interested in what you were saying, back there, about it being a "demoralizing philosophy",' said Kiki, and at the same time carefully scanned the ground before her for any black ice. 'I mean, *I* certainly wasn't done any favours in my life — nor was my mother, nor was *her* mother . . . and nor were my children . . . I always gave them the opposite idea, you know? Like my mamma said to me: You gotta work *five times as hard* as the white girl sitting next to you. And that was sure as hell true. But I feel torn . . . because I've *always* been a supporter of affirmative action, even if I personally felt uncomfortable about it sometimes — I mean, obviously my husband has been heavily involved in it. But I was interested in the way you expressed that. It makes you think about it again.'

'Opportunity,' announced Monty, 'is a right — but it is not a gift. Rights are earned. And opportunity *must* come through the proper channels. Otherwise the system is radically devalued.'

A tree in front of them shuddered a shelf of snow from its branches on to the street. Monty held a protective arm out to stop Kiki passing. He pointed to a runnel between two ice banks, and they walked along this into the open road, only rejoining the sidewalk at the fire station.

'But,' protested Kiki, 'isn't the whole point that here, in America — I mean I accept the situation is different in Europe — but here, in *this* country, that our opportunities have been severely retarded, *backed up* or however you want to put it, by a legacy of stolen rights — and to put *that* right, some allowances, concessions and support are what's needed? It's a matter of redressing the balance — because we all know it's been unbalanced a damn long time. In my mamma's neighbourhood, you could still see a *segregated bus* in 1973. And that's true. This stuff is *close*. It's recent.'

'As long as we encourage a culture of victimhood,' said Monty, with the rhythmic smoothness of self-quotation, 'we will continue to raise victims. And so the cycle of underachievement continues.'

'Well,' said Kiki, holding on to a fence-post so she could hop heavily over a big puddle, 'I don't know . . . I just think it stinks of a kind of, well, a kind of *self-hatred* when we've got black folks arguing against opportunities for black folks. I mean — we don't need to be arguing among ourselves at this point. There's a war on! We got black kids dying on the front line on the other side of the world, and they're in that army 'cos they think college has got nothing to offer them. I mean, that's the reality here.'

Monty shook his head and smiled. 'Mrs Belsey — are you informing me that I am to let unqualified students into my classes to prevent them from joining the United States Army?'

'Call me Kiki — well, OK, maybe that's not the argument I want to pursue — but this *self-hatred.* When I look at Condoleezza, and *Co*-lin — *God!* I want to be *sick* — I see this *rabid* need to separate themselves away from the rest of us — it's like "We got the opportunity and now the quota's full and thank you very much, adios." It's that right-wing black self-hatred — I'm sorry if I offend you by saying that,

652

but I mean . . . isn't that a part of it? I'm not even talking politics now, I'm talking about a kind of, of, of *psychology*.'

They had reached the top of Wellington Hill and now heard the various church bells ring in the midday. Laid out beneath them, tucked up in its bed of snow, was one of the most peaceful, affluent, well-educated and pretty towns in America.

'Kiki, if there's one thing I understand about you liberals, it's how much you like to be told a fairytale. You complain about creation myths — but you have a dozen of your own. Liberals never believe that conservatives are motivated by moral convictions *as profoundly held* as those you liberals profess *your*selves to hold. You choose to believe that conservatives are motivated by a deep self-hatred, by some form of . . . *psychological flaw*. But, my dear, that's the most comforting fairytale of them all!'

9

Zora Belsey's real talent was not for poetry but persistence. She could dispatch three letters in an afternoon, all to the same recipient. She was the master of redial. She compiled petitions and issued ultimatums. When the city of Wellington served Zora with (in her opinion) an undeserved parking ticket, it was not Zora but the city — five months and thirty phone calls later — which backed down.

In cyberspace, Zora's powers of perseverance found their truest expression. Two weeks had passed since the faculty meeting, and in that time Claire Malcolm had received thirty-three — no, thirty-four — e-mails from Zora Belsey. Claire knew this because she had just got Liddy Cantalino to print them all out. Now she shuffled them into a neat pile on her desk and waited. At exactly two o'clock, there came a knock on her door.

'Come in!'

Erskine's long umbrella entered the room and rapped twice upon the floor. Erskine followed, in a blue shirt paired with a green jacket, the combination of which did strange things to Claire's vision.

'Hi, Ersk — thanks so much for coming. I know this is not your problem at all. But I really appreciate your input.'

'At your service,' said Erskine, and bowed.

Claire threaded her fingers together. 'Basically, I just need back-up — I'm being lobbied by Zora Belsey to help this kid stay in class, and I'm willing to lend my voice, but ultimately I'm powerless here, really — but she simply won't take my word for it.'

'Are these they?' asked Erskine, reaching for the printouts on the desk and then sitting down. 'The collected letters of Zora Belsey.'

'She's driving me *crazy*. She's totally obsessed with this issue — and, I mean, I'm *behind* her. Imagine what it would be like to be *against* her.'

'Imagine,' said Erskine. He took his reading glasses from his top pocket.

'She's got this enormous petition going that the students are signing — she wants me to overturn the rules of this university overnight — but I can't *create* a place for this kid at Wellington! I really enjoy having him in my class, but if Kipps gets the board to rule against discretionaries, what can I do? My hands are tied. And I just feel like I never stop working at the moment — I've got unmarked papers coming out of my ears, I owe my publishers three different books now — I'm conducting my marriage through e-mail, I just —'

'Shhhh, shhhh,' said Erskine and laid his hand over Claire's. His skin was very dry and puffy and warm. 'Claire — leave it with me, will you please? I know Zora Belsey well — I have known her since she was a small girl. She loves to make a fuss, but she is rarely very attached to the fuss she makes. I will deal with this.'

'Would you? You're a *darling!* I'm just so *exhausted.*'

'I must say, I *do* rather like these subject titles she uses,' said Erskine whimsically. 'Very dramatic. Re: *Forty Acres and a Mule.* Re: *Fighting for the Right to Participate.* Re: *Can Our Colleges Purchase Talent?* Well: is the young man very talented?'

Claire scrunched up her little freckled nose. 'Well, *yes.* I mean — he's completely untutored, but — no, yes, he is. He's extremely charismatic, very good-looking. *Very* good-looking. Carl's a rapper, really — he's a very good rapper — and he *is* talented — he's enthusiastic. He's great to teach. Erskine, please — is there anything you can do here? Something you can find this kid to do on campus?'

'I have it. Let's give him tenure!'

They both laughed, but Claire's laugh slid to a whimper. She propped her elbow on the desk and rested her face in her hand.

'I just don't want to kick him back out on to the street. I really don't. We both know the likelihood is that next month the board is going to vote against discretionaries and then he'll be out on his ass. But if he had something else to do that . . . I *know* I probably should never have accepted him into the class in the first place, but now I've made this undertaking and I'm feeling like I've bitten off more . . .' Claire's phone started to ring. She held up her index finger in front of her face and took the call.

'Can I . . . ?' mouthed Erskine, standing and holding the printouts up in the air. Claire nodded. Erskine waved goodbye with his umbrella.

Erskine's great talent — aside from his encyclopedic knowledge of African literature — lay in making people feel far more important than they actually were. He had many techniques. You might receive an urgent message from Erskine's secretary on your voicemail, which arrived simultaneously with an e-mail and a handwritten note in your college box. He might take you aside at a party and share with you an intimate story from his childhood that, as a recently arrived female graduate from UCLA, you could not know had already been intimately shared with every other female student in the department. He was skilled in the diverse arts of false flattery, empty deference and the appearance of respectful attention. It might seem, when Erskine praised you or did you a professional favour, that it was you who were benefiting. And you might indeed benefit. But, in almost every case, Erskine was benefiting more. Putting you forward for the great honour of speaking at the Baltimore conference simply saved Erskine from having to attend the Baltimore conference. Mentioning your name in connection with the editorship of the anthology meant that Erskine himself was free of one more promise he had made to his publisher, which, due to other commitments, he was unable to fulfil. But where is the harm in this? You are happy and Erskine is happy! Thus did Erskine run his academic life at Wellington. Occasionally, however, Erskine came across difficult souls whom he could *not* make happy. Mere praise did not pacify their tempers or ease their dislike and suspicion of him. In these cases, Erskine had an ace up his sleeve. When someone was determined to destroy his peace and well-being, when they refused to either like him or to allow him to live the quiet life he most desired, when they were, as in the case of Carl Thomas, giving someone a headache who was in turn giving *Erskine* a headache, in situations like this, Erskine, in his capacity as Assistant Director of the Black Studies Department, simply gave them a job. He *created* a job where before there had been only floor space. *Chief Librarian of the African-American Music Library* had been one such invented post. *Hip-Hop Archivist* was a natural progression.

Never in his life had Carl had a job like this one. The pay was basic admin wage (Carl had been paid a similar amount to file papers in a lawyer's office and to answer calls on the desk of a black radio station). That wasn't the point. He was being hired because he knew about *this* subject, *this* thing called hip-hop, and knew much more about it than the average Joe — more maybe than anyone else in this university. He had a skill, and this job required his particular skill. He was an *archivist.* And when his pay cheques came to his mother's apartment in Roxbury they came in Wellington envelopes printed with the Wellington crest. These Carl's mother left in conspicuous spots around their kitchen for guests to see. *And* he didn't even have to wear a suit. In fact, the more casual he looked, the better everybody in the department seemed to like it. His workplace was a closed-off corridor at the back of the Black Studies Department with three small rooms leading from it. In one of these rooms was a circular desk, and this he shared with a Ms Elisha Park, the Chief Librarian of the Music Library. She was a little fat black girl, a graduate student from a third-rate college way down South, whom Erskine had met on one of his book tours. Like Carl, she felt a mixture of awe and resentment faced with the grandeur of Wellington, and together they formed a gang of two, always steeled for the contempt of the students and faculty, but equally appreciative when 'they' treated 'us' kindly. They worked well together, both quietly industrious, each on their own computer, although, while Elisha beavered away at her 'context cards' — earnest vignettes of black music history that were to be filed next to the CDs and records themselves — Carl barely ever used his computer for anything except Googling. *Useful* Googling — part of his job was to research new releases and buy them in if he thought the archive should include them. He had a certain amount to spend each month. *Buying records he loved was now part of his job.* Within one week of being thus employed he'd already spent the greater part of his budget for the month. Elisha didn't bawl him out, though. She was a calm, patient boss and, like most of the women Carl had come across in his life, was always trying to help him out, covering for him when he messed up. She kindly fiddled the figures a little and told him to be more careful next month. It was amazing. Carl's other task was to photocopy, alphabetize and file the covers from the older part of the archive, the 45s. There were some classics in there. Five guys with big afros in tiny pink shorts, hugging themselves, posing by a Cadillac that was being driven by a monkey in shades. Classics. When Carl's boys from the neighbourhood got to hear about Carl's new job, they couldn't believe it. Money for buying records! Getting paid to listen to music! *Dog, you stealing they dollars from under they noses! Damn, that's sweet!* Carl surprised himself by getting a little pissed at this kind of congratulation. Everybody kept telling him what a great gig he had, getting paid for doing nothing. But it wasn't nothing. Professor Erskine Jegede himself had written Carl a welcome letter that said he was part of the effort to 'make a public record of our shared aural culture for future generations'. Now: how is that nothing?

The job was three days a week. Well, that was what he was *expected* to do, but actually he came in every day of the week. Sometimes Elisha looked at him a little worriedly — there just wasn't enough work for him to fill five days. That is, he could photocopy the backlog of album covers for the next six months, but this had begun to seem pointless work, work they were giving him because they didn't think him capable of anything more. In fact, he had all kinds of ideas on how to improve the archive, how to make it more student-friendly. He wanted to get it set up like the big record stores, where you can walk in, pick up a pair of earphones and have access to hundreds of different songs — except in Carl's archive, the earphones would be attached to computer equipment that automatically displayed the research articles that Elisha wrote and collated about the music in the archive.

'That sounds expensive,' said Elisha, upon hearing this plan.

'OK, sure, but somebody please tell me what the point of a library resource is if you can't even access the resources? Ain't nobody gonna borrow the old records — most kids don't even know what a record player is any more.'

'Still sounds expensive.'

Carl tried to get a meeting with Erskine to discuss his ideas, but the brother was never available, and when Carl bumped into him by chance in a hallway, Erskine appeared confused as to who Carl even was, and suggested he address all queries to the librarian — what was her name? Oh, yes, Elisha Park. When Carl retold this story to Elisha, she took off her glasses and said something to Carl that resonated deeply with him, something he grasped and held to his heart like a lyric.

'This is the kind of job,' said Elisha, 'that you have to make something of for *yourself* It's all very well walking through those gates and sitting in the lunchroom and pretending that you're a Wellingtonian or whatever —' Here, if Carl's skin could blush, it would have. Elisha had his number. He *did* thrill to walk under those gates. He *did* love walking across the snowy quad with a knapsack on his back or sitting in that bustling cafeteria, for all the world as if he *were* the college student his mother had always dreamed he would be. 'But people like you and me,' continued

Elisha severely, 'we're not really a part of this community, are we? I mean, no one's gonna help us feel that way. So if you want this job to be something special, you got to *make* it something special. No one's gonna do it for you, that's the truth.'

So, in his third week of work, Carl started to get into the research end of things. Economically and time-wise it didn't make any sense to do this — no one was going to pay him more for the extra work. But for the first time in his life he found he was interested in the work he was doing — he *wanted* to do it. And what was the point, after all, of Elisha (whose area of expertise was the Blues) always asking him this and that about rap artists and rap history, when he had a brain in his head and a keyboard at his disposal? The first thing he sat down to write was a context card on Tupac Shakur. All he meant to do was write a thousand-word bio, as Elisha had asked him to, and then pass it on to her so that she could notate it with one of her mini-discographies and bibliographies, pointing students to further listening and related reading. He sat down at the computer at ten in the morning. By lunchtime he'd written five thousand words. And all this without even getting to the bit where teenage Tupac leaves the East Coast for the West. Elisha suggested that instead of taking whole people as subjects he could take one aspect of rap music in general, and make a note of all incidences of that aspect, so people could cross-reference. That didn't help. Five days ago, Carl had elected the subject of *crossroads*. All mention of crossroads, imagery on album covers of crossroads, and raps based on the idea of a crossroads in someone's life journey. Fifteen thousand words and counting. It was like suddenly he had a typing disease. Where was this disease when he was in school?

'Knock, knock,' said Zora pointlessly, as she stuck her head into his office and tapped his door. 'Busy? I was just passing by, so.'

Carl pushed his cap off his face and looked up from his keyboard, annoyed by the disruption. Certainly, his intention was always to be nice to Zora Belsey, for she had always been nice to him. But she did not make it easy. She was the kind of person who never gave you enough time to miss her. She 'passed by' his office pretty much twice a day, usually with news of her campaign to keep him in Claire Malcolm's poetry class. He hadn't been able to tell her yet that he no longer gave a damn if he stayed in that class or not.

'Hard at work — as always,' she said and stepped into the room.

He was taken aback by the large amount of cleavage he was confronted with, pushed up and together in a tight white top that could not quite contain the goods it had been entrusted with. There was also a silly shawl-like thing around her shoulders instead of a coat, and this Zora was forced to keep rearranging, as the left side slipped down her back.

'Hello, *Professor* Thomas. Thought I'd pay you a visit.'

'Hey,' said Carl, and instinctively pushed his chair a little further from the door. He took his earphones out. 'You look kinda different. You heading somewhere? You look very . . . aren't you *cold?*'

'No, not really — where's Elisha? Lunch?' Carl nodded and looked at his computer screen. He was in the middle of a sentence. Zora sat in Elisha's chair, and moved it round the desk until it was next to Carl's own.

'You want to get some lunch?' she asked. 'We could go out. I've got no class till three.'

'You know . . . It's like I *would,* 'cept I

got all this shit to do . . . I might as well just stay and do it . . . and then it'll be done.'

'Oh,' said Zora. 'Oh, OK.'

'No, I mean, another time'd be cool — but I'm having trouble concentrating — I keep on getting a lot of noise from outside. People hollering for an hour. You happen to know what's going on out there?'

Zora stood, went to the window and opened the blind. 'Some kind of Haitian protest thing,' she said, pulling open the sash. 'Oh, you can't see it from this angle. They're in the square handing out leaflets. It's a big deal, lots of people. I guess there's a march later.'

'I can't *see* them, but I can hear them, man, they *loud.* What's their beef anyway?'

'Minimum wage, getting shit on by everybody all the time — a lot of stuff, I guess.' Zora closed the window and sat down. She leaned into Carl's body to look at his computer. He covered the screen with his hands.

'Aw, man — don't be doing that — I ain't even spellchecked it, man.'

Zora peeled his fingers from the monitor. '*Crossroads* . . . The Tracy Chapman album?'

'No,' said Carl, 'the motif.'

'Oh, I see,' said Zora in a teasing voice. 'Pardon me. The *motif.*'

'You think I can't know a word 'cos you know it, is that it?' demanded Carl, and immediately regretted it. You couldn't get angry with middle-class people like that — they got upset too quickly.

'No — I — I mean, no, Carl, I didn't mean it like that.'

'Oh, man . . . I know you didn't. Calm down, there.' He patted her hand softly. He couldn't know about the electric whoosh that went through her body when he did that. Now she looked at him funny.

'Why're you looking at me weird like that?'

'No, I was just . . . I'm so *proud* of you.'

Carl laughed.

'Seriously. You're an amazing person. Look at what you've achieved, what you're achieving every day. That's so my whole point. You *deserve* to be at this university. You're about fifteen times as brilliant and hard-working as most of these over-privileged assholes.'

'Man, shut up.'

'Well, it's true.'

'What's *true* is that I wouldn't be doing none of this if I hadn't met you. So there you go, if you're gonna start getting all

Oprah about the situation.'

'Now, *you* shut up,' said Zora beaming.

'Let's *both* shut the hell up,' suggested Carl, and touched his keyboard. His screen, which had gone to sleep in the last few seconds, came back to life. He tried to retrace the thread of his last half-written sentence.

'I got fifty more signatures on the petition — they're in my bag. Do you want to see them?'

It took Carl a moment to remember what she was talking about. 'Oh, right . . . that's cool . . . no, don't bother taking them out or nothing . . . that's cool, though. Thank you, Zora, I really appreciate what you're doing for me there.'

Zora said nothing, but audaciously followed through on a plan she had been hatching since before Christmas: the reciprocal hand pat. She touched the top of his hand twice, quickly. He did not scream. He did not run from the room.

'Seriously, I'm interested,' she said, nodding at the computer. She inched her chair still closer to him. Carl leaned back in his own chair and casually explained to her a little about the image of the crossroads and how frequently rappers use it. Crossroads to represent personal decisions and choices, to represent 'going straight', to represent the history of hip-hop itself, the split between 'conscious' lyrics and 'gangsta'. The more he spoke, the more animated and absorbed he became by his subject.

'See, I was using it all the time myself — never even thought about why. And then Elisha says to me: *'member that mural in Roxbury, the one with the chair hanging from that arch?* And I'm like, yeah, of course, man, 'cos I live right by there — you know the one I'm talking about?'

'Vaguely,' said Zora, but she had only been to Roxbury once on a walking tour, during Black History Month back when she was in high school.

'So you got the crossroads painted there, right? And the snakes and this guy — who obviously I now know is Robert Johnson — I lived my whole life next door to this mural, never knew who the brother was . . . *anyway:* that's Johnson in the picture, sitting at the crossroads waiting to sell his soul to the devil. And that's why (*man, there's a lot of noise out there*). *That's* why there's a *real* chair hanging from the archway in that alley. My whole life I been wondering why someone hung a chair in that alley. It's meant to be Johnson's chair, right? *Sitting at the crossroads.* And that's totally filtered through hip-hop — and that, like, reveals to me the essence of rap. YOU GOTTA PAY YOUR DUES. That's what's written on the top of that mural, right? Near the chair? And that's the first *principle of rap music.* You gotta pay your dues, man. So, it's like . . . I'm tracing that idea through — *man,* those brothers make a lot of noise! I can't hear myself thinking in here!'

'The top bit of the window is open.'

'I know, I don't how to close that — these windows don't close right.'

'Yeah, they do, you just can't do it — there's a knack to it.'

'Now, what would I do without my Boo, huh?' asked Carl, as Zora stood up. He smacked her playfully on her big butt. 'You always got my back. Knows everything 'bout *everything.*'

Zora took her chair to the window and demonstrated the technique.

'*That's* better,' said Carl. 'Little peace for a brother when he's working.'

You never know what the hotels are like in your hometown because you never have to stay in them. Howard had been recommending the riverside Barrington to visiting professors for ten years, but, aside from a slight familiarity with the lobby, he really knew nothing about the place. He was about to find out. He was sitting on one of their reproduction Georgian sofas, waiting for her. From a window he could see the river and the ice on the river and the white sky reflected in the ice. He was feeling absolutely nothing. Not even guilt, not even lust. He had been compelled to come here by a series of e-mails she'd sent in the past week, liberally illustrated with the kind of home-made digital camera pornography that every teenage girl now seems so expert at. Her motivations were obscure to him. The day after the dinner she had sent him a livid e-mail, in reply to which he had sent a feeble apology, with no expectation of hearing from her again. But this was not like being married, as it turned out: Victoria forgave him at once. His disappearing act at the dinner seemed only to have intensified her determination to repeat what had happened in London. Howard felt himself too weak to fight anyone who had resolved to have him. He opened all her attachments and passed a lusty week of intense hard-ons at his desk — lurid visions of letting her do what she had asked to do. Crawl under your desk.

Open my mouth. Suck it. Suck it. Suck it. How sexy the words are! Howard, who had almost no personal experience of pornography (he had contributed to a book denouncing it, edited by Steinem), was riveted by this modern sex, hard and shiny and fluid-free and violent. It suited his mood. Twenty years ago, maybe, he would have been repelled. Not now. Victoria sent him images of orifices and apertures that were simply *awaiting* him — with no conversation and no debate and no conflicting personalities and no sense of future trouble. Howard was fifty-seven years old. He had been married for thirty years to a difficult woman. Entering waiting orifices was about as much as he felt he could handle now, in the arena of personal relations. There was nothing left to fight for or rescue. Soon, surely, he would be sent off to find an apartment of his own, to live as so many of the men he knew lived, alone and defiant and always slightly drunk. And so it was all much of a muchness. It was inevitable, what was coming. And here it — *she* — was. The revolving doors spat her out looking predictably lovely, in a high-collared, very yellow coat with big, square buttons made of horn. They barely spoke. Howard went to the desk to get the key.

'It's a street-facing room, sir,' said the hotel guy, because Howard had pretended he was staying overnight. 'And it may be a bit noisy today. A march is going through town — if you find it unbearable, please call down to us and we'll see if we can fix you up with something on the other side of the building. Have a nice day.'

They took the elevator up alone and she pressed her hand against his crotch. Room 614. At the door, she pushed him up against the wall and started to kiss him.

'You're not going to run away again, are you?' she whispered.

'No . . . wait, let's get inside first,' he said, and slid the credit-card key into its sheath. The green light came on, the door clicked. They found themselves in a musty, afternoon room with the curtains closed. There was a cutting little breeze, and Howard could hear muffled chanting. He went over to find the open window.

'Leave the curtains closed — I don't want everybody to see the floor show.'

She dropped her yellow coat to the floor. She stood there in all her youthful glory in the dust-flecked light. Corset, stockings, G-string, *garters* — not one dreary detail had been neglected.

'Oh! Pardon! Excuse me, please!'

A woman in her fifties, a black woman, in a T-shirt and sweatpants, had emerged from the bathroom with a bucket in her hand. Victoria screamed and sank to the floor to retrieve her coat.

'Sorry, please,' said the woman. 'I clean — later, I come —'

'Didn't you *hear* us come in?' asked Victoria heatedly, rising swiftly.

The woman looked to Howard for mercy.

'I'm *asking* you a question,' said Victoria, coat draped like a cape over her now. She stepped in front of her quarry.

'My English — sorry, can you — repeat, please?'

Outside a flurry of whistle-blowing started up.

'For fuckssake — we were clearly in here — you should have made yourself known.'

'Sorry, sorry, pardon,' said the woman, and began to back herself out of the room.

'*No,*' said Victoria. 'Don't leave — I'm *asking* you a question. Hello? Speak English?'

'Victoria, please,' said Howard.

'Excuse me, sorry,' continued the maid; she opened the door and, bowing and nodding, made good her escape. The door eased itself slowly to its click. They were left together in the room.

ference for you here has been invited. It's all done. Nothing to worry about. Just need that *pah*-point finished and we're ready to roll.'

'Did you invite my wife?'

Smith swapped his case to his other hand and looked perturbedly at his employer.

'Kiki? Sorry, Howard . . . I mean, I just sent out professional invitations as usual — but if there's a list of friends and family y'all want me to —'

Howard waved the idea away.

'OK, then.' Smith saluted Howard. 'My work here is done. Three o'clock.'

Smith left. Howard clicked around the website left open for him. He found the list of paintings Smith had mentioned and opened *The Sampling Officials of the Drapers' Guild*; more popularly known as *The Staalmeesters.* In this painting, six Dutchmen, all about Howard's age, sit around a table, dressed in black. It was the Staalmeesters' job to monitor cloth production in seventeenth-century Amsterdam. They were appointed annually and chosen for their ability to judge whether cloth put before them was consistent in colour and quality. A Turkey rug covers the table at which they sit. Where the light falls upon this rug, Rembrandt reveals to us its rich, burgundy colour, the intricacy of its gold stitching. The men look out from the painting, each adopting a different pose. Four hundred years of speculation have spun an elaborate story around the image. It is supposedly a meeting of shareholders; the men are seated on a raised dais, as they might be in a modern panel discussion; an unseen audience sits below them, one member of which has just asked the Staalmeesters a difficult question. Rembrandt sits near, but not next to, this questioner; he catches the scene. In his rendering of each face the painter offers us a slightly different consideration of the problem at hand. This is the moment of cogitation as shown on six different human faces. This is what *judgement* looks like: considered, rational, benign judgement. Thus the traditional art history.

Iconoclastic Howard rejects all these fatuous assumptions. How can we know what goes on beyond the frame of the painting itself? What audience? Which questioner? What moment of judgement? Nonsense and sentimental tradition! To imagine that this painting depicts any one temporal moment is, Howard argues, an anachronistic, photographic fallacy. It is all so much pseudo-historical storytelling, disturbingly religious in tone. We want to believe these Staalmeesters are sages, wisely judging this imaginary audience, implicitly judging us. But none of this is truly *in* the picture. All we really see there are six rich men sitting for their portrait, expecting — *demanding* — to be collectively portrayed as wealthy, successful and morally sound. Rembrandt — paid well for his services — has merely obliged them. The Staalmeesters are not looking at anyone; there is no one to look at. The painting is an exercise in the depiction of economic power — in Howard's opinion a particularly malign and oppressive depiction. So goes Howard's spiel. He's repeated it and written about it so many times over the years that he has now forgotten from which research he drew his original evidence. He will have to unearth some of this for the lecture. The thought makes him very tired. He slumps in his chair.

The portable heater in Howard's office is turned up so high he feels himself to be held in place by hot, thick air. Howard clicks his mouse, enlarging the image of the painting until it is as big as his computer screen. He looks at the men. Behind Howard, the icicles that have decorated his office window for two months melt and drip. In the quad the snow is retreating, and small oases of grass can be seen, although it is important not to derive hope from this: more snow is surely on its way. Howard regards the men. Outside there are bells ringing to mark the hour. There is the clunking sound of the tram linking with its overhead cables, there is the inane chatter of students. Howard looks at the men. History has retained a few of their names. Howard looks at Volckert Jansz, a Mennonite and collector of curiosities. He looks at Jacob van Loon, a Catholic clothmaker, who lived on the corner of the Dam and the Kalverstraat. He looks at the face of Jochem van Neve: it is a sympathetic, spaniel face with kind eyes for which Howard feels some affection. How many times has Howard looked at these men? The first time he was fourteen, being shown a print of the painting in an art class. He had been alarmed and amazed by the way the Staalmeesters seemed to look directly at him, their eyes (as his schoolmaster put it) 'following you around the room', and yet, when Howard tried to stare back at the men, he was unable to meet any of their eyes directly. Howard looked at the men. The men looked at Howard. On that day, forty-three years ago, he was an uncultured, fiercely bright, dirty-kneed, enraged, beautiful, inspired, bloody-minded schoolboy who came from nowhere and nothing and yet was determined not to stay that way — *that* was the Howard Belsey whom the Staalmeesters saw and judged that day. But what was their judgement now? Howard looked at the men. The men looked at Howard. Howard looked at the men. The men looked at Howard.

Howard pressed the 'zoom' option on his screen. Zoom, zoom, zoom until he was involved only with the burgundy pixels of the Turkey rug.

'Hey, Dad — what's up? Daydreaming?'

'Christ! Don't you knock?'

Levi pulled the door to behind himself. 'Not for family, no . . . can't say I do.' He perched on the end of Howard's desk and reached out a hand for his father's face. 'You OK? You sweating, man. Your forehead's all wet. You feel OK?'

Howard batted Levi's hand away. 'What do you want?' he asked.

Levi shook his head disapprovingly but laughed. 'Oh, man . . . that's real cold. Just because I come to see you, you think I want something!'

'Social call, is it?'

'Well, yeah. I like to see you at work, see what's going on with you, you know how it is, being all *intellectual* in college land. You're like my role model and all that.'

'Right. How much is it, then?'

Levi shrieked with laughter. 'Oh, man . . . you're cold! I can't believe you!'

Howard looked at the little clock in the corner of his screen. 'School? Shouldn't you be in school?'

'Well . . .' said Levi, stroking his chin. 'Technically, yeah. But see they got this rule — the city has a rule that you can't be in class if the temperature in the room is below a certain, like, temperature — I don't know what it is, but that kid Eric Klear knows what it is — he brings this thermometer in? And if it drops below that specific temperature, then — well, basically, we all just go home. Not a thing they can do about it.'

'Very enterprising,' said Howard. Then he laughed and looked at his son with fond wonder. What a period this was to live through! His children were old enough to make *him* laugh. They were real people who entertained and argued and existed entirely independently from him, although he had set the thing in motion. They had different thoughts and beliefs. They weren't even the same colour as him. They were a kind of miracle.

'This isn't traditional filial behaviour, you know,' said Howard jovially, already reaching for his back pocket. 'This is being mugged in your own office.'

Levi slipped off the desk and went to look out of the window. 'Snow's melting. Won't last, though. Man,' he said, turning around. 'As soon as I have my own greens and my own life, I'm moving somewhere so *hot*. I'm moving to, like, *Africa*. I don't even care if it's poor. Long as I'm warm, that's cool with me.'

'Twenty . . . *six, seven, eight* — that's all I have,' said Howard holding up the contents of his wallet.

'I really appreciate that, man. I'm dry and dusty right now.'

'What about that *job*, for God's sake?'

Levi squirmed a little before confessing. Howard listened with his head on the table.

'Levi, that was a *good* job.'

'I got another one! But it's more . . . ir-regular. And I'm not doing it right now, 'cos I got other things cooking, but imma go back to it soon, 'cos it's like —'

'Don't tell me,' insisted Howard, closing his eyes. 'Just don't tell me. I don't want to know.'

Levi put the dollars in his back pocket. 'Anyway, so in the meantime I got a bit of a cash flow *situation.* I pay you back, though.'

'With other money I'll have given you.'

'I got a job, I told you! Chill. OK? Will you chill? You gonna give yo'self a heart attack, man. *Chill.*'

Sighing, he kissed his father on his sweaty forehead and closed the door softly on his way out.

Levi did his funky limp through the department and out into the main lobby of the Humanities Faculty building. He stopped here to select a tune that would fit the experience of stepping out of this building and facing the freeze outside. Somebody called his name. He couldn't see at first who it was.

'Yo — *Levi.* Over here! Hey, man! I ain't seen your ass in the *longest* time, man. Put it there.'

'*Carl?*'

'Yeah, Carl. Don't you even know me now?'

They touched fists, but with Levi frowning all the time.

'What you doing here, man?'

'Damn — didn't you know?' said Carl,

smiling cheesily and popping his collar. 'I be a *college* man now!'

Levi laughed. 'No, seriously, bro — what you doing here?'

Carl stopped smiling. He tapped the knapsack on his back. 'Didn't your sister tell you? I'm a college man now. I'm working here.'

'*Here?*'

'Black Studies Department. I just started — I'm an archivist.'

'A *what?*' Levi transferred his weight to the opposite foot. 'Man, you screwing with me?'

'Nope.'

'You *work* here. I don't get it — you cleaning?'

Levi didn't mean this the way it came out. It was just that he had met a lot of Wellington cleaners on the march yesterday, and it was the first thing that came to his mind. Carl was offended.

'No, man, I manage the *archives* — I don't clean shit. It's a music library — I'm in control of the hip-hop and some R & B and modern urban black music. It's an amazing resource — you should come check it out.'

Levi shook his head, disbelieving. 'Carl, bro, I'm tripping . . . you gotta run this past me again. You're working *here?*'

Carl looked up over Levi's head at the clock on the wall. He had an appointment to get to — he was meeting someone in the Modern Languages Department who was going to translate some French rap lyrics for him.

'Yeah, man — it's not that complicated a concept. I'm working here.'

'But . . . You *like* it here?'

'Sure. Well . . . it's a little tight-assed sometimes, but the Black Studies Department is cool. You can get a lot done in a place like this — hey, I see your dad *all* the time. He works just down there.'

Levi, concentrating on the many strange facts being put before him, ignored this last. 'So, wait: you ain't making music no more?'

Carl shifted the knapsack on his back. 'Aw . . . I'm doing a little but . . . I don't know, man, the rap game . . . it's all gangstas and playas now . . . that's not my scene. Rap should be all about *proportion,* for me, as I see it. And it's like, you go to the Bus Stop these days, it's all these really angry brothers kinda . . . *ranting* . . . and I'm not really feeling that, so, well . . . you know how it is . . .'

Levi unwrapped a gum and put it in his

mouth without offering Carl one. 'Maybe they got shit they angry about,' said Levi frostily.

'Yeah . . . well — look, man — I actually got to run, I got this . . . thing — hey, you should come by the library sometime — we're gonna start this open-listening after-noon, where you can pick any record and play it through — we got some really rare shit, so, you should come by. Come by to-morrow afternoon. Why don't you do that?'

'It's the second march tomorrow. We marching all week.'

'March?'

Just then the front doors opened and they were joined, for a moment, by one of the most incredible-looking women either boy had ever seen. She was walking at high speed, past them and on towards the Hu-manities departments. She was dressed in tight jeans and pink polo neck and high tan boots. A long silky weave fell down her back. Levi did not connect her with the weeping, short-haired girl dressed in black that he had seen a month ago, walking, in more sedate and pious mode, behind a coffin.

'Sister — *damn!*' murmured Carl, loud enough to be heard, but Victoria, practised in ignoring such comments, simply continued along her way. Levi stared after the incendiary rear view.

'Oh, my *God* . . .' said Carl, and held his hand to his breast. 'Did you see that booty? Oh, *man,* I'm in pain.'

Levi had indeed seen that booty, but suddenly Carl was not the person with whom he wanted to discuss it. He had never known Carl well, but, in the way of a teenage crush, he had thought a great deal of him. Just shows what happens when you mature. Levi had obviously matured a hell of a lot since last summer — he'd sensed that about himself and now saw it was true. Feckless brothers like Carl just didn't impress him any more. Levi Belsey had moved on to the next level. It was strange to think of his previous self. And it was *so* strange to stand next to this ex-Carl, this played-out fool, this *shell* of a brother in whom all that was beautiful and thrilling and true had utterly evaporated.

Howard was preparing to nip out for a bagel from the cafeteria. He rose from his desk — but he had a visitor. She smashed the door open and smashed it closed. She didn't come far into the room. She stood with her back pressed against the door.

'Could you sit down, please?' she said,

looking not at him but to the ceiling, as if addressing a prayer upwards. 'Can you sit down and listen and not say anything? I want to say something and then I want to go and that's it.'

Howard folded his coat in half and sat down with it on his lap.

'You don't *treat* people like that, right?' she said, still talking to the ceiling. 'You don't do that to me *twice.* First you make me look like a *fool* at that dinner and then — you don't leave someone in a hotel by themselves — you don't act like a fucking *child* — and make someone feel that they're not worth anything. You don't *do* that.'

She brought her gaze down at last. Her head was wobbling wildly on her neck. Howard looked to his feet.

'I know you think,' she said, each word tear-inflected, making her hard to understand, 'that you . . . *know* me. You *don't* know me. This,' she said and touched her face, her breasts, her hips, 'that's what you know. But you don't know *me.* And you were the one who wanted *this* — that's all anybody ever . . .' She touched the same three places. 'And so that's what I . . .'

She wiped her eyes with the hem of her polo neck. Howard looked up.

'Anyway,' she said, 'I want the e-mails I sent you destroyed. And I'm dropping out of your class, so you don't have to worry about *that*.'

'You don't need —'

'You don't have any idea what I need. You don't even know what *you* need. Anyway. Pointless.'

She put her hand to the door handle. It was selfish, he knew, but before she left Howard was desperate to secure from her the promise that this disaster should stay between them only. He stood up and put his hands on the desk but said nothing.

'Oh, and I know,' she said, scrunching her eyes closed, 'that you're not interested in anything I have to say, because I'm just a fucking idiot girl or whatever . . . but as someone who's relatively objective . . . basically, you just need to deal with the fact that you're not the only person in this world. In my opinion, I have my own shit to deal with. But you need to deal with that.'

She opened her eyes, turned and left, another noisy exit. Howard stayed where he was, gripping his coat by its collar. At no point during the past month's debacle had he harboured any genuinely romantic feelings for Victoria, nor did he feel any now, but he did realize, at this late stage, that he actually liked her. There was something courageous there, flinty and proud. It seemed to Howard to be the first time she had spoken to him truthfully, or at least in a manner that he experienced as true. Now Howard put his coat on, shaking as he did so. He came to the door, but then waited a minute, not wanting to risk bumping into her outside. He felt peculiar: panicked, ashamed, relieved. *Relieved!* Was it so awful to feel that he had escaped? Must she not feel it too? Alongside the physical tremors and psychological shock of having been party to such a scene (and how strange it is to be spoken to that way by someone who, in truth, you barely know), was there not, on the other side of the explosion, the satisfaction of survival? Like a street confrontation, where you are physically threatened and dare to stand up to the threat and are then left alone. You walk away quivering with fear and joy at the reprieve, relief that things did not become worse. In such a mood of equivocal elation, Howard walked out of the department. He strolled past Liddy at the front desk, through the hall, past the drinks machines and the internet station, past the double doors of Keller Libr—

Howard took a step back and pressed his cheek against the glass of one of the doors. Two significant details — no, actually three. One: Monty Kipps at a podium, speaking. Two: the Keller Library packed with people, more people than any Wellington audience Howard had ever managed to amass. Three — and this was the detail that had initially arrested Howard's attention: a few feet from the door, sitting up tall in her chair, holding a notepad, apparently alert and interested, one Kiki Belsey.

Howard forgot about his appointment with Smith. He went straight home and awaited his wife. In his rage, he sat on the couch holding Murdoch tightly on his lap, scheming upon the many ways he might open the coming conversation. He lined up a pleasing selection of cool, emotionally detached possibilities — but when he heard the front door open, sarcasm vanished. It was all he could do not to leap from his seat and confront her in the most vulgar way. He listened to her footsteps. She passed the doorway of the living room ('Hey. You OK?') and kept walking. Howard internally combusted.

'Been at work?'

Kiki retraced her steps and stopped in the doorway. She was — like all long-married people — immediately alerted to trouble by a tone of voice.

'No . . . Afternoon off.'

'Have a nice time?'

Kiki stepped into the room. 'Howard, what's the problem here?'

'I think,' said Howard, releasing Murdoch, who had grown tired of being partially strangled, 'I would have been marginally — *marginally* — less surprised to see you at a meeting of . . .'

They began to speak at the same time.

'Howard, what is this? Oh, *God* —'

'. . . of the Klu Klux *fucking* Klan — no, actually, that would have made a bit more —'

'Kipps's lecture . . . Oh, Jesus Christ, that place is like Chinese whispers . . . Look, I don't need —'

'I don't know what other neo-con events you've got planned — no, darling, *not* Chinese whispers, actually; I *saw* you, taking notes — I had no *idea* you were so taken with the great man's work, I wish I'd realized, I could have got you his collected speeches, or —'

'Oh, *fuck* you — leave me alone.'

Kiki turned to leave. Howard flung himself to the other end of the couch, knelt up and caught her by the arm. 'Where are you going?'

'Away from here.'

'We're talking — you wanted to talk — we're talking.'

'This isn't talking — this is you ranting. *Stop* it — let go of me. *Jesus!*'

Howard had successfully twisted her arm, and therefore her body, moving her round the couch. Reluctantly she sat down.

'Look, I don't need to explain myself to you,' said Kiki, but then immediately went on to do so. 'You know what it is? Sometimes I feel it's always the same viewpoint in this house. And I'm just trying to get all points of view. I don't see how that's a crime, just trying to *expand* your —'

'In the interest of balance,' said Howard in the nasal voice of an American TV commentator.

'You know, Howard, all you *ever* do is rip into everybody else. You don't have any *beliefs* — that's why you're scared of people with beliefs, people who have dedicated themselves to something, to an *idea*.'

'You're right — I *am* scared of fascistic *loons* — I'm — my mind is *boggling* — Kiki, this man wants to *destroy* Roe v. Wade. That's just for starters. This man —'

Kiki stood up and started shouting.

'That is *not* what this is about — I don't give a rat's ass about Monty Kipps. I'm talking about *you* — you're terrified of anyone who believes anything — look how you treat *Jerome* — you can't even *look* at him, because you know he's a Christian now — we *both* know it — we never talk about it. *Why?* You just make jokes about it, but it's not funny — it's not funny to *him* — and it just seems like you used to have some idea of what you . . . I don't know . . . what you *believed* and what you *loved* and now you're just this —'

'Stop shouting.'

'I'm not shouting.'

'You're shouting. Stop shouting.' A pause. 'And I don't know *what on earth* Jerome has to do with *any* of this —'

With two bunched fists Kiki thumped the sides of her legs in frustration. 'It's *all* the same thing, I've been thinking about *all* of this — it's part of the same . . . just, veil of *doom* that's descended on this house — we can't talk about anything seriously, everything's ironic, nothing's serious — everyone's scared to *speak* in case *you* think it's clichéd or dull — you're like the thought police. And you don't care about anything, you don't care about *us* — you know, I was sitting there listening to Kipps

— OK, so he's a nutcase half the time, but he's standing up there talking about something he *believes* in —'

'So you keep saying. Apparently it doesn't matter *what* he believes in, as long as it's *something.* Will you listen to yourself? He believes in *hate* — what are you *talking* about? He's a miserable, lying —'

Kiki stuck a finger right in Howard's face. 'I *don't* think you want to talk about lies, OK? I do *not* think you want to sit there and *dare* talk to me about lies. If he's nothing else, that man is a more honourable man than you will *ever* be —'

'You've lost your mind,' muttered Howard.

'Don't do that!' screamed Kiki. 'Don't undermine me like that. *God* — it's like . . . you can't even . . . I don't feel I even *know* you any more . . . it's like after 9/11 when you sent that ridiculous e-mail round to everybody about Baudry, Bodra—'

'Baudrillard. He's a philosopher. His name is Baudrillard.'

'About simulated wars or whatever the fuck that was . . . And I was thinking: *What is wrong with this man?* I was *ashamed* of you. I didn't say anything, but I was. Howard,' she said, reaching out to him but not far enough to touch, 'this is *real.* This life. We're really here — this is really happening. Suffering is *real.* When you hurt people, it's *real.* When you fuck one of our best friends, that's a *real* thing and it *hurts* me.'

Kiki collapsed into the couch and started to weep.

'Comparing mass murder to my infidelity seems a tad . . .' said Howard, quietly, but the storm was over, and there was no point. Kiki cried into a pillow.

'Why do you love me?' he asked.

Kiki kept on crying and did not answer. A few minutes later he asked her again.

'Is that some kind of trick question?'

'It's a genuine question. A *real* question.'

Kiki said nothing.

'I'll help you out,' said Howard. 'I'll put it in the past tense. Why *did* you love me?'

Kiki sniffed loudly. 'I don't want to play this game — it's stupid and aggressive. I'm tired.'

'Keeks, you've been holding me at arm's length for so long, and I can't remember if you even *like* me — forget love, *like.*'

'I have *always* loved you,' said Kiki, but in such a furious way that words and sentiment disconnected. '*Always.* I didn't change. Let's remember who changed.'

'I am honestly, *honestly* not picking a

fight with you,' said Howard wearily and pressed his eyes with his fingers. 'I am asking you why you loved me.'

They sat and said nothing for a while. In the silence, something thawed. Their breathing slowed.

'I don't know how to answer that — I mean, we both know all of the good stuff and it doesn't help,' said Kiki.

'You say you want to talk,' said Howard. 'But you don't. You stonewall me.'

'*All* I know is that loving you is what I did with my life. And I'm terrified by what's happened to us. This wasn't meant to happen to us. We're not like other people. You're my best friend —'

'Best friend, yes,' said Howard wretchedly. 'That's always been the case.'

'And we're co-parents.'

'And we're *co-parents*,' repeated Howard, chafing against an Americanism he despised.

'You don't have to say that sarcastically, Howard — that's part of what we are now.'

'I wasn't being . . .' Howard sighed. 'And we were in love,' he said.

Kiki let her head flop back on the couch.

'Well, Howie, that was your past tense, not mine.'

They were silent again.

'*And,*' said Howard, 'of course we were always very good at the Hawaiian.'

It was now Kiki's turn to sigh. *Hawaiian,* for reasons private and old, was a euphemism for sex in the Belsey household.

'Actually, we *excelled* at the Hawaiian,' added Howard — he was out on a limb and he knew it. He put a hand to his wife's coiled hair. 'You can't deny it.'

'I never did. You did. When you did what you did.'

This sentence — with its overabundance of 'dids' — was problematically comic. Howard struggled to rein in a smile. Kiki smiled first.

'Fuck you,' she said.

Howard took both his hands and put them under his wife's cataclysmic breasts.

'Fuck *you,*' she repeated.

He brought his hands round to their summits, and massaged the handful he could manage. He touched his lips to her neck and kissed her there. And again on her ears, which were wet from tears. She turned her face to his. They kissed. It was a burly, substantial, tongue-filled kiss. It was a kiss from the past. Howard held his wife's lovely face in both of his hands. And now the same journey of so many nights over so many years: the kiss trail down her throat's chubby rings of flesh, down to her chest. He undid the buttons of her shirt, as she attended to the hardy clip of her bra. The silver-dollar-sized nipples, from which occasional hairs sprouted, were the familiar deep brown with only a hint of pink. They protruded like no other nipples he had ever seen. They fitted perfectly and properly into his mouth.

They moved on to the floor. Both thought of the children and the possibility that one of them would come home, but neither dared go to the door to lock it. Any movement away from this spot would be the end. Howard lay on top of his wife. He looked at her. His wife looked at him. He felt known. Murdoch, in disgust, left the room. Kiki reached up to kiss her husband. Howard pulled off his wife's long skirt and her substantial, realistic underwear. He put his hands under her lovely fat ass and squeezed. She let out a soft hum of contentment. She sat up and began to unwind that long plait of hers. Howard lifted his hands up to help her. Coils of long afro hair came free and sprang wide and short until the halo from the old days surrounded her face. She undid his zip and took him into her hands. Slowly, steadily, sensuously, expertly, she manipulated him.

She began whispering in his ear. Her accent grew thick and Southern and filthy. For reasons private and old she was now in character as a Hawaiian fishwife called Wakiki. The fatal thing about Wakiki was her sense of humour — she'd bring you to the edge of abandon and then say something so funny that everything fell apart. Not funny to anyone else. Funny to Howard. Funny to Kiki. Laughing hard now, Howard lay back and pulled Kiki on top of him. She had a way of hovering closely there without putting all her weight on him. Kiki's legs had always been strong as hell. She kissed him again, straightened up and crouched over him. He reached out like a child for her breasts and she placed them in his hands. She lifted her belly with her own hand and then pushed her husband inside herself. Home! But this happened sooner than Howard had expected, and he was partly saddened, for he knew like she knew that he was out of practice and therefore doomed. He could survive on top, or behind, or spooning, or any of the many other marital familiars. He was a stayer in those positions. He was a champion. They used to spend hours spooned next to each other, moving gently back and forth, speaking of the day, of funny things that had happened, of some foible of Murdoch's, even of the children. But if she crouched above him, the giant breasts bouncing and developing their coating of sweat, her beautiful face working intently on what she wanted, the strange genius of her muscles clasping and unclasping him — well, then he had three and a half minutes, tops. For ten or so years, this was a cause of enormous sexual frustration between them. Here was her favourite position; here was his inability to withstand the pleasure of it. But life is long, and so is marriage. There came a breakthrough one year when Kiki found herself able to work with his excitement so as to somehow stimulate new muscles, and these sped her along in time with him. She once tried to explain to him how she did this, but the anatomical difference between our genders is too great. The metaphors won't work. And who cares, anyway, for technicalities when that starburst of pleasure and love and beauty is taking you over? The Belseys got so good at it that they grew almost blasé, more proud than excited. They wanted to demonstrate the technique to the neighbours. But Howard did not feel blasé just now. He lifted his head and shoulders off the floor, grappled with her backside and pulled her tighter on to him; he apologized to her as his release came early, but in fact she joined him seconds later as the last ripples of the thing went through them both. The back of Howard's head connected with the carpet, and he lay there breathing frantically, saying nothing. Kiki moved off him slowly and sat cross-legged like a big Buddha beside him. He reached out his hand, the open flat palm awaiting hers, the way they used to. She did not take it.

'Oh, *God,*' she said instead. She picked up a cushion and buried her face in it.

Howard didn't hesitate. He said: 'No, Keeks — this is a good thing. It's been hell —' Kiki pushed her face further into the cushion.

'I know it has. But I don't want to be without . . . *us.* You're the person I — you're my life, Keeks. You have been and you will be and you are. I don't know how you want me to say it. You're for me — you *are* me. We've always known that — and there's no way out now anyway. I love you. You're for me,' repeated Howard.

Kiki had not raised her face from the cushion and now she spoke into it. 'I'm not sure you're the person for me any more.'

'I can't hear you — what?'

Kiki looked up. 'Howard, I love you. But I'm just not *interested* in watching this *second adolescence.* I had my adolescence. I can't go through yours again.'

'But —'

'I haven't had my period in *three months* — did you even *know* that? I'm acting crazy and emotional all the time. My body's telling me the show's over. That's real. And I'm not going to be getting any *thinner* or any *younger,* my ass is gonna hit the ground, if it hasn't already — and I want to be with somebody who can *still see me in here.* I'm still *in* here. And I don't want to be *resented* or *despised* for changing . . . I'd rather be alone. I don't want someone to have *contempt* for who I've become. I've watched *you* become too. And I feel like I've done my best to honour the past, and what you were and what you are now — but you want something more than that, something new. I can't *be* new. Baby, we had a good run.' Weeping, she lifted his palm and kissed it in the centre. 'Thirty years — almost all of them *really happy.* That's a lifetime, it's incredible. Most people don't get that. But maybe this is just over, you know? Maybe it's over . . .'

Howard, crying himself now, got up from where he lay and sat behind his wife.

He stretched his arms around her solid nakedness. In a whisper he began begging for — and, as the sun set, received — the concession people always beg for: a little more time.

II

Spring break arrived, budding pink and violet in the apple trees, streaking orange through the wet sky. It was still as cold as ever, but now Wellingtonians permitted themselves hope. Jerome came home. Not for him Cancún, or Florida, or Europe. He wanted to see his family. Kiki, tremendously touched by this, took his hand in hers and led him into their chilly garden to witness the changes there. But she had other motives besides the simply horticultural.

'I want you to know,' she said, bending down to pluck a weed from the rose bed, 'that we will support you in each and every choice that you will ever make.'

'Well,' said Jerome mordantly, 'I think that's beautifully and euphemistically put.'

Kiki stood up and looked helplessly at her son and his gold cross. What else could she say? How could she follow him where he was going?

'I'm joking,' Jerome assured her. 'I appreciate it, I do. And vice versa,' he said, and gave his mother the same look she'd given him.

They sat on the bench under the apple tree. The snow had peeled the paint and warped the wood, making it unsteady. They spread their weight to settle it. Kiki offered Jerome a portion of her giant shawl, but he declined.

'So there's something I wanted to talk to you about,' said Kiki, cautiously.

'Mom . . . I *know* what happens when a man puts his thing in a woman's —'

Kiki pinched him in his side. Kicked him on his ankle.

'It's *Levi.* You know that when you're not around he's got no one . . . Zora won't spend any time with him, and Howard treats him like some piece of — I don't know what — *moon rock.* I worry about him. Anyway, he's got in with these *people* — it's fine, I've seen them around — it's a big group of Haitian and African boys, they sell things on the street — I guess they're traders.'

'Is it legal?'

Kiki pursed her lips. She had always been sweet on Levi, and nothing he ever did could be completely wrong.

'Oh, boy,' said Jerome.

'I don't know that it's especially *illegal.*'

'Mom, it either is or it —'

'No, but that's not . . . it's more that he seems so *involved* with all of them. Suddenly he has no other friends. I mean, in a lot of ways it's been interesting — he's a lot more politically aware, for example. He's in the square pretty much every weekend with leaflets helping this Haitian support-group campaign — he's there now.'

'Campaign?'

'Higher wages, unfair detention — a lot of issues. Howard's very proud *of course* — proud without actually thinking about what any of it might *mean.*'

Jerome stretched his legs out across the grass and crossed one foot over the other. 'I'm with Dad,' he had to admit. 'I don't see the problem, really.'

'Well, OK, it's not a *problem,* but . . .'

'But what?'

'Don't you find it a little strange that he's so interested in *Haitian* things? I mean, *we're* not Haitian, he's never been to Haiti — six months ago he couldn't have pointed to Haiti on a map. I just think it seems a little . . . *random.*'

'Levi *is* random, Mom,' said Jerome, standing up and moving around to get warm. 'Come on, let's go in, it's cold.'

They walked quickly back across the grass, through squelchy mounds of blossom forced off the trees by the previous night's rainstorm.

'Will you just hang out with him a little, though? Promise? Because he tends to go *all in* for one thing — you know how he is. I worry that all the crap that's been going on in this house has been . . . throwing him off balance somehow. And it's an important school year.'

'How . . . how *is* all the crap?' asked Jerome.

Kiki put her arm round Jerome's waist. 'Truthfully? It's *damn* hard work. It's the hardest work I've ever done. But Howard's really trying. You have to give him that. He is.' Kiki noted Jerome's doubtful face. 'Oh, I know he can be an almighty pain, but . . . I do *like* Howie, you know. I may not always show it, but —'

'I know you do, Mom.'

'But will you promise that, about Levi? Spend some time with him — find out what's up with him?'

Jerome made the typical maternal promise casually, imagining that it might be casually attended to, but, as they stepped back into the house, his mother revealed her true face. 'Yes, he's down there right now, in the square,' she said, as if Jerome had asked her. 'And poor Murdoch needs a walk . . .'

Jerome left his packed bags in the hallway and obliged his mother. He clipped a lead to Murdoch, and together they enjoyed the pretty walk through the old neighbourhood. It was a surprise to Jerome how happy he was to be back. Three years ago he had thought he hated Wellington: an unreal protectorate; high income, morally complacent; full of spiritually inert hypocrites. But now his adolescent zeal faded. Wellington became a comforting dreamscape he felt grateful and fortunate to call home. It was certainly true that this was an unreal place where nothing ever changed. But Jerome — on the brink of his final college year and he knew not what — had begun to appreciate exactly this quality. As long as Wellington stayed Wellington, he could risk all manner of change himself.

He walked into a lively late-afternoon square. A saxophonist playing over a tinny backing track alarmed Murdoch. Jerome picked the dog up. A small food market had been set up on the east side, and this competed with the usual chaos of the taxi rank, students at a table protesting the war, others campaigning against animal testing and some guys selling handbags. Near the T-stop, Jerome saw the table his mother had described. It was covered with a yellow cloth embroidered with the words HAITIAN SUPPORT GROUP. But no Levi. Jerome stopped at the newspaper concession outside the station and bought the latest *Wellington Herald.* Zora had sent three e-mails urging him to buy a copy. He stayed in the relative warmth of the newsstand and flicked through the paper, looking for a tell-tale Z. He found his sister's name on page 14, heading the weekly campus column 'Speaker's Corner'. The mere name of this column aggravated Jerome: it smacked of that wearisome Wellingtonian reverence for all things British. The British flavour spread to the contents of the column itself, which, no matter the student who happened to be writing it, always retained a superior, Victorian tone. Words and phrases that the student had never before had cause to use ('indubitably', *'I cannot possibly fathom'*) came from their pen. Zora, who had been in Speaker's Corner four times (a record for a sophomore), did not waver from the house style. The arguments of these columns were always presented as if they were motions being put before the Oxford Union. To-day's title, 'This Speaker Believes that Wellington Should Put Its Money Where Its Academic Mouth Is', by Zora Belsey. Just below this, a large photo of Claire Malcolm *in medias res,* animated, at a round table of students, in the foreground of which photo was a handsome face Jerome faintly recognized. Jerome paid a dollar twenty to the guy in the newspaper booth and walked back into the square. *Whither* <u>real</u> *affirmative action?* read Jerome. *That is the question I put before all fair-minded Wellingtonians this day. Are we truly steadfast in our commitment to the equality of opportunity or no? Do we presume to speak of progress when within these very walls our own policy remains so shamefully diffident? Are we satisfied that the African-American youth of this fair city . . .'*

Jerome gave up and tucked the paper under his arm. He resumed his search for Levi, spotting him at last in the doorway of Wellington Savings Bank, eating a burger. As Kiki had predicted, he had friends with him. Tall, skinny black guys in baseball caps, evidently not Americans, also intent on their burgers. From ten yards off, Jerome hollered at Levi and held up his hand, hoping that his brother would save him from an awkward set of introductions. But Levi waved him in.

'Jay! Hey, this is my brother, man. My *brother,* brother.'

Jerome now learned the grunted names of seven inarticulate guys who seemed little interested in learning his.

'This is my crew — and *this* is Choo, he's my main man, he's cool. He's got my back. This is Jay. He's all . . .' said Levi, tapping both of Jerome's temples, 'he's a deep thinker, always analysing shit, like you.'

Jerome, uneasy in this company, shook the hand of Choo. It drove Jerome nuts that Levi always assumed that everyone felt as comfortable as Levi did himself in any given situation. Now Levi left Choo and Jerome to stare blankly at each other as he crouched down and gathered up Murdoch in his arms.

'And *this* is my little foot soldier. He's my lieutenant. Murdoch *always* got my back.' Levi let the dog lick his face. 'So, how are you, man?'

'Good,' said Jerome. 'I'm good. Glad to be home.'

'Seen everybody?'

'Just saw Mom.'

'Cool, cool.'

They were both nodding a lot. Sadness swept over Jerome. They had nothing to say to each other. A five-year age gap between siblings is like a garden that needs constant attention. Even three months apart allows the weeds to grow up between you.

'So,' said Jerome, trying weakly to fulfil his mother's brief, 'what's going on with you? Mom said you got lots going on.'

'Just . . . you know . . . hanging with my boys — getting things done.'

As usual, Jerome tried to sieve Levi's elliptical language for any specks of truth concealed within.

'You all involved in the . . . ?' said Jerome, motioning to the little table across the way. Behind it two young black men with glasses were handing out leaflets and newspapers. A banner was propped up behind them: FAIR PAY FOR WELLINGTON'S HAITIAN WORKERS.

'Me and Choo, yeah — trying to get the voice heard. Representing.'

Jerome, who was finding this conversation increasingly irritating, stepped around the other side of Levi so as to get out of earshot of the silent burger-eating men beside him.

'What did you put in his coffee?' Jerome

joked stiffly to Choo. 'I couldn't even get him to vote in his school elections.'

Choo clasped his friend around his shoulders and had the gesture returned. 'Your brother,' he said affectionately, 'thinks of all his brothers. That's why we love him — he's our little American mascot. He fights shoulder to shoulder with us for justice.'

'I see.'

'Take one,' said Levi, and pulled a double-sided piece of paper printed like a newspaper from his voluminous back pocket.

'You take this, then,' said Jerome, handing him the *Herald* in return. 'It's Zora. Page 14. I'll get another one.'

Levi took the newspaper and forced it into his pocket. He tucked the last lump of burger into his mouth. 'Cool — I'll read it later . . .' Which meant, Jerome knew, that it would be found torn and screwed up with the rest of the trash in his room a few days from now. Levi handed the dog over to Jerome.

'Jay, actually — I got something I gotta do just now — but I'll see you later . . . you coming to the Bus Stop tonight?'

'Bus Stop? No . . . no, um, supposedly Zora's taking me to some frat party or other, down in —'

'Bus Stop tonight!' said Choo over him and whistled. 'It will be incredible! You see all those guys?' He pointed to their silent companions. 'When they get on stage, they tear up *everything*.'

'It's deep,' confided Levi. 'Political. Serious lyrics. About struggle. About —'

'Getting back what is *ours*,' said Choo impatiently. 'Taking back what has been stolen from our people.'

Jerome winced at the collective term.

'It's profounding,' explained Levi. 'Deep lyrics. You'd really be into it.'

Jerome, who doubted this very much, smiled politely.

'Anyway,' said Levi, 'I'm out.

He touched fists with Choo and each of the men in the doorway. Last was Jerome, who received not a touched fist, nor the hug of Levi's younger days, but rather an ironic chuck on the chin.

Levi crossed the square. He went through Wellington's main gate, across the quad, out the other side, into the Humanities Faculty site, into the building, along the halls, into the English Department, out the other side, down another hallway, and arrived finally at the door of the Black Studies Department. It had never struck him before how *easy* it was to walk these hallowed halls. No locks, no codes, no ID cards. Basically, if you looked even vaguely like a student, nobody stopped you at all. Levi shouldered open the Black Studies door and smiled at the cute Latino girl on the desk. He walked through the department, idly mouthing the names on each door. The department had that last-Friday-before-a-vacation feeling — people hurrying to finish off their odds and ends. All these industrious black folk — like a mini-university within a university! It was crazy. Levi wondered whether Choo realized that Wellington had this little black enclave. Maybe he would speak more kindly of it if he knew. A familiar name now arrested Levi's stroll. Prof. M. Kipps. The door was closed, but to the left a half-pane of glass revealed the office inside. Monty was not in. Levi lingered here, none the less, taking in the luxurious details to relay to Choo later. Nice chair. Nice table. Nice painting. Thick carpet. He felt a hand on his shoulder. Levi jumped.

'Levi! Cool — you came —'

Levi looked puzzled.

'The library — it's through here.'

'Oh, yeah . . .' said Levi, knocking the fist that Carl offered to him. 'Yeah — that's right. You . . . you said come, so I came.'

'You just caught me, man — I was just about to quit for the day. Come in, man, come in.'

Carl walked him into the Music Library and sat him down.

'You wanted to hear something? Name it.' He clapped his hands. 'I got *every* damn thing.'

'Er . . . yeah . . . hear something . . . OK, well, actually there's this group I been hearing a lot about . . . they Haitian . . . their name is hard to say — I'll write it down like how I hear it.'

Carl looked disappointed. He bent over Levi as Levi phonetically wrote the name on a Post-it. Afterwards Carl took up the little piece of paper and frowned at it.

'Oh . . . well, that ain't my area, man — I bet you Elisha'll know, though — she does the world music. *Elisha!* Let me go find her — I'll ask her. This is the name?'

'Something like that,' said Levi.

Carl left the room. Levi hadn't been comfortable in his seat for a few minutes — now he remembered why. He lifted up and pulled the newspaper from his pocket. He was still restless. He hadn't brought his iPod out with him today, and he had no personal resources to cope with being alone without music. It never even occurred to him that the paper in front of him might afford a distraction.

'You Levi?' said Elisha. She stretched out her hand, and Levi stood up and shook it. 'I can't believe it — you're one of the first visitors to this *fine* resource,' she said chidingly. 'And then you got to go and make some *rare* request. Couldn't just ask for Louis Armstrong. No, sir.'

'But don't be searching if it's like a big hassle or a problem,' said Levi, embarrassed now to be here.

Elisha laughed easily. 'Isn't either. We're glad to have you. It'll take a little while for me to have a look through our records, that's all. We're not completely computerized . . . not *yet*. You can go and come back if you like — it might be about ten, fifteen minutes, though.'

'Stay, man,' pressed Carl. 'I been going stir crazy in here today.'

Levi did not especially want to stay, but it was more effort to be rude. Elisha left to go through her archives. Levi sat back down in her seat.

'So — what's up?' asked Carl. But just then a loud beep came from Carl's computer. A look of hungry anticipation broke out over his face.

'Oh, Levi — sorry, man, one minute — e-mail.'

Levi sat back in his chair, bored, as Carl typed frantically with two fingers. He felt the despondency universities had long inspired in him. He had grown up in them; he had known their book stacks and storage cupboards and quads and spires and science blocks and tennis courts and plaques and statues. He felt sorry for the people who found themselves trapped in such arid surroundings. Even as a small child he was absolutely clear that he would never, ever enrol at one himself. In universities, people forgot how to live. Even in the middle of a music library, they had forgotten what music was.

Carl hit 'Return' with a pianist's flourish. He sighed happily. He said, 'Oh, *man.*' He seemed to have overestimated Levi's curiosity about the lives of other people.

'Know who that was?' he prompted finally.

Levi shrugged.

'Remember that girl? I first saw her when I was with you. The one with the booty that was just . . .' Carl kissed the air. Levi did his best to look unimpressed. One thing he couldn't *stand* was brothers boasting about their ladies.

'That was *her,* man. I asked someone her name and found her in the college book. Easy as that. Victoria. *Vee.* She driving me crazy, man — she e-mails like . . .' Carl lowered his voice to a whisper. 'She so dirty. Photos and all'a that. She got a body like . . . I don't even have any *words* for what she got. She be like sending me . . . well — you want to see something? Takes a minute to download.' Carl clicked his mouse a few times and then began to turn his screen round. Levi had seen a quarter of a breast when they both heard Elisha coming down the hall. Carl whipped his computer back to face him, switched off the screen and picked up the newspaper.

'Hey, Levi,' said Elisha. 'We got lucky. I found what you're looking for. You want to come with me?'

Levi stood up and, without saying goodbye to Carl, followed Elisha out of the room.

'Baby, you can't lie to me. I can see it in your face.'

Kiki took Levi by the chin, tilted his head back and examined the swollen pockets of skin under the eyes, the blood that had leaked into his corneas, the dryness of his lips.

'I'm just tired.'

'Tired my *ass.*'

'Let go of my chin.'

'I *know* you've been crying,' insisted Kiki, but she didn't know the half of it: couldn't know, would never know, the lovely sadness of that Haitian music, or what it was like to sit in a small dark booth and be alone with it — the plangent, irregular rhythm, like a human heartbeat, the way the many harmonized voices had sounded, to Levi, like a whole nation weeping in tune.

'I know things at home haven't been good,' said Kiki, looking into his red eyes. 'But they're going to get better, I promise you that. Your daddy and I are *determined* to make it better. OK?'

There was no point in explaining. Levi nodded and zipped up his coat.

'The Bus Stop,' said Kiki, and resisted the urge to deliver a curfew that would only be ignored. 'You go and have fun.'

'You want a ride?' asked Jerome, who was passing through the kitchen with Zora. 'I'm not drinking.'

Just before they got in the car, Zora took off her coat and turned her back to Levi. 'Seriously, do you think I should wear this

722

— I mean, does it look OK?'

Her dress was a bad colour and it had no back and it was the wrong material for her lumpy body and it was too short. Normally, Levi would have bluntly told his sister all of this, and Zoor would have been upset and angry, but at least she would have gone back in and changed, and, as a consequence, arrived at the party looking a hell of a lot better than she did now. But tonight Levi had other things on his mind. 'Beautiful,' he said.

Fifteen minutes later they dropped Levi off in Kennedy Square and continued on to the party. There was nowhere to park. They had to leave the car several blocks from the party itself. Zora had specifically worn the shoes she was wearing because she had not anticipated any walking. To make progress she had to grip her brother around his waist, take little pigeon-steps and lean far back on her heels. For a long time Jerome restrained himself from commentary, but at the fourth pit stop he could keep silent no longer. 'I don't get you. Aren't you meant to be a feminist? Why would you cripple yourself like this?'

'I *like* these shoes, OK? They actually make me feel powerful.'

Finally they reached the house. Zora had

never been so happy to see a set of porch steps. Steps were easy, and with joy she placed the ball of her foot on each wide wooden slat. A girl they did not know answered the door. At once they saw that it was a better party than either had been expecting. Some of the younger grads and even a few faculty members were there. People were already boisterously drunk. Pretty much everybody Zora considered vital for her social success this coming year was present. She had the guilty thought that she would do better at this party without Jerome hanging at her heels in his slacks with the T-shirt tucked in too tightly.

'Victoria's here,' he said as they left their coats in the pile.

Zora looked down the hall and spotted her, simultaneously overdressed and half naked.

'Oh, *whatever,*' said Zora, but then a thought came to her. 'But Jay . . . If, I mean, if you want to go . . . I'd understand, I could get a taxi back.'

'No, it's fine. Of course it's fine.' Jerome went over to a punch bowl and scooped them a drink each. 'To lost love,' he said sadly, taking a sip. 'One glass. Did you see Jamie Anderson? He's *dancing.*'

'I *like* Jamie Anderson.'

It was strange being at a party with your sibling, standing in a comer, holding your plastic tumblers with both hands. There's no small talk between siblings. They bopped their heads ineptly and stood slightly turned out from each other, trying to look not alone and yet not with each other.

'There's Dad's Veronica,' said Jerome, as she passed by in an unflattering 1920s flapper dress complete with headband. 'And that's your rapper friend, isn't it? I saw him in the paper.'

'Carl!' called Zora, too loudly. He was fiddling with the stereo, and now turned and came over. Zora remembered to put both hands behind her back and pull down her shoulders. Her chest looked better that way. But he did not look in that direction. He patted her chummily on the arm as usual and shook Jerome's hand vigorously.

'Good to see you again, man!' he said and shot out that movie star smile. Jerome, now recalling the young man he had met that night in the park, registered the pleasant change: this open, friendly demeanour, this almost *Wellingtonian* confidence. In answer to Jerome's polite question as to what Carl had been up to recently, Carl prattled on about his library, neither defensively nor particularly boastfully, but with an easy egotism that did not for a moment consider asking Jerome a similar question. He spoke of the Hip-hop Archive and the need for more Gospel, the growing African section, the problem of getting money out of Erskine. Zora waited for him to mention their campaign to keep discretionaries in class. No mention came.

'So,' she said, attempting to keep her own voice casual and cheery, 'did you see my op-ed or . . . ?'

Carl, in the middle of an anecdote, stopped and looked confused. Jerome, peacemaker and trouble-spotter, stepped in.

'I forgot to tell you I saw that in the *Herald* — Speaker's Corner — it was really great. Really *Mr Smith Goes to Washington* . . . it was great, Zoor. You're lucky you got this girl fighting in your corner,' said Jerome, knocking his tumbler against Carl's. 'When she gets her teeth into something, she doesn't let go. Believe me, I know.'

Carl grinned, 'Oh, I *hear* that. She's my Martin Luther King! I'm serious, she be — sorry,' said Carl, looking away from them towards the outdoor balcony. 'Sorry, I just saw someone I gotta speak to . . . Look, I'll talk to you later, Zora — good to see you again, man. I'll catch you both later.'

'He's very charming,' said Jerome generously, as they watched him go. 'Actually he's almost slick.'

'Everything's going so well for him right now,' said Zora uncertainly. 'When he's gotten used to it, he'll get more focus, I think. More time to tune in to other important stuff. He's just a little busy right now. Believe me,' she said, with more conviction, 'he'll be a real addition to Wellington. We need more people like him.'

Jerome hummed in an ambivalent way. Zora rounded on him. 'You know, there's other ways to have a successful college career than the route you went down. Traditional qualifications are *not* everything. Just because —'

Jerome mimed zipping up his lip and throwing away the key.

'I'm a hundred and ten per cent behind you, Zoor, as ever,' he said, smiling. 'More wine?'

It was the kind of party where every hour two people leave and thirty people arrive. The Belsey siblings found and lost each other several times that night, and lost new people they found. You'd turn to eat from a bowl of peanuts and not see the person you'd been talking to again until you met them forty minutes later in the line for the toilets. Around ten, Zora found herself on the balcony smoking a joint in an absurdly cool circle consisting of Jamie Anderson, Veronica, Christian and three grads she didn't know. In normal circumstances she would have been ecstatic at this, but, even as Jamie Anderson was taking her theory about women's punctuation seriously, Zora's busy brain was otherwise occupied, wondering where Carl was, if he'd already left, and whether he'd liked her dress. Out of nerves she kept drinking, filling her cup from an abandoned bottle of white wine by her feet.

Just after eleven, Jerome stepped out on to the balcony, interrupting the impromptu lecture that Anderson was giving and plonked himself upon his sister's lap. He was badly drunk.

'Sorry!' he said, touching Anderson's knees. 'Carry on, sorry — don't mind me. Zoor, *guess* what I saw? I should say *who*.'

Anderson, piqued, moved away and took his acolytes with him. Zora bumped Jerome off her lap, stood up and leaned against the balcony, looking out on to the quiet, leafy street.

'*Great* — and how are we going to get home? I'm way over the limit. There's no taxis. You're meant to be the designated driver. Jesus, Jerome!'

'Blasphemer,' said Jerome, not entirely unserious.

'Look, I'll start treating you like a Christian when you start acting like one. You *know* you can't handle more than a glass of wine.'

'But so,' whispered Jerome and put his arm around his sister, 'I come with news. My darling heart ex-whatever is in the coat room getting it on with your rapper friend.'

'What?' Zora shook his arm off. 'What are you *talking* about?'

'Miss Kipps. Vee. And the rapper. That's what I love about Wellington — everybody knows *everybody.*' He sighed. 'Oh, well. No, but it's OK . . . I really couldn't care less. I mean I *care,* obviously I care! But what's the point? It's just pretty tacky — she *knew* I was here, we said hi an hour ago. It's just tacky. But you'd think she could at least *try* to . . .'

Jerome kept on talking but Zora was not listening any more. Something alien to Zora was taking her over, starting in her belly and then rocketing like adrenalin through the rest of her system. Maybe it *was* adrenalin. It was certainly a rage physical in nature — never in her life had she experienced an emotion as corporal as this. She seemed to have no mind or will; she was only resolute muscle. Afterwards she could in no way account for how she got from the balcony to the coat room. It was as if fury transported her there instantaneously. And then she was in the room, and it was as Jerome had described. He on top of she. Her hands embracing his head. They looked perfect together. So perfect! And then, a moment after that, Zora herself was outside on the porch with Carl, with Carl's hood in her hand, for she had — as was explained to her afterwards — physically dragged him down the hallway and out of the party. Now she released him, pushing him away from her, on to the wet wood. He was coughing and working his hand around his throat, which had been constricted. She had never known how strong she was. Everyone had always told her she was a 'big girl' — was *this* why she was big? So she might drag grown men by their hoods and throw them to the floor?

Zora's brief physical elation was soon replaced by panic. Out here it was cold and wet. The knees of Carl's jeans were soaked.

What had she done? *What had she done?*
Now Carl knelt before her, breathing
heavily, looking up, enraged. Her heart
justly broke. She saw she had nothing further to lose.

'*Oh, man, oh, man . . . I can't believe . . .*'
he was whispering. Then he stood up and
became loud: 'What the *FUCK* do you
think —'

'Did you even *read* that piece?' cried
Zora, shaking madly. 'I spent so *long* on
that, I missed my dissertation deadline, I've
been working *constantly* for *you* and —'

But of course without the secret piece of
the narrative in Zora's head — the one that
connected 'writing pieces for Carl' with
'Carl kissing Victoria Kipps' — no sense
could be made of what she was saying.

'What the hell are you talking about,
man? What did you just do?'

Zora had shamed him in front of his girl,
in front of a whole party. This was no
longer the charming Carl Thomas of
Wellington's Black Music Library. This was
the Carl who had sat out on the front
porches of Roxbury apartments on steamy
summer days. This was the Carl who could
play the Dozens good as anybody. Zora had
never been spoken to like this in her life.

'I — I — I'

'Are you my *girlfriend* now?'

Zora began to weep wretchedly.

'And what the *fuck* has your article got to do with . . . Am I meant to be *grateful?*'

'All I was trying to do was help you. That was all I wanted to do. I just wanted to *help.*'

'Well,' said Carl, putting his hands on his hips, reminding Zora, absurdly, of Kiki, 'apparently you wanted to do a little more than help me. Apparently you expected some payback. Apparently I had to sleep with yo' skank ass as well.'

'*Fuck* you!'

'*That's* what it was all about,' said Carl and whistled satirically, but the hurt was clear to read in his face, and this hurt grew deeper as he stumbled over further realizations, one after the other. 'Man, oh, *man.* Is *that* why you helped me? I guess I can't write at all — is that it? You were just making me look an idiot in that class. Sonnets! You been making a fool of me since the beginning. Is that *it?* You pick me up off the streets and when I don't do what you want, you turn on me? Damn! I thought we was *friends,* man!'

'So did I!' cried Zora.

'*Stop* crying — you *ain't* gonna get out of this by crying,' he warned heatedly, and yet Zora could hear concern in his voice. She dared to hope that this still might end well. She reached out a hand to him, but he took a step back.

'Speak to me,' he demanded. 'What *is* this? You got some problem with my girl?' Upon hearing this formulation, a snotty clump of tears flew spectacularly from Zora's nose.

'Your girl!'

'Have you got some problem with her?'

Zora wiped her face on the neck of her dress. 'No,' she snapped indignantly. 'I haven't got a problem with her. She's not worth having a problem with.'

Carl opened his eyes wide, shocked by this answer. He pressed a hand to his forehead, trying to figure it out. 'Now, what the fuck does that mean, man?'

'Nothing. *God!* You totally deserve each other. You're both trash.'

Carl's eyes grew cold. He brought his face right up to hers, in an awful inversion of what Zora had spent six months hoping for. 'You know what?' he said, and Zora prepared to hear his judgement on what he saw. 'You're a fucking *bitch*.'

Zora turned her back to him and began her difficult journey down the porch steps, minus her coat and purse, minus her pride and with a good deal of trouble. These shoes took stairs in only one direction. At last she made it to the street. She wanted to go home now desperately; the humiliation was beginning to outweigh the rage. She was experiencing the first inklings of a shame she sensed would live with her for a long, long time. She needed to get home and hide under something heavy. Just then Jerome appeared on the porch.

'Zoor? You OK?'

'Jay, go back in — I'm fine — *please* go back in.'

As she said this Carl ran down the stairs and confronted her again. He was not willing to leave her with this last, ugly image of himself; it still, somehow, mattered to him what she thought of him.

'I'm just trying to understand why you would act so crazy,' he said earnestly, coming close to her again and searching for an answer in her face; Zora almost fell into his arms. From where Jerome was standing, however, it appeared that Zora was cringing in fear. He rushed down the steps to put himself between his sister and Carl.

'Hey, buddy,' he said unconvincingly, 'back off, OK?'

The front door opened once more. It was Victoria Kipps.

'Great!' shouted Zora, throwing her head back and spotting the little audience on the balcony who were watching these events. 'Let's sell tickets!'

Victoria closed the door behind her and skipped down the stairs with the style of a woman well practised at walking in impossible heels. 'What are you *on?*' she asked Zora as she reached the ground, and seemed more curious than angry.

Zora rolled her eyes. Victoria turned instead to Jerome.

'Jay? What's this about?'

Jerome shook his head at the floor. Victoria approached Zora again.

'Have you got something to say to me?'

Usually Zora feared confrontation with her peers, but Victoria Kipps's composed radiance standing right opposite her own snot-faced breakdown was simply too maddening. 'I've got NOTHING to say to you! Nothing!' she yelled, and began the march down the street. At once she stumbled on her heel and Jerome steadied her, getting her by the elbow.

'She jealous — that's her problem,' taunted Carl. 'Just jealous 'cos you finer than her. And she can't *stand* that.'

Zora spun back round. 'Actually, I look for a little more from my partners than just a nice *ass*. For some reason I thought you did too, but, my mistake.'

'Pardon me?' said Victoria.

Zora hobbled a little way further along the road, accompanied by her brother, but Carl followed.

'You don't know *anything* about her. You're just uppity about *everybody*.'

Zora stopped once more. 'Oh, I *know* about her. I know she's an airhead. I know she's a *slut*.'

Victoria reached out for Zora, but Carl restrained her. Jerome grabbed hold of Zora's pointing hand.

'Zoor!' he said, raising his voice. 'Stop it! That's enough!'

Zoor wrenched her wrist from her brother's grasp. Carl looked disgusted with them both. He took Victoria's hand and began to walk her towards the house.

'Take your sister home,' he said, without looking back at Jerome. 'She's drunk as hell.'

'And I also know about guys like *you*,' said Zora, shouting impotently after him. 'You can't keep your dick in your pants for five minutes — that's all that's important to you. That's all you can *think* about. And you haven't even got the *good taste* to stick it in something a little more classy than Victoria *Kipps.* You're just one of those kind of *assholes.*'

'Fuck you!' screamed Victoria and began to cry.

'Like your old man?' yelled Carl. 'An asshole like that? Let me tell you something —'

But Victoria began to speak frantically over him. 'No! Please, Carl — *please,* just leave it. There's no point — please — no!'

She was hysterical, placing her hands all over his face, apparently trying to stop him speaking. Zora frowned at her, not understanding.

'Why the hell not?' Carl asked, peeling a hand from his mouth and holding Victoria at the shoulders as she continued to weep loudly. 'She's so damn superior all the time, she should have a little home truth told to her — she thinks her daddy's such a —'

'NO!' screamed Victoria.

Zora put her hands on her hips, utterly bemused, almost entertained, by this new scene passing in front of her. Someone was making a fool of herself, and, for the first time tonight, it wasn't Zora. A window someplace down the street was thrown up.

'Keep the goddamn noise down! It's the middle of the goddamn night!'

The clapboard houses, prim and shut-

737

tered, silently seemed to support the departure of the street's noisy visitors.

'Vee, baby, go back in the house. I'll be in in a minute,' said Carl and tenderly wiped some tears from Victoria's face with his hand. Zora abandoned her curiosity. She felt the fury double inside her. She didn't stop to consider the meaning of what had just passed, and so did not follow Jerome as his mind wandered down a formerly concealed path to a dark destination: the truth. Jerome put his hand against the soggy trunk of a tree, and this alone kept him upright. Victoria rang the bell to get back in the house. For a moment Jerome met her eye with all that he felt: disappointment because he had loved her; grief because she had betrayed him.

'Can you keep it down out here?' requested a kid at the door and let a distraught, broken Victoria back into the house.

'I think that's enough now,' said Jerome firmly to Carl. 'I'm going to take Zoor home. You've upset her enough as it is.'

Of all the things he had been accused of so far, this reasonably voiced charge struck Carl as the most unfair. 'This was *not* me, man,' said Carl adamantly, shaking his head. 'I did *not* do this. Damn!' He kicked a step hard. 'You people don't behave like human beings, man — I ain't never *seen* people behave like you people. You don't tell the *truth,* you *deceive* people. You all act so superior, but you're not telling the truth! You don't even know a thing about your own father, man. My daddy's a worthless piece of shit too, but at least I *know* he's a worthless piece of shit. I feel sorry for you — you know that? I really do.'

Zora wiped her nose and cut her eyes at Carl imperiously. 'Carl, please don't talk about our father. We *know* about our father. You go to Wellington for a few months, you hear a little gossip and you think you know what's going on? You think you're a *Wellingtonian* because they let you file a few records? You don't know a thing about what it takes to belong here. And you haven't got the *first idea* about our family *or* our life, OK? Remember that.'

'Zoor, please don't —' cautioned Jerome, but Zora took a step forward and felt a pool of water seep into her toeless shoes. She bent down and removed her heels.

'I ain't even talking about that,' whispered Carl.

Everywhere around them in the darkness

the trees dripped. In the main road, far off from this one, the splatter and screech of wheels speeding through puddles.

'Well, what *are* you talking about?' said Zora, using her shoes to gesticulate. 'You're pathetic. Leave me alone.'

'I'm just saying,' said Carl darkly, 'you think everybody you know is so pure, so perfect — *man,* you don't know anything about these Wellington people. You don't know how they do.'

'That's *enough,*' insisted Jerome. 'You can see the state she's in, man. Have a little pity. She doesn't need this. Please, Zoor, let's go find the car.'

But Zora wasn't finished yet. 'I know that the men I know are *grown-ups.* They're *intellectuals* — not children. They don't act like hound-dog teenagers every time some cute piece of ass comes shimmying up to them.'

'Zora,' said Jerome, his voice cracking, for the thought of his father and Victoria had begun to overwhelm him. There was a very real possibility that he was going to be sick here in the street. 'Please! Let's just get in the car! I can't do this! I need to be *home.*'

'You know what? I've tried being patient with you,' said Carl, lowering his voice.

'You need to hear some truth. All of you people, you *intellectuals* . . . OK, how about Monty Kipps? Victoria's pop? You know him? OK. He been *screwing* Chantelle Williams — she lives in my street, she told me about it. His kids don't know a thing about it. That girl you just made cry? She don't know a thing about it. And everybody thinks he a saint. And now he wants Chantelle out of the class, for why? Cover *his* ass. And it's *me* that gotta know that — I don't *want* to know *any* of this shit. I'm just trying to get a stage higher with my life.' Carl laughed bitterly. 'But that's a *joke* around here, man. People like me are just toys to people like you . . . I'm just some experiment for you to play with. You people aren't even black any more, man — I don't know *what* you are. You think you're too good for your own people. You got your college degrees, but you don't even live right. You people are all the same,' said Carl, looking down, addressing his words to his own shoes, 'I need to be with *my people,* man — I can't do this no more.'

'Well,' said Zora, who had stopped listening to Carl's speech halfway through, 'that's basically what I'd expect from somebody like Kipps. Like father like daughter.

So is *that* your level? Is that your model? I hope you have a nice life, Carl.'

It had started to rain properly, but at least Zora had won the argument, for Carl now gave up. With his head hanging, he walked slowly back up the steps. Zora wasn't sure at first if she was hearing correctly, but when he spoke again, she was gratified to find she was right. Carl was crying.

'You *so* sure of yourself, you so superior,' she heard him splutter as he rang the doorbell. 'All you people. I don't know why I even got myself caught up with any of you, it can't come to no good anyway.'

Zora, splashing along in her bare feet, heard the thud of Carl slamming the door.

'*Idiot,*' she muttered, and hooked her arm around her brother as they walked away.

Only when Jerome leaned his head on her shoulder did she realize that he too was crying.

12

The next day was the first day of spring. There had been blossom before today, and the snow had already departed, but it was *this* new morning that broadcast a blue sky to every soul on the East Coast, *this* day that brought with it a sun that spoke not simply of light but of heat. The first Zora knew of it was in slices — her mother twisting open the Venetian blinds.

'Baby, you got to wake up. Sorry, honey. Honey?'

Zora opened her other eye and found her mother sitting on her bed.

'The college just called me. Something's happened — they want to see you. Jack French's office. They sounded pretty het up. Zora?'

'It's a *Saturday* . . .'

'They wouldn't tell me anything. They said it was urgent. Are you in trouble?'

Zora sat up in bed. Her hangover had vanished. 'Where's Howard?' she asked. She could not remember ever feeling as focused as she did this morning. The first day she wore glasses had been a little like this: lines sharper, colours clearer. The whole world like an old painting restored. Finally, she understood.

'Howard? The Greenman. He walked in 'cos the weather's nice. Zoor, do you want me to come with you?'

Zora declined this offer. For the first time in months, she got dressed without attention to anything else except the basic practical covering of her body. She didn't do her hair. No make-up. No contact lenses. No heels. How much time she saved! How much more she would get done in this new life! She got into the Belsey family car and drove with hostile speed into town, cutting up other cars and swearing at innocent traffic signals. She parked illegally in a faculty space. It being a weekend, the department doors were locked. Liddy Cantalino buzzed her in.

'Jack French?' demanded Zora.

'And good morning to you too, young lady,' Liddy snapped back. 'They're all in his office.'

'All? Who?'

'Zora, dear, why don't you go on in there and see for yourself?'

For the very first time in a faculty building, Zora walked in without knocking. She was confronted with a bizarre composition of people: Jack French, Monty Kipps, Claire Malcolm and Erskine Jegede. All had taken up different poses of anxiety. Nobody was sitting, not even Jack.

'Ah, Zora — come in,' said Jack. Zora joined the standing party. She had no idea what it was all about, but she was not in any way nervous. She was still flying on fury, capable of anything.

'What's going on?'

'I'm extremely sorry for dragging you out this morning,' said Jack, 'but it is an urgent matter and I did not feel it could wait until the end of spring break . . .' Here Monty snorted derisively. 'Or indeed even until Monday.'

'What's going on?' repeated Zora.

'Well,' said Jack, 'it seems that last night, after everybody had left for the evening — at about 10 p.m. we think, although we're looking at the possibility that one of our own cleaners was still here at a later point and did, in some capacity, aid whoever it was who —'

'Oh, for God's sake, Jack!' cried Claire Malcolm. 'I'm sorry — but *Jesus Christ* — let's not spend all day here — I, for one, would like to get back to my holiday — Zora, do you know where Carl Thomas is?'

'Carl? No — why? What's happened?'

Erskine, tired of having to pretend he was more panicked than he was, took a seat. 'A painting,' he explained, 'was stolen from the Black Studies Department last night. A very valuable painting belonging to Professor Kipps.'

'I find out only *now*,' said Monty, his voice twice as loud as everybody else's, 'that one of the *street-children* of Dr

Malcolm's collection has been working three doors away from me for a month, a young man who evidently —'

'Jack, I am *not,*' said Claire, as Erskine covered his eyes with his hand, 'going to stand around being insulted by this man. I'm just not going to do it.'

'*A young man,*' bellowed Monty, 'who works here without references, without qualifications, without anybody knowing *anything whatsoever about him* — never in my long academic life have I EVER experienced anything as incompetent, as slap-dash, as —'

'How do you know that this young man is responsible? What evidence do you have?' barked Claire, but seemed terrified of hearing the answer.

'Now, please, *please,*' said Jack, gesturing towards Zora. 'We have a student here. Please. Surely it behooves us to . . .' But Jack wisely thought better of this digression and returned to his main theme. 'Zora — Dr Malcolm and Dr Jegede have explained to us that you are close to this young man. Did you happen to see him yesterday evening?'

'Yes. He was at a party I was at.'

'Ah, *good.* And did you happen to notice what time he left?'

'We had a . . . we kind of argued and we both . . . we both left quite early — separately. We left separately.'

'At what *time?*' asked Monty in the voice of God. 'At what time did the boy leave?'

'Early. I'm not sure.' Zora blinked twice. 'Maybe nine thirty?'

'And was this party far from here?' asked Erskine.

'No, ten minutes.'

Now Jack sat down. 'Thank you, Zora. And you have no idea where he is now?'

'No, sir, I don't.'

'Thank you. Liddy will let you out.'

Monty banged Jack French's desk with his fist. 'Now one minute please!' he boomed. 'Is that all you intend to ask her? Excuse me, Miss Belsey — before you cease to grace us with your presence could you tell me what kind of young man — in your estimation — is this Carl Thomas? Did he strike you, for example, as a thief?'

'Oh, my *God!*' complained Claire. 'This is really repulsive. I don't want any part of this.'

Monty glared at her. 'A court might find you party to this matter whether you liked it or not, Dr Malcolm.'

'Are you *threatening* me?'

Monty put his back to Claire. 'Zora, could you answer my question, please? Would it be an unfair description to describe this young man as from the "wrong side of the tracks"? Are we likely to find a criminal record?'

Zora ignored Claire Malcolm's attempt to catch her eye.

'If you mean, is he a kid from the streets, well, *obviously* he is — he'd tell you that himself. He's mentioned being in . . . like, trouble before, sure. But I don't really know the details.'

'We will find out the details, soon enough, I'm sure,' said Monty.

'You know,' said Zora evenly, 'if you really want to find him you should probably ask your daughter. I hear they're spending a lot of quality time together. Can I go now?' she asked Jack, as Monty steadied himself with a hand to the desk.

'Liddy will let you out,' repeated Jack faintly.

An (almost) empty house. A bright spring day. Birdsong. Squirrels. All the curtains and blinds open except in Jerome's room, where a beast with a hangover remains under his comforter. Afresh, afresh, afresh! Kiki did not consciously

748

begin a spring clean. She merely thought: Jerome is here, and in the storeroom beneath our lovely home boxes and boxes of Jerome's things lie, awaiting the decision to be kept or destroyed. And so she would go through all of these things, the letters, the childhood report cards, the photo albums, the diaries, the home-made birthday cards, and she would say to him: *Jerome, here is your past. It is not for me, your mother, to destroy your past. Only you can decide what must go and what must stay. But please, for the love of God, throw away something so I can free up some space in the storeroom for Levi's crap.*

She put on her oldest track pants and tied a bandanna round her head. She went into the storeroom, taking nothing but a radio for company. It was a chaos of Belsey memories down here. Just to get in the door Kiki had to clamber over four massive plastic tubs that she knew to be full of nothing but photographs. It would be easy to panic when confronted with such a mass of the past, but Kiki was a professional. Many years ago she had loosely divided this space into sections that corresponded with each of her three children. Zora's section, at the back, was the largest, simply because it was Zora who had put more words on paper than anyone else, who had joined more teams and societies, garnered more certificates, won more cups. But nor was Jerome's space inconsiderable. In there were all the things Jerome had collected and loved over the years, from fossils to copies of *Time* to autograph books to an assortment of Buddhas to decorated china eggs. Kiki sat legs crossed among all this and got to work. She separated physical things from paper things, childhood things from college things. Generally she kept her head down, but on the occasions she raised it she was treated to the most intimate of panoramic views: the scattered possessions of the three people she had created. Several small items made her cry: a tiny woollen bootie, a broken orthodontic retainer, a woggle from a cubscout tie. She had not become Malcolm X's private secretary. She never did direct a movie or run for the Senate. She could not fly a plane. But here was all this.

Two hours later, Kiki lifted a box of sorted Jerome papers and carried it into the hallway. All these journals and notes and stories he had written before he was sixteen! She admired the weight of it in her arms. In her head she was making another speech to the Black American Mother's

Guild: *Well, you just have to offer them encouragement and the correct role models, and you have to pass on the idea of entitlement. Both my sons feel entitled, and that's why they achieve.* Kiki accepted her applause from the assembly and went back into the clutter to retrieve two bags of Jerome's pre-growth-spurt clothes. She carried these sacks of the past on her back, one over each shoulder. Last year, she had not thought she would still be in this house, in this marriage, come spring. But here she was, here she was. A tear in the garbage bag freed three pairs of pants and a sweater. Kiki crouched to pick these up and, as she did so, the second bag split too. She had packed them too heavy. The greatest lie ever told about love is that it sets you free.

Lunchtime came round. Kiki was too involved in her work to stop. And while the radio jocks pushed the country to extremity and the voices of white housewives encouraged her to take advantage of the spring sales, Kiki made a pile of all the photographic negatives she could find. They were everywhere. At first she held each one up to the light and tried to decode the inverted brown shadows of ancient beach holidays and European landscapes. But there were too many. The truth was, nobody would ever reprint them or look at them again. That didn't mean you threw them away. This was why you freed up floor space — to make room for oblivion.

'Hey, Mom,' said Jerome sleepily, poking his head round the doorframe. 'What's going on?'

'You. You're going out, buddy. That's your stuff in the hallway — I'm trying to free up some space, so I can put some of the crap from Levi's room in here.'

Jerome rubbed his eyes. 'I see,' he said. 'Out with the old, in with the new.'

Kiki laughed. 'Something like that. How are you?'

'Hung over.'

Kiki tutted chidingly. 'You shouldn't have taken the car, you know.'

'Yeah, I know . . .'

Kiki stuck her arm into a deep box and pulled out a little painted half-mask, the kind you would wear to a masquerade ball. She smiled at it fondly and turned it over. Some of the glitter around the eyes came off in her hands. 'Venice,' she said.

Jerome nodded quickly. 'That time we went?'

'Hmm? Oh, no, before then. Before any of you were born.'

'Some kind of romantic holiday,' said Jerome. He tightened his tense grasp on the edge of the door.

'The *most* romantic.' Kiki smiled and shook her head free of some secret thought. She put the porcelain mask carefully to one side. Jerome took a step into the storeroom.

'Mom . . .'

Kiki smiled again, her face upturned to listen to her son. Jerome looked away.

'You . . . you need some help, Mom?'

Kiki kissed him gratefully.

'*Thanks,* honey. That'd be so great. Come and help me move some stuff out of Levi's. It's a nightmare in there. I can't face it alone.'

Jerome put his hands out for Kiki and lifted her up. Together they crossed the hall and pushed Levi's door open, working against the piles of clothes on its other side. Inside Levi's room the smell of boy, of socks and sperm, was strong.

'Nice wallpaper,' said Jerome. The room was newly plastered with posters of black girls, mostly big black girls, mostly big black girls' butts. Interspersed with these here and there were a few vainglorious portraits of rappers, mostly dead, and a massive photograph of Pacino in *Scarface.*

But big black girls in bikinis was the central decorating scheme.

'At least they're not starving half to death,' said Kiki, getting down on her knees to look under the bed. 'At least they've got some flesh on their bones. OK — there's *all kinds of crap* under here. You take that end and lift.'

Jerome hiked up his end of the bed.

'Higher,' requested Kiki and Jerome obliged. Suddenly Kiki's right knee slipped and her hand went to the floor. 'Oh, my God,' she whispered.

'What?'

'Oh, my *God.*'

'*What?* Is it porn? My arm's getting tired.' Jerome lowered the bed a little.

'DON'T MOVE!' screamed Kiki.

Jerome, terrified, lifted the bed high. His mother was gasping, like she was having some kind of a fit.

'Mom — what? You're scaring me, man. What is it?'

'I don't understand this. I DON'T UNDERSTAND THIS.'

'Mom, I can't hold this any longer.'

'HOLD IT.'

Jerome saw his mother get a grip on the sides of something. She slowly began to pull out whatever it was from under the bed.

'What the . . . ?' said Jerome.

Kiki dragged the painting into the middle of the floor and sat next to it, hyperventilating. Jerome came up behind her and tried to touch her to calm her, but she slapped his hand away.

'Mom, I don't understand what's going on. What *is* that?'

Then came the sound of the front door clicking and opening. Kiki leaped to her feet and left the room, leaving Jerome to stare at the naked brown woman surrounded by her Technicolor flowers and fruit. He heard screaming and yelling from upstairs.

'OH, REALLY — OH, REALLY — NOTHING GOING ON!'

'LET GO OF ME!'

They were coming down the stairs, Kiki and Levi. Jerome went to the door and saw Kiki smack Levi round the head harder than he'd ever seen.

'Get *in* there! Get your ass in there!'

Levi fell into Jerome and then both of them almost fell on to the painting. Jerome steadied himself and pulled Levi aside.

Levi stood dumbfounded. Even his powers of rhetoric could not obscure the evidence of a five-foot oil painting hidden underneath his own bed.

'Oh, *shit,* man,' he said simply.

'WHERE DID THIS COME FROM?'

'Mom,' tried Jerome quietly, 'you need to calm down.'

'Levi,' said Kiki, and both boys recognized her coming on 'all Florida', which was the same thing, in Kiki terms, as 'going postal', 'you'd better open your mouth with some kind of explanation or I am *gonna strike you down where you stand,* as God is my witness, I will *wear* your ass out today.'

'Oh *shit.*'

They heard the front door open and slam again. Levi looked in that direction hopefully, as if some intervention from upstairs might save him, but Kiki ignored it, yanking him by his sweatshirt to face her. 'Because I *know* no son of mine steals ANYTHING — no child I ever raised took it into his head to steal ANYTHING FROM ANYBODY. Levi, you better open your mouth!'

'We didn't steal it!' managed Levi. 'I mean, we took it, but it ain't stealing.'

'*We?*'

'This guy and me, this . . . guy.'

'Levi, give me his name before I break your neck. I am *not* playing with you today, young man. There ain't no games here today.'

Levi squirmed. From upstairs came the noise of shouting.

'What's . . . ?' he said, but that was never going to work.

'Never *mind* what's going on up there — you better start worrying about what's going on down *here.* Levi, tell me the name of this man *now.*'

'Man . . . it's like . . . I can't do that. He's a guy . . . and he's a Haitian guy and —' Levi took a breath and began to speak extremely quickly. 'Trust me, you don't even understand, it's like — OK, so, *this painting is stolen anyway.* It don't even *belong* to that guy Kipps, not really — it was like twenty years ago and he just went to Haiti and got all these paintings by lying to poor people and buying them for a few dollars and now they be worth all this money and it ain't *his* money and we're just trying to —'

Kiki pushed Levi hard in the chest. 'You *stole* this from Mr Kipps's office because some *guy* told you a lot of *bullshit?* Because some brother spun you a load of conspiracy bullshit? Are you an *idiot?*'

'No! I'm not an idiot — and it's not bullshit! You don't know anything about it!'

'Of *course* it's bullshit — I happen to know this painting, Levi. It belonged to

Mrs Kipps. And *she* bought it herself, before she was even married.'

This silenced Levi.

'Oh, Levi,' said Jerome.

'And that isn't even the point, the point is you *stole.* You just *believed* anything these people say. You just gonna believe them all the way to jail. Just want to be cool, show you the big man around a load of *no-good Negroes* who don't even —'

'IT AIN'T LIKE THAT!'

'That's *exactly* what it's like. It's those guys you been spending all your time with — you can't lie to me. I am so angry at you right now. I am so MAD right now! Levi — I'm trying to understand what you think you've achieved by stealing somebody's property. Why would you *do* this?'

'You don't understand anything,' said Levi very quietly.

'What was that? *Excuse* me? WHAT WAS THAT?'

'People in Haiti, they got NOTHING, RIGHT? We living off these people, man! We — we — living off them! We sucking their blood — we're like vampires! *You* OK, married to your white man in the land of plenty — *you* OK. *You* doing fine. You're living off these people, man!'

Kiki stuck a shaky finger in his face. 'You

758

crossing a line right now, Levi. I don't know what you're talking about — I don't think you do either. And I *really* don't know what any of this has to do with you becoming a *thief.*'

'Then why don't you *listen* to what I'm talking about. That painting don't belong to him! Or his wife! These people I'm talking about, they remember how things went *down,* man — and now look how much it's worth. But that money belongs to the Haitian people, not some . . . some *Caucasian art dealer,*' said Levi, confidently remembering Choo's phrase. 'That money needs to be redis— to be shared.'

Kiki was briefly too astounded to speak.

'Umm, that's not the way the world works,' said Jerome. 'I study economics and I can tell you that isn't the way the world works.'

'That's *exactly* the way the world works! I know you all think I'm some kind of a fool — I'm not a fool. And I been reading, I been watching the news — this shit is *real.* With that money from that painting you could go build a hospital in Haiti!'

'Oh, is *that* what you were intending to do with the money?' asked Jerome. 'Build a hospital?'

Levi made a face both sheepish and defiant. 'No, not zackly. We was going to *re-distribute*,' said Levi successfully. 'The funds.'

'I see. So how exactly were you gonna sell it? Ebay?'

'Choo had people on that.'

Kiki found her voice again. 'Choo? *Choo?* WHO IS CHOO?'

Levi covered his face with both hands. 'Oh, *shit*.'

'Levi . . . I'm trying to understand what you're telling me,' said Kiki slowly, making an effort to calm herself. 'And I . . . I understand that you had concerns about these people, but, baby, Jerome's right, this is not the way you go about solving social problems, this is not how you —'

'So how *do* you do it?' demanded Levi. 'By paying people four dollars an hour to clean? That's how much you pay Monique, man! Four dollars! If she was American you wouldn't be paying her no four dollars an hour. Would you? Would you?'

Kiki was stunned.

'You know what, Levi?' she said, her voice breaking. She bent down to put her hands to one side of the painting, 'I don't want to talk to you any more.'

' 'Cause you ain't got no answer to that!'

'*Because* the only thing that comes out of your mouth is *bullshit.* And you can save it for the poh-leese when they come and drag your ass off to jail.'

Levi sucked his teeth. 'You ain't got no answer,' he repeated.

'Jerome,' said Kiki, 'take the other side of this. Let's try to get it upstairs. I'll call Monty and see if we can sort this out without a lawsuit.'

Jerome went to the other side and hitched the painting up on to his knee. 'I think longwise. Levi — get out of the damn way,' he said, and together they turned themselves a hundred and eighty degrees. As they were completing this manoeuvre, Jerome began to yank at something on the back of the canvas.

Kiki let out a little scream. 'No! *No!* Don't pull at it! What are you *doing?* Have you damaged it? Oh, *Jesus Christ* — I don't believe this is happening.'

'No, Mom, no . . .' said Jerome uncertainly. 'It's just there's something stuck here . . . it's fine . . . we can just . . .' Jerome brought the painting upright and rested it against his mother. He pulled again at a piece of white notecard tucked into the frame.

'Jerome! What are you doing? Stop doing that!'

'I just want to see what . . .'

'Don't tear it,' yelled Kiki, unable to see what was going on. 'Are you tearing it? Leave it!'

'Oh, my God . . .' whispered Jerome, forgetting his own blaspheming rule. 'Mom? *Oh, my God!*'

'What are you doing? Jerome! *Why are you tearing it more?*'

'Mom! Oh, shit, Mom! Your name's written here!'

'*What?*'

'Oh, man, this is too fucking weird . . .'

'Jerome! What are you *doing?*'

'Mom . . . look.' Jerome pulled the note free. 'Here, it says *To Kiki — please enjoy this painting. It needs to be loved by someone like you. Your friend, Carlene.*'

'*What?*'

'I'm reading it! It's right here! And then, under that, *There is such a shelter in each other.* This is too weird!'

Kiki lost her legs, and it was only Levi's intervention, hands at her waist, which prevented both Kiki and painting from hitting the floor.

Ten minutes earlier, Zora and Howard had arrived back home together. After driving around Wellington for most of the afternoon, thinking things over, Zora had spotted Howard walking back from the Greenman. She gave him a lift. He was in chipper spirits after a good afternoon's work on his lecture and spoke so much and so continually that he didn't notice that his daughter was not responding. Only when they came through the front door did it dawn on Howard that a cold front was coming off Zora in his direction. They walked silently into the kitchen, where Zora threw the car keys on to the table with such vigour that they slid the length of it and fell off the other side.

'Sounds like Levi's in trouble,' said Howard cheerfully, nodding towards the sound of shouting coming from the basement. 'He had it coming. I can't say I'm surprised. There're sandwiches developing into life forms in that room.'

'Ha,' said Zora. 'And ha.'

'Sorry?'

'Just admiring your ironic gift for comedy, Daddy.'

Sighing, Howard sat down in the rocking chair. 'Zoor — have I pissed you off? Look, if it was that last grade, let's discuss it. I think it was fair, darling, that's why I gave it. The essay was just badly structured. Ideas-wise it was fine, but — there was a lack of . . . concentration, somehow.'

'It's true,' said Zora. 'My mind's been elsewhere. I'm real focused now, though.'

'Good!'

Zora rested her backside on the lip of the kitchen table. 'And I've got a bombshell for the next faculty meeting.'

Howard put on his interested face — but it was spring, and he wanted to go into the garden and sniff the flowers, and maybe take his first swim of the year and towel off upstairs, and lie naked on the marital bed he had so recently been allowed to return to, and pull his wife on to that bed with him and make love to her.

'The discretionaries?' said Zora. She lowered her eyes to avoid the bright, reflected sun streaming through the house. It dappled the walls and made the whole place look like it was underwater. 'I don't think that's going to be a problem any more.'

'Oh, no? How so?'

'Well . . . it turns *out* that Monty's *fucking* Chantelle — a student,' said Zora, speaking the expletive with particular vulgarity. 'One of the discretionaries he was trying to get rid of.'

'No.'

'Yes. Can you believe it? A student. He

was probably *fucking* her before his wife even died.'

Howard slapped the sides of his chair jubilantly. 'Well, my *God.* What a tricky bastard. Moral majority my *arse.* Well, you've got him. My God! You should go in there and *spit-roast* him. Destroy him!'

Zora forced her fake nails, left over from the party, into the underside of the table top. 'That's your advice?'

'Oh, absolutely. How could you resist? His head's on a platter! Deliver him up.'

Zora looked up to the ceiling, and when she looked down a tear was working its way down her face.

'It's not true, *is* it, Dad?'

Howard's face stayed the same. It took a minute. The Victoria incident was so happily concluded in his mind that it was a mental stretch to remember that this did not mean the incident was not a real thing in the world, capable of discovery.

'I saw Victoria Kipps last night. *Dad?*'

Howard held his expression in place.

'And Jerome thinks . . .' said Zora, with difficulty, 'somebody said something and Jerome thinks . . .' Zora hid her wet face behind her elbow. 'It's not true, is it?'

Howard put a hand over his mouth. He had just seen the step after this and the step after that, all the way to the awful end.

'I . . . oh, God, Zora . . . oh, God . . . I don't know what to say to you.'

Here Zora used an ancient English expletive, very loudly.

Howard stood up and took a step towards her. Zora put her arm out to stop him.

'Defended,' said Zora, opening her eyes very wide in amazement, letting the tears course down. 'Defended and defended and defended *you*.'

'Please, Zoor —'

'Against Mom! I took your *side!*'

Howard took another step forward. 'I'm standing here, asking for you to forgive me. It's real *mercy* I'm asking for. I know you don't want to hear my *excuses*,' said Howard, whispering. 'I know you don't want that.'

'When have you *ever*,' said Zora clearly, taking another step back from him, 'given a *fuck* about what *anyone* wants?'

'That's not fair. I love my family, Zoor.'

'*Do* you. Do you love Jerome? How could you *do* this to him?'

Howard's head shook mutely.

'She's my *age*. No — she's *younger than me*. You're fifty-seven years old, Dad,' said Zora and laughed miserably.

Howard covered his face with his hands.

'IT'S SO BORING, DAD. IT'S SO FUCKING *OBVIOUS*.'

Zora now reached the top of the stairs leading down to the basement. Howard begged her for a little more time. There was no more time. Mother and daughter were already calling for each other, one running upstairs and one running down, each with her rich, strange news.

13

'What? What am I looking at exactly?'

Jerome directed his father to the relevant section of the letter from the bank that had been placed in front of him. Howard put his elbows either side of it and tried to concentrate. The air-conditioning was still not up to the job of summer in the Belsey house, so the sliding doors were pulled across and every window open, but only warm air circulated. Even reading seemed to bring on a sweat.

'You need to sign there and there,' said Jerome. 'You have to do this stuff yourself. I'm late.' A heavy smell lingered over the table: a putrid bowl of pears that had expired in the night. Two weeks earlier Howard had let go of Monique, the cleaner, describing her as an expense they could no longer afford. Then the heat came and everything began to rot and swelter and stink. Zora took a seat far from these pears rather than move the bowl herself. She finished what was left of the cereal and pushed the empty box towards her father.

'I still don't see what the point of separating the bank account is,' grumbled Howard, his pen hovering above the document. 'It just makes things twice as difficult.'

'You're separated,' said Zora factually. 'That's the point.'

'Temporarily,' said Howard, but wrote his name on the dotted line. 'Where are you going?' he asked Jerome. 'Need a lift?'

'Church, and no,' replied Jerome.

Howard restrained himself from comment. He stood and walked across the kitchen to the doors, stepping out on to the patio, which was too hot for his bare feet. He stepped back on to the kitchen tiles. Outside smelled of tree sap and swollen brown apples, of which maybe a hundred were scattered over the lawn. It had been like this every August for ten years, but only this year did Howard realize something might be done to improve the situation. Apple cobbler, apple crumble, candied apples, chocolate apples, fruit salads . . . Howard had surprised himself. There was nothing now that he didn't know about making food from apples. He had an apple dish for every day of the week. But it just didn't make as much difference as he'd hoped. Still they kept falling. Worms spent their days passing through them. When they turned black and lost their shape, the ants came crawling.

It was now about time for the squirrel to make its first appearance of the day. Howard leaned against the doorframe and waited. And here he came, scuttling along the fence, intent on destruction. He stopped halfway along and made the acrobatic leap over to the bird feeder, which Howard had spent yesterday afternoon reinforcing with chicken wire to protect it from this very predator. He watched with interest as the squirrel now set about methodically tearing his defences apart. He would be more prepared tomorrow. Howard's forced sabbatical had brought with it a new knowledge of the life cycles of his house. He now noticed which flowers closed themselves when the sun set; he knew the corner of the garden that attracted ladybugs and how many times a day Murdoch needed to relieve himself; he had identified precisely the tree in which the bastard squirrel lived and had considered cutting it down. He knew what sound the pool made when the filter needed changing, or when the air-conditioning unit needed a thump to its side to quieten it down. He knew, without looking, which of his children was passing through a room — from their intimate noises, their treads. Now he reached out for Levi, who he correctly sensed was right behind him.

'You. You need your allowance. Don't you?'

Levi, in his shades, was giving nothing away. He was taking a girl out to brunch and a movie, but Howard didn't need to know that. 'If you're giving it,' he said carefully.

'Well, did your mother already give you some?'

'Just give him the money, Dad,' called Jerome.

Howard came back into the kitchen.

'Jerome, I am merely *interested* in how your mother manages to pay for the secret "bachelor pad" *and* go out with her girlfriends every night *and* fund a court case *and* provide Levi with twenty dollars every other day. Is that all out of the money she's

770

siphoning off me? I'm simply interested in how that works.'

'Just give him the money,' repeated Jerome.

Howard tightened the cord of his bathrobe indignantly. 'But then of course *Linda* — she's the lesbian one, isn't she?' asked Howard, knowing the answer. 'Yes, the lesbian one — she's *still* squeezing half of Mark's money out of him, five years later, which seems a bit rich, really, what with their children being grown, Linda a lesbian . . . marriage having been just a small blip in her lesbian career.'

'Do you have any *idea* how many times you say the word lesbian *in a day?*' asked Zora, switching on the television.

Jerome laughed quietly at this. Howard, happy to amuse his family even incidentally, smiled too.

'So,' said Howard, clapping his hands, 'money. If she wants me bled dry, so be it.'

'Look, man, I don't want your money,' said Levi resignedly. 'Keep it. If it means I don't have to listen to you talk about it.'

Levi lifted his sneaker up, a request for his father to do that special triple knot thing with the laces. Howard braced Levi's foot against his thigh and began tying.

'Soon, Howard,' said Zora breezily, 'she

won't need your money. Once the case is won she can sell the painting and buy a goddamn island.'

'No, no, no,' said Jerome confidently, 'she won't sell that painting. You don't understand anything if you think that. You have to understand the way Mom's *brain* works. She could have kicked *him* out' — Howard expressed alarm at this nameless characterization of himself — 'but she's like, "No, *you* bring up the kids, *you* deal with this family." Mom's perverse like that. She doesn't go the way you think she's going to go. She's got a will of iron.'

They had this discussion, in different variants, several times a week.

'Don't you believe it,' contributed Howard, and with exactly the morose intonation of his father. 'She'll probably sell this *house* from under us an' all.'

'I really *hope* so, Howard,' said Zora. 'She totally deserves it.'

'Zora, haven't you got to get to work?' asked Howard.

'None of you knows anything,' said Levi, hopping to swap feet. 'She's gonna sell that picture, but she won't keep the money. I was round there yesterday, talked to her about it. The money's going to the Haitian Support Group. She just doesn't want Kipps to have it.'

'You were round there . . . Kennedy Square?' queried Howard.

'Nice try,' said Levi, because they had all been instructed not to give Howard any details as to Kiki's exact location. Levi put both feet on the floor and evened up the legs of his jeans. 'How do I look?' he asked.

Murdoch, fresh from a short-legged scramble through the long grass, came scuffling into the kitchen. He was overwhelmed by attention from all sides: Zora ran over to pick him up; Levi played with his ears; Howard offered him a bowl of food. Kiki had wanted desperately to take him, but her apartment was not dog-friendly. And now the remaining Belseys being nice to Murdoch was, in some way, *for* Kiki; there was the unspoken, irrational hope that, although not with them in this room, she could somehow sense the care they were lavishing upon her beloved little dog, and that these good vibes would . . . it was ridiculous. It was a way of missing her.

'Levi, I can give you a lift into town if you like, if you can wait a minute,' said Howard. 'Zoor — aren't you late?'

Zora didn't move.

'*I'm* dressed, Howard,' she said, pointing

to her summer waitress's uniform of black skirt and white shirt. 'It's *your* big day. And you're the one with no pants on.'

This much was true. Howard picked Murdoch up — although the dog had barely tasted the meat put in front of him — and took him upstairs to the bedroom. Here Howard stood before his closet and considered how smart he could possibly look given the humidity. In the closet, from which all the real clothes — all the colourful silk and cashmere and satin — had been removed, a solitary suit hung, swinging above a jumble of jeans and shirts and shorts. He reached out for the suit. He put it back. If they were going to take him, they could take him as he truly was. He pulled out black jeans, dark blue short-sleeved shirt, sandals. Today, supposedly, there would be people from Pomona in the audience, and from Columbia University and from the Courtauld. Smith was excited about all these possibilities, and now Howard did his best to be too. *This is the big one,* read Smith's e-mail of this morning, *Howard, it's time for tenure. If Wellington can't give you that, you move on. This is how it's supposed to be. See you at ten thirty!* Smith was right. Ten years in one place, without tenure, was a long time. His children were grown. They would soon leave. And then the house, if it were to stay as it was, without Kiki, would be intolerable. It was in a university that he must now put all his remaining hope. Universities had been a home for him for over thirty years. He only needed one more: the final, generous institution to take him in his dotage and protect him.

Howard pulled a baseball cap on to his head and hurried downstairs, Murdoch struggling behind him. In the kitchen, his children were hooking their various bags and knapsacks round their shoulders.

'Wait —' said Howard, padding his hand around the empty sideboard. 'Where're my car keys?'

'No idea, Howard,' said Zora callously.

'Jerome? Car keys!'

'Calm down.'

'I'm not going to calm down — no one's leaving until I find them.'

In this way, Howard made everybody late. It's strange how children, even grown children, will accept the instruction of a parent. Obediently they tore up the kitchen hunting for what Howard needed. They looked everywhere likely and then in stupid unlikely places because Howard went ballistic if anyone, for a moment, appeared to have ceased looking. The keys were nowhere.

'Aw, man, I'm done with this, it's too *hot* — I'm out,' cried Levi, and left the house. A minute later he returned, having found Howard's car keys in the door of his car.

'Genius!' cried Howard. 'OK, come on, come on, everybody out — alarm on, everyone get keys, *come on,* people.'

Out on the scorching street, Howard opened the door of his baking car by wrapping the corner of his shirt round his hand. The leather interior was so hot he had to sit on his own bag.

'I'm not coming,' said Zora, protecting her eyes from the sun with her hand. 'Just in case you thought I was. I didn't want to change my shift.'

Howard smiled charitably at his daughter. It was in her nature to come across a high horse and ride it for as long as it would carry her. She was certainly riding high at the moment, for she had recast herself as the angel of mercy. It had been in her power, after all, to get both Monty and Howard fired. To Howard she had strongly suggested a sabbatical, which reprieve he had taken, gratefully. Zora had two years left at Wellington, and, the way she saw it, the college was no longer big enough for the both of them. Monty had been allowed to keep his job but not his principles. He did not contest the discretionaries and the discretionaries stayed, although Zora herself dropped out of the poetry class. These epic acts of unselfishness had lent Zora a genuinely unassailable moral superiority that she was enjoying immensely. The only cloud on her conscience was Carl. She had left the class so that he might stay, but in fact he never returned. He disappeared from Wellington altogether. By the time Zora felt brave enough to ring his cell it was out of order. She enlisted Claire's help in trying to find him; they got his home address from the payment records, but letters sent there received no reply. When Zora dared a visit, Carl's mother said only that he had moved out; she would say no more. She wouldn't let Zora past the doorstep, and talked to her guardedly, apparently convinced that this light-skinned woman who spoke so properly must be a social worker or a police officer, somebody who could cause the Thomas family trouble. Five months later Zora continued to see Carl's many doppelgängers in the street, day after day — the hoodie, the baggy jeans, the box-fresh sneakers, the big black earphones —

and each time she spotted a twin she felt
his name soar from her chest to her throat.
Sometimes she let it out. But the boy always walked on.

'Anybody for a lift into town?' asked
Howard. 'I'm happy to drop everybody
where they need to go.'

Two minutes later Howard rolled down the
passenger window and beeped his horn at his
three half-naked children walking down
the hill. All of them gave him the finger.

Howard drove through Wellington and
out of Wellington. He watched the blis-
tering day undulate outside his windshield;
he heard the crickets' string section. He
listened, on his car stereo, to the
Lacrimosa and, like a teenager, turned it
up high and kept his windows down.
Swish dah dah, swish dah dah. As the
music slowed, he slowed, entering Boston
and meeting up with the Big Dig. He sat in
its maze of unmoving cars for forty minutes. After finally emerging from a tunnel
as long as life itself, Howard's phone rang.

'Howard? Smith. Gosh, it's great you finally went and got yourself a phone. How
you gittin' on there, buddy?'

It was Smith's artificial voice of calm. In
the past it had always worked, but recently

Howard had grown better at attuning himself to the reality of his own situation.

'I'm late, Smith. I'm now very late.'

'Oh, it's not rilly that bad. You've got time. *Pah*-point's all set up there ready for you. Where you at exactly?'

Howard gave his coordinates. A suspicious silence followed.

'You know what ah'll do?' said Smith. 'Just make a little announcement. And if you can get here in about twenty minutes or under, that would be just fine.'

Thirty minutes after that call, the Big Dig spat an apoplectic Howard out into the city. Huge flowers of sweat bloomed beneath each armpit on his dark blue shirt. Panicking, Howard decided to avoid the one-way system by parking five blocks from where he needed to be. He slammed the door of the car and began to run, locking it remotely over his shoulder. He could feel sweat dribbling between his buttocks and slooshing in his sandals, readying his instep for the two water blisters that would surely have formed by the time he reached the gallery. He had given up smoking soon after Kiki walked out, but now he cursed that decision — his lungs were in no way better at coping with this exertion than they would have been five months ago. He had also put on twenty-three pounds.

'The loneliness of the long-distance runner!' called Smith, upon spotting him staggering round the corner. 'You did it, you did it — it's OK. Take a moment, you can take a moment.'

Howard leaned against Smith, unable to speak.

'You're OK,' said Smith convincingly. 'You're just fine.'

'I'm going to be sick.'

'No, no, Howard. That is the very *last* thing you're gonna do. Come on now, let's git in.'

They walked into the kind of air-conditioning that freezes sweat on contact. Smith led Howard by the elbow down one hallway, and then another. He stationed his charge just by a door that was slightly ajar. Through the gap Howard could see the thin slice of a podium, a table, and a jug of water with two lemon slices floating in it.

'Now, to make the *pah*-point work, you just click the red button — it'll be right by your hand on the podium. Each time you press that button, a new painting will appear, in the order that they're mentioned in the lecture.'

'Everybody in there?' asked Howard.

'Everybody who's anybody,' replied Smith and pushed open the door.

Howard entered. Polite but fatigued applause greeted him. He stood behind the podium and apologized for his lateness. He spotted at once half a dozen people from the Art History Department, as well as Claire, Erskine, Christian and Veronica, and several of his students past and present. Jack French had brought his wife and children. Howard was touched by this support. They didn't need to come here. In Wellington terms, he was already a dead man walking, with no book coming any time soon, surely heading for a messy divorce and on a sabbatical that looked suspiciously like the first step towards retirement. But they had come. He apologized again for his tardiness and spoke self-deprecatingly of his inexperience and inability with the technology he was about to use.

It was halfway through this preliminary speech that Howard visualized with perfect clarity the yellow folder that remained where he had left it, on the back seat of his car, five blocks from here. Abruptly he stopped speaking and remained silent for a minute. He could hear people moving in their seats. He could smell the tang of himself strongly. What did he look like to these people? He pressed the red button. The lights began to go down, very slowly, on a dimmer, as if Howard were trying to romance his audience. He looked out across the crowd to find the man responsible for this special effect and found instead Kiki, sixth row, far right, looking up with interest at the image behind him, which was beginning to refine itself in the coming darkness. She wore a scarlet ribbon threaded through her plait, and her shoulders were bare and gleaming.

Howard pressed the red button again. A picture came up. He waited a minute and then pressed it once more. Another picture. He kept pressing. People appeared: angels and staalmeesters and merchants and surgeons and students and writers and peasants and kings and the artist himself. And the artist himself. And the artist himself. The man from Pomona began to nod appreciatively. Howard pressed the red button. He could hear Jack French saying to his eldest son, in his characteristically loud whisper: *You see, Ralph, the order is meaningful.* Howard pressed the red button. Nothing happened. He had come to the end of the line. He looked out and spotted Kiki, smiling into her lap. The rest of his audience were faintly frowning at the back wall. Howard turned his head and looked at the picture behind him.

'*Hendrickje Bathing*, 1654,' croaked Howard and said no more.

On the wall, a pretty, blousy Dutch woman in a simple white smock paddled in water up to her calves. Howard's audience looked at her and then at Howard and then at the woman once more, awaiting elucidation. The woman, for her part, looked away, coyly, into the water. She seemed to be considering whether to wade deeper. The surface of the water was dark, reflective — a cautious bather could not be certain of what lurked beneath. Howard looked at Kiki. In her face, his life. Kiki looked up suddenly at Howard — not, he thought, unkindly. Howard said nothing. Another silent minute passed. The audience began to mutter perplexedly. Howard made the picture larger on the wall, as Smith had explained to him how to do. The woman's fleshiness filled the wall. He looked out into the audience once more and saw Kiki only. He smiled at her. She smiled. She looked away, but she smiled. Howard looked back at the woman on the wall, Rembrandt's love, Hendrickje. Though her hands were imprecise blurs, paint heaped on paint and roiled with the brush, the rest of her skin had been expertly rendered in all its variety — chalky whites and lively pinks, the underlying blue of her veins and the ever present human hint of yellow, intimation of what is to come.

author's note

Thank you to Saja Music Co. and Sony/ATV Music Publishing Ltd for permission to quote from 'I Get Around' by Tupac Shakur. Thank you to Faber and Faber for permission to quote from the poems 'Imperial' and 'The Last Saturday in Ulster', and also for allowing the poem 'On Beauty' to be reprinted in its entirety. All three poems are from the collection *To a Fault* by Nick Laird. Thank you to Nick himself for allowing the last poem to be Claire's. Thank you to my brother Doc Brown for some of Carl Thomas's imaginary lyrics.

There are a number of real Rembrandts described in this novel, most of them on public display. (Claire is right about *The Shipbuilder Jan Rijksen and His Wife Griet Jans,* 1633. If you want to see that, you have to ask the Queen.) The two portraits that lead to trouble between Monty and Howard are *Self-Portrait with Lace Collar*, 1629, Mauritshuis, The Hague, and *Self-Portrait,* 1629, Alte Pinakothek, Munich. They are not as alike as the author suggests. The painting that Howard uses for his first class of the semester is *The Anatomy Lesson of Dr Nicolaes Tulp*, 1632, Mauritshuis, The Hague. The painting that Katie Armstrong examines is *Jacob Wrestling with the Angel*, 1658, Gemäldegalerie, Berlin; the etching is *Woman on a Mound*, *c.* 1631, Museum het Rembrandthuis, Amsterdam. Howard is stared at by *The Sampling Officials of the Drapers' Guild*, 1662, Rijksmuseum, Amsterdam. It is from Simon Schama's detailed account of the Staalmeesters' hermeneutic history that I draw my own sketched account. Howard has nothing at all to say about *Hendrickje Bathing*, 1654, National Gallery, London.

Carlene's Jean Hyppolite painting is also a real one and can be seen in the Centre d'Art, Haiti. The painting Kiki imagines walking down is Edward Hopper's *Road in Maine*, 1914, Whitney Museum of American Art, New York. Howard thinks that Carl looks like Rubens's *Study of African Heads*, *c.* 1617, Musées Royaux des BeauxArts, Brussels. I don't agree.

About the Author

ZADIE SMITH was born in northwest London in 1975 and still lives in the area. She is the author of *White Teeth* and *The Autograph Man*.

The employees of Thorndike Press hope you have enjoyed this Large Print book. All our Thorndike and Wheeler Large Print titles are designed for easy reading, and all our books are made to last. Other Thorndike Press Large Print books are available at your library, through selected bookstores, or directly from us.

For information about titles, please call:

(800) 223-1244

or visit our Web site at:

www.gale.com/thorndike
www.gale.com/wheeler

To share your comments, please write:

Publisher
Thorndike Press
295 Kennedy Memorial Drive
Waterville, ME   04901